COLORADO Wings

Four Inspirational Love Stories with a Dash of Intrigue

TRACIE PETERSON

BARBOUR
PUBLISHING, INC.
Uhrichsville, Ohio

ISBN 1-57748-828-8

Published by Barbour Publishing, Inc., P.O. Box 719, Uhrichsville, Ohio 44683 http://www.barbourbooks.com

Member of the
Evangelical Christian
Publishers Association

Printed in the United States of America.

TRACIE PETERSON

Tracie Peterson, best-selling author of over forty fiction titles and one nonfiction title, lives and works in Topeka, Kansas. As a Christian, wife, mother, and writer (in that order), Tracie finds her slate quite full.

First published as a columnist for the *Kansas Christian* newspaper, Tracie resigned that position to turn her attention to novels. After signing her first contract with Barbour Publishing in 1992, her first novel appeared in 1993, and the rest is history. She has over twenty-three titles with Heartsong Presents' book club and stories in six separate anthologies from Barbour, including the best-selling *Alaska*. From Bethany House Publishing, Tracie has a historical three-book Westward Chronicles series dealing with the Harvey Girls, and three contemporary intrigue romances. Other titles include two historical series cowritten with Judith Pella. Tracie's women's fiction title *A Slender Thread* is her latest release from Bethany.

Voted favorite author for 1995, 1996, and 1997 by the Heartsong Presents readership, Tracie enjoys the pleasure of spinning stories for readers and thanks God for the imagination He's given. "I find myself blessed to be able to work at a job I love. I get to travel, study history, spin yarns, spend time with my family, and hopefully glorify God. I can't imagine a more perfect arrangement."

Tracie also does acquisitions work for Barbour Publishing and teaches workshops at a variety of conferences, giving workshops on inspirational romance, historical research, and anything else that offers assistance to fellow writers.

See Tracie on the Internet at http://members.aol.com/tjpbooks/

A Wing and a Prayer

Dedicated to Keith and Charlene,
with thanks for tolerating my multiple calls,
teaching me about flying, sending flight maps,
and throwing in all the little extras that made this book fun.

Chapter 1

C J stared at her reflection in the mirror. Why did she always turn introspective in the bathroom? She reached into her purse, pulled out a compact to adjust her makeup, and grimaced. Her serious expression made her look older than her twenty-one years. Time was not her friend, she decided.

Pulling out her lipstick as well, CJ touched the Burgundy Frost to her lips, blotted the better part of the color onto a tissue, and restored the makeup to her purse.

Glacier, ice blue eyes stared back at her from the mirror, while long, coppery rings of hair cascaded from her head like a waterfall. Before yesterday, CJ had worn her hair parted on the side and straight. The thick red mass had reached nearly to her waist. Now a stranger stared back at her. Why had she let Cheryl talk her into getting a permanent?

"CJ?" Cheryl's voice called from the other side of the closed door. "Can you be free at three o'clock tomorrow for the final dress fitting?"

"Three is fine," CJ called back. She could hear her friend's voice continue on the telephone with the dressmaker. She and Cheryl Fairchild had been friends since childhood. In fact, Cheryl was CJ's best friend. Correction—her only friend.

CJ stepped back from the hotel mirror for a quick survey of her new, khaki-colored outfit. Cheryl had talked her into purchasing it, telling CJ that it complemented her skin and hair color. It reminded CJ of an outfit you might wear on a safari. With a shrug of her shoulders that sent curls bobbing and dancing, CJ reached for the handle on the door.

When nothing happened, she stared dumbly for a moment. She turned the handle again, but it wouldn't catch to open the door. Instead it turned freely. CJ pulled at the door, then pushed. Finally, she gave up and called out for Cheryl.

"The door handle is broken," CJ explained when Cheryl answered from the other side.

"It won't budge out here," Cheryl answered. "Did you lock it?"

"I suppose I did," CJ replied. "I tried to turn the handle, but all it does is spin." Then a little louder and with a hint of disgust, CJ added, "Things are made pretty cheaply these days. Anything to save a buck."

"I guess I'd better call maintenance," Cheryl called. "Given the cost of everything in this hotel, you'd expect the door handles to work."

"Just get somebody up here," CJ said, starting to realize for the first time that she was trapped.

She pressed her ear against the door and could hear Cheryl trying to explain her problem, via the telephone, to the front desk personnel. Much to CJ's utter frustration, it didn't sound as though Cheryl was making much headway.

CJ felt the air grow stuffy. It always started that way. She looked around the small room. Veined-marble sink and counter, toilet, shower stall. The entire room was no larger than eight by eight. *Make that six by eight,* CJ thought as the walls seemed to visibly move closer together.

"No one in maintenance is answering," Cheryl called to CJ.

"What do you mean, no one is answering?" The nervousness was evident in her voice. A cold sweat dampened her brow.

"Look, CJ, just sit tight and I'll go find someone."

"No! Don't go!" CJ exclaimed.

"I can't just leave you in there," Cheryl answered. "You'll be okay. Just keep telling yourself that nothing bad can happen to you."

"Cheryl, please don't leave me!" CJ's voice was near to hysteria. She braced her hands against the door, hoping to steady herself. "I don't want to be alone." The words sounded like a moan.

"Look, I've seen maintenance and housekeeping people all over this place. Someone out there will know how to help us. Take some deep breaths and get a towel wet and wipe your face. I'll be just a second. You wait right here," Cheryl insisted.

"Where did you expect me to go? It's not like I can tunnel out." CJ was beginning to feel desperate. "Would if I could, though."

Cheryl's lyrical laughter sounded from outside the door, breaking a bit of the tension. "Guess you're right. I'll be back in a minute."

"Cheryl?" CJ called, but there was no answer.

CJ returned to her evaluation of the small hotel bathroom. She wouldn't even be here if it hadn't been for Cheryl. She could still hear her friend's animated voice when she'd called to announce her arrival in Denver.

CJ leaned against the wall and forced herself to remember every detail of their conversation. She knew from experience that concentrating on something other than the circumstance at hand would help to stave off her claustrophobia.

Cheryl had been so excited that day, and CJ had been more than a little surprised to hear her friend announce her upcoming wedding. Cheryl had always been the one to adamantly declare herself a most content and liberated woman. That liberation had taken a backseat, however, when Cheryl had fallen hard for CJ's brother, Curt. CJ had always hoped that Cheryl and Curt would carry through with their plans and marry, but that had been before the accident. After that, everything changed. Now, two years CJ's senior, Cheryl was marrying a man she'd known for only a few months.

Shaking off the vision, CJ tried her best to forget. "Cheryl's getting married," she reminded herself. "If she's committed to him enough to get married, he must be special."

CJ tried desperately to remember her conversation with Cheryl. "His name is Stratton McFarland," Cheryl had gushed over the phone. "He's tall and handsome and absolutely perfect for me. He even works for Daddy."

CJ had laughed at that reference. As an only child, Cheryl had been her father's pride and joy, especially after the death of Cheryl's mother. If Stratton worked for Benjamin Fairchild and had passed his close scrutiny, he must indeed be a most unique specimen of man.

CJ felt her head begin to swim. Her cheeks felt hot, but she knew from experience that the blood was, in all actuality, draining from her face. She imagined that it pooled somewhere in the tightening ball that had become her stomach. It was, she concluded, the reason she generally vomited when the sensation of being closed in got to be too much.

She slid down the wall to crouch with her head on her knees. Her vision narrowed as the black walls inside her mind closed in.

Then it began.

At first it was just the pulsating hum of her blood, rushing to leave her head. Then it changed and grew louder. Now it was the drone of her father's airplane.

The noise increased. They were flying back from an air show in the Midwest when something happened. CJ could feel the vibrations of that fatal moment. After years of training with her father and piloting a variety of planes, she'd known instinctively that something was desperately wrong with her father's aircraft.

"We're going to crash!" she could hear her father tell her mother. The look they had exchanged put more fear into CJ's heart than she had ever known. More words were spoken, and then her father had glanced back at her. It was for only a second. He fought to control the plane and offered her a parting smile. "Better get down into position, Squirt," he'd said as easily as if he were telling her to take the dog for a walk.

"Daddy!" CJ wondered if she'd said the word aloud or if it was only a ghostly murmuring from the past. The droning in her head brought her back to reality. "I can't pass out," she moaned and slumped onto the bathroom floor.

❧

Cheryl wasn't having any luck. In a hotel as big as this one, it seemed incomprehensible that no one could help her. She was beginning to get quite agitated when she spotted a man in coveralls and felt a wave of relief. Poor CJ would no doubt be frantic by now.

"Excuse me," Cheryl said and took possessive hold of the man's tan-colored jumpsuit.

An oil-smudged face with twinkling green eyes looked down at her. "Yes?" the man questioned.

"I have an emergency upstairs, and I need you to grab your maintenance tools. My friend is stuck in the bathroom. . .the handle broke off on the door. You have to hurry. She's got a real problem when it comes to tight spaces," Cheryl said, paying no attention to the man's surprised reaction. Dropping her hold on his arm, Cheryl turned to punch the up button for the elevator.

"My, ah, tools," the man said with a note of amusement in his voice, "are downstairs, not up. Why don't you tell me the room number, and

I'll follow you after I get my things."

Cheryl glanced first to the elevator and back to the man. Her shoulder-length blond hair flipped from side to side as she tried to make up her mind.

"We have to hurry," she emphasized. The elevator doors opened and the burgundy-uniformed operator waited for her to enter. Looking back to the maintenance man, Cheryl seemed genuinely distressed.

He smiled sympathetically. "Look, miss. I understand the urgency. In fact, I'll take the stairs down and you go ahead to your room. What's the number?" the man asked softly.

Cheryl bit her lower lip and gave in to his suggestion. "Six hundred eighteen," she answered and stepped into the elevator. "You will hurry, won't you?"

"It won't take me but a minute."

Cheryl hoped he was telling the truth. He seemed sincere enough, but she knew CJ would be half out of her mind by now. Glancing at her watch, Cheryl could see that she'd been gone for over twenty minutes.

"Poor CJ," she whispered.

❦

CJ could feel the twisted metal binding her body to the small enclosure toward the back of the plane's fuselage. She had been sixteen when her father's plane crashed, claiming both his life and her mother's. Yet in spite of the severity of their accident, CJ had never lost consciousness. She could smell fuel all around her and frantically wondered if she would survive the crash only to be consumed by a fire.

After what had seemed like hours, she could hear the rescue vehicles screaming their way to the field where her father had fought to land the plane. More evident than any other sensation, however, was the helpless feeling of being tied to the wreckage. CJ had never been the same after the experience. Claustrophobia had emerged as the result of the crash, that and three years of rehabilitation for her shattered left leg.

Lying on the cold marble floor, CJ fought to remain awake. The flashback to the crash was so vivid that for a moment she could almost smell the aviation fuel. Curling into a fetal position, CJ pulled her knees to her chest and rocked slightly on her side. *Why doesn't Cheryl come back? Where is she?*

CJ opened her eyes for a moment, saw the room spin, and closed them tightly again.

"CJ!" a voice called to her. Was it a memory?

"CJ!" the voice came again, and she struggled to concentrate.

"Cheryl?" she asked weakly.

"Yes, it's me," Cheryl called from outside. "Maintenance is on their way. You okay?"

"I'm sick, Cheryl. You know, same old stuff."

"I know and I'm sorry. I hurried and. . ." Cheryl paused. "He's here, CJ. The maintenance guy is here. You hang on. He's going to have you out of there in just a minute."

CJ forced herself to sit up. Somehow, even in her state of mind, it seemed more than a little degrading to think of the hotel maintenance man finding her on the bathroom floor. She leaned back against the wall just under the towel rack and waited.

When the door opened moments later, CJ didn't have the strength to get up. Why did she have to be such a baby about these things?

Cheryl rushed into the bathroom, pushing the bewildered man aside. "CJ! CJ, talk to me, honey!" she exclaimed.

CJ looked up and, when she did, she caught sight of the man who stood vigil in the doorway. She tried to smile her thanks, but Cheryl was pulling at her arm.

"Come on; try to stand. We'll get you out of here and get you something cold to drink. You can lie down on my bed and rest until you feel better," Cheryl was saying. "Did you hear me, CJ? Come on; help me out here."

CJ tried to stand with Cheryl's help, but her knees buckled under her, just as the maintenance man reached out and pulled her into his arms.

"I'll go turn the covers down," Cheryl said, pushing past the man. "You bring her, okay?" Obviously used to getting whatever she demanded, Cheryl left without waiting for him to answer.

"Sorry," CJ barely whispered. "It's this claustrophobia thing."

"Don't worry about it," he replied with a warm smile. "I think your friend has the best plan, though. You'll feel better after you lie down."

CJ felt her stomach lurch and knew she was going to throw up.

When the man started to lift her, she shook her head adamantly. "No—wait. I think I'm going to be sick."

The man never hesitated. Pulling CJ against his left side, he lifted the toilet lid and centered her over it. CJ unceremoniously lost her breakfast while the maintenance man held back her long, copper hair with one hand and with the other firmly encircled her waist.

"What's keeping you two?" Cheryl called from the other room.

CJ struggled to compose herself and straightened up to face her rescuer. It was hard to be dignified, given her current state, and she felt like laughing for the first time since she'd arrived at the hotel. The man beside her sensed her amusement. "Just give her a minute," he answered Cheryl.

Cheryl appeared in the doorway as CJ was rinsing her mouth. She realized at once what had happened. "Oh, CJ. I'm so sorry. I forgot how badly these things affect you."

CJ was aware that the man's hands never left her. One minute they held her upright, the next they easily lifted her against his chest.

"Really, I'm much better now," CJ protested. "I can walk."

"No sense in pushing yourself," he declared, following Cheryl.

The scents of musky cologne and oil filled CJ's senses. "I'm grateful," she said, lifting her ice blue eyes to meet his warm, green ones. "My name is CJ."

"I'm Brad," he replied and deposited her on the bed.

"I'll bring you some tea to settle your stomach," Cheryl said after removing CJ's shoes and pulling the sheet up under her chin.

"Look," CJ said, propping herself up on an elbow, "I'm really sorry about this. Thank you for everything." In complete exhaustion, she fell back against the pillow and closed her eyes.

Brad stood for a moment, mesmerized by the pale-faced woman. How could two people share such a moment as they had just minutes before and know nothing more about each other than first names? Pulling the door closed, he went back to the bathroom door and began to repair the handle.

"I've called room service," Cheryl announced, coming up from behind. She peered over Brad's shoulder as if inspecting his work. "But if they don't respond any faster than anyone else does in this place, I could be married and moved out before the tea arrives."

"Having trouble with the service, eh?" Brad questioned casually.

"If I hadn't come down for you myself, I'd still be sitting here with CJ passed out in the bathroom."

"I guess I had best let the management know," Brad offered good-naturedly.

"I already plan to," Cheryl replied, adding, "Can you see to it that this doesn't happen again?"

Brad gave the perky blond an appraising glance, then winked to break the tension. "I thought it might be more to my advantage to see to it that all the handles fell apart. Then I'd have a good reason to come back and see our friend more properly. She seems to be quite an intriguing woman."

Cheryl laughed. "You certainly move fast, but you might as well save your time and energies. CJ is a wall of ice. She wants only to hide out in that apartment of hers and listen to classical music."

"Doesn't she work?" Brad questioned. He finished with the door handle and stood to receive Cheryl's answer.

"She doesn't have to," Cheryl said with a coy smile. "Bet that makes her even more attractive, eh?"

Brad didn't take offense. He picked up his things and turned at the door. Matching Cheryl's smile, he said, "Just let me know if you need anything else repaired. In the meantime, I'll let the management know about the door."

❧

Later that afternoon, a completely recovered CJ sat quietly reading while Cheryl rushed around the room and made at least fifty phone calls. When a knock sounded at the door, the two women exchanged glances.

"I didn't order anything!" Cheryl exclaimed with the telephone halfway to her ear.

"Don't worry about it," CJ said. "You just work on getting to your hair appointment. I'll get the door."

CJ opened the door and found a huge bouquet of red roses being thrust forward. She immediately noted the card addressed to Cheryl and presumed the flowers must be from the perfectly romantic Stratton

McFarland. Taking the flowers in hand, CJ was surprised when the delivery boy didn't wait for a tip but sauntered off down the hall.

"Wow!" Cheryl exclaimed, hanging up the phone. "Who are they for?"

"Well, who do you think?" CJ answered with a laugh. "This isn't my room."

"I'll bet they're from Stratton!" Cheryl put the flowers on the coffee table and ripped open the envelope. "Well, I'll be," she muttered.

"What?" CJ couldn't resist asking.

"We've been invited to dinner in the penthouse."

"I didn't know Stratton was staying in the penthouse," CJ said, retaking her seat.

"He isn't." Cheryl glanced up from the letter, then handed it to her friend.

CJ read the note, uncertain of what to expect:

> *The management regrets the unfortunate accident that befell you this morning. Please accept this expression of our sincerest best wishes for your speedy recovery. We would also like to extend an invitation to both of you for dinner in the penthouse suite, this evening at seven o'clock.*

CJ looked up and met Cheryl's bewildered expression. "A bit much for a broken door handle, don't you think?"

Cheryl laughed. "I can't imagine receiving this kind of welcome. Especially after all the things I said downstairs in the lobby and on the telephone."

CJ grinned. "Gave them a bit of a hard time, did you?"

Cheryl nodded. "I think dinner sounds like fun. Shall we go and let them make their apologies in person?"

"I didn't bring anything with me to change into," CJ said, getting to her feet. "I hardly think this African safari getup would be appropriate, and there certainly isn't time for me to get home and back before seven."

"You can wear something of mine," Cheryl replied.

"Your dresses are too short on me," CJ protested.

"Not my green tea-length," Cheryl said, already planning the evening in her mind. "It'll go perfectly with your hair, too."

"I don't know."

"Come on. It'll be fun. The best part is," Cheryl said, pulling CJ to the bedroom, "it'll get us out of here and give us a reason to dress up!"

An hour later, CJ appraised herself in the dressing room mirror. Cheryl was right. The richness of the forest green material clung to her in all the right places.

The sound of the telephone ringing caused CJ to abandon her examination. Cheryl was just hanging up the phone when CJ poked her head through the door. "Problems?" she questioned.

"It seems my plans have changed. Stratton has just come back to town and wants to take me out to dinner. He'll be here in about fifteen minutes."

"Oh, well," CJ said. "So much for that."

"You're still going to go, aren't you?"

"By myself?" CJ asked. "You expect me to go sit with some stuffy old hotel manager and listen to him drone on about the virtues of his resort, while you dine in the pleasant company of Mr. Perfect?"

"But it's too late for both of us to bow out gracefully," Cheryl insisted. "Just go and stay for a short time, then excuse yourself and come back here. Here, take the extra key card and wait until I get back."

CJ shook her head. "It isn't my style, Cheryl."

"Look, they're really trying to make amends for what happened. I'll bet that maintenance guy. . . What was his name?"

"Brad," CJ filled in absentmindedly.

"Yes, Brad," Cheryl confirmed with a nod. "He probably went back to his boss and told him how you lost it and now they're worried that you'll sue them or something. Just go and enjoy yourself and accept their gesture of apology."

CJ stared at Cheryl's determined face. "Oh, all right," she finally sighed in exasperation. "I'll go."

Chapter 2

CJ took the elevator to the penthouse, but only because it was glassed-in on one side and allowed her to look out on the Denver skyline. It also helped to have the companionship of the elevator's operator.

"Penthouse suite," the operator announced when the doors opened into a brass and glass vestibule.

CJ stepped out of the elevator and glanced around hesitantly. The only way seemed to be down a short corridor to where double oak doors waited. Taking a deep breath, she walked slowly, with images of a martyr being led to her execution coming to mind. Smiling at her own misgivings, CJ refused to notice her surroundings. *The sooner this is over,* she thought, *the better.*

CJ knocked on the door and smoothed the skirt of her already-perfect dress. She was still looking down when the door opened.

"Feeling better, I see."

CJ's head snapped up to meet Brad's dark green eyes. He was dressed impeccably in a navy suit. . .a very expensive navy suit. Gone were the oil smudges and grease-monkey coveralls. His brown hair was neatly parted on the side and stylishly combed back, while the sweet musky scent of his cologne wafted a greeting.

"I don't understand," CJ murmured.

"Brad Aldersson III, hotel and resort owner," he said with a charmingly boyish grin, "and occasional maintenance man." He extended his well-manicured hand to take CJ's slim arm. "Come inside, Miss CJ. . ." He purposefully fell silent and waited for her to fill in the rest.

"O'Sullivan."

"Ahh," he replied with a grin. "Irish and a redhead."

CJ couldn't resist a smile. "Hotheaded, too. My father said it just went with the territory."

"That's all right," Brad said, pulling CJ gently into the suite. "I'm descended from stubborn Swedes, myself."

"Oh, really? Did it rub off?" CJ asked. Brad closed the door and shrugged.

"I guess I'll let you be the judge of that. By the way, where is Miss Fairchild?"

"Her fiancé called at the last minute, so she had to cancel. I was going to beg off, too, but Cheryl said that would be unquestionably rude. So, here I am."

"I'm glad you came," Brad said, offering her a seat in the spacious living room. "I feel very badly about what happened to you. I pride my resorts on being first-rate."

"You have others?" CJ asked, hoping to keep the conversation steered away from anything personal.

"I have seven altogether," Brad replied. "Six are here in Colorado and one is in Jackson Hole, Wyoming. I hope to continue expanding in the future."

"How interesting."

"Oh, it can be," Brad answered. "But it's also a big headache at times. Good help is hard to get and keep. Up until two weeks ago, I had a fantastic executive assistant, but he hired on with a national chain and left me to handle my own problems."

"So here you are, trying to fix broken doorknobs and entertain claustrophobics," CJ said and laughed.

"I guess you could say that, but enough about me. What about you?"

"What about me?" CJ asked rather defensively.

Brad sensed her withdrawing a bit. "Well, why don't we start with your name. What does CJ stand for?"

"Curtiss Jenny." She said it in a matter-of-fact way that suggested everyone was named after aircraft.

"You mean like the biplane?" Brad questioned curiously.

"Exactly like it," CJ said with a smile. "My father gave it to me. When I was little, I was called Jenny, but as I got older, CJ seemed to work better."

"I love it!" Brad exclaimed, surprising CJ. "I adore the Jenny biplane, and I think it a most unique name for a girl."

"Unique wasn't quite the term my mother used. She used to say, 'Doug, you're saddling that girl with a terrible burden.' But," CJ paused, feeling a bittersweet pain at the memory of her parents, "as you can see, I fared just fine."

"I'll definitely second that." Brad couldn't resist the compliment. "Where are your folks now?"

"Dead. They were killed in a plane crash." The pain it caused her to remember was evident in her expression.

A sudden revelation dawned on Brad. "You said your father's name was Doug?"

"That's right." CJ grew apprehensive, wondering if she should have kept quiet.

"Douglas O'Sullivan, the famous flyer?" Brad asked with a raised eyebrow.

"Yes." CJ steeled her nerves for the assault that was bound to come. It was always the same. Whenever someone familiar with her father's career found out that she was his daughter, they deluged her with questions about his life and death.

"Well, I'll be." Brad sat back in genuine awe.

CJ sat in silence. She fidgeted with the beaded cuff of her sleeve, waiting uncomfortably for Brad to say something.

"The accident was five or six years ago, wasn't it?" Brad more stated than questioned.

"Yes," CJ replied softly. "It was five."

"The world lost a truly great man when he died. I'm not ashamed to say he was my inspiration. I started flying after attending one of his air show performances." Brad went on, but CJ barely heard him.

The same things that always crossed her mind when people learned of her true identity began to play themselves out in her head. *He knows now that I'm rich,* CJ thought. It was a well-publicized fact that she was an heiress, having inherited, along with her older brother, millions of dollars and property.

She tried to rationalize away her fears. Brad obviously had his own money or at least he had his investments in the resorts.

"CJ?" Brad quietly spoke her name.

"I'm sorry," she said with a start. "I don't like to dwell on my parents.

19

I was just sixteen when I lost them, and it's still hard."

Brad nodded and tried to lighten the conversation. "So that would mean you're twenty-one, right?"

CJ nodded with a look somewhere between a smirk and a smile. "Think you're pretty smart, eh?"

"At least it got you smiling again. For a few minutes there, you looked too serious, almost worried." Brad noticed her discomfort. "I told Miss Fairchild, in a roundabout way, that I'd like to get to know you better. You aren't spoken for by anyone else, are you?"

Surprise registered on CJ's face. "That's a pretty straightforward, if not old-fashioned, question to ask someone you just met. But, the answer is no. I'm not seeing anyone."

Brad's face lit up. "Good. I wouldn't want to step on any toes."

CJ shook her head. "You are a most unusual man, Mr. Aldersson."

"You aren't going to keep calling me that, are you?"

"It is your name."

"So's Brad, and I prefer we use it," he replied. "I can't imagine us getting very far using formalities like Mr. Aldersson."

"And just how far did you expect us to get, Brad?" she asked, sizing up the man before her.

"I guess I'll leave that up to you," he answered with a sheepish grin. Strange feelings surfaced for just a moment, before CJ recovered from her surprise.

"How about something to drink?" Brad offered, getting to his feet.

CJ steadied herself once again. "I don't drink." She waited for the inevitable goody-two-shoes comments.

"Not even water?" Brad questioned in mock sarcasm.

His approach surprised CJ, but flipping her long curls over one shoulder, CJ faced the situation as she would any other battle. Surrounding herself with a wall of indifference, she spoke. "Look, I don't want this to sound presumptuous, but I would just as soon put aside any misgivings you might have."

She paused and drew a deep breath. "I don't drink liquor. I also don't smoke, dance, do drugs, or believe in having sex before marriage." She blurted the rhetoric out in the same routine fashion she'd used since finding herself on her own at sixteen.

Lowering her eyes, CJ felt almost embarrassed by her declaration. *Oh well*, she thought, *let him think me strange. I don't need him or anyone else.* Mustering her courage, CJ raised her eyes to meet his gaze. Instead of the disgust she expected, she was stunned to find his amused stare.

"You're different," he finally said with a lightheartedness that put CJ on edge, wondering what he'd say next. "And I find you fascinating."

"Most people find heiresses to be so," CJ said without thinking.

This only served to broaden Brad's smile. "Tell me, Heiress," he said, with a roguishness that instantly put her off guard, "are you a Christian?"

CJ hadn't expected the question. Her mouth dropped open for a moment before she regained her composure. "Yes," she finally replied, "I am."

"That's wonderful!" Brad declared. "I am, too. Would you by any chance be interested in attending a Bible study with me? We have a great group going on at my church. We meet once a week and most everybody there is single."

"I don't know. I've not been all that interested in starting new relationships. Besides, I really don't know you," CJ stated.

Brad refused to let her withdraw. "I've never shared a more intimate moment with anyone than the one I shared with you earlier today."

CJ shook her head. "Holding someone's head while they vomit can hardly constitute the foundation for a relationship."

Brad laughed out loud. "Why don't we share dinner and stretch that meager foundation?" He extended his hand to help her to her feet. For a moment they stood facing each other, almost as if ready to step into a waltz.

Brad smiled. "Don't dance, huh?"

CJ countered his grin. "Never learned how."

"We'll have to remedy that," Brad replied.

CJ grew uncomfortable at the low, husky tone of his voice. "What's for dinner?" she asked, hoping to break the spell.

"How do you feel about Italian?"

"Love it," CJ admitted.

"Good, then what we don't eat tonight, we can take with us on our picnic tomorrow."

"What picnic?" CJ questioned. Forgetting the effect of looking into his eyes, she lifted her gaze to meet Brad's.

"The one I intended to suggest for our second date."

"I see." CJ heard her voice tremor slightly. He was too close and too impressive. She wanted to draw back her hand, but he held it so possessively that CJ was certain he'd never willingly release it.

"Does that mean you'll say yes?"

"Let me see how good the food is first," CJ said with a grin. For some reason, it all seemed very right.

Dinner proved to be wonderful, and even CJ had to admit that she was quite comfortable in Brad's company. They took their tea with them to the balcony, and CJ enjoyed the warm summer breeze.

"Do you live here in Denver?" Brad suddenly asked.

"I have an apartment here," CJ admitted. "My parents also left me a couple of cabins. One is in the Sangre de Cristo range near Westcliffe, Colorado. The other is just outside of Skagway, Alaska."

"I know Skagway quite well," Brad replied. "Wonderful town! I flew for a commuter company out of Juneau when I was nineteen. One of my regular flights was in and out of Skagway."

"Daddy loved the challenge," CJ remembered. "It used to scare me every time we made the final approach."

Brad nodded. "It was a thrill and a half, to be sure. There I was, coming down the passageway. . ." He began one of those infamous pilot stories that always began with the three words "There I was." He used his hand to simulate his approach. "Mountains on both sides and a narrow harbor strip to land on."

"We hugged the mountain so close on the one side that I thought I could very nearly reach out and touch the trees," CJ added. She was drawn into the story against her will. *Dear God, don't let me get sick again*, she prayed silently.

"There were times when I thought it would be necessary to do just that. You nearly had to embrace the mountain, then pull a one-eighty, turning completely back the way you'd come in, and head almost straight down," Brad elaborated.

CJ nodded. "Daddy called it wing-and-a-prayer flying."

"I remember reading that somewhere. I always liked that better than seat-of-your-pants flying. Seemed closer to God."

"True," CJ admitted. "I think that was Daddy's sentiment, as well." Somehow, sharing the memory with Brad wasn't quite as painful as she'd feared it might be. Nevertheless, the old apprehension was there, and CJ longed to change the subject. She had no desire to explain her inability to deal for very long with memories of her parents.

"It's getting late," she began and took a final drink of tea. "I think I'd better go." She started to move toward the sliding glass door when Brad reached out to stop her.

"I've really enjoyed sharing this evening with you, CJ. Will you come with me tomorrow?"

"On the picnic?"

Brad smiled. "Yes, on the picnic. I know a terrific place, and I think you'll love it."

CJ contemplated the idea for a moment. She had enjoyed Brad's company. What harm could there be in a picnic? "All right," she finally answered. "It sounds like fun."

"Great. Where can I pick you up?"

"I'll meet you in the lobby." CJ wasn't yet ready to reveal her address to Brad.

"Okay, let's say eleven?"

"Eleven is good for me." CJ waited for Brad to open the balcony door. "Thank you for dinner. It was some of the best lasagna I've ever had."

"Mrs. Davis is a woman of many talents. It also helps that she comes from a long line of Italian cooks. I'll have her make us a special dessert for tomorrow," Brad said, walking CJ to the suite's double doors.

"Sounds wonderful," CJ admitted.

Brad walked her to the elevator, then lifted her hand to his lips and lightly kissed her fingers. "Until tomorrow, then," he whispered.

CJ wanted to say something, but the words wouldn't come. She felt strange emotions return. Frantically, she searched for something that wouldn't sound awkward. Instead, the elevator doors opened and she found herself stepping inside without a word to Brad. The look on his face told her that he understood. . .maybe too much.

Chapter 3

The following morning, CJ found Cheryl more than a little amused at having mistaken Brad for a maintenance man.

"I suppose I should be embarrassed at all the things I said to him about the poor management and such. But in truth, I'd have probably said those things even if I'd known," Cheryl admitted.

"No doubt," CJ laughed, playing with the handle of her coffee cup.

Cheryl looked through her calendar of events. "Now don't get so wrapped up in Brad that you forget about your dress fitting. I don't want my maid of honor looking shabby on the happiest day of my life."

"I won't forget," CJ assured her friend. "Now remind me where it is I'm supposed to go."

"Designs By Christy." Cheryl pulled out a piece of paper and jotted down the address while CJ looked at her watch for the tenth time.

"Relax. It takes only five minutes to get down to the lobby," Cheryl teased, handing the address to CJ. "And I'm sure he'll wait. . .even if you're late."

CJ stuffed the piece of paper into the back pocket of her jeans. "Do you think I look okay?" she suddenly asked, surprising both Cheryl and herself.

"You look smashing!" Cheryl said, feigning a British accent. "Jolly good, I say. Just like the good old days."

CJ nodded seriously. "I've missed them. When you went to Europe and Curt moved away, I thought I'd go crazy."

It was Cheryl's turn to sober at the mention of CJ's brother. "How is Curt?"

CJ shrugged her shoulders. "Beats me. I hardly ever heard from him after you two broke off your engagement. He never calls. Never writes. I suppose someday I'll pick up a newspaper and read that he's won a Nobel prize or something. I'd be the last to know."

"Where's he living now?"

"Florida," CJ replied. "At least he was still there a month ago. I never find out anything until he's already relocated. He's lived in seven different places in the last five years."

"The accident was hard on him. It was the end of your close-knit family," Cheryl remembered. "It was the end of our relationship, as well."

CJ nodded. "Mind if we change the subject?"

"Nope. Besides, if my watch is right, you have just a few minutes to get downstairs and meet Mr. Hotel. Or should I say Prince Charming?"

CJ stuck her tongue out in feigned disgust. "I'm going to go comb my hair or whatever you do with it. I'm still not sure why I ever let you talk me into getting it curled."

"Because you needed the change," Cheryl said firmly. "You've been stuck in a rut for five years, and if I have anything to say about it, you won't be stuck there much longer."

"Well, changing my hair is one thing," CJ replied, heading for the bathroom. "Rearranging my life is totally different." She glanced at the bathroom door handle and smiled. "Totally different."

❧

Downstairs in the lobby, Brad was already pacing back and forth when CJ stepped off the elevator. He was dressed casually and holding a wicker basket.

"You look great," Brad said and added, "I hope you're hungry."

"Starved," CJ confessed. "You'll think all I ever do is eat."

"Not with a figure like yours," Brad answered, casting CJ an appreciative once-over. He directed her out the front door, where a Jeep stood ready and waiting. "Ownership has its privileges." Brad grinned and opened the car door for her.

"Where to?" CJ asked.

"It's a surprise," Brad announced and started the Jeep.

CJ realized she'd not get anything more out of him and decided, instead, to sit back and enjoy their drive. She loved Denver and lost her thoughts in the passing city streets.

"You haven't heard a word I've said," Brad proclaimed, startling CJ. With an embarrassed nod, she admitted that he'd caught her daydreaming.

"Sorry," she offered. "I got a little caught up in memories."

"Why don't you share them with me?" Brad suggested.

"I'd only bore you."

"Hardly," Brad replied. "I want to know everything about you."

"Why?"

"You're a unique woman and I want to get all the details. . .the scoop, so to speak."

CJ laughed. "It won't stop the presses, I assure you. I'm just a nobody."

"I'm just a nobody," Brad mimicked. "You've lived a lifetime of events, no doubt, following your father and mother around the world. You're no ordinary woman, CJ. You're Doug O'Sullivan's daughter."

CJ turned to size Brad up with a frown. "Is that all you care about? Is that all I represent. . .the daughter of your dead hero?" She hadn't meant to be so frank, but she reasoned it was better to be honest than hide her feelings.

"I'm sorry," Brad began, "that was rather callous and rude. I didn't mean it that way, I assure you. I just figured that you must have experienced a lot in your life because of the life your father lived. Maybe you didn't. Maybe you stayed home, safe and sound with a nanny, or perhaps you were tucked away in boarding school."

CJ smiled and instantly forgave him the indiscretion. "No such luck. I'm guilty of the gypsy lifestyle you purport me to have lived."

"You sound like it was an awful thing."

"I guess in some ways it was. I never knew where we'd be from one week to the next. Oh, I'm sure someone had that all mapped out, but I didn't know about it."

"What did you do about school?"

"My mother home-schooled me. I never saw the inside of a classroom until I was grown." The tightening in her stomach made CJ wish Brad would change the subject.

Brad didn't sense that anything was amiss and continued to quiz her. "What was your first memory of childhood? I mean, do you have one thing that sticks out in your mind above the rest?"

"I suppose I do." CJ remembered flying with her father and forced the image away.

"Well?" Brad pushed for an answer.

Just then, as if to rescue her from having to speak, Brad screeched on the brakes to avoid running a red light. CJ was amused to find his arm shoot out in front of her, as if to offer her additional protection.

"Whew! That was a close one," he sighed. "I guess I should do less talking and more driving."

"This isn't a town to fall asleep at the wheel in," CJ quickly answered. "I remember once. . ." The words tumbled out over themselves as CJ recalled some insignificant near miss. She was grateful to avoid thinking of her parents and hoped to keep Brad's mind occupied with other stories. Maybe he'd forget about Doug O'Sullivan and the fact that his only daughter was sitting beside him on the way to a picnic. Maybe, but not likely.

They drove slowly through the city until they were able to catch Interstate 25 north, and then the pace picked up dramatically. CJ forgot to pay attention to the surrounding scenery as Brad broke into a story about one of his resort hotels.

"You wouldn't believe the things people take back home with them. We leave the complimentary stationery, pens, coffee, and tea. We even anticipate the cheating that goes on with the wet bar and snacks. We bill them after the fact, but we always anticipate the possibility of it happening."

CJ laughed. "But I take it this involved something much bigger."

"You might say that," Brad replied dryly. "This particular time they took a huge, cherry highboy. The thing weighed enough to require two grown men to move it, and when I finally caught up with the thief, I found myself face-to-face with a sixty-year-old woman who told me she simply had to have it."

CJ couldn't suppress a giggle. "What was her reason for that?"

Brad shrugged and rolled his eyes. "She said it matched her own bedroom furniture and she'd looked all over for one."

CJ broke into a hearty laugh. "How did she ever get it out of the hotel unobserved?"

"She waited until two in the morning, and then, with the help of some hired hands, moved it down the service elevator and out into a waiting truck. After that, we card coded all the service elevators."

"Did you let her keep it?" CJ couldn't resist asking.

"Yeah," Brad said with a nod. "For thirty-six hundred dollars." At this, they both laughed until CJ felt tears come to her eyes. She hadn't even realized they'd left the interstate until Brad stopped the car and jumped out.

"Well, we're here. Now, don't look up until I help you out," he pleaded, his earnestness reminding CJ of a little boy who'd prepared a special surprise.

CJ pulled her compact out of her purse and cast a quick glance at her hair. Deciding it was still presentable, she waited for Brad to open the door.

Lord, she prayed silently, *don't let him bring up the subject of Mom and Dad again. I just can't deal with it right now.* She breathed an "Amen" and tucked her purse under the seat.

Brad opened the door and offered CJ a hand out. Her eyes met his, and a moment of weakness washed over her at his expression. How could anyone look at her so tenderly, so. . .well, almost like he could see clear to her soul?

"Still hungry?" he asked, and his voice was barely a whisper.

CJ could hardly force herself to speak. What was wrong with her? "Yes," she finally answered. "Did Mrs. Davis make dessert?"

"You bet she did," Brad smiled. "I know you're starving, but I'd like to show you something first. It's the reason I brought you here."

CJ realized for the first time that she had no idea where "here" really was. Looking around her, she felt a feeling of dread begin to seep in.

"What do you think?" Brad questioned. "I live over there," he continued, without waiting for her answer. "But my hangar is back here. That's where I keep my vintage biplanes. Of course, I keep a twin-engine Beech closer to the house because I use it so often. Isn't this place great?" Brad was too absorbed in the moment to notice CJ's reaction. "You can very nearly taxi right up to the front door. I'll bet your dad would have loved coming home to a place like this."

His words trailed off in her mind. CJ felt her stomach tighten. The sound of a Cessna 180 coming in for a landing behind them made her head swim with memories. Bile rose in the back of her throat.

Brad watched the color drain from her face. "CJ? Are you all right? CJ?"

The plane's wheels touching down, the engine's tireless droning, and the ominous realization that she stood in the middle of an airfield were suddenly too much for CJ.

Slapping Brad's arm away from her, she began to walk away.

"CJ? What is it?" she heard him call behind her.

She looked around her and realized that the posh airstrip had been designed to allow pilots to live in-residence where they could simply get into their airplanes for transportation, like normal folks would their cars.

"No!" she exclaimed, shaking her head. Memories of another time were everywhere. No matter where she turned, CJ faced the things she'd avoided for the last five years. Her steps increased to a run, and she lost all reasoning.

"No! No! No!" she sobbed and ran in the only direction that seemed void of life.

"CJ!" Brad easily caught up to her and whirled her around to face him.

"No!" she exclaimed and pushed away from the shock-faced man. Instantly she brought her hands to her ears, hoping to block out the sounds.

"CJ, stop. Tell me what's wrong. Talk to me!" Brad demanded, pulling her arms down.

CJ felt her knees give way. She collapsed in a heap on the ground with Brad still firmly gripping her arms. She buried her face in her hands and cried uncontrollably.

Brad could only stare in amazement for a moment. What had happened?

Reaching down, Brad gently lifted the crying woman into his arms. He cradled her against him as he might a small child and tried to soothe the obvious heartache.

"Shhh," he whispered against her ear. "It's all right. I'm here, CJ; just tell me how I can help you."

CJ gasped for air. She could feel herself growing faint. "Take. . . me. . .home," she pleaded and fell back against his arms in unconscious blackness.

Chapter 4

CJ fought her way through the endless mire that held her captive. When she finally opened her eyes, she found Brad's concerned face hovering over her. His green eyes were intent on her every move.

For a moment, CJ couldn't remember what had happened. Then everything came rushing back at once. Brad was still holding her tightly, as if he were afraid of what might happen if he let her go.

CJ couldn't think of anything to say and so she said nothing. It was Brad who finally broke the tense silence.

"You want to tell me about it?" he questioned gently.

CJ stared blankly for a moment, then shook her head. "No," she whispered. "I just want to go home. I need to be alone."

"I don't think that would be wise," Brad said. Tenderly he put her in the Jeep, even fastening her seat belt before standing back. "I don't know what's going on with you, but I'm not about to let you go off by yourself. We may not be that close of friends, but I wouldn't let a total stranger wander off alone after a scene like I just witnessed."

He came around and got in the Jeep, causing CJ to turn her tear-streaked face to the window.

"Does this kind of thing happen all the time?" he asked, starting the Jeep.

Silence met his concern.

"CJ, I'm not the type to give up. You might as well talk to me and get it over with. Besides, maybe I can help."

Still, CJ refused to respond. She stared in silence out the window, looking beyond the airfield to the distant Rockies. "I lift up my eyes to the hills," the psalmist had said. Now CJ found herself doing that very thing. . .the same thing she'd done a million times before.

Brad drove back to the hotel in dejected silence. He wanted so much to help the troubled young woman, yet she kept a wall of protection firmly in place between them. What was it that troubled her so? When they'd first met, it was the claustrophobia and now this incident at the airstrip. What was grieving her so that she was given to these bizarre episodes?

Brad drove the Jeep under the archway and parked in the same place as before. Without a word, he turned off the engine and came around to help CJ out of the vehicle.

"Come on," he said firmly. "I'm taking you upstairs to Miss Fairchild. I don't think you're in any condition to drive yourself home."

CJ wanted to protest, but in truth she couldn't find the energy for it. "Brad," she finally managed to speak.

Brad stopped and looked down. CJ refused to look at him and instead lowered her gaze to the patterned carpet of the hotel's lobby.

"I'm sorry."

"Don't be," he replied. "Just know that I'm here and I'll be happy to listen whenever you're ready to talk."

Upstairs, Brad knocked loudly on the door to 618 and prayed silently that Cheryl Fairchild would answer. Cheryl pulled open the door in a burst of energy and enthusiasm. Her face, however, dropped the animated look when she caught sight of Brad's worried expression and CJ's lack of color.

"What happened?" she questioned, taking hold of CJ possessively. She eyed Brad suspiciously over CJ's bent head.

Brad shrugged his shoulders with a look of pure confusion on his face. "I wish I knew," he answered. "I think you should put her to bed, though. She's not in any shape to drive."

Cheryl nodded. "You wait here, Mr. Aldersson. I'll be right back."

Brad paced the room nervously while waiting for Cheryl to return. He went over every detail of his actions and couldn't begin to figure where things had gone wrong. When Cheryl came through the door and closed it firmly behind her, Brad urgently asked, "Is she all right?"

Cheryl nodded. "I managed to get enough out of her to figure out what happened. Why don't we sit down and talk?"

"I'd love to," Brad replied. "I have to know what I did wrong."

"It has nothing to do with you." Cheryl took a seat on the sofa and waited for him to join her. "In fact, if CJ hadn't agreed to my telling you, I wouldn't be talking to you now. She's a very introverted, private person. She always has been, but even more so after the accident."

"Telling me what? What accident?" Brad questioned.

"The crash that took her parents' lives."

"I never thought about it," Brad admitted. "Do you mean to tell me that she still isn't over it? Was it the airfield that upset her so much?"

Cheryl nodded. "CJ's never been the same. Even though the crash took place five years ago, she can't talk about it and she can't handle anything to do with flying."

Brad rubbed his chin and shook his head. "I never for one minute intended to cause her pain."

"She knows that, and so do I."

"Please call me Brad," he urged. "I guess I knew that CJ's father was killed in the crash but, until she mentioned it, I didn't remember that she'd lost her mother, as well."

"That's not the half of it," Cheryl admitted. "CJ, herself, was on that flight. They were coming back from an air show in the Midwest."

Brad's head snapped up and met Cheryl's worried expression. "She was on the plane when it went down? I've seen pictures of the wreckage. How could anyone have lived through that?"

"She was the sole survivor," Cheryl replied. "She was conscious the whole time and pinned in the wreckage for hours. They eventually had to cut her out in order to take her to the hospital. She very nearly lost her leg, but they managed to piece it back together after several surgeries. Then, years of rehab followed in order to get her walking again."

"No wonder she never learned to dance," Brad muttered.

"What?"

"Oh, nothing," Brad said, meeting Cheryl's eyes. "Go on. What else happened to her?"

Cheryl seemed to relax. "It was the hardest thing I've ever seen anyone bear. A shattered leg, multiple injuries, and the realization that both of her parents were dead. She couldn't deal with the knowledge that she'd been left behind. She hated the fact that she was still alive.

"Then the reporters and FAA people came. They drilled her for information and hounded her relentlessly until her brother, Curt, arrived and drove them off. CJ wouldn't speak to anyone, not even me. That went on for several weeks, and the doctors began to worry that maybe she couldn't talk. They thought perhaps it was hysterical laryngitis or something like that. Then one day, CJ announced to them all that she'd simply had enough and wanted to be moved from the hospital immediately. Curt arranged for her to convalesce at home, and that was that."

"She never told me," Brad said softly.

"No," Cheryl admitted, "she wouldn't. That would require facing the problem, and CJ hasn't begun to do that. It's something that has worried me greatly over the years. In fact, I have to confess that I spent a lot of time abroad because I couldn't handle the situation here at home. It came between us in a big way because I wanted to force her to deal with it, and CJ absolutely refused to consider the matter at all."

"But she'll never be free of it if she doesn't try."

"I'm not sure she wants to be free of it, Brad. Although she can't face her memories, they are, as far as CJ is concerned, all she has left. She has a storage unit filled with memorabilia and family mementos. Curt and I tried on several occasions to get her to bring the stuff home or get rid of it, and CJ acted like we were both off our rockers. Curt finally gave up and moved off, and I guess in my own way, I gave up, too."

"But all we did was visit an airstrip. It wasn't even a place she'd ever been with her parents. It's a relatively new area—"

"But don't you see?" Cheryl interrupted. "It doesn't matter! She can't even fly on a commercial airliner. CJ turns the TV off if there's an advertisement for flying. She won't visit a travel agency or go to movies or the mall—all because she's afraid she might have to encounter something to do with flight."

"But she's a grown woman. Surely she sees the need of getting past this thing. There are counselors who could help her," Brad protested.

"You have to want to be helped, Brad, and CJ doesn't want to be helped."

"Maybe I can help her," Brad said with a new resolve. He was beginning to formulate an idea in his mind.

"Would you risk being responsible for sending her into complete seclusion?"

Brad's shoulders slumped. "What do you suggest? I can't just leave her alone."

"Just be yourself. Show her that you care, in spite of her trauma, and let nature take its course."

"Cheryl," he paused, "may I call you that?" She nodded and he continued. "I don't mean to seem harsh, but isn't this style of ignoring the problem the same thing that everyone else has already tried? It obviously isn't working."

"No, it isn't working." Cheryl's voice betrayed her anguish.

"Then doesn't it stand to reason that someone has to make her face up to the problem?"

"I don't know," Cheryl answered honestly.

"Look, I have a friend at church who happens to be a counselor. Maybe he'll have some ideas." Brad got to his feet. "I really appreciate your taking the time to explain this to me. I know God can get CJ through this."

Cheryl shrugged. "He doesn't appear to be too concerned at this point."

Brad turned in surprise, but said nothing. *One problem at a time*, he told himself. *One problem at a time.*

❧

CJ had no intention of falling asleep. She hated to sleep because when she did, the old dream came back to haunt her. Always, she was falling. Falling and falling, as though it would never end. It was always the same. Always the crash. But, to her surprise, when she awoke two hours later, she felt much better. She hadn't dreamed the dream. Instead, she had the vaguely familiar sensation of being held in warm, masculine arms.

All at once she remembered Brad. No doubt he'd be long gone after having to face two episodes of her inability to cope with the past.

Getting out of bed, CJ walked calmly into the living room and confronted her friend.

"How did it go?"

Cheryl looked up from the list of wedding guests and eyed CJ suspiciously. "Are you sure you ought to be out of bed? Brad said you had a very nasty spell."

"I did," CJ conceded. "But I'm better now, and I need to get home.

Did you talk to Brad? Did you tell him everything?"

"Yeah, he was really worried about you. I don't think you've heard the last from him."

"Well, I'd be surprised to learn that he wanted to go another round with me," CJ replied, searching the room with her gaze. "Do you know where my purse is?"

"No. I didn't see that you had it when Brad brought you in. Do you suppose it's still in his car?"

"That'd be just my luck," CJ replied. "Oh well, I'm not going to worry about it. There wasn't much of anything in it, and my license is in the car. I guess I'll manage."

"But what about the car keys?" Cheryl asked, getting up to walk CJ to the door.

"I used the valet parking," CJ answered. "They have my keys."

Cheryl nodded, then reached out to touch CJ's arm. "Are you sure you can drive home?"

"Stop worrying, Cheryl. It's a car, not an airplane."

Chapter 5

B rad's interest in helping CJ didn't wane with the consideration that he was really getting into something about which he knew little. He prayed in detail for the wisdom to deal with the matter and asked God over and over to show him what direction to take in order to be a help and not a hindrance.

He called Cheryl the very next day to inquire about CJ's recovery.

"She was fine, Brad. Drove herself home and everything," Cheryl answered in a distracted voice.

"I want her address," Brad suddenly said. "I checked with directory assistance for a phone number, but it's unlisted. Can you help me?"

"It wouldn't be right to give it to you without CJ's permission."

"Look, I promise I won't go over there; I just want to send her some flowers, maybe a letter or card. Please, Cheryl."

Cheryl felt torn. The man obviously cared, and it wasn't like he was some kook off the streets. Her loyalty to CJ was fierce, however, and won out. "I can't."

Brad's exasperated sigh filled the receiver. "I know she'll never call me."

"She will if she wants her purse back," Cheryl said, still wondering how she could help Brad without betraying CJ.

"What?"

"CJ thinks she left her purse in your Jeep."

"I didn't see it anywhere," Brad said. He tried to remember what CJ had done with it when she got in the car.

"All I know is, when she got ready to leave here yesterday, she told me she'd probably left her purse in your Jeep."

Brad smiled for the first time that day. "I'll find it, Cheryl, and I'll see to it that it makes its way home."

"Brad, please be careful. CJ is precious to me, and I won't stand by and see her needlessly hurt."

"I won't hurt her," Brad promised. "At least not the way you're implying. I want to see her beat this phobia of hers. I want to get to know the real woman inside and clear out that scared, sixteen-year-old girl. It might be a bit painful, but in the long run, CJ will be better off for it.

"Look, I'll send a bonded courier over with her purse and I'll attach a letter to it. Is that acceptable?"

"Of course. I guess it's perfectly logical that you were bound to find the purse sooner or later. I just don't want CJ thinking that I betrayed her."

"She'll never know that you even mentioned it," Brad assured. "You have my number, so don't hesitate to call me if I can be of help."

❧

Over the next few days, Brad tried to get some kind of response from CJ. He had the courier require a signed receipt for the purse and letter—and the receipt was returned to him the same day—but there had been no other response.

Then he went to work trying to woo her with gifts. He'd sent flowers, balloons, stuffed animals, and candy, but they were consistently refused and returned with the delivery man back to the shop of origin. Next, he tried overnighting and same-day-delivering letters and cards, still without a single response or acknowledgment. At least they weren't refused. Finally, Brad decided enough was enough. Picking up the phone, he dialed his friend, Roger Prescott.

❧

CJ nervously paced her apartment. Why wouldn't Brad just leave her alone? She'd refused his gifts and the stack of unopened letters sat on the entryway table as evidence that she wasn't the slightest bit interested in what he had to say to her. But she was. At least a hundred times a day, she had to force herself not to open the envelopes.

He'll either feel one way or the other, CJ told herself. *Either he'll want to draw me out of my shell or he'll want to pursue a relationship in spite of it.* Neither one seemed acceptable.

"I've tried to be a good person," CJ reasoned aloud. Since her parents' deaths, she had convinced herself that accepting Christ as her Savior was simply not enough. She had deemed it necessary to be as perfect as she could in order to go to heaven. But in this situation with Brad, she felt she was failing miserably. She wasn't being good to Brad. She wasn't even being kind.

When the doorbell rang, CJ was certain it would be yet another of Brad's deliveries. She glanced down at her striped top and navy shorts with indifference as she opened the door to her apartment.

CJ's eyes widened at the sight of Brad Aldersson on her doorstep. "Brad!" she exclaimed and stepped back a bit. "What are you doing here?"

"You wouldn't call me," he offered to begin with, "and I was worried. I brought a friend with me, and I thought you might like to talk to him, since you don't seem inclined to talk to me."

CJ shook her head. "I don't need to talk to anyone."

"CJ, please just listen to me for a minute," Brad pleaded. "I know the letters may have sounded a bit forward—"

"I never read them," CJ interjected. Brad's eyes registered disappointment, but he refused to give into it.

"Then I guess I really need to start from scratch," he continued. "My friend is a Christian counselor from my church. Roger, this is CJ O'Sullivan. CJ, this is Roger Prescott."

CJ only stared at the man's extended hand.

"I'm glad to meet you, CJ. Brad tells me that you're a sister in the Lord."

CJ didn't dare be rude with a man of God. "Yes," she finally answered and reached out to shake Roger's hand. She glanced hesitantly at Brad and then again to Roger. "Won't you come in?"

"Are you certain that you want us to?" Roger asked. "We aren't about to barge in, if you'd rather we leave."

"No, it's all right. I don't know for sure what Brad hopes to accomplish here, but I won't be inhospitable."

"May I call you CJ?" Roger asked informally.

"I suppose so," CJ replied in an agitated manner. "Won't you sit down?"

Roger shook his head and turned instead to Brad. "Brad, I know that you want to help CJ, but if it's all right with her, I'd like to talk to CJ alone."

Brad looked stunned but nodded his cooperation. He turned to meet CJ's eyes. "I would like to call you sometime," Brad said softly as he turned to leave.

CJ hated the pained expression on his face. She knew she'd caused it with her cold-shouldered attitude. "Do you have the number?" she asked.

"No."

"I won't promise anything," CJ announced. She jotted down her number and handed it to Brad. "But you have my permission to call."

Chapter 6

CJ listened in awkward silence as Roger Prescott explained the role he would like to have in CJ's life.

"I know this is all very strained, and I must admit I don't usually make this kind of house call—"

"But Brad was no doubt very persistent," CJ interjected.

Roger smiled. "Yes, as a matter of fact, he was."

"He can be like that, at least from what I've seen."

"He just cares, CJ. I'm convinced that he's genuinely concerned for your welfare and that he has a deep desire to get to know you better."

"I understand that," CJ said firmly. "What I don't understand is why he feels he has to fix me. I'm just fine."

"You know, CJ," Roger began, "many times people find that they can't deal with things from their past. The mind shuts out the horrific. Psychologists once tested people by showing them pictures of Nazi concentration camps. The photos explicitly revealed hundreds of the innocent dead. After viewing the pictures, people were asked to write down one thing they remembered in particular. More often than not, what those people wrote had nothing to do with the atrocities they'd witnessed in those pictures.

"Usually," Roger continued with a soft expression of compassion, "people noted some unusual thing that had nothing to do with the death and destruction. Some noted the existence of words or markings on the buildings. One photo prompted a common response from people as they noted a child's single shoe lying in the mud. They couldn't handle the scene of the dead child in his mother's arms, right beside that shoe. Their mind picked out something neutral and refused the rest."

"I don't understand what this has to do with me," CJ replied defensively.

"When faced with monumental ordeals in which the mind finds itself having to register unpleasantries or even horrifying situations, we do what we must to protect ourselves. In your case, if I understand correctly, you had to endure a tragic plane crash. The crash resulted in the deaths of your parents and injury to yourself. Now, you find that even the association of things related to flight and the lifestyle you knew before the accident are unbearable. Is that a fair assessment?"

"It hurts too much."

Roger nodded. "Yes, I know. But, CJ, if you don't deal with this now, it will continue to hurt you over and over again. You must realize that burying your pain and suffering over all these years has resulted in a deep-rooted fear."

"I'm getting by," CJ replied and hugged her arms to her chest.

"Getting by isn't always enough. Is that all you want for your life?"

CJ looked up at the ceiling, refusing to meet his eyes. "It's not a matter of what I want," she whispered. "It's all I can handle."

"I'd like to help you handle it in another way," Roger said evenly. "Brad would like to help, too. You know, he thinks quite highly of you."

"No, he thinks highly of Doug O'Sullivan, my father," CJ said, snapping her head back down. "I'm just the left-behind daughter of Brad's hero."

"Brad came and talked to me extensively," Roger continued. "At first, I point-blank refused to become involved. Like I told Brad, a person has to want to be helped. Otherwise, it isn't help—it's interference —and accomplishes absolutely nothing. Sometimes it hurts the person even more."

He paused and looked at CJ sympathetically. "However, I've known Brad for a long time, and the more he talked, the more I could see the genuine concern and respect he held for you. CJ, he never once mentioned your father, except to say that you two were very close and that he'd died in the crash."

CJ got to her feet, unable to sit still any longer. She paced out a few steps in front of Roger and turned. "I was left a small fortune," she confided. "In fact, it wasn't that small. My brother and I are well set financially and, unfortunately, this has made me a very popular woman. The first time any man learns of my true identity, he usually starts seeing dollar signs. Add to this my determination to do what is right in the eyes of the Lord and, all of a sudden, the simplest relationship becomes impossibly complicated."

"And you think Brad is after your money and that his only other interest is a kind of far-off hero worship of your father?"

Again she paced. "I don't know. I really don't know!" Her auburn hair whirled around her face as she turned on her heel. "Why does he have to care so much? He doesn't even know me. I threw up while he held me over the toilet. Then I broke down in complete hysteria when he tried to take me on a picnic. How can he possibly care whether I deal with this issue or not?"

"So you realize there is an issue to deal with?" Roger questioned gently.

CJ froze. Her face contorted into several expressions before her protective mask went back into place.

"CJ, no one is trying to hurt you or use you. We only want to help. I'm offering to set aside counseling time for you, if you want that help. And I've a feeling Brad is offering much more than that. Are you so confident that you can make it through this without help? Is there never a time when the demons haunt you so severely that you just want out?"

CJ's eyes registered acknowledgment. "How could you know?"

Roger got up and walked to where CJ stood. "It's my job to know, for one thing. For another, we all have our demons to contend with. Christ told us it wouldn't be easy here on earth. But, CJ, Christ overcame the world and He's already dealt with this problem, as well. He's given you a path to find the way home. It's up to you to set your feet on the trail."

CJ nodded slowly. "It's so hard," she whispered faintly.

"I know. But you have people who care, and you don't have to walk that path alone. You have a Savior Who loves you and Who will always be with you. Even when times get rough and things are as bad as they can be, you won't be alone."

Roger's words permeated the hard façade CJ had lived behind for five years. By listening to the things he had said, CJ recognized the truth and realized that God had brought her to a very important crossroad.

"I'll think about it, okay?" CJ said with tears in her eyes.

Roger handed her his card. "Call me anytime. Oh, and on the back is Brad's number. I think he'd like to know that you aren't angry with him."

CJ took the card and nodded. She had a great deal to consider.

∞

Sitting in his Jeep, Brad waited impatiently for Roger. He'd wanted to be there. No, the truth was Brad wanted to be the one to whom CJ talked. He gripped the steering wheel, then released it, wishing he could feel at peace with what he'd done. In his mind he kept seeing CJ's frightened expression.

"Why can't this be easy?" he questioned with an impatient fist to the steering wheel.

After nearly an hour, Roger reappeared in the parking lot and made his way to Brad's Jeep. When he got inside, he smiled.

"I think we made a bit of progress," he said confidently.

"You honestly think so?"

"I can't be certain, but I believe CJ is ready to deal with this thing. She needs some time to think, but I left her my card and told her to call me anytime and that I'd set up appointments to counsel her. I also left her your phone number. I knew you wouldn't mind."

"Of course I don't mind. I want to help her," Brad said sharply.

"I know. So do I. But we see only a little bit of the picture that makes up CJ O'Sullivan. God has the blueprints, and He's the One in charge. We must take our direction from Him or we'll only be interfering with His plan."

Brad slumped back in the seat in complete dejection. "I've never been one to just sit back and do nothing."

"I don't expect for you to do nothing. You have access to information about CJ and her family. Do a little research and learn what you can. Pull out books, newspaper articles, whatever it takes, and learn about her. The more you know about CJ as a child before the accident, the better you can help. The accident forever changed her life. She not only lost her parents, she also lost a part of herself when that plane went down. If she lets you into her life, you might be the one to help her recover that."

"I'll get right on it," Brad said with renewed hope.

"Oh, and Brad," Roger said as he fastened his seat belt, "spend a good amount of time in prayer, as well."

Brad smiled. "Of course."

ᏚᏋ

Almost a week later, the telephone on Brad's desk in the penthouse began to ring. Brad picked it up absentmindedly, his eyes still focused on the column of figures before him.

"This is Brad Aldersson."

"Brad, it's CJ."

The feminine voice brought Brad's full attention to the call. "CJ? How are you?"

"Better, I think."

"Good," he replied. "I've been worried about you."

"Why?" CJ asked without thinking.

"Because I care."

"Why?"

"Do I have to have a reason?"

"I guess not." CJ paused. "Look, this isn't why I called."

"Why did you call?" Brad questioned, almost afraid of the answer.

"Actually, I wondered if you could come over and talk. I'm not good at explaining myself under any circumstances, but on the phone, I'm even worse."

Brad could hardly contain his excitement. He fought to speak evenly. "Of course. When?"

"Whenever is convenient for you."

"I'm free right now. Is that too soon?"

"No. Now would be fine. Do you remember the address?"

"I certainly do. Would you like me to bring anything? Mrs. Davis has been working up a feast in the kitchen. I could pack some of it up and bring it along."

CJ laughed, and the sound was like music to Brad's ears. "You know me and food," she answered. "Bring whatever you like, and I'll scout around in the refrigerator and see if I have anything appropriate to add."

"Don't you dare," Brad replied. "I owe you this meal. I'll bring everything we need. You just sit tight."

CJ hadn't long to wait. When she opened the door, she burst out laughing. Two large grocery sacks with legs sticking out from beneath stood at attention. "Is that you, Brad?"

The deep chuckle from behind the food told CJ it was. "Mrs. Davis got a bit carried away, but I think you'll be pleased."

"Well, come on in. You can put the stuff in the kitchen or on the dining room table, whichever you prefer."

"Do you want to eat while we talk?" Brad questioned.

"That'd be good. At least if things get bad, I won't miss out on dinner again."

"Then lead me to the dining room table and we'll just lay all this food out," Brad directed. "Then, if you'll get some plates and silverware, we should be ready to eat."

"Okay, right this way," CJ replied and led Brad to her small but neatly ordered dining room.

Placing the sacks on the table, Brad looked at CJ for a moment. Self-conscious of the attention, CJ glanced down. "I'll get the dishes," she finally said. "Is tea all right to drink?"

"Tea sounds good to me," Brad answered.

CJ quickly retrieved the pitcher and brought out a woven bamboo tray from under the sink to put it on. She pulled down her everyday dishes and pale blue glasses and went to the silverware drawer to finish out the setting.

Taking a deep breath, CJ walked back into the dining room, carrying the tray. Brad looked up and smiled.

"Everything's ready here."

CJ noted the table and gasped in surprise. "There's enough food here for an entire dinner party."

"I wanted to make sure you had a choice. I still know so very little about you. I wasn't sure what you liked," Brad offered.

CJ looked the food over and laughed. "I don't see a single thing here that I don't like," she said good-naturedly and took the seat that Brad offered her. They were rapidly running out of idle chatter.

Taking the place across from her, Brad stared deeply into her blue eyes. "Thank you for asking me over," he said in a tone that left no doubt as to his pleasure in the matter.

CJ nodded and dropped her head in embarrassment. But the thought of praying came to mind, and she quickly covered her discomfort by suggesting they offer thanks.

"Would you say the blessing?" she whispered in request.

"Of course," Brad replied and bowed his head. "Father, I thank You for this day and the meal we are about to share. I ask Your blessing on the food and those who partake of it. Amen."

CJ filled her plate in silence, knowing that Brad was waiting for her to say something to start them off. Finally, she choked back her discomfort and spoke.

"I guess I owe you a bit of an explanation, if not an apology."

Brad shook his head. "No apologies are necessary."

CJ folded her hands in her lap and looked at the food on her plate. "I know Cheryl told you about the accident. I'm certain that beyond that, given your love of my father, you must have read about it, as well."

Brad nodded, and CJ continued. "I don't remember a lot about the actual crash. I do remember being pinned in the wreckage and feeling so helpless. There was fuel everywhere," she said, remembering the smell. "I just knew that at any minute the whole plane would burst into flames. I don't remember seeing my parents, but somehow I knew that they were dead. Don't ask me how. I just sensed it, I guess." CJ fell silent, wondering if it had been such a good idea to have this talk, after all.

"You don't have to push yourself, CJ. It's good that you're willing to deal with it at all."

"I know," she answered softly. "I know that you and Roger want to help me, and I do appreciate that."

"But. . . ," Brad interjected.

CJ looked up and met his dark green eyes. "But I'm not sure I'm up to the task. I've thought a lot about what Roger said, but I don't feel comfortable going to a stranger and baring my life."

"What about me?" Brad questioned.

"You're nearly as much a stranger as he is," CJ responded.

"And do you want to keep it that way?" he asked.

CJ found his eyes fixed on hers. They held her captive in a way that was not at all unpleasant. "I'm not saying that," she finally answered. "I'm just saying that I don't know what I want. I've been chained to these emotions and problems for so long, I'm not sure I can break away from them. Or," she added in a barely audible voice, "that I even want to. Does that sound horrible?"

"Sometimes the things that bind us feel almost comforting," Brad said in a knowing way. "Kind of like the evil we know is better than the evil we don't."

"I suppose that's what I mean," CJ said, lowering her eyes once again. She toyed with her fork for a minute before adding, "I guess it just comes down to the fact that I'm afraid."

Brad reached out and stilled her restless hand. "We're all afraid at one time or another. But, if you'll let me, I'd like to be there for you. I want to help."

"Why? I don't understand how you can just walk into my life from nowhere and want to help me. I'm nothing to you."

Brad tightened his hold on her hand. "I can't explain it all. I don't know for sure why you've come to be so important to me. Maybe it's just that I don't like to see anyone hurting as much as you are. Maybe it's because you seem so lost and scared. I don't know. All I know is that I want to help. I want to get to know you better. Will you give us a chance to be friends?"

CJ swallowed the lump in her throat and fought back the tears that threatened to spill. It was the moment she knew would come. Could she make the right decision? Could she put aside her fears and break the chains?

"I'd like very much to keep seeing you," she finally managed to whisper. "Is that enough to start with?"

Brad smiled. "You bet it is."

Chapter 7

Brad fairly soared on wings of his own. He went straight to Roger's house after leaving CJ and explained her acceptance of his help.

"What do I do now?" Brad questioned, as Roger set a cup of coffee in front of him.

"You must earn her trust," Roger answered, taking a seat. "She doesn't know you, and you really don't know her. Establish a friendship, first and foremost. And," he added in a stern tone, "I mean friendship. Don't try to fall in love with her or make her fall in love with you. That would be disastrous. You need to be friends first. I can't stress that enough."

Brad took a long drink of the steaming black liquid. "I'm already drawn to her physically as well as emotionally," Brad admitted. "I may have already lost my heart to her."

"No," Roger stated firmly, "you feel sorry for her. You have sympathy for her plight and you care about her recovery. You aren't in love with her; you're merely a concerned observer at this point."

Brad grinned and put the cup on the table. "Keep talking. Maybe you'll convince me."

Roger shook his head. "Brad, this is most serious. I know it's hard, but you need to find a common ground with CJ that doesn't revolve around a physical attraction. Bring her to church. Take her to the Bible study. Offer her friendship, but don't get physical. You'll never be able to help her objectively if you do."

"I don't think I follow you," Brad confessed.

Roger leaned forward. "If you fall in love with her, you won't allow yourself to cause her pain and, unfortunately, most healing starts with that very thing. If you fall in love with her, you will only build her a bigger wall. You will convince yourself that you can keep her from the pain of the past and then she'll never deal with it. Do you understand?"

Brad frowned. He did, indeed, see the logic in Roger's words. Not that he wanted to. Much to his disappointment, Roger's advice held that solid foundation of truth that Brad couldn't ignore.

☙

CJ wasn't at all sure what to expect when Brad suggested she come to his penthouse at the hotel. She weighed her options carefully and finally accepted, realizing that she had agreed to take on his help.

She lingered in the corridor outside the penthouse, studying the brass and glass fixtures and objets d'art. Plush, mauve carpeting seemed the perfect balance to the entryway. It was refined, but not overdone. CJ ran her hand lightly across the frame of a Renoir replica. It was a painting she'd always enjoyed. DÉJEUNER DES CANOTIERS—THE LUNCHEON OF THE BOATING PARTY was printed in bold letters on the plaque at the bottom. She stared for a moment at the painted figures.

There were men in straw hats and a red-haired woman, cooing at a fluffy dog. The table was set for the luncheon, the wine goblets just catching the light. CJ's eyes were drawn to the woman in the background. She leaned casually against the railing, listening or pretending to listen to the gentleman in front of her. CJ thought perhaps she was daydreaming. Of all the characters there, the leaning woman was the one most distant. She was a part of the boating party, yet she was alone. It was almost as if the woman observed what was going on around her without truly being a part of it. It reminded CJ hauntingly of herself. Shaking off the sorrow, CJ knocked on the door.

Brad opened it and smiled broadly. "Come in. Come in." CJ returned his smile with timid warmth. "Have you eaten yet?"

"Yes," CJ replied and nervously plunged her hands into her skirt pockets. Would there ever come a time when she could face Brad with an emotion other than dread?

"There are some things I wanted to say," Brad began, "and I thought perhaps it would be best to say them here."

"I see."

"Why don't you make yourself comfortable?" He motioned to a chair. "I want to say up front that I want to help you just because I care about you. It doesn't have anything to do with your father, and I don't expect anything out of it."

CJ's brow furrowed. "Be real, Brad. Everyone expects something. No one does anything without anticipating an end result."

Brad nodded. "Maybe I should reword that to say your welfare is my uppermost goal. If you are better able to deal with life and can put the pain of your past behind you, then I will have accomplished what is most important to me at this point."

"I see. A real humanitarian, eh?"

"CJ, I can't honestly say why it's so important to me," Brad admitted. "But from the moment I found you cowering there in Cheryl's bathroom, it seemed overwhelmingly necessary to be a part of your life. I propose friendship. Nothing more. Nothing less. I won't overstep those bounds, at least not until you progress to the place where you feel comfortable considering such a thing."

"Is this Roger's idea or yours?" CJ questioned.

Brad smiled. "I have to admit it was Roger's at first. But I quickly saw the logic and reasoning in what he suggested. I can't be objective if I fall in love with you." His green eyes were intense.

"Go on," she whispered.

"It's just that I want everything to be on the level with you. Roger says trust is the most important element in our beginning a friendship. I figure, first of all, that you have to feel confident that I'm not after your money or your body. I've made arrangements for my business office to open its books to your scrutiny."

"Brad, that's hardly necessary," CJ protested. She was touched that he would do such a thing, but it embarrassed her greatly for him to think her so insecure about her money.

"I insist. This is one matter in which I won't take no for an answer," Brad stated firmly. "Another area I insist be clear between us is that any time you feel I'm moving too fast or expecting too much, I want you to tell me so. I'm not porcelain, and I won't be hurt. I promise."

CJ smiled at his insistence. "All right," she agreed. "But I have some demands of my own." The words surprised CJ. In all honesty, she hadn't considered such things until just then.

"When you check in with Roger for advice on how to help me, I want to know what he says. Just because I don't feel comfortable enough to see him on my own doesn't mean I want you two discussing me behind my back. I'm willing to try and deal with this thing, but I've never held much store in shrinks. That goes for Christian ones, as well. Fact is, I've always thought the two things kind of conflicted with each other. But that's another issue. Do you agree?" CJ asked.

"Agreed. It's only fair that you know what advice Roger offers. In fact, we can discuss that right now, if you like."

"All right, what does the good doctor say?"

Brad grew serious. "He says that this won't be easy. It will be painful and slow, and if you aren't a willing participant, all of my caring in the world won't matter.

"Furthermore, Roger stresses that you must deal with the past or go on suffering. I think you have to recognize that, right off the bat. You have to make yourself understand that we are trying to address the deaths of your parents, the crash itself, and your resulting phobias and sorrows."

CJ swallowed hard. Her face paled slightly. "You're asking quite a bit," she responded.

Brad's serious expression softened. "I know I am. It may sound stupid, but there's this image of the real Curtiss Jenny O'Sullivan that I see in my mind, and I'd very much like to get to know her. But only if you want it that way."

CJ took in Brad's words and sorted them into an acceptable form. "I want to know how you plan to do this. I want to know the details. That's another of my demands." Her words hit their mark, and now it was Brad's turn to swallow hard.

"I thought we'd start with some books. You can come over here or I can come to your place. I have a great many books on flying, air shows, and. . . ," he paused, "your father."

CJ steadied herself. "Go on."

"Well, I figured we could read about different flight-related activities, then graduate up to videos, and eventually pull in more personal items."

"Such as?" CJ questioned curiously.

"For starters, Cheryl tells me you have a storage unit filled with memorabilia. When you feel up to it, we could go through it. I also have some videotape that deals exclusively with your father's career and includes some family shots, as well."

CJ could only nod. It all seemed overwhelming. "I'd rather we meet here," she finally said. "My place seems too personal, and I'm not sure I'm ready for that. And we both know your house at the airfield is out of the question."

"Meeting here is fine. But let's keep it as informal and friendly as possible. We are friends, after all. No set appointments. . .just get-togethers."

CJ smiled. "That does sound better."

A couple of nights later, CJ sat beside Brad on the sofa.

"Did you have your people check out my financial status?" he asked, surprising CJ.

She nodded. "I did what you asked of me. Everything checked out, just like you said it would. My accountant, in fact, was very impressed. He kept going on and on about your portfolio. Maybe you two should spend some time together."

Brad chuckled at her teasing mood. How he wished she could maintain that lightheartedness throughout the evening ahead.

"Do you feel more comfortable about spending time with me? Are you convinced that I'm not after your money?"

CJ smiled. "My accountant assured me I could only benefit by spending time with you. I think he's hoping for trade secrets. Shall I play the spy?"

"Don't invest in hotels," Brad offered. "That's the best advice I can give."

Amusement lit up CJ's eyes. "Yes, I can see how you've suffered."

Brad rolled his eyes. "This is the longest I've stayed in one place. If it weren't for you, I'd probably be in Vail or Telluride."

"Do you have resorts there, as well?"

"Didn't you check that out?" Brad questioned.

"Umm. . . ," CJ tried to remember what her accountant had told her. "I guess I remember something about it. It wasn't all that important." She stopped abruptly and apologized. "I'm sorry. That didn't come out the way I meant it."

"It's all right, CJ. I don't offend easily. Is there anything you'd like to know about me that your accountant didn't find out?"

CJ leaned back against the plush couch and sighed. "Do you have brothers or sisters?"

"No."

"Do you have a college education?"

"Yes. I have two bachelor degrees. One in business administration, the other in hotel management. And I have a master's in public administration, as well."

"What? No doctorate?" CJ teased.

"Give me time. I'm only thirty," he said, feigning exasperation.

"Ah, now things are getting interesting. When is your birthday?"

"February 24," he replied. "Yours?"

CJ grinned. "I'm the one who's supposed to ask the questions."

Brad leaned back and folded his arms. "We're supposed to be friends. Can't friends know when each other was born?"

CJ took pity on him. "July 17."

"Been to college?"

"Yes." CJ couldn't help but grin at him. "Art history degree. Now there's something that will take you far."

Brad laughed. "Anything else?"

CJ sobered. "Are your parents still alive?"

Brad shook his head. "I lost them both when I was twenty-three."

"How?" she questioned softly.

"My father suffered a massive heart attack. He died instantly."

"What about your mother?" CJ forced herself to ask.

"I believe she died of a broken heart. She went downhill in a big way after Dad passed on. There was nothing I could do to comfort her. Within six months she was gone."

"I'm sorry, Brad." CJ's voice held tenderness and compassion.

"They're in heaven, and it's not the end," he said in a poignant way that CJ understood.

For several minutes, they sat in silence. Brad wanted CJ to have plenty of time to deal with the information, while CJ came face-to-face with another person's tragedies.

"Are you ready to look at some books?" Brad finally asked.

CJ nodded. "Maybe you could tell me what you have planned."

"I have a coffee-table book filled with beautiful photographs of airplanes. Some are in flight and some are on the ground. I thought for tonight, we could just look at the pictures and if you wanted to talk about anything, that'd be fine, too. If not, we'll just enjoy each other's company. Okay?"

CJ took a deep breath and looked at Brad. Enjoying his company wouldn't be hard. Keeping her emotions under control would be the major battle. "All right," she replied and forced herself to add, "let's get started."

Chapter 8

CJ found Brad's patience could very nearly disarm her concerns and fears. He was gentle with his questions and always eased up when he felt that probing into the past was becoming too difficult for her to handle.

She finally agreed to attend a Bible study with him and enjoyed the event in a way she'd not expected. The people gathered at the church were mostly singles, and before the study began, Roger Prescott led the group in a discussion of their concerns and problems for that week.

CJ listened in earnest interest as one person after another relayed the frustrations they had endured. Some spoke of loneliness or fears of being alone. Others mentioned difficulties at work or pressures to settle down and marry. One woman spoke of the lingering illness of her mother and how hard it was to watch her die, little by little, each day. For the first time, CJ could see merit in a quick and painless death such as her parents had shared.

When everyone had voiced something, with the exception of CJ and Brad, Roger led the group in prayer and asked God to surround each person individually with His protection and to bless them each in a special way. CJ felt the prayer go straight to her soul, and she clung to each word as though it were prayed for her alone.

"If everyone will open their Bible," Roger began, "we'll get started. Last week we moved into the second chapter of Ephesians. Does anyone recall something special about our study?"

One petite, dark-haired woman raised her hand. "I had never read this part of the Bible before, and I guess I was pretty amazed by the clarification that Satan really is at work on earth. I guess I knew from things I'd been told that Satan was genuine, but the idea of him working in those around me was a concept I couldn't make real. That is, until we read that verse."

Roger nodded. "Let's all look again at the second chapter, verses one and two. I'll read out of the *New International Version,* so those of you who are following in another version, bear with me. 'As for you, you were dead in your transgressions and sins, in which you used to live when you followed the ways of this world and of the ruler of the kingdom of the air, the spirit who is now at work in those who are disobedient.' I guess we all recognize Satan in that passage. We can also see here that 'the ways of this world' are not God's ways. Anyone else have something they want to share?"

The man seated beside CJ spoke up. "I liked the fact that verse six says we've already been raised up with Christ."

"Good," Roger agreed. "Verse six says, 'And God raised us up with Christ and seated us with him in the heavenly realms in Christ Jesus.' We need to understand, folks, salvation began when we accepted Christ, and with salvation, eternity also begins for us as Christians. We don't need to keep waiting for our eternal blessings. We can take possession of them now!"

CJ tried to take it all in. Not only had it been a long time since she'd given any real attention to the Scriptures, but she'd never experienced this kind of Bible study in her life. Sunday sessions of church had left a great deal unanswered, and it was easy to see why people were drawn to more in-depth readings of the Word. For CJ, it was like a feast of spiritual food, and she was nearly starved to death for it.

"If no one else wants to add anything, we'll start tonight's study with verse eight and read through to ten." Roger waited for everyone to find their place, then continued. " 'For it is by grace you have been saved, through faith—and this not from yourselves, it is the gift of God—not by works, so that no one can boast. For we are God's workmanship, created in Christ Jesus to do good works, which God prepared in advance for us to do.' Who would like to comment on this section of Scripture?"

"I'd like to say, 'Thank God!' " one man replied, and the group chuckled in unison before the man continued. "I'd be in a bad way if I had to get to heaven on my own."

"We all would be," Roger admitted. "Paul, the writer of this letter, above everyone else seemed to recognize this. He makes comments throughout his letters of how hard he tried to do the right thing, only to fail. If our salvation depended on whether or not we could tow the line and be perfect, as Christ is perfect, no one would make it into heaven. That's not to say we don't try to be like Christ."

CJ was stunned. It was as if Roger's words were aimed directly at her heart, yet this was a concern she'd shared with no one. Not even Cheryl or Brad.

Roger continued with CJ's eyes fixed intently upon him. "Let's break it down. We are saved by grace. What is grace?" Silence met the question and Roger did what he often did when this happened—he pulled out a dictionary.

"The closest definition I find here would be, 'Divine love and protection bestowed freely upon mankind. A virtue or gift granted by God.' We are saved by divine love and protection. We are saved through a gift God freely bestowed upon mankind. He didn't offer it with the expectation that we should pay something in return. He didn't offer it because of what we could do. He gave us salvation because He loves us.

"Now, look further at that verse," Roger continued. " 'Through faith—and this not from yourselves, it is the gift of God.' We just established that, didn't we?" Several people murmured affirming words before Roger continued. "Now we've gone over this before, but who can tell me what faith is?"

The woman whose mother was dying raised her hand. "Hebrews 11:1 says, 'Now faith is being sure of what we hope for and certain of what we do not see.' Sometimes," she admitted, "that verse is all that gets me through."

"Exactly. Now, Paul knew there would be those do-gooders who would try to convince people otherwise. People who would proclaim that unless you performed sacrificial acts of worthiness and deeds of devoted worship, you would lose your salvation. He covers that neatly in verse nine when he says, 'not by works, so that no one can boast.'

"We can't work ourselves into heaven. However, God does expect us to live for Him, and in doing so, we find verse ten applies to how we are to go about it: 'For we are God's workmanship, created in Christ Jesus to do good works, which God prepared in advance for us to do.' "

CJ reread the words until she knew them by heart. *Not by works!*

Her pulse quickened. She'd always believed that she had to be good, do good, in order to get to heaven and see her parents again. Now, she was hearing and reading that this wasn't the case. God expected her, as His child, to do good works that He had prepared for her, but not in order to earn her salvation.

The study continued, but CJ was lost in thought. She barely heard Roger announce that it was time to end in prayer. Everything seemed overwhelming.

❧

On the ride home, Brad chanced a question. "Tell me about your brother."

CJ flashed a bittersweet smile. "Curt is five years older than me. Even so, we were very close. He used to hang around with Cheryl and me and tease us unmercifully."

Brad said nothing. He recognized the fragile web that CJ spun.

"Whenever we were on a circuit of air shows and his college breaks coincided with a performance," CJ continued, "Curt would fly in and join us. Daddy always liked to have him along. . .said it made his job a whole lot easier. Our last performance was in Kansas. We finished up and had a really great meal of Chinese food with Cheryl and her dad. Curt had already gone back to college, and Cheryl was pining away for him." CJ glanced up suddenly. "I don't remember. . .did I tell you that Cheryl and my brother were engaged to be married?"

"No, but it sounds like you were all a close-knit family."

CJ nodded. "We were, until the accident. Now, in the five years that have passed, I've managed to drive both Cheryl and Curt away."

"What makes you think you had that responsibility?" Brad pulled into the parking lot of CJ's apartment complex and shut off the engine.

"Curt left shortly after bringing me home to recuperate. I'm afraid I wasn't a good patient. I insisted he move me to a new house. I couldn't bear to be in the old one without my mom and dad. All the responsibilities of the funeral. . ." CJ felt her throat tighten. "I couldn't even go to my parents' funeral.

"My leg was shattered in the accident. Mangled might be a better word. I had to have fourteen separate pieces of debris surgically removed from my leg. Some were pieces of metal, others wood and fiberglass. The

58

bone was broken in seven places, and the doctor wasn't even sure he could save it. Curt flew in a team of the best orthopedic surgeons in the country and wouldn't allow them to amputate. I had over three years of physical therapy, and I guess that only helped to make me more reclusive."

"What about Cheryl and Curt? Did they marry?"

"No. Curt changed after the accident. He tried to keep it inside, but I knew he was just as devastated as I was. When the press and the FAA came to my hospital room, Curt was most protective. Everything was so stressful. He and Cheryl started fighting. She couldn't understand why he'd shut her out. He couldn't deal with her constant clinging and questions. After Curt managed to get me and the estate settled, he took off—without a word—for three weeks."

"That must have frightened you a great deal," Brad declared.

"It was all of my worst nightmares come true. All I had left was Cheryl, and she grew distant and eventually began to travel with her jet-set friends. She'd get so upset with me and say, 'You'll have to fly again sometime, CJ; why not just come along with me to Rio or Paris?' "

CJ paused and grew even more introspective. "It really wasn't Cheryl's fault, though. She also had to deal with her father. He and Daddy were best friends. They even invested in the air show business together and started their own aviation company. In fact, when Daddy put together a performance team, Ben Fairchild put together an impressive ground crew, just to see to our needs."

" 'Our needs'?" Brad questioned, sitting up and leaning forward. "Do you mean you were a part of the performance team?"

CJ smiled. "You couldn't be Doug O'Sullivan's daughter and not pilot a plane. I could handle a plane before I could ride a bicycle, even if I couldn't fly legally by myself. I'm still not all that good at riding a bicycle."

"And you performed in the air shows?" Brad was completely taken aback.

"In whatever way I could. Daddy said a child behind the stick always brought in the crowd, and the crowd was everything to my father." CJ closed her eyes for a moment, and when she opened them again, tears streamed down her cheeks. "Missing them just isn't an adequate enough word."

Brad patted the seat beside him and CJ automatically scooted closer. CJ allowed Brad to encircle her with his arms. "No words can fill the void it leaves behind when we say good-bye to someone we love. Just remember, CJ," Brad whispered against her ear, "you've only said good-bye for a little while."

CJ said nothing. She let the tears fall in a quiet state of mourning while Brad rocked her gently in his arms. It was a slow release of pain and sorrow, and only the first in many steps that would be necessary to free herself from the accident.

❧

Days later, CJ found herself thinking back to that moment in Brad's car. She hadn't gotten sick from reliving some of the past, and that, to her, was one of the very best signs. She began to feel better about herself almost immediately.

After donning cream-colored slacks and a burgundy silk blouse, CJ hurriedly attached gold dangling hearts to her ears and took a final look in the mirror. Hating the way her hair looked, CJ grabbed her brush, swept her hair back from one side, and secured it with a barrette. Deciding the results were acceptable, she repeated the action with the other side.

She was going to spend the day with Brad, and for some reason, she felt like dressing up for him. She knew he'd stressed that they should be only friends but, in truth, part of her disliked the limitation. *Maybe he's not attracted to me,* CJ thought. *Maybe I should dress up more and really turn on the charm.*

She smiled to herself. It was the first time in her life she'd ever considered trying to attract a man's attention. She hadn't felt this good in years and, for once, CJ could actually say she felt hopeful.

Mrs. Davis had created another of her culinary delights. Sweet-and-sour meatballs were served on beds of steaming white rice, with stir-fried vegetables on the side. CJ couldn't remember when food had tasted so good.

After lunch, Brad led CJ into one of the side rooms, dominated by a big-screen television. A VCR sat conspicuously on the coffee table, and Brad motioned her to take a seat.

"I found something really special. I know I promised to tell you everything ahead of time, so I'm going to explain myself here and now," Brad began.

CJ looked warily around the room. Up until now, things had been going her way. She could only guess what Brad had planned. She watched suspiciously as he walked over to a handcrafted, oak sideboard and pulled open a drawer.

"I found a movie that had been made at one of the air shows when you were quite young. It's a very personal film, devoted to your family, especially your father. I had it transferred to videotape and thought we could watch it together. Are you game?"

CJ paled a bit and sat back hard. She hadn't even looked at photographs of her parents since the accident. "I don't know, Brad. I mean, we've watched other videos and that went all right, but this is different."

"Look, I promise I'll turn it off if it gets to be too much. In fact, here." He reached over and handed her the remote control. "You're in charge."

CJ stared at the black-and-silver remote in her hand. She was in charge? Since when? She would have laughed out loud if it weren't for the serious expression on Brad's face.

Taking a deep breath, CJ decided to risk it. "Put the tape in."

The film started and for several minutes a narrator extolled the virtues of Douglas O'Sullivan in grand style. He told of her father's birth into a flying family. Her grandfather had barnstormed in his early days and later maintained one of the better flying circuses in America. Doug O'Sullivan was just as much a natural at flying as his father had been.

CJ smiled when they showed photographs of her father and grandparents. "They called him 'Scrappy' when he was a boy," CJ told Brad in a whisper. "On account of the fact he was so small."

The narrator spoke of other events in the life of Doug O'Sullivan. A distinguished career in the military, an honored war hero, and later, one of the forerunners in organizing international fly-ins, where people from all over the country could compete for prizes and laurels in flight performance. That brought the narrator to the place where he introduced the background.

CJ vaguely remembered the scene. It was one of the gatherings at

Oshkosh, Wisconsin. Here was competition at its best. The camera panned the painted wooden banner. INTERNAT'L EXPERIMENTAL AIRCRAFT ASSOC., proudly labeled the top, and just beneath that, big, bold, yellow letters stated, FLY-IN CONVENTION. Flags from several nations, including the U.S., Canada, Britain, and France, graced the top of the banner and added an air of patriotic festivity to the day.

CJ was mesmerized as the tape rolled back the years. She felt her stomach tighten as the camera zoomed in on a Curtiss Jenny biplane her father had called his baby. Usually, he flew the Jenny in ahead of the family while Curt and CJ's mother, Jan, would fly in later, bringing all the needed supplies for their stay.

"Nearly one million people will share the experience of this fly-in, and over fifteen thousand planes will take off and land on this runway before the week is out," the narrator was saying. The aerial view of the field was impressive, with row after row of planes anchored at the side of the airstrip.

"The numbers are staggering," the narrator continued. "They must find it quite a task to organize all of these aircraft."

"I'd imagine finding space to park the thirty or forty thousand campers that accompany folks here is more of a chore." CJ tensed and gripped the arm of the sofa. The voice belonged to her father.

The narrator continued. "Doug O'Sullivan, you've been flying most all of your life, isn't that true?"

"It sure is. Flying is my life," he was saying. CJ forced herself to look at the screen as the camera caught the tanned, leathery face of her father. "Of course," Doug O'Sullivan added, "I wouldn't have a life at all if it weren't for God. He's always been my copilot and always will be."

Tears blurred CJ's vision. *Oh, Daddy,* she thought, *why did you have to go away? Why did God take you from me?*

"You have quite a family, I understand," the narrator said. "I know folks would love to meet them."

"Well, over here is my oldest, Curtiss." CJ saw her dad put a possessive arm around Curt. "He's seventeen and handles the second biplane in our simulated dogfights. I'm sure you'll be able to catch us in the air later this afternoon."

Curt hammed for the camera and answered the questions directed at him before the men moved on to focus on Jan O'Sullivan, Doug's beloved wife. CJ felt her heart breaking. Her mother was radiant, youthful, and happy. She missed her so much, remembering their girl talks and the tenderness her mother had for her.

"There's not a gal around who can beat her. She's remembered by most for her multiple participations in the Powder Puff Derby," her father was saying of his wife. CJ watched her father lovingly pull her mother into his arms. "A pretty, young, talented woman is always good for the show, right?" Doug winked at the narrator, then planted a firm kiss on his wife's lips.

"Oh, Doug!" Jan exclaimed and feigned disgust. "You'll have to excuse him for his lack of manners," she laughed. "He's eaten and slept biplanes for so long, he doesn't know how to act in front of respectable people."

The film broke away to some previously recorded footage of her parents' earlier days as a team. The narrator told of the couple's harrowing experiences and triumphant successes. CJ wiped away the tears with her hand, then gratefully took a handkerchief Brad offered her.

"Last, but certainly not least," the reporter said, bringing the viewers back to Oshkosh, "is the youngest member of this flying team. I understand your daughter is only twelve, but already she flies like a pro."

"She certainly does. She's a great mechanic, too," Doug O'Sullivan said with pride. He was seated beside the narrator beneath a tent awning. "CJ!" he called. It was more than she could bear. CJ softly sobbed into the handkerchief, not even aware that Brad had slipped his arm around her.

A twelve-year-old CJ appeared on the screen. She was giggly and pigtailed and totally devoted to her father. She threw herself onto her father's lap in little-girl abandonment. Doug O'Sullivan tickled his daughter, until a laughing CJ yelled, "Oh, Daddy, stop!" Settling down, CJ faced the interviewer like she'd done it all her life.

"CJ O'Sullivan, I understand you have quite an interesting story behind your name," the narrator said.

"My daddy named me after his biplane," the little girl answered. CJ could barely hear the words. "I'm Curtiss Jenny O'Sullivan." Until that moment, CJ hadn't remembered even doing the interview. Now it all came flooding back to her.

"What a name and what a young lady!" the man replied.

"That she is," CJ heard her father say. "She's my special angel, and I love her very much."

CJ, the little girl on the screen, giggled and kissed her father. "I love you, too, Daddy." She laughed and danced away from the camera.

CJ, the woman, lifted the remote and murmured two words, "No more!"

Chapter 9

CJ broke down and cried with all her heart. Five years of pent-up loneliness and hurt came pouring out with the tears. Brad held her close, whispered comfortingly into her ear, and refused to let her bear the sorrow alone.

Little by little, instead of easing, CJ's pain intensified. Then came anger and resentment that CJ could no longer bury. Without warning, she pushed away from Brad and threw the remote control across the room. Her eyes caught the book on the end table, and she threw it, too.

Jumping up from the couch, CJ was like a wild, crazed animal, hurt and wounded so deeply that she refused to be consoled.

"He could have let them live!" she raged. "God didn't have to take them. I lived! They could have survived, as well. Why? Why did I have to be left behind? It isn't right! It isn't fair!"

By this time, Brad had gotten to his feet and closed the distance between them. "CJ, you've got to calm down."

"Stay away from me. Don't touch me," she managed to say between her clenched jaws. "I don't want to feel better. I don't want to be comforted. I can't bear the way you're looking at me now! I don't want your pity, and I don't want your sympathy."

Brad froze in midstep. "Is that what you think I want to give you? Pity? Sympathy? Grow up a little, CJ. Your temper tantrum at God won't change a thing. They're still dead."

CJ's mouth dropped open in surprise, but the tirade halted, at least momentarily. Brad used the opportunity to continue.

"I care about you, CJ. I thought highly of your father, but he's beyond caring about my devotion. He's at peace with His Savior, and he would want you to be, as well." Brad walked toward her in slow, deliberate steps.

"I want to give you many things, CJ, but pity is not one of them.

Pity cripples and kills, and I will not be part of it. I offer you friendship. Take it or leave it, but please don't spoil my heartfelt concern with your own self-pity." He stood directly in front of her. He could see the terror and rage in her eyes.

CJ drew a ragged breath. Everything Brad had said was right. "I don't want to be left behind," she whimpered. "I have nothing. Even my brother ran away to be rid of me. I'm alone, and it scares me."

Brad opened his arms, waiting for her move. CJ hesitated for only a moment, then threw herself into the welcoming embrace. "You're not alone anymore, CJ. I'm here, and I'll be here as long as you want me to be."

CJ said nothing. It was enough just to hear the declaration of faithfulness. She reveled in it. She embraced it. In that moment, she wanted nothing more than to feel the blanket of protection that Brad Aldersson offered her.

She lost track of how long they stood there, but finally Brad led her back to the couch and sat down with her.

"Being angry at God is probably the biggest guilt you've buried inside," Brad whispered. "You wanted so much to be good in order to earn your way into heaven, but deep down inside, you knew you harbored this horrible thing. You blame God for taking your parents. You blame God for your pain."

CJ nodded. He was right. How could he know so much about her? It was if she had laid her soul open for him to read, page by page.

"They're gone, and I'm here," she said hoarsely.

"But you aren't alone," Brad stressed.

"But I feel alone," CJ responded, looking deep into his eyes. She placed her hand over her heart. "I'm alone and lost inside, and I don't know how to find my way back."

Brad reached out and took her hand. Slowly, never taking his eyes from hers, he pulled her hand to his chest. "You're not alone," he repeated. "God never left you alone, CJ. You may have walked away, but He didn't. . .and neither will I."

❧

When CJ had finally calmed down enough to meet with Brad's approval, she made her way home and took a long, hot shower. Knowing she should call Cheryl but feeling unable to deal with her friend, CJ unplugged her phone and went to bed early.

For several hours, she stared at the ceiling. Her head was flooded with images from the past. In spite of how she tried to block their entry, the memories were there, and they forced her attention from every corner of her mind.

Tossing and turning, CJ struggled to find peace. It was clear that God was dealing with her, she realized, but what did He want? Absolution? He certainly didn't need forgiveness from her. After all, God hadn't held the grudge all these years; CJ had. God was innocent of the ugliness that bred contempt within her.

God was innocent!

The words hit her like a wall of stone. God had done nothing wrong. CJ was to blame for her own misery. She had allowed Satan a foothold, and now she was paying the price. Misery, paranoia, phobias, loneliness, anger—these were all things by which Satan could benefit. His purpose was served in these scornful attitudes—his and no one else's. CJ didn't have a life to call her own. She served those feelings as clearly as angels served their Lord in heaven.

No, she reasoned, *God doesn't need my forgiveness, but I need His.*

Yet, even knowing her need, CJ couldn't bring herself to ask for forgiveness. She felt the wall of protection going up around her. God, she rationalized, would understand just where she was coming from. God knew what pain she'd suffered and the battles she'd had to fight. *And ultimately*, CJ told herself, *God has allowed everything that happened to me. How could He still be a loving and merciful God and do that?*

There was no peace for CJ that night. Nor in the nights that followed. She refused to plug her phone back in, and when Brad finally showed up at her door, she told him to go home.

CJ moved restlessly from room to room, never leaving the apartment for any reason. She wanted to make things right. She wanted to believe God was sovereign and righteous and loving, but her heart felt hardened with each day that passed, and her mind told CJ she was justified to feel that way.

When finally she could bear no more of the alienation she'd created, CJ cried out to God, "I don't know what You want from me! You've already taken all that I loved. What more can I give?"

The resounding silence only made CJ feel worse. She paced a bit more, then settled down at her desk. Pushing up the roll top cover, CJ's eyes caught sight of her Bible. She hadn't picked it up in days. Now, even though she fought the urge, CJ reached out and opened it.

Lamentations, a requiem of sorrow, greeted CJ's eyes, and she was drawn to the words that were spread out before her in the third chapter. "So I say, 'My splendor is gone and all that I had hoped from the Lord.' I remember my affliction and my wandering, the bitterness and the gall. I well remember them, and my soul is downcast within me. Yet this I call to mind and therefore I have hope: Because of the Lord's great love we are not consumed, for his compassions never fail. They are new every morning; great is your faithfulness."

Her eyes backed over the words, "I remember my affliction and my wandering, the bitterness and the gall." CJ not only remembered them, she wore them about her like a suit of armor that kept her from feeling or thinking or living.

CJ forced herself to concentrate on the last sentences: "Therefore I have hope: Because of the Lord's great love we are not consumed, for his compassions never fail." She stopped.

"But I feel like they've failed," CJ whispered. "I feel consumed." She read the last words: "They are new every morning; great is your faithfulness." CJ put her head upon the Bible and wept softly.

"I do want to believe that. I do want to trust You, God. I don't want this thing between us. Forgive me," she cried. "Just send me a sign. Show me what I must do in order to heal. I give up, God. I give up. There's nothing left."

It was almost startling the way peace began to infiltrate the rockhard wall she'd placed around her heart. Slowly, CJ composed herself and got up. She'd wasted a great deal of time, not only during the last few days in her fight with God, but in her struggles against Him for over five years. What now? Recognizing the situation didn't make it disappear.

CJ wasn't surprised by the knock at her door, nor by the fact that it was Brad. Brad, however, was astonished at CJ's ragged appearance.

"Are you all right?" he questioned with a critical eye. Her eyes were puffy and swollen, with dark circles spoiling her perfect complexion.

"Yes and no." CJ pulled back from the doorway to add, "Want to talk about it?"

Brad smiled in a slight, almost impish way. "What do you think?"

CJ wearily stepped aside, letting Brad close the door behind him. She took herself to the couch and collapsed. Brad followed her in mute scrutiny. His face bore the concern that poured out from his heart.

CJ glanced up and almost laughed at his expression. "I look pretty bad, don't I?"

"Actually, you're a welcome sight. I was afraid I'd have to tear down that door. What have you been doing with yourself these past few days? You don't look like you've slept or eaten."

"I haven't," CJ admitted. "But I have been busy."

"Doing what?"

"Fighting." CJ's reply said it all.

"And who have you been fighting?" Brad questioned softly. The worried look faded into compassion.

"God. Myself."

"Who won?" Brad asked with a grin.

"Who do you suppose?" CJ countered with a laugh.

"Are you ready to try again?"

CJ pulled her knees up under her chin. She looked like a little girl, so vulnerable and lost. "I have to be," she answered. "I promised to go on."

"So now you're pulling yourself up by the bootstraps, is that it?"

CJ raised her head and shook it slowly. "I have no bootstraps," she replied. "All that is left in me is this weak, very tiny flicker of hope. Hope that God is really Who He says He is and that I can rest in that."

Brad reached out and squeezed her hand. "He's all that He says and much, much more." Spying her Bible on the desk, he got up and walked over to retrieve it. "Lamentations?" he questioned, not really needing an answer.

CJ shrugged. "It's what I opened up to. I read from chapter three, through verse twenty-three."

Brad glanced down, then turned back to CJ with a smile. "You should have moved on down to the twenty-fifth and twenty-sixth verses."

"Well, don't just stand there," she replied. "Read it."

" 'The Lord is good to those whose hope is in him, to the one who seeks him; it is good to wait quietly for the salvation of the Lord.' " Brad closed the Bible, put it on the coffee table, and smiled. "That tiny flicker of hope is all you need, CJ. God will do the rest."

"I asked Him to show me what to do," CJ shared. "I asked for a sign."

"Come with me, then," Brad whispered. "Come see my biplanes."

CJ looked apprehensive. "You haven't forgotten how I reacted the last time, have you?"

"I haven't forgotten."

"Are you sure?"

Brad reached down and pulled her to her feet. "CJ, come see my planes. Let go of your fear and bank on that hope. God won't let you down."

"Because of the Lord's great love, we are not consumed," CJ murmured.

"What?"

"Nothing," CJ said, losing herself in his warm, green eyes. "Let's go see your planes."

Chapter 10

Moving down the interstate, CJ felt her apprehension grow. Could she really do this? Now that they were nearing the airstrip, she silently questioned the sensibleness of the trip.

"Penny for your thoughts," Brad whispered.

"A penny's worth would take an hour," she replied, paying close attention to their approach to the airfield. She tried not to grimace, but Brad saw her expression before she carefully concealed it.

"If you don't feel up to getting out of the Jeep, we can just sit and talk."

CJ said nothing. She forced her gaze across the field to where someone was shooting touch-and-goes in a Piper Cub. Watching the plane land, circle the field, and take off again brought back memories of when her father had taught her to fly. Touch-and-goes were an important part of the routine in order to teach technique and hone skills for landings and takeoffs. She'd spent hours at the controls, with her father's gentle instructions helping her to correct each mistake.

Brad parked the Jeep and turned to face CJ. "Are you all right?"

She took a deep breath. Trepidation was a companion she knew well. Glancing back at the runway, she swallowed hard. "I think so," she finally replied.

"I meant what I said. I don't want you to force yourself. There's no sense in passing out again."

CJ tried to be lighthearted. "You're just afraid you'll have to carry me back to the car." Her blue eyes met his amused stare.

"That would be my pleasure," he said with a grin. "I couldn't possibly pass up the chance to get that close to you."

CJ lost herself for a moment. His eyes twinkled in a dazzling display that made her feel like laughing. The tiny crow's-feet that edged them only made his smile more pronounced. Her heart quickened and pounded in a way she'd never noticed before. Fearing the truth, she

71

told herself it was from apprehension and anxiety. But part of her wasn't convinced. Was she losing her heart to this man?

"Are you ready?" he asked and reached his hand out to cover hers.

CJ entwined her fingers with his and squeezed them tightly. "I'm so afraid," she whispered. "Inside the car it doesn't seem so bad, but out there. . ." She lifted her chin. "Out there, it's real and it's frightening."

"I'll stay right by your side. I'll even hold your hand. You won't be alone. God and I will be with you."

CJ searched Brad's face to confirm his declaration. Finding the affirmation she needed to see, CJ took another deep breath. "I'm ready."

Brad opened the door for her and pulled her close. "How's this?" he asked. CJ looked up, offered him a weak smile, but said nothing. They walked out toward the hangar, and Brad began to speak. "Anytime you want to go back to the car, just tell me."

CJ nodded. Her head was already filled with the sights, sounds, and smells of the private airport.

"I bought extra property here so that I could keep all my planes in one place," Brad informed her. "I have six altogether. The four biplanes I want to show you are on the front side, over here." He pulled her along with him to an ultramodern, prefab metal hangar.

Dropping his arm for a moment, Brad fished out a set of keys and unlocked the building. As he swept aside the doors, CJ gasped in surprise. The dimly lit interior of the hangar stood in sharp contrast to the contemporary exterior.

Brad flipped on the lights and drew CJ to his side. She let her eyes travel over the individual stalls where some of history's finest aviation wonders were housed. Memories rushed back in waves that threatened to drown her in sorrow.

Not even realizing it, CJ reached across and grabbed Brad's hand. Her breath caught in her throat.

"I'm sure you recognize them," Brad said softly against her ear. Indeed she did. They were some of her father's favorites.

"It's been a long time," CJ whispered, feeling the years fall away.

They walked by each plane, giving a cursory evaluation. The blue-and-white Waco with its enclosed cockpit and passenger cabin was similar to one that CJ's father had bought shortly before the accident.

The red-and-white Travel Air, product of the business marriage between Cessna, Stearman, and Beech in 1924, waited regally. The model had always been one of CJ's favorites. Putting aside the horrors of her past, she reached out and touched the eight-foot prop.

"It's just like Daddy's," she murmured.

"I know. It was one of the first I purchased. Reading your father's first book, I fell in love with his description. He talked about how big and cumbersome most pilots thought the Travel Air was, but he didn't feel that way."

"That's true," CJ joined in, forgetting to be upset. "Daddy said it was all a matter of perspective. He loved the way it handled, and when I was with him in the Travel Air, I thought it was the most glorious plane in the world."

Brad smiled, knowing that for a brief moment, CJ was twelve years old again, with the wind in her hair and Doug O'Sullivan at the stick.

"Over here's the old standard," Brad said, moving her on before she became morose.

"A Stearman," she said with a grin. "Daddy said you could fly them standing on your head."

"From the looks of some of the air show films, I'd say he did that once or twice," Brad laughed.

CJ found the experience much better than she'd thought it would be. All the years of worry were far more oppressive than the actual deed of standing there before the planes her father loved.

"And last, but not least," Brad said, "is this beauty. She's my favorite."

CJ stood before the de Havilland Tiger Moth. "Oh, Brad!" she exclaimed. "I can see why. What a beautiful plane!"

The plane had been restored to perfection, and CJ admired the hard work that had resulted in the masterpiece before her. "Dope and fabric never looked so good," she complimented.

"It took a lot of hours, but I enjoyed it all," Brad admitted. "Here, look at this," he said and led CJ to the place where a photograph was pinned up on the wall. "This is how she came to me."

"Now I'm really impressed," CJ said, looking at the photo. The plane in the picture barely resembled the majestic wonder that graced the hangar.

"They brought her in on the back of a truck. She couldn't even fly."

"Kind of like me," she murmured absentmindedly.

CJ looked away from the picture to find Brad's face only inches from her own. She wondered for the briefest second if he would kiss her, and then the moment passed, unfulfilled.

Brad stepped away with a look of discomfort, and CJ wondered if she'd somehow done something wrong. She tensed up, feeling the tightness in her chest for the first time since entering the hangar. She put her hand to her throat, taking a deep breath.

Brad didn't notice the look on her face as he moved back toward the Waco. "This is my newest in the collection," he said as though nothing had happened.

CJ moved to the Waco, working hard to keep her emotions under control.

"I've had to make some adjustments and repairs," Brad said, sounding very casual. "I put in a new engine, but I'm still having trouble with. . ."

Brad's words faded into CJ's imagination and took on the voice of her father. For a moment she was a little girl again, working alongside him, seeing the engines through his eyes, and touching them with his hands.

Without thinking, CJ voiced several suggestions for the problem at hand, and before Brad could answer, she continued, "I remember once when you were working on. . ." Her words fell into silence, as her eyes refocused on the hangar. CJ's head began to swim. The old feelings of weakness were making her legs rubbery.

"Brad," she whispered weakly.

He turned with a look of questioning, but quickly saw the problem. "Come on, let's get out of here," he suggested.

CJ nodded. "I'm sorry. I don't know why—"

"Shhh," Brad interrupted, putting his finger to her lips. "We both knew this wouldn't be easy. I'm proud of you for even trying. Most folks wouldn't."

Once they were outside, CJ felt a little better. The Piper was no longer shooting touch-and-goes, and, for the most part, everything was quiet. For the first time, CJ realized it was a weekday, and she turned to Brad.

"Don't you ever work?" she asked.

Brad laughed. "Actually, it's funny that you should ask. I am planning on being out of town the rest of the week. I have to fly over to Telluride and see to some matters at the resort there. Want to come?"

CJ shook her head. "I'm not ready for that." She paused reflectively. "But ask me again, later."

"Don't worry, I will. Until then, what would you suggest we do next?"

CJ wanted to say something about their encounter in the hangar when she thought he might kiss her, but instead she shrugged and turned away.

"Did you have something in mind?" she asked, refusing to look at him.

"The Waco still needs work. How about coming out here on the weekends and helping me?"

CJ wondered how it would feel to work on planes again. She'd spent many hours with her father, tightening cylinder-base nuts, patching tears, replacing broken struts. She doubted there was a single part of any one of those planes that she hadn't worked on, in another time.

Summoning up her courage, CJ replied, "I suppose it would be a logical way to proceed. Also," she added, only now making up her mind, "I'm going to call Roger. I think I'm ready to talk with him."

Brad surprised them both by pulling CJ into his arms. He hugged her briefly, then set her away as though just realizing what he'd done. "That's fantastic news, CJ. I know you won't regret it."

"I'm sure I won't," CJ replied. "What I regret are the wasted years in between."

🐾

More problems awaited CJ when she returned to her apartment. The telephone answering machine had a message on it from Cheryl. *Poor Cheryl*, CJ thought. *I really need to make up some time with her.*

Picking up the phone, CJ dialed her friend's hotel room.

"Hello," Cheryl answered without her usual enthusiasm.

"Cheryl? It's CJ."

"CJ! Are you all right? Where have you been? I've tried and tried to call. I couldn't even locate Brad to ask him whether he knew where you were."

"I'm really sorry," CJ apologized. "I've been working through the past, as you well know, and the other day, things just got to be too much. I'm better now, and I'm really sorry to have neglected you."

"As long as you're okay," Cheryl replied.

"So the big day is just a week away, eh?" CJ asked and got comfortable on the couch.

Cheryl didn't reply, and the silence from the other end of the line caused CJ to realize something was wrong.

"Cheryl?"

"There is no wedding. At least not for a while," she finally answered. "Stratton and I had a fight and he walked out. He called me several days later and asked me to postpone things until he could clear his head."

"Sounds like he has a hole in it if he's letting you get away," CJ countered.

"I just feel so. . ."

"Disappointed?" CJ suggested.

"Yeah, and lonely," Cheryl replied.

"Say, I have an idea," CJ began. "Why don't you move in with me for a while? It would take care of the lonely part, anyway."

Cheryl didn't say anything for a moment, but then with a childlike voice, she questioned, "When?"

CJ laughed. "Today. Right now. As soon as we hang up, just load up and come ahead. I'll be here."

"Are you sure a certain hotel owner wouldn't be a bit miffed? After all, he won't have you all to himself anymore."

"Brad and I are just good friends," CJ said sternly.

"Yeah, sure."

"Cheryl, are you trying to get me to change my mind?" CJ didn't wait for an answer. "I'll expect you by five. Now get packing."

CJ hung up the phone, but Cheryl's call had caused her to think. For the first time she realized that her feelings for Brad were quite strong. She depended on their friendship in a way she'd never depended on anyone before. The phone rang again, breaking her concentration.

"Hello?"

"Hi, it's Brad. I just wanted to tell you good-bye. I've got the plane packed, and I'll be taking off for Telluride today instead of tomorrow."

CJ felt a lump in her throat. "It'll be dangerous, flying over the mountains and all. I remember all about wind shears and downdrafts. Stay away from the ridges," she instructed.

Brad laughed. "Yes, Mother."

CJ tried to be as amused, but she was startled at the feelings that surfaced inside her. "Sorry," she finally said.

"Don't be. I like your being concerned for me. Take care, and I'll see you Saturday."

"Brad!" She said his name in near panic. Had he already hung up?

"Yeah?" His voice calmed her nerves.

"Please be careful."

"Stop fretting, CJ. I've got a twin-engine Beech, and she's a real honey of a plane. . .plenty of power and I've had her for some time. It's going to be all right. I'll call you tonight, okay?"

"Okay, bye."

CJ hung up the phone feeling strangely calm. Brad was a good pilot, and he could handle himself just fine. *Of course, a few prayers couldn't hurt,* CJ thought, and immediately offered one up for his safety.

Chapter 11

S ummer waned, moving into autumn with a golden glow of quaking aspen. The mountainsides turned colorful in shades of red, orange, and yellow, as the season placed its mark on the land. Amid this change, CJ found her Saturdays consumed with the sights and sounds of Brad's private hangar. She relished their time together, realizing that for the first time since the accident she actually felt happy.

On three different occasions, when they labored for several hours in the hangar, Brad suggested they move up to his house for refreshment and a rest, but CJ refused. In spite of her security with Brad, she felt the house signaled something too personal. It was one thing to go to his office/apartment at the hotel penthouse, but for some reason the three-story, native-stone residence made CJ uneasy.

Brad didn't seem to mind, but CJ still felt she owed him an explanation. One day, after several hours of silent work over the Travel Air, CJ found the words.

"I feel like I should explain to you about the house," CJ began. "I guess it sounds crazy, but it's just too much for me," she said softly and added, "at least, right now."

Brad smiled and reached out with a rag to wipe grease from her chin. "I wasn't offended. I figure when the time is right, you won't be uncomfortable. When it's important to you, you'll show up under your own steam, and I probably won't even have to extend the invitation."

Brad quickly moved on to another subject, and CJ breathed a sigh of relief.

The situation with the house did bother Brad, but what could he say? Days passed and he contemplated CJ's fears with a deep, dreaded kind of concern. Maybe she was put off by him. Maybe she was just seeking to keep things from becoming too familiar. . .too personal.

That night, to his surprise, CJ telephoned. It was the first time she'd ever called him directly at home.

"This is a treat," he said, recognizing her voice.

"I thought it was about time," CJ admitted.

"Indeed," he replied. "I suppose I can expect a visit to the house to be not far behind."

"Don't rush me," CJ answered in a light manner. "You, above everyone, should know I work at my own pace."

"Speaking of paces, I've been thinking about something, and I wanted to talk to you about it."

"Sounds ominous," CJ said in a hesitant voice. "I'm not sure I want to hear it."

"Well, just listen and don't interrupt," Brad said sternly. "I think it's time you tried to fly again. I don't expect you to pilot or anything like that. Just a simple buzz around the field. I wouldn't make you stay up very long, and you could call it quits when you'd had enough."

There was dead silence on the other end of the phone. Brad's forehead furrowed in frustrated worry, anticipating her response. Finally, CJ spoke.

"I don't know."

Brad felt elated. She hadn't said no. "Well," he said, "maybe you could just think it over and we'll pray about it, too."

"All right."

"Thatta girl!" he exclaimed.

❧

When Saturday arrived, CJ drove up to the airfield and parked beside Brad's hangar. She got out of the car and stared back at the house for several minutes. *It's a beautiful home*, she thought. Three floors of sandy brown, native stone, with balconies on the second and third levels. Beamed cathedral ceilings could be seen in the lower level through full-story, arched windows. CJ thought it a masterpiece of architecture.

Turning away, she moved to the hangar. Finding the doors already pushed back, CJ entered, fully expecting to find Brad already at work.

"I'm here," she called. Silence met her declaration, and CJ frowned slightly. "Brad?"

Nothing. CJ reasoned that he must have gone up to the house for some reason, and she decided to wait until he returned. She moved from plane to plane, feeling on an intimate level with each one. No one could spend the hours she had working on these planes' bodies and engines without feeling a special kinship with them.

Reaching the Travel Air, CJ put her hand out and ran it along the back portion of the fuselage. It was sleek with its multiple coats of hand-rubbed butyrate dope and paint. CJ moved up to the wing, and before she gave herself time to think, she stepped up onto it and propelled herself into the cockpit.

For a minute, she did absolutely nothing. Sitting in the silence, CJ squeezed her eyes closed and concentrated on the feel of the cockpit. It felt like the arms of an old friend encircling her as she sat there, yet she still felt uncomfortable. Without opening her eyes, CJ reached forward and felt the stick, the instrument panel—old memories blended with new feelings. It was all coming back.

Brad had heard the car pull in and finished with the phone call that had taken him from the hangar. He stood in the entryway to the building, afraid to say a word as he focused on CJ's coppery head peaking out from the cockpit of the Travel Air.

He didn't know if she'd heard him enter or felt his presence, but CJ opened her eyes and met his as he waited there for her. She pushed back her hair and stood to get up. Brad quickly came to the plane and helped her down from the wing.

It was one of those moments that both Brad and CJ realized had been intended for something more than words. Brad wrapped her in his arms and swung her out away from the plane and then refused to let her go. Feeling her melt against him, Brad nearly moaned aloud. Instead, he pulled back slowly, knowing that he was about to cross the barrier line he'd put in place between them. CJ turned her face upward as if the whole thing were choreographed by someone else. Brad lowered his lips to hers, hesitating only a brief second before they touched and sealed the moment. The line had been crossed!

"I'm so proud of you," Brad whispered. "You've worked so hard to put your fears to rest. I know your folks are smiling down from heaven. You've almost made it, CJ."

"I couldn't have done it without you," she admitted and stepped away. "You've taught me a great deal these past months, and I'm grateful."

Brad thought he noted hesitation in her voice and hurried to ask, "So do we fly today?"

She looked from the plane to Brad and then turned away. "I don't think I can."

Brad came up behind her and pulled her back against him. He just held her.

"I know you're afraid," he finally whispered. "I can wait for you to deal with it. But I have a suggestion that might help."

CJ took a deep breath. "What is it?"

"Why don't we just taxi out and back? We won't even leave the ground, and you can just get used to the sound and feel of the plane again."

"That doesn't sound so bad," she replied. Then a look of doubt crossed her face. "But what would keep you from taking off, anyway?" She turned and stepped back. "I couldn't stop you if you decided to force the situation."

Brad frowned. "You don't trust me? Have I ever done anything that would prove to you that I'm other than a man of my word?"

She put out her hand, intending to do nothing more than touch his shoulder. Instead she allowed her fingers to reach up and trace the tense line of his jaw.

"Can we take the Travel Air?" she asked in a voice that reminded Brad of a little girl.

He took hold of her fingers and kissed them before letting go. A smile replaced the frown, revealing that all was forgiven. "We'll take whichever one you like."

CJ smiled. "Do you have any airsickness bags?"

Brad threw back his head and laughed. "I don't think so, but we'll find something suitable if it means the difference between your scratching the mission and going through with it."

CJ shook her head, still smiling. "I just didn't want to make a scene. I figure I can pass out, and being strapped into the plane, I won't cause much of a problem. But since I have to work on these things, I didn't want to have a mess to clean up."

"You won't get sick," he stated firmly.

"I won't get sick," she repeated, feeling a bit of confidence in the declaration.

81

"Come on," he said and held out his hand. "You'll see."

They taxied to the end of the runway with CJ tightly gripping the seat, eyes closed. She clenched her jaws together until her gums ached in protest. Her stomach tightened, but only for a moment. Then Brad gave the engine a little power and CJ realized it was a pleasant sound, not a painful one.

The wind rushed up to meet her face, and CJ was grateful for the goggles that held her hair down against her head. She opened her eyes and realized that all was well. Relaxing against the bouncing motion as they moved back toward the hangar, CJ felt she'd once again met and conquered an important hurdle.

"Thank You, God," she breathed against the wind. "Thank You for helping me and thank You for Brad's patience with me."

Chapter 12

In the days that followed, CJ gave heavy consideration to Brad's suggestion that she fly with him. She weighed the situation carefully, concluding that sooner or later she would have to face this final leg of recovery or forget about it all together.

This isn't going to get any easier, she told herself. *You've put things off for too long as it is.*

It was very early, and having no idea whether Brad would be home or at the penthouse, CJ drove out to the airfield. She parked beside the hangar and, noting that Brad's Jeep was in its usual spot, bolstered her conviction with prayer.

"Father," she began, "I feel this is the direction You are leading me, but if it's not. . .if somehow I have misunderstood. . .please, let Brad be too busy to fly today. Amen."

With slow, determined steps, CJ walked up the cobblestone walkway to the front of the house. For a moment she stood before the arched, double doors, hesitating in her mission. She reached out her hand, took a deep breath, and pressed the button to ring the doorbell.

Silently, she counted to ten to keep her mind from insisting that she bolt and run. She'd just reached six when a rather disheveled Brad opened the door. For a moment he just stared in stunned disbelief, and then his look changed to amusement as he ran his hand back through his uncombed hair.

"You would show up today," Brad said with a chuckle. He quickly tucked in the tails of his long-sleeved shirt.

CJ wrinkled her nose, shrugged her shoulders, and turned to go. Brad quickly reached out and turned her back around.

"Oh, no, you don't. You aren't going anywhere. You think I don't know why you're here today, but I do."

CJ raised a questioning eyebrow. "Oh, really?"

Brad pulled her toward the door. "You wouldn't have come to the house if it weren't very important, and I can only think of one very important issue that you would bring to me," he said, pulling her into the stylish entryway and closing the door behind her. "Now you can't run away," he grinned.

CJ leaned back against the door and smiled. "Well, if you can really read my mind, you'd know I have no intention of running away."

"I was just getting ready for the day. Why don't you come in and have some coffee while I finish?"

CJ glanced around to take in the small vestibule. "I suppose I could," she replied slowly. "But only if it won't take too long. I'm on a mission, you know."

"Yes, I know." His words were very nearly serious, and CJ didn't want the atmosphere to change from the lighthearted banter that she was enjoying.

"Do you make decent coffee?" she questioned.

Brad smiled, sensing her mood, and took hold of her arm. "Why, Miss O'Sullivan, I make the best coffee in the world. It's a very special blend that keeps busy pilots awake and on their toes."

CJ tucked her arm around his and allowed him to guide her to the kitchen. She noticed that the breakfast bar was covered with papers and a small notebook computer. "If I'm keeping you from working, I can come back," she offered.

Brad tightened his hold. "You know better. Now, sit here." He directed her to a stool and moved the papers aside. Bringing the pot and a mug bearing his hotel logo, Brad poured a cup of coffee and handed it to CJ.

"So you take cups from hotels?" she mused, examining the mug. "Most people go for the towels or an occasional highboy."

Brad laughed. "I know the owner and he doesn't mind at all."

"He does seem to be an awfully patient sort," CJ agreed, taking a long sip of the hot liquid. She put the cup down and met Brad's amused stare. "And very considerate," she added.

"Sounds like you're kind of fond of this guy," Brad teased. "I might have competition."

CJ feigned shock. "Well, he certainly isn't as brash and forward as you, but alas," she paused and took another drink, "I'm certain he can't make coffee anywhere near this good." She batted her eyes, enjoying the game.

"You like it, then?"

"What?" CJ asked innocently. "The coffee or the maker?"

"You have my permission to elaborate on both," Brad said and leaned back against the butcher block that dominated the center of the room.

"I thought you had something to do," CJ said. "Looks to me like you could use a shave."

Brad grinned broadly. "Looking out for your own interests, I see."

Confusion registered on CJ's face, confirming that she didn't catch his meaning. Brad walked to where she sat, leaned down, and kissed her cheek, making certain that his whiskery chin rubbed against it lightly.

"I see what you mean," she said and blushed deeply. She hadn't expected the kiss or the suggestive teasing.

Brad reached out and touched his fingers to her coppery curls, letting one wrap around his finger. "I'll go shave, and then we'll discuss where you want to fly to."

CJ sat waiting for Brad to return, still contemplating his words. He seemed to know automatically that she was here to fly. How could he know her so well?

She drained the cup of coffee and felt a little less nervous as she allowed her gaze to travel around the room. Copper-bottomed pots and pans hung over the butcher block in the center of the room, with a multitude of spices and condiments lining the middle of the broad workstation.

The room was light and airy. CJ thought it very much what she would like for her own, if she ever bought a house.

"I told you I wouldn't be long," Brad said minutes later. He reappeared, pulling on a navy blue sweater.

CJ blushed, noting that he had shaved. She lowered her head, pretending to concentrate on the empty cup, hoping that Brad hadn't seen her embarrassment.

She thought she'd pulled it off until he joined her at the table with the pot and his own cup. "You look very charming when you blush. More coffee?"

CJ started to laugh, although she wasn't really sure why. It suddenly all seemed so funny. There she sat, trying so hard to be professional and disengaged from her emotions while they screamed to be recognized from every portion of her being. There was no sense in trying to conceal her feelings from Brad. He always seemed to know exactly what she was thinking and feeling.

Brad didn't say a word. He poured them both more to drink, then sat down beside CJ at the table. He enjoyed her laughter and even more so, her embarrassment, for it spoke loudly of what CJ wouldn't say with words. He knew she cared for him, but he wanted quite badly to know how much. Breaking all of Roger's rules, Brad lost his heart completely when CJ lifted her ice blue eyes to meet his. She was everything to him, and Brad could no longer ignore his feelings for her.

"So you've decided to fly," he stated, refusing to drop his gaze.

"I, uh. . . ," she stammered. "Yes."

Brad nodded. "And where would you like to go, and which plane shall we take?"

CJ shook her head. "I don't want to go anywhere, and I'd just as soon we take the Travel Air."

Brad laughed and the spell was broken. "You don't want to go anywhere, but you want to get there in the Travel Air?"

"I just thought maybe we could shoot touch-and-goes or just circle the field. I don't want to get so far that I can't get back down. I don't want to move too fast and mess everything up."

Brad wondered if her words had a double meaning. "Okay," he answered. "We'll just circle and land. If you want more, we'll go again."

❧

Moments later, CJ found herself in the cockpit of the Travel Air. "Are you ready?" Brad yelled above the plane's roar.

CJ couldn't really hear him, but she knew he was waiting for her okay. Without looking back, CJ waved her arms forward, knowing that Brad would understand. He did.

The plane moved forward as it had the time before when they'd taxied out and back. CJ forced herself to keep her eyes open. Reaching up, she adjusted the goggles and wondered what it would feel like to rush down the runway and feel the plane lift up into the air.

Because the Travel Air was a tail dragger, the nose of the plane was elevated and obstructed CJ's view down the runway. Nevertheless, she glanced out to the side and past the struts. Biplanes looked so frail compared to the modern mono-wing plane. Especially when you sized them up against the commercial planes, with their metallic glow and powerful jet engines. In reality, however, the biplane was a very reliable ship, and CJ took comfort in that fact as Brad revved up the engine.

In the next minute, they were rushing down the runway in a burst of energy. Autumn gave the wind a bite as it slammed against CJ's face. Twenty feet rolled by, then one hundred, then two hundred. CJ lost track and braced herself as she felt the familiar sensation of the plane lifting up from the ground.

In a flash of memory, she was a little girl again—five, maybe six years old. She felt the buckles that held her snug against the cockpit. "Whatever you do, Jenny," she could hear her father say, "don't unbuckle these."

As the plane climbed higher, Brad leveled the nose a bit. CJ looked down across the valley and held her breath. *Dear God,* she thought, *I'm really here and You are, too.* God was still God, and CJ sighed in relief.

Brad circled the airfield in a wide sweep. The plane moved through the skies with the grace and elegance of a refined old woman.

"Planes fly through the air, not over the ground, Jenny darlin'," her father would say, feigning an Irish brogue. He'd taught her important properties of flight from her earliest years. Bernoulli's theory was pounded in, explaining the way an airplane achieved lift as the air moved over the wing.

"Remember, Jenny, airplanes don't stall at a speed, they stall at an angle," he would say. It came back to her as though it'd been just yesterday.

Lost in thought, CJ panicked when the plane began to descend. She tried to throw herself forward, anticipating a crash. The harness held her fast and made her realize that all was well. Brad was simply landing the plane.

Brad was a gifted pilot, and he touched the Travel Air down as though kissing the earth with the landing gear. They were level for several feet until the tail snapped down and the plane rolled to a stop at the end of the runway.

CJ felt like shouting. She'd done it! She'd actually flown, and she hadn't gotten sick or frightened. Well, not much, anyway.

Brad taxied back to his hangar and jumped from his seat as the propeller slowed and then stopped. He was at CJ's side instantly.

"You okay?"

CJ undid her harness and nearly leaped into his arms. "I did it, Brad! I really did it!" The enthusiastic smile on her face told him everything he needed to know.

He lifted her out of the cockpit and helped her off the wing. When they were both on the ground, he pulled her into his arms and whirled her around and around.

"I did it. I flew again!" she exclaimed over and over.

"You sure did!" Brad's enthusiasm matched her own.

When he stopped turning her around and her feet touched the ground once again, CJ lifted her face to his and waited for the inevitable to happen. She knew he would kiss her. She wanted him to. And then he did.

Taking her face in both hands, Brad looked at her lovingly for several heartbeats. His green eyes were dancing with laughter, but they were also bright with passion.

"I love you, CJ," he whispered, then lowered his lips to hers.

CJ's mind exploded in a riot of emotions and thoughts. *He loves me?* Had she heard him correctly?

The kiss deepened as if in answer, and CJ found her fears and concerns melting away. She wrapped her arms around his neck and, for the first time in her life, kissed a man in return.

When Brad pulled away, CJ kept her eyes closed and sailed away on wings all her own.

"CJ, did you hear me?"

"Ummm?"

"I said, I love you."

CJ's eyes snapped open. "Of course I heard you."

Brad laughed nervously. "I really do," he said, sobering slightly. "And not just because you got in that plane today and not simply because of all the hard work you did to defeat the ghosts of your past."

"No?" she questioned, needing and wanting to hear more.

"No. I love you for so many more reasons, and I can't even begin to tell you all of them."

"You could try," CJ said, dancing away with a teasing smile. "You could try." She picked up speed, threw a glance over her shoulder, and gave Brad a departing wink.

She ran out across the fading lawn and past the hangar, but by that time, Brad had caught up with her, grabbed her around the waist, and pulled her to him in a giant embrace. CJ laughed as she hadn't laughed since before the accident. She was happy and, for the first time in her life, she felt secure and free.

"I love your laugh. I love your hair when the sunlight hits it and makes it sparkle. I love the way your eyes light up when you're happy and the way you blush when you're embarrassed," Brad said, pulling away from her to look intently into her eyes.

Some of CJ's braid had pulled loose and several copper ringlets framed her face. A chill wind blew down from the Rockies, causing her to shiver.

"Come on," Brad said, putting his arm around her shoulders and steering her toward his home. "I'll make some more pilot coffee."

CJ thought he sounded strangely disappointed. Perhaps he had hoped that she'd return his declaration of love. Gently, she reached out to halt him. "Brad," she said softly, "thank you for taking me up and," she lowered her head and blushed, "for loving me."

Brad gave her shoulder a squeeze and walked on toward the house. "Getting you in the plane was real work, but loving you wasn't hard at all," he whispered and added a wink when CJ raised her face to his.

"Well, so much for just being friends," CJ laughed.

"Roger will no doubt chastise me for my lack of discipline," Brad replied, feigning sternness. "Good thing I didn't become a psychologist, eh?"

"I think you would have been great at helping people," CJ countered, enjoying the lazy walk back to the house.

"But then, I might have fallen in love with someone else," Brad said flatly.

They stopped walking and CJ felt her heart skip a beat. She warmed under the look he gave her, and she felt her breath catch in her

throat. "I don't think I would have cared for that," she managed to say.
"No?"

"No." The firmness of her reply was all the hope she would give him.

Unable to resist the windblown woman with glacier blue eyes, Brad encircled her waist with his hands and kissed her briefly once again.

"Can we do this every weekend?" CJ murmured as he pulled away.

Brad's laughter filled the air. "Kiss or fly?"

"Both," CJ responded boldly. "I think I need to get used to both."

❧

It was late evening when CJ finally returned to her apartment. She'd enjoyed spending the entire day with Brad and felt only marginally guilty when she returned to find Cheryl somewhat concerned about her long absence.

"I had the most glorious day," CJ told her friend. "I flew, Cheryl. I flew in the Travel Air, and it was wonderful."

Tears filled Cheryl's eyes. She knew what this had cost CJ and how hard the choice had been.

"Oh, CJ," she said, embracing her friend, "I'm so happy. It's like a totally new start for you."

"The flight was only part of what made the day glorious," CJ admitted.

Cheryl stepped back with a questioning look. "Well?"

CJ laughed and pushed past her friend and down the hall. She stood outside her bedroom door and looked back at the puzzled Cheryl.

"He told me he loves me, Cheryl." Her giggles sounded like a child at play. "Brad loves me."

Chapter 13

Brad turned out the lights and made his way upstairs. His mind was filled with the image of copper curls, blue eyes, and warm, responsive lips. CJ!

He turned down the covers of his bed, grabbed his briefcase, and settled down to read quarterly reports from his resorts. He scanned the papers, noting with interest that additional land adjoining his Jackson Hole, Wyoming, property had come up for sale. The manager had been good enough to let him know before the property had been placed on the open market. It would make a great piece for a golf course or recreation center. He'd fly up there tomorrow or the next day and check it out.

Brad put the papers down. Maybe he could interest CJ in going. No, he reasoned, it was still too early to expect that. He would ask, but if she turned him down, it would still be all right.

Brad's concentration was completely broken. He tried three times to turn his attention back to the papers, but it was impossible. Getting up, he walked to the french doors that opened onto his balcony. The night air was cold and assaulted his skin through the silk pajamas he wore.

Staring out across the moonlit valley to the shadowed mountains in the distance, Brad prayed. "God," he began, "I love her. I think I've loved her from the first minute I saw her. I tried to do as Roger suggested, I really did. I think we have a good friendship, but Father, I want much more. I want to love CJ in the way that she needs to be loved, but the past still stands between us. Help her, please, to deal with the pain and the things that haunt her mind. Heal her and make her whole, and God," Brad paused, concentrating hard on the words he would pray, "if it's Your will. . .let CJ be the one I'll marry. Amen."

The whispered prayer seemed to catch on the night winds, drifting out across the open land and ever upward to the starry heavens. Brad stood there for a long time, watching and wondering. How would he know? How would he know for sure if it was right to marry CJ?

❧

Mondays were devoted to cleaning house, at least for CJ. Monday was the day she put everything in order—her house and her emotions. It was also the day she saw Roger Prescott and walked back through time to the moments that had held her prisoner for so many years.

CJ smiled to herself as she opened the glass doors of the administrative building where Roger's office was. Today, she decided, would be her last visit. She'd come so far in the few months since she'd met Brad and Roger. It was hard to imagine the woman who'd existed back then, and CJ had no desire to dwell on her too much.

"You look as though you have the world by the tail," Roger said when CJ entered the room.

CJ's smile broadened. "I guess I feel that way, too."

"I take it the weekends are working out well and that flying hasn't caused you any problems," he said, casually opening their session.

CJ smoothed the skirt of her navy jumper and took a seat. "I feel wonderful, and I can't thank you and Brad enough. I guess I never realized what I was missing in life until Brad forced me to face it head-on."

"And you feel now that you've put it all behind you?"

CJ toyed with the burgundy bow that trimmed her print blouse. "I know things aren't completely perfect, but I'm working on it."

"It's good that you still see room for improvement. God doesn't want us to stagnate." Roger paused, then changed the subject. "What about you and Brad? He tells me that he stepped outside the boundaries of friendship and lost his heart to you." Roger's face showed the delight he held for his friend. "How do you feel about that?"

"I'm not sure," CJ responded. "No, that's not true. It thrills me to pieces and scares me to death."

"Do you want to talk about it?"

"No," CJ said, shaking her head. "I don't think so. It's too new and I'm not sure what I feel or what to do with it."

"All right." Roger smiled and leaned back in his chair. "I know you've been coming regularly to the Bible study. Have you found it helpful?"

CJ nodded. "I know it's helped tremendously. I lost a good portion

92

of guilt the day I realized I could never be good enough or do enough to earn my salvation."

"Guilt has played a heavy role in your life, hasn't it?"

Roger's words impacted CJ in a strange way. She really hadn't considered the guilt aspect for a very long time. "There was a time," she said in a faraway voice, "when I felt guilty for being alive. No matter what I did or how I looked at life, I was alive and they weren't, and for that I felt somehow to blame."

"Why?" Roger asked softly.

"You tell me." CJ laughed nervously. "You're the shrink."

Roger smiled. "You know it doesn't work that way."

"I guess I do." She paused and shifted in the seat to cross her legs. "Life is difficult to understand. I guess no one would dispute that." She didn't wait for Roger to comment before moving on. "Still, it seems odd that a sixteen-year-old girl could take so much on her shoulders. I hated being left behind. I hated feeling the loss and knowing that everyone looked at me as the survivor of the crash that took Douglas O'Sullivan from the world. I wasn't a survivor." CJ slowly added, "In many ways, I was just as much a fatality of the crash as they were."

"And now?" Roger questioned.

"Now?" CJ shrugged. "Now, I'm not sure. I don't feel the same guilt, and the loss is easier to deal with. I'm more mature in my thinking and realize that of course the world would mourn my father while paying little attention to me."

"But?" Roger pressed.

"But?" CJ repeated the question.

"But there's something more. At least, that's how it sounded to me," Roger replied.

CJ swallowed hard. "I guess there is. I guess somewhere out there, there's a little girl still wandering around, trying to piece her life back together."

"Do you ever try to picture her?" Roger asked.

"What?" CJ asked, sounding surprised.

"Picture her. See yourself at sixteen again. What do you see?"

CJ closed her eyes. She focused on the girl she saw herself as before the crash. "I'm naïve. I believe the world is a good place and that nothing can hurt me. I'm happy because I don't know that there is anything more than what I'm experiencing, and what I'm living is wonderful in my mind." CJ fell silent and felt tears come to her eyes.

"Go on, CJ. Tell me what else you see."

"I can't," she whispered.

"Is that where you want to leave her. . .naïve, happy, living a wonderful life? Is she safe there?" Roger questioned.

"No," CJ answered and opened her eyes. "She's not safe. She's just waiting for the other shoe to drop."

"What do you mean?"

"She. . ." CJ shook her head. "I loved them so much. My folks were everything to me. My brother, too. Then one day, they just got into an airplane and flew out of my life. Even Curt flew away."

"And now you're afraid to give your heart to Brad because he just might do the same thing?"

CJ's eyes opened wide in surprise. "The other shoe," she whispered. "I never saw it that way before."

"Now that you do, what do you want to do about it?"

"I don't know," CJ said and shifted again in the seat. "I thought I was coming here today to tell you I was finished with these sessions. Now I don't think I will."

"It's up to you, CJ. You alone know when they stop being helpful. Some people rely on counseling for years and eventually it becomes as much a crutch as other things do. If you want to keep coming, I'm here. If you're ready to move on, that's fine, too."

CJ shook her head. "I thought the physical aspect of flying was my biggest problem to overcome. That and my anger at God. Now I see a whole new slate of problems, and I guess I'm confused. I can't stop now and leave in the middle." With a weak smile, she looked up at Roger. "It'd be too much like putting down a good book before reading the last chapter."

Roger laughed. "You're just beginning to write that book, CJ. You won't reach the last earthly chapter until God calls you home."

When the session ended, Roger walked with CJ out to her car. The air was colder than it had been the day before, and CJ wished she'd thought to bring her jacket.

"CJ," Roger said as she unlocked her door. "I'd like to say something, but not as a counselor. . .just as a friend."

"Go ahead," CJ replied, a look of curiosity punctuating her words.

Roger shoved his hands into his pants pockets and smiled in a sheepish way. "I've known Brad a while now, and I don't mind saying he's a good guy. He's participated in the church with more enthusiasm than most, and anytime there's a special project, he's more than willing to do his part. And," Roger added with a wink, "the single gals have been mighty disappointed to see him devote so much time to you."

CJ laughed but wondered what Roger was getting at. Roger grew quiet for a moment, then looked past CJ to the mountains. "I guess what I want to tell you is that he's worthy of your trust. I know I warned him not to fall in love with you, but you have to understand, that was purely on a professional level. Frankly, I knew he was already headed there when we talked, but I didn't want him to concentrate on the love interest so much that he protected you from dealing with the real issue of your fear. If I wronged you in that, I hope you'll forgive me."

CJ reached out and put her hand on Roger's arm. "I don't believe you wronged me at all. I wasn't ready to fall in love then. I'm not even sure about now, but I do know that I cherish the friendship I have with Brad, and I think it makes a good foundation for whatever else might come."

Roger nodded. "You're pretty smart, CJ O'Sullivan."

✌

The phone was ringing as CJ opened the door to her apartment. Juggling groceries, she answered breathlessly.

"Hi, thought I'd check in with you."

"Brad! Where are you? Did you have to fly back from Jackson Hole in the storm?" CJ sounded panicked.

"What storm?" Brad asked. Thunder crashed loudly, and before CJ could reply, Brad's voice answered nonchalantly, "Oh, that storm."

"Where are you?" CJ asked again.

"Wyoming. By the time my meeting ended, it was too late to fly back, so I decided to give my own hotel a try."

CJ sighed and sounded much relieved when she spoke. "I was worried. I kept watching that storm move in from the north, and I just knew you'd be foolish enough to try and beat it in."

"Never worry about things like that CJ," Brad assured. "I take my flight safety very seriously. I've seen too many things go wrong to chance it. In fact, I'm probably overcautious."

"Good. Keep it that way."

"You growing fond of me or something?"

CJ laughed. "Or something," she replied. Another loud crash of thunder rocked the panes in her windows. "It sure is a nasty storm for this time of year. I was totally surprised. One minute the weather was perfect; the next thing I knew I was nearly drenched. I was outside, bringing in groceries, when you called."

"Where's Cheryl?"

"She was supposed to meet Stratton. I hope he kept the date. He's sure treated her strangely lately. I think Cheryl's honestly questioning whether she'll marry him at all."

"Marriage is an important commitment," Brad remarked.

CJ found the opportunity to discuss the subject too tempting to ignore. "That's what I told Cheryl," she began, using Cheryl to distance herself from harm. "I told her she needed to be able to trust Stratton with her life, as well as her emotions. If he doesn't look out for her over-all well-being, then he just doesn't care the way he should."

"I think that's a very important point. You should probably tell Cheryl, as well, that most men find women somewhat of a mystery. She should be straightforward with him and let him know exactly what she expects out of marriage."

"True," CJ said, knowing that Brad realized her game. "A man should be no different. Say for instance, he expects a wife to give up all her other interests in life for his, he should tell her before they walk down the aisle together."

"Or if he'd just like to see her get some interests in life," Brad retorted.

"Well, maybe if she had problems that kept her from seeking outside influences, then she'd be justified in having very few interests. But I think she's working all that out." CJ realized how stupid she sounded and laughed. "After all, Cheryl went to the art gallery with me just yesterday, and she told me that she thought my art history degree would be best put to use in owning my own gallery."

"An art gallery, huh?" Brad questioned. "I didn't know you even had an interest in such a thing."

"There's a lot about me you don't know," CJ quipped. A quick glance out the kitchen window showed that the storm was abating.

"Guess I'd better be straightforward then."

"I guess you'd better." CJ liked their coded banter. "Now tell me, how did your meeting go?"

"Pretty well," Brad admitted. They talked on for several minutes about his plans, when suddenly CJ realized he'd not had supper.

"You'd better go get something to eat," she stated firmly.

"Yes, dear," he replied in a teasing voice.

"And if you're flying back at the crack of dawn, you'll want to get to bed early."

"Yes, dear."

"Just being straightforward," CJ replied with a laugh.

"Yes, dear." Brad's voice betrayed his amusement. "Good night, dear."

"Good night," CJ said, then quickly added, "Brad?"

"Yeah?"

"Thanks for letting me know you were all right. Be careful tomorrow." There was no teasing in her voice.

"I will be. Don't worry, just pray."

With a smile, Brad hung up the phone. "She loves me," he whispered to the room. "She doesn't realize it yet, but she loves me." He patted his chest in a self-satisfied way and whistled while he browsed through the room service menu. Things were definitely looking up.

Chapter 14

Brad's trip home was delayed when a heavy rain and overcast skies developed in the night and continued through the next day. Clear skies finally came late the next morning, and Brad flew out for Denver shortly before noon. He questioned the sensibility of leaving that late. Turbulence over the mountains would be greater as the day wore on and the temperatures warmed the air. But he wanted to be home more than anything else in the world.

Hours later he dialed the now-familiar number. "Honey, I'm home," he said in a teasing, singsong voice.

"Brad?" CJ said in a questioning tone.

"Who else would call you honey?" Brad asked earnestly. "There isn't anyone else, is there?"

CJ smiled. "Now why would I tell you if there were?"

Brad sobered a bit, realizing that it was suddenly very important to him that he be the only man in CJ's life. "What happened to being straightforward? There isn't anyone else, is there?" His voice took on a pleading note.

A strange sensation overcame CJ. "No, you know there isn't." Her voice was completely serious.

Brad exhaled in relief. "Good. Now, let's keep it that way."

"Sounds kind of possessive," CJ replied.

"I feel very possessive when it comes to you. I think I'm only coming to realize how important you are to me. I kept thinking about you all the time I was in Jackson, and I couldn't keep my mind on what I was doing."

"Now that sounds dangerous. I hope you were concentrating on the plane when you were flying back home."

Brad laughed. "Well, most of the time. Say, can you come over?"

CJ glanced at the clock. "Right now?"

"Sure. Come on out and I'll fix my famous Chicken à la Brad and we can have a nice cozy fire. Maybe we could watch some mushy, romantic movie and I could tell you how wonderful you are and you could tell me—"

"How wonderful you are," CJ filled in. "All right. You talked me into it. Can I bring anything?"

"Just yourself. That's really all I want." Brad's words sent out a clear message.

❧

CJ rang the bell and waited for Brad to open the door. She was grateful for the wool coat she'd thought to wear and hugged it close against the unseasonably cold breezes. Was it more than the wind that made her tremble? Seeing Brad again was more than a little exciting. She wondered nervously if she'd be able to act reasonably.

It's only been two days, she chided herself. But, for some reason, it had been two very important days. Deep down, CJ had come to realize she cared quite deeply for Brad.

Brad opened the door, wearing a broad smile. "How good of you to come, Miss O'Sullivan." He bowed low and stepped back.

"Good of you to have me, Mr. Aldersson."

Brad took her coat and hung it up. When he turned back around, he pulled CJ into his arms. With a sigh, she melted against him. She lifted her face to his and let her arms travel up his, until her hands met behind his neck. For the first time, CJ initiated their kiss, pulling his face down to meet hers. Brad didn't hesitate for a moment.

"I love you so very much, CJ O'Sullivan," Brad whispered against her ear.

CJ smiled and put her head against his sweatered chest. She wanted to return his words, but the image Roger had concocted of Brad, flying away, came back to haunt her. She was suddenly afraid and pulled back rather quickly.

"What's wrong?" Brad asked, fearing that he'd done something to offend her.

"Nothing. Honestly, nothing at all," CJ protested, knowing she sounded startled. Before Brad could press her further, CJ threw up her hands. "It's just my insecurities. Please, bear with me."

Brad reached out and pulled her back to him. "Come on, I have a nice fire crackling away on the grate and no one to enjoy it with."

They sat and talked for hours, and at one point Brad served them dinner on a checkered tablecloth on the floor in front of the fireplace.

CJ kicked off her boots and relaxed against the coffee table, while Brad cleared away the dishes. It was nice to be cared for in such a completely giving way. In the back of her mind, however, a thought struck CJ. Brad was doing all the giving, and she, in her needy way, was taking all that he offered.

Feeling guilty, CJ patted the space beside her when Brad returned with coffee. "I'm afraid I should apologize," she began. "You've done so much for me this evening, and I've done very little for you."

Brad smiled provocatively and put the coffee on the table behind CJ. "I can think of many ways you could repay me," he whispered, kneeling beside her.

CJ smiled. "So can I, but most of them are totally inappropriate, and I think maybe I should go home."

Brad laughed. "Relax; you're safe with me. I honor the same values and principles you do, remember?"

"Yes," CJ mused, "but it's difficult at times like this to remember just what all those principles are."

"Good point," Brad said solemnly. "I think our relationship is coming to the place where we need to make some important decisions."

CJ lowered her head. "I don't know if I can."

Brad reached out and ran a finger along CJ's jaw. It came to rest under her chin, lifting her face to meet his. "I'm not asking you to marry me, at least not just yet. But I would like a commitment between us. Something I can count on as solid and trustworthy."

"I thought we already had that," CJ whispered.

"In a sense, but I just want to know that you belong to me. Does that sound terribly chauvinistic?"

"Terribly," CJ said with a slow, sweet smile. "But I like it, and you can count on it, as far as I'm concerned. There's no one else I'm interested in, nor do I desire to be this close to anyone but you."

❧

Friday night, Brad called to tell CJ to bring an overnight bag for their flight the following morning.

"What do you have planned?" CJ questioned. "We've never gone flying anywhere that would require we stay over. I'm not sure I'm up to the distance and—"

"Nonsense," Brad interrupted. "I have to go up to Jackson, and I want you to come with me. It will be the perfect time for you to put your fears to rest, once and for all. We'll have fun, CJ, and we can stay at the resort and go swimming or sightseeing. . .whatever you want to do."

"I don't know," CJ said apprehensively.

"Well, I do and, if I have to, I'll come pack you myself. Now, take warm clothes and meet me at the hangar at six."

"Okay," she said, getting her courage up. "I'll go."

"You promise?"

"Promise."

CJ faced her decision with a great deal of turmoil. It shouldn't bother her so much, but it did. When morning came, she got up before the sun, wrote out a note for Cheryl, who hadn't returned the night before, and took off for the airport.

"Please, Father," she prayed as she drove up to park beside Brad's Jeep. "Please give me the strength and courage I need for this day. Amen."

When she looked up, Brad stood in the doorway of the hangar. For a moment, all CJ could do was stare. He was gorgeous. *He is everything a man should be,* she thought. Tall and tanned. Brown hair glinting gold from the sun, blowing in the light breeze. Passionate, intense eyes that seemed to stare through to her soul. He wore insulated flight coveralls, and a ball cap with "O&F Aviation" written across it was in his hands. It was the company CJ's father had co-owned with Cheryl's.

Shyly she stepped out of the car, thinking the scene looked like something out of the movies. As if sensing his effect on her, a lopsided grin broke the serious expression on his face.

"Welcome to Aldersson Airlines. I have insulated coveralls for you inside. I'm going to finish the preflight check," he said, taking her bag. "I'm on the backside of the hangar. Just come on around when you're dressed."

CJ nodded and did as she was told, grateful for the extra warmth of the one-piece suit. Brad had just completed his inspection when she came around the corner and spotted the plane. CJ froze. It was a replica of her parents' plane—the same one that had taken them from her.

She felt the color drain from her face. The blue-and-white Cessna greeted her like an apparition from the past.

"I thought if you were going to put this behind you once and for all, we might as well put you in the same kind of plane. I know I should have told you, but honestly, CJ, it's no different than the Travel Air. It's just an airplane," Brad said firmly.

CJ stared at the Cessna as though she expected her parents to wave back from the cockpit. "I can't do this," she said and turned to leave.

"Yes, you can," Brad insisted, and his arm shot out to stop her flight. "It's just a bad memory. That's all it is. Your parents are in heaven, safe and happy. You have to put this to rest. You have to let go of that accident."

CJ leaned her back against Brad's chest and took a deep breath. Dread overwhelmed her in a tidal wave of emotion. Trembling and weak-kneed, she nodded. "I know you're right. I want to let go. I truly do."

"Then fly with me today and give it over to God. It's only two hours and forty minutes to Jackson. You can do it, CJ. I know you can, and you know God can help you do it. Remember Philippians 4:13."

"I can do everything through him who gives me strength," CJ whispered in reply.

"That's right. Everything. . .through Christ." Brad's words neutralized her fears. "You'll work in Christ's strength, CJ. Not your own."

Pushing Brad's arms aside, CJ squared her shoulders and turned to face both Brad and the plane. "Everything through Christ," she repeated. "Everything."

Chapter 15

Even climbing into the plane caused a rush of memories to fill CJ's mind. She eyed the cockpit knowingly. She'd flown in her father's Cessna 180 many times. Now, here she was, in the one place she'd vowed never to be again.

CJ could very nearly see her father in the pilot's seat beside her. She could almost hear her mother's laughter as they prepared to go on one of their many adventures.

"Are you okay?" Brad's voice broke through the madness.

"Uh-huh," she murmured with a slight nod of her head.

Brad checked over a self-made list and radioed out on common frequency to begin their journey. CJ was lost again in thought. Voices from the past filled her head. It was her father making the radio announcement of takeoff, not Brad. It was his smiling face that looked over at her.

"CJ, you look as white as a ghost. Are you going to be sick? CJ?" Brad reached over and touched her hand.

She looked up. "I'm fine. Really. Just a lot of memories to work through."

Brad nodded and moved the aircraft down the runway. In a matter of seconds, they were airborne, and only then did CJ realize she'd been holding her breath the entire time. Exhaling loudly, she tried to ignore Brad's grin.

"You're still alive and well," he said, trying to lighten her spirits. "You may as well relax and enjoy the view."

CJ tried. The day was perfect, and the air was clear and cold. She could see for miles around her in the cloudless sky. The mountains glimmered from their new toppings of snow, and CJ reminded herself how comforting these majestic markers had always been in her life.

"Life is like climbing those peaks," her father had told her. "You see only your side of the mountain, and while you climb and trudge through, there is no other side. But once you get to the top, you can look down around you and see where you came from and where you're going to. When we're in the valleys, just climbing out and up, we can't believe there will ever be that viewpoint. Just remember it, though, and don't get discouraged when things get hard. Climb to the top, CJ. The view from there is fantastic!"

She nodded to herself as though the voice had reached across the years. Her father and mother had taught her so much about living. They'd truly hate knowing that she'd spent so much of her young life focused on death. Especially their deaths.

CJ glanced over at Brad. He was perfectly at ease doing his favorite job. He loved to fly and had told her so on many occasions. Once or twice when they'd talked about flying, CJ had allowed herself to remember the way it felt.

Her eyes moved from Brad to the dual control in front of her. It moved with unison rhythm as Brad maneuvered them through the air. She reached out a finger and let it ride on the control, just feeling the pulsating moves.

Brad looked over and smiled. "You want to give it a try?"

CJ pulled her hand back as though she'd touched a flame. "No!" she exclaimed more quickly than she'd intended. Calming her nerves, she smiled. "I was just remembering."

"You really ought to get your pilot's license. You could become involved with your father's enterprise again, instead of letting Curt run things by proxy."

"Even Curt doesn't spend that much time with it. Cheryl's father has everything under control. The air show business isn't what it used to be. It's much more complicated, and that, coupled with the way the aviation company has grown, makes me pretty useless. It's probably best that I stay out of it. Maybe I'll open that art gallery like Cheryl suggested."

"Think you could be happy, grounded?" Brad questioned. "You are Doug O'Sullivan's daughter, after all. Five years without the things you cut your teeth on are bound to have taken their toll in more than the obvious ways. I think you love all of this as much as he did."

CJ recoiled a bit into the seat. Love the thing that killed her parents? "That was before," she murmured.

"Before the crash, you mean?"

"Yes," CJ answered. "I doubt my father would think too highly of this profession now."

"You mean if he'd lived through the crash, as you did?"

"Exactly."

Brad laughed and surprised CJ even more. "You don't remember your father very well then. CJ, he went through a dozen near misses and minor crashes. He even experienced a pretty bad one during the war. You should know. He teetered between life and death for weeks."

"I don't know what you're talking about," CJ replied in complete shock. "Sure, Daddy had some risky moments, but I don't know anything about an accident like what you're telling me about."

Brad shook his head. "I'm sorry. I didn't know. They must have kept it from you. It happened before you were born. My point, however, is that Doug knew the risks related to flying, and after each disaster, he got back into the cockpit and did it all over again. The last accident wouldn't have kept Doug O'Sullivan grounded, even if it had taken the lives of those he loved. Flying was his life, and you, your mother, and brother were all a part of it."

CJ looked at Brad as though she couldn't believe the words he spoke. "I know he loved flying, but I can't imagine wanting to be a part of something that took away those you cared for so deeply."

Brad's expression softened. "Ignoring the pleasures of something you love to do wouldn't bring them back. It's no different for you now. Just because you won't pilot a plane, doesn't balance out the fact that they can't be here with you. Let them go, CJ. They aren't far away, and you'll see them again. Just let it all go."

CJ grew quiet and turned to stare out the window as if by doing so, she could block out Brad's words. She hated the logic of it all. Why was it so hard to admit that she'd buffered herself for years behind the false assumption that her parents would have reacted the same way?

❦

The trip to Jackson was perfect. The winds were cooperative and turbulence was low. Even when they had to fly close to dangerous ridges and downdrafts, Brad was able to position the plane in such a way that they sailed through, high above, without difficulties.

CJ had never been to Jackson Hole before, and she enjoyed the time she and Brad shared there. The scenery was spectacular with the rugged Teton peaks rising heavenward. Already dressed in heavy snowcaps, they looked much more rustic than CJ's beloved mountains in Colorado.

The view from her hotel room was impressive, and CJ enjoyed relaxing there when Brad left for his meeting with the real estate agent. He was quite optimistic about his purchase, and CJ was happy that his plans were coming together. As she stretched out on the queen-sized bed, she daydreamed about what it would be like if Brad's plans and aspirations were her own.

The thought was a pleasant one, and CJ giggled to herself in little-girl fashion, all the while contemplating what it might be like to be Mrs. Brad Aldersson. Then a cloud of frustration shadowed the fantasy. Brad would no doubt continue to fly all over the country, especially if his resorts expanded in the manner he hoped. She'd have to fly with him or be left home a great deal of the time. Maybe he'd even expect her to get her pilot's license and help with the flying.

Her mind raced with images of treacherous mountain blizzards and freak thunderstorms. She could imagine the tiny Cessna or twin-engine Beech being tossed mercilessly through the air. Shaking her head, CJ forced the picture from her mind.

"Oh, Brad," she sighed. "If I love you, will I always have to confront this thing?"

If I love you? CJ laughed aloud. She knew full well that it was too late. She already did love Brad Aldersson; she just couldn't find the words to tell him. Then, too, maybe she was afraid of what would happen once she made that declaration. Would he push her to marry immediately? Did she want that?

That evening, she enjoyed his company with guarded emotions. Brad was the exuberant new owner of prime acreage in Jackson Hole. They celebrated in grand style at the finest restaurant in town, then slowly made their way back to the hotel.

"Weather still looks good for tomorrow's flight," Brad stated, walking CJ to her door. "There's a cold front moving in, but it's dragging a bit, so we've got plenty of time. I've got someone watching the weather, and they'll give me a call if the conditions deteriorate."

CJ tried to approach the subject enthusiastically. "I hope the return trip is as wonderful as the one coming up. Everything was so pretty and—"

Brad put a finger to her lips. "Don't. You don't have to pretend with me. I know you're afraid, but I'll take every precaution to ensure that we stay safe."

"Daddy did that, too," CJ argued softly.

Brad smiled and pulled her into his arms. "Yes, he did. But God called him home, and when He calls us, it will be no different. We'll be ready to go and walk jubilantly into the arms of our Savior. Is there any fear in that?"

CJ trembled in his arms, and a single tear slid down her cheek. "But what if it only takes one of us? What then?"

Brad kissed the wet spot on her face. "Either God is God, or He isn't. We trust, and we go on. We live life and expect the best in His will for us. There are no guarantees, CJ, except that through Christ, we defeat death."

CJ felt a bit of peace in his words. She knew Brad was right. She had to let God be in control. She had to let go of the past, her fears, and her worries. But how very hard it was to trust!

※

That night CJ dreamed she was falling. The ground raced up to meet her, but she never came to a stop. She just kept falling and falling. Pain in her left leg woke her up once. She shifted positions and fell back asleep, thinking of how the old dream never seemed to fade from her mind.

Around five-thirty in the morning, her phone rang. "Sorry to wake you, CJ, but the front's picked up speed and there's another behind it. I'd suggest we wait it out, but from the looks of it, we could be here a while."

"So what other choice do we have?" CJ asked in a sleepy voice.

"We leave right now," Brad replied. "The weather's good, and by the time we get up and running, it'll be light. Can you be ready to go in five minutes?"

CJ came awake instantly. "Sure. I'll meet you downstairs."

"No, I'll come get you. I don't want you wandering around the hotel by yourself at this hour." Brad's protectiveness made CJ feel good. "Just stay put. I'll be over shortly."

CJ scurried around the room, grateful that she'd thought to pack everything the night before. She pulled on her blue jeans and tucked in a dark green T-shirt before pulling a heavy wool sweater over her head. Grimacing, she didn't even take time to put on makeup and was just doing up the laces on her hiking boots when Brad knocked on the doorway.

"I'm ready," she said, thrusting her bag through the door into Brad's waiting arms.

"What? No good morning kiss?" Brad teased.

CJ leaned across the bag and placed a light kiss on Brad's lips. "Good morning," she said. She pushed her hair back only to realize that she'd forgotten to brush it. "Oh, no!" she exclaimed. "My hair must look frightful. Well, this is the best you get with a five-minute warning. No makeup and no combed-out hair." She shrugged good-naturedly and stared up into Brad's twinkling eyes.

"You look fine," Brad said with a wink. "I kind of like it all tossed around like that."

CJ rolled her eyes. "Just let me borrow your cap, okay?"

Brad laughed out loud, forgetting the hour. He quieted down when CJ put a finger to her lips. Shifting the bag, he pulled the baseball cap from his jacket pocket and handed it to her.

"Are you ready now, or is there something else you want before we go?" he asked with a sardonic grin.

"Breakfast would have been nice," she countered.

"I've already arranged for the kitchen to have something waiting for us to take along. We can pick it up on our way out."

CJ shook her head and reached out to open the unzipped front of Brad's coat.

"What are you doing?" His confusion was apparent.

"Just looking."

"For what?" Brad questioned in earnest.

"Your cape," CJ replied.

"My cape?"

"Your hero cape. You know. . .Superhero Brad! Defender of the weak!

Nourisher of the hungry! Pilot for the cowardly!"

It was Brad's turn to roll his eyes, and with a low chuckle he asked, "Are you finished?"

CJ adjusted the cap, pushing her long red hair inside. "Yes, Super Brad," she replied. "Lead on."

❧

Brad made an engine run-up and double checked to make certain the radio was on the 123.0 frequency for Jackson Hole.

"Jackson Hole traffic," he announced on the common frequency, "this is Cessna Four-Kilo-Mike departing runway one-niner."

CJ tensed in the seat as Brad moved the craft down the runway. They lifted gracefully into the air, and once again CJ felt relieved to see they were up and on their way. It was more the anticipation of the thing that bothered her.

Brad turned the plane to the right and radioed once again. "Jackson Hole traffic, Cessna Four-Kilo-Mike departing to the east." He replaced the mike and turned to CJ. "Look, we're greeting the morning." He pointed to the rush of color that lit up the eastern horizon.

CJ watched as he maneuvered the plane and climbed to 9,500 feet. Leveling off, Brad seemed relaxed and content, almost like an extension of the Cessna. *He loves it,* CJ thought. He was just like her father. Sitting back, CJ finally gave in to her fatigue and dozed.

The first turbulence hit them about the same time Brad was contemplating the breakfast they'd brought along. He contacted the nearest flight service station and updated the altimeter setting before making a climb to calmer air space. CJ instantly awoke at the disturbance, but Brad assured her all was well.

"We just passed the cabins at Fremont Lake," he announced. "We're up to 13,500 and things seem a little calmer here. Hungry?"

She shook her head. The nerves in her stomach were suddenly tight. "No, I think I'll wait."

"There's a thermos of coffee back there. Maybe that would help settle your stomach."

She looked at him wonderingly and again shook her head. "I'm fine. You want me to get you something?"

"Yeah, I think they packed some donuts and I don't know what

109

else," he replied. He started humming while CJ frowned ever so slightly.

"What's that song?" she asked, unbuckling herself.

" 'Have a Little Talk With Jesus,' " Brad sang out just as the plane lurched.

"Looks like you'd better have more than a little talk," CJ suggested.

Brad laughed while CJ reached around behind his seat to where the small box of food had been placed. The plane bumped up and down, causing CJ to lose her grip on the plastic thermos. It rolled back behind her and wedged out of reach. She watched the skies with a sense of dread. To the east was the Wind River Mountain range, with its twelve- and thirteen-thousand-foot peaks. It seemed most intimidating to CJ. Even worse was the fading visibility to the south.

"On second thought," Brad said, trying not to appear overly concerned, "I think I'll wait on that donut."

CJ nodded, buckled herself back in, and resumed her vigil of the skies. Things weren't good, and there was no way Brad could keep it from her. She was, after all, Douglas O'Sullivan's daughter. She'd grown up in planes and probably had logged more air miles than most pilots.

They covered another one hundred miles or so before Brad radioed for another updated setting. It was critical for a pilot to keep track of the local pressure in order to reset the altimeter. Otherwise, he might actually believe he was at one altitude when, in fact, he could be much lower. Flying over mountain terrain made this little inconvenience even more important.

CJ sat in silence while Brad and flight service discussed the changing weather. It seemed the easterly front, which had been expected to move through by this time, had stalled out over Denver and built back.

Brad weighed his options. Very few existed. Visual Flight Rules, or VFR, required a three-mile visibility, and Jackson Hole was now socked in with the low-pressure system pushing forward and picking up speed. Turning back was out of the question.

Finally, a course was plotted that would take them over some rough mountain terrain, but even then Brad wasn't worried. He'd flown the area many times before and anticipated the dangers in advance—at least as much in advance as mountain flying allowed for. They'd simply fly high and take no chances.

Things seemed to settle down for a time, and although problems existed, CJ tried to remind herself that Brad was a capable and experienced flyer. With a wing and a prayer, they'd surely get through; wasn't that what her father had always said?

They passed the miles in silence, but eventually Brad seemed to sense her tension worsening, and he reached across with a quick pat on her arm.

"A walk in the park," he teased, knowing that CJ knew full well how bad things could get.

"Right," she replied and sarcastically added, "you could probably do it with your eyes closed."

"Not and fly VFR," Brad laughed. The plane jumped a bit and settled back down. CJ's knuckles were white from gripping the edge of the seat.

"Relax," Brad tried to encourage. "Remember what Luke 4:10 says, 'He will command his angels concerning you to guard you carefully.' Maybe He could stake one or two under the wings."

"I wonder if angels have to worry about turbulence and downdrafts," CJ quipped.

Brad laughed. "Just keep your sense of humor, honey. We'll be fine."

The word "fine" was barely out his mouth when the plane ran into another bouncing bout with the elements. It reminded CJ of a roller coaster ride, and she worried for a brief moment that she'd get sick.

Brad had worries of his own when Mt. Zirkel came into view after they crossed into Colorado airspace. He checked the altimeter. At 13,500 feet, he should be well above the landmark, but for some reason the mountain looked much higher than usual. Maybe CJ's paranoia was getting to him. He glanced over and gave her a smile.

Heading toward the Medicine Bow Mountain range, Brad tried to make radio contact, but received only static. He was quickly reaching the point where he'd have to make serious decisions on his own.

"We're going to go higher," he told CJ. She only nodded and cowered into her corner. Brad felt badly that he couldn't cajole or comfort her in the midst of the frightening situation, but he had his hands full, and his mind was more than a little bit preoccupied.

The plane fought to pick up altitude, while the wind campaigned in equal earnest to push it back down. To CJ, the plane seemed too frail to endure much more. She alternated between pleading with God and raging against Him at the injustice of it all.

All of a sudden, a tremendous blow came against them, and CJ knew they were falling from the sky. The plane kept plummeting with Brad working at the controls to somehow achieve the lift they needed. Nothing worked.

"You'd better get down," Brad said with an authoritative sternness that left CJ no hope that he'd recover the descent.

CJ shook her head. This just couldn't be happening. How could God be so cruel as to make her go through it again?

"I love you, Brad!" she exclaimed, knowing that if she didn't say it now, she might never get a chance.

Brad laughed. "Now you tell me."

The mountain peaks rushed up to meet them, then something miraculous happened and Brad managed to pull them up just a bit. It was too late to keep them from crashing, but they had more control, and he banked them ever so diligently toward an open valley.

"Get down!" Brad ordered, and CJ quickly complied.

"Dear God," she whispered, "forgive me my sins and deliver us from death." Her mind drifted into the memory of another crash. "He's done us in, Jan," she suddenly remembered her father saying just before the noise of the crash tore through the plane. *Oh God,* she thought, *I don't want to die.* It was her last conscious thought.

Chapter 16

The landing gear broke up and scattered across the mountain. Brad fought for some kind of control and quickly realized there was little to be had. When they finally skidded to a stop, the plane had flipped several times and finally landed upside down.

Brad, though dazed, never lost consciousness. He was aware of a burning pain in his side and the fact that he was half lying, half hanging against the cockpit door. The haze gradually lifted from his mind, and the cold of the snow-spotted valley brought him fully awake.

"CJ!" he cried her name and fought the harness that bound him to the cockpit seat.

The wreckage left Brad frustrated as he struggled to free himself. CJ was unconscious. A trickle of blood marred her otherwise peaceful-looking face. Sometime during the crash, she'd lost his baseball cap, and now copper hair spilled out everywhere in tangled disarray.

"CJ!" Brad said her name over and over, trying to evoke some response as he managed to free himself.

He knew without checking that she was alive. CJ's rhythmic breathing confirmed his assumptions. Remembering the bit of control he'd had over the plane right before the crash, Brad felt certain that God had brought them both through for a purpose. But what could it possibly be?

Working CJ's jammed seat belt, Brad freed her and pulled her from the wreckage. Tenderly, he put her on the ground several feet from the fuselage and looked around to survey the damage.

The plane looked like a turtle, stranded on its back. The landing gear had been ripped away and the wing on one side was lying at an angle. It was a miracle that they were alive.

Still a bit stunned, Brad managed to locate one of the blankets he'd kept in the plane. He spread it out on the ground next to CJ, and then gently rolled her onto it. He gave her a cursory going-over to see if she was injured. There were no stains of crimson to give him reason for concern, and Brad sat down hard, sighing with relief. The bump on her head had already begun to turn purple, but the bleeding was barely noticeable.

Twisting around to get his bearings, Brad cried out in pain. His hand went to his side, where something had punctured him during the crash. He unzipped his coveralls and reached in his hand, bringing it out bloody. Struggling to his feet, he went to search the fuselage for their bags and the first-aid kit.

The winds picked up, and heavy clouds began to lower over the valley while Brad worked to find their things in the jumbled mess. He tried the radio to no avail and glanced again to the sky. Hopefully the ELT, Emergency Locator Transmitter, would already be sending out signals that someone flying overhead could pick up. Brad silently thanked God he'd taken the time to file a flight plan and that the flight service knew their whereabouts after their last altimeter update. It would greatly reduce the time in locating them.

Pulling together what he could, Brad managed to dress his wound and stop the bleeding. His next concern was CJ. When he knelt beside her, she was already coming to.

In her mind, CJ was sixteen again. She felt the pain and the fear. The smell of fuel assailed her nose and, for the first time since the accident, she could see the twisted, bleeding bodies of her parents.

"No!" she screamed. "Daddy, no!" She struggled to fight the wreckage and flailed her arms against its hold.

"CJ, calm down. It's okay. We're okay!" Brad said, holding her down.

CJ was unable to shake the image. "They're dead! They're dead! Somebody help me!"

"Shhh," Brad soothed and pulled her close. "It's all over, CJ. Wake up, honey."

CJ opened her eyes. The wreckage of her parents' plane was gone. Brad's concerned face replaced the horrors of contorted death. "What's happened?" she questioned in a whisper. Her mind refused to accept the accident they'd just endured.

"Rough landing," Brad quipped. CJ struggled to sit up, but Brad held her fast. "How's your head?"

"My head?" CJ questioned. "My head is fine. Why is it so cold?"

"Perhaps because we're on top of a mountain with a storm about to hit," Brad replied sarcastically, letting her sit up.

CJ stared around in disbelief. Then it all started to come back. The downdrafts. . .the plane going down. It was suddenly very clear.

"Oh, Brad!" she exclaimed and clung to him as though she were about to drown. She moaned his name over and over, while he held her tightly and stroked her hair.

"It's okay," he whispered. "We made it. God protected us through the crash. Are you hurt anywhere?"

CJ refused to answer his questions. She refused to let go. It was too much. How could God do this to her twice in one lifetime? *I trusted You, Lord,* she thought. *I trusted You.*

The wind picked up, a sure sign that the storm was nearly upon them. Brad knew if the weather continued to build, search and rescue would be unable to locate them, much less pick them up. He needed to make a shelter of some kind. Prying himself away from CJ's grip, he glanced around.

"CJ, we have to get to work. I have a feeling we're about to be pelted with rain or snow, and we've got to get out of the elements. I want you to try to stand and see if you're hurt."

"No, don't leave me. I can't bear it!" She reached out and grabbed him again.

"Honey, I'm not going anywhere. I just want to see if you're hurt, and if not, you can help me fix up a shelter." CJ was still unconvinced. She refused to loosen her hold on Brad.

He wanted to go on holding her—anything to take the fear from her eyes. Brad remembered Roger's words about love marring objectivity. Feeling cruel, he forced CJ away from him.

"We have to get to work. I'm serious, now." He hated himself for the words. "Stand up," he ordered, getting to his own feet. He refused to wince even though the pain in his side was more than he wanted to admit.

CJ stared up at him, from the ground. "No," she said, refusing to budge. "I won't. I can't."

"Yes, you can," Brad insisted and pulled her to her feet. "Now, walk around and see if anything hurts."

CJ glared at him for a moment, tossed her hair over her shoulder, and walked. Brad saw the rage in her face and felt the anger that was barely contained.

"Move your arms around," Brad said, watching her carefully.

CJ flapped them like a bird, with a scowl on her face. "If I were dying I wouldn't tell you. You're acting like a real. . ." She paused as if trying to think of something bad enough to call him. When nothing came, she simply retorted, "I'm fine!"

"Then why are you so mad?" he questioned with a grin.

"I'm not mad!" CJ yelled at him.

"Then why are you shouting?" The grin broadened into a smile.

His calm irritated her. "I just want to make sure you can hear me!" she yelled.

"I don't think it's that at all. You're mad. I think it's that Irish temper getting the better of you."

"I think you stubborn Swedes have the compassion and manners of goats! You're supposed to help me feel better. You know. . .comfort and kindness. I've just been through—"

"We've just been through," Brad interjected. "Stop feeling sorry for yourself. We're in this together."

CJ suddenly stopped her ranting. She was rather embarrassed to realize she was taking out her emotions on Brad. She looked him square in the face and felt her indignation fade away. "Oh, Brad," she breathed and came to him. Wrapping her arms around him, CJ heard him grunt when she tightened her hold. "You're hurt, aren't you?"

"It's nothing much. I've already taken care of it," Brad replied.

CJ stepped back in disbelief. She surveyed the bloodstained rips in the side of his coveralls. "Nothing much? Sure. People lose blood like that all the time."

Brad laughed. "Stop fretting. I promise to let you tend to it later. You can fuss all over me and tell me how brave I was and what a good pilot I am." His eyes were twinkling. "Right now, though," he said and turned her to face the craggy peaks behind them, "we've got to make a shelter."

CJ took a deep breath, nodding at the heavy, gray sky. "Daddy always said, stay with the plane. People die because they wander away from the wreckage and get disoriented. Stay with the plane."

"What's left of it will hardly offer much comfort," Brad replied. "We won't venture far, though. Why don't you look around in the plane and find our things? Just make a pile so we can utilize what we have. I'll go scout out that rock face. Maybe we can hole up there."

CJ nodded and watched Brad cross over to the rocks. She looked at the angry, snow-heavy sky and then across to the man who'd managed to save her life. "Why, God?" she whispered. "Why this? Why now?" The wind whipped across her face with an icy chill, and CJ shivered. Suddenly she questioned everything. Her faith. Her life. Her death. How did it all figure together?

Rubbing her hands over her arms, CJ turned her attention to the plane and grimaced. She wondered how Brad had managed to keep it in relatively one piece. *He must be some kind of pilot*, she thought, then laughed nervously. Maybe angels had helped out.

CJ silently searched the plane, located their bags, and pulled them from the wreckage. After a little more investigation, she managed to turn up another blanket. Glancing around her, she suddenly realized that she couldn't see Brad anywhere. Apprehension gnawed at her shattered nerves. Where had he gone?

Standing alone on the mountaintop, CJ was reminded of her father's analogy about mountain peaks. "You never told me, Daddy, what to do when the peaks were covered with clouds and you can't see behind you and you can't see ahead," CJ whispered to the wind.

The cold numbed her fingers, and CJ began to shake. Pacing in a circle to keep her blood circulating, the truth of what had happened began to sink in. They were stranded! Trapped on top of a rocky fortress. A most unforgiving one, at that.

CJ started to cry but pushed the tears back. Her throat ached from the denial of emotions that rode so close to the surface. The wind blew harder, biting into the thick, insulated coveralls. If she was already this cold, how would they ever survive the night?

Once again, CJ scanned the rocks for Brad. When she spotted him coming back to the wreckage, she breathed a sigh of relief.

Brad returned with a broad smile, as if he'd done nothing more strenuous than to check them into the nearest hotel. "There's a place over there where two rocks lean together. Right behind that is solid rock. It's not a cave, but very nearly. We could probably use the blanket to block the wind and scoot up under the overhang."

It sounded hopeless to CJ, but she grabbed the blankets and bags while Brad took the first-aid kit and some emergency lights he'd found earlier in the plane. Silently, they made their way to the refuge he'd found.

Finding that the mountain tundra yielded little in the way of wood, they used pieces of the plane to stake up the blanket and ward off the wind. Crawling inside, the space proved wider than Brad had originally thought and offered a decent escape from the snow that had started to fall.

CJ rubbed her aching fingers and tried to keep her teeth from chattering too loudly. She played a game with herself of trying to imagine things that were warm. Warm baths, hot towels right out of the dryer, electric blankets—nothing seemed to help.

"I don't think the temperatures will drop too much, but we have to stay dry and warm. We can snuggle up here and do both," Brad said, tossing the remaining blanket around them. "What a hardship."

CJ refused to be humored. "Will they start looking for us right away?"

Brad shook his head. "They can't in this weather. They'll have to wait it out until it clears. That could be hours or days."

"We could be dead by then."

Brad shook his head. "CJ, I don't think God brought us through the crash just to let us die on this mountain. Where's your faith?"

"I lost it at about twelve thousand feet," she replied seriously.

Brad put his arm around her, and CJ scooted close to avoid him hurting himself by pulling her. "Don't be angry at God, CJ. It won't change a thing, and it'll leave you miserable and bitter."

"Get real, Brad!" she exclaimed, pushing away. "Don't you ever get upset? Don't you ever question why God let something happen?"

Brad looked thoughtful. "Sure. When things like this happen, I ask plenty of questions. But I know that sometimes I don't get to know all the details. We're sitting here in the middle of a mountain, survivors of what could have been a fatal airplane crash, and I can't help but wonder how this works into Romans 8:28."

"Romans what?" CJ questioned with a raised brow.

"Romans 8:28. 'And wc know that in all things God works for the good of those who love him. . . .' I have a questioning mind, just like you do. Nevertheless, here we are." He looked down at her with a mischievous grin and added, "Alone."

"Brad, how can you joke at a time like this?"

"It beats the alternative."

"Which is?" CJ questioned.

"We could cry. We could lament the situation until our faces turned blue."

"That wouldn't take long. Our faces are already blue from the cold," grumbled CJ. She eased back into Brad's arms, needing to feel his warmth.

" 'Survival is 50 percent attitude, 30 percent mind-set, and 20 percent perspective,' a wise man once said." The words sounded familiar to CJ. Brad continued. "In other words, you're going to have to change your way of thinking if you don't want to spend your time up here in misery."

"You talk as though we were at one of your resorts. We're stranded on the side of a mountain. Correction, the top of a mountain. A blizzard is moving in; the temperature is dropping. We're cold, hungry, bruised, and battered. Now I ask you, what part of that should I turn my attention toward in order to get a better attitude?"

Brad shrugged his shoulders. "I guess that would be entirely up to you. Each person finds value in different things. As for myself, I'm grateful we're both alive. It could be very different. I could be standing over your dead body, mourning the loss or vice versa." All trace of humor was gone.

CJ knew he was right. Wasn't that her biggest fear? That had been the reason she was afraid to love him. Fear that he might be taken and she would be left behind had kept her from saying what she really felt. But then, as they were about to face death, she had told him. She wondered if he remembered. As if reading her mind, Brad tightened his hold.

"Wait just a minute, CJ. I seem to remember one good thing that came out of this situation."

"What?"

"I recall you telling me something just before we went down. Now, what was it? My mind's just a bit foggy on this. You might have to help me," Brad said, staring up at the rock overhead.

CJ would have elbowed him, but she was up against his injured side. "I'm sure I don't know what you're talking about," she stated stubbornly and looked away. *So he does remember!*

Brad laughed and brought his hand up to her face, forcing her to look at him. "Did you mean it?"

CJ grew serious. The warmth in Brad's eyes was too much. The feel of his hand on her face was more than she could bear. Emotions welled up and threatened to flood her mind and soul. "Yes," she confessed in a whisper. "I meant it with all my heart. I love you, Brad."

"It took you long enough to admit to it," he said rather dryly.

"I know," she said, lowering her face against the blanket. "I'm sorry."

"Don't be," he replied, his voice low and husky. "I knew what you felt for me, but I also knew you needed time to admit it to yourself."

An uncomfortable silence fell between them as the wind howled outside. CJ didn't know what else to say. What could she say that could possibly explain the way she felt? It was all so new to her. It left her feeling helplessly out of control, a feeling she hated. It was all a matter of attitude, Brad had told her.

"Who was the wise man you quoted a minute ago?" CJ questioned softly.

"Douglas O'Sullivan," Brad replied without looking at her.

CJ nodded and grew quiet again at the mention of her father.

Brad didn't push her to talk. He was content to just sit and wait for her to feel like telling him her thoughts. Closing his eyes, Brad saw the crash again in his mind. The loss of altitude, the mountainside coming up fast. The certainty of death as it loomed before his eyes. No wonder CJ had struggled through the years.

Shaking off the image, he tried to concentrate on what they should do next. CJ wiggled down against his shoulder, breaking all thoughts of their predicament. Instantly, the realization of her body sitting next to his, dependent upon his for warmth, caused Brad's heart to pound. They were as isolated as people could get. Whatever might happen, or not happen, would be a matter of determination and willpower, he quickly realized.

CJ's voice came in a soft, childlike tone. "I've never been in love before," she admitted.

Brad was surprised at the statement and instantly took interest. "Never? Come on, surely there was some sweetheart of a boy way back there, somewhere."

"Nope. Nobody measured up to my standards," CJ said flatly.

"Which were?"

CJ felt her face flush. "You'll laugh at me."

"No, I won't. I promise. I'm just curious to know what standards you hold. Especially if I made it within their tight boundaries."

CJ shook her head and refused to look up. "I wanted a guy like my dad."

"That's quite a compliment. I thank you."

"I suppose," she said, barely breathing the words, "that it's quite strange to be twenty-one and know nothing of falling in love, but it's the truth. Nobody else even interested me. Not in college or even after that. You're the first one." She couldn't take her eyes away from his.

"And the last," he whispered hoarsely before lowering his lips to hers.

CJ's heart raced and her stomach knotted, but this time it was a good feeling. She felt her fears slip away as Brad's kiss deepened. All she wanted to do was forget everything that had happened—the accident, her parents, everything. She began kissing him back with a passion she'd not known existed. She hoped the kiss would go on forever, and she wrapped her arms tightly around Brad's neck.

Suddenly, with a noise that was something between a growl and grunt, Brad pushed her away. CJ felt hurt and almost afraid. Brad's frowning face didn't help. With all that she'd endured that day, she couldn't stop her tears from flowing. She sobbed softly into her hands and lay down, turning away so that he couldn't see her cry.

Brad stared down at the crying woman. Why had he done that? Why had he allowed his passions to rule his thinking? Now he was hesitant to even touch her, yet he couldn't leave her in tears. Brad reached out and pulled CJ up. He forced her to sit next to him and brushed her hands away from her face. "I'm sorry," he whispered. "I should never have started that. I don't have much willpower when it comes to you."

"What are you talking about? You told me back at your house that I was always safe with you."

Brad smiled. "You are, but I'm only human. I've wanted to take you in my arms a million times. I've wanted to hold you and caress you and much, much more. Every time you look at me with that helpless, lost expression, I just want to wrap you up and love you." He paused, taking in her surprised expression. "Does that shock you? Have I lost my cape?"

"Your what?"

"My cape. You know. . .Superhero Brad. Didn't you think I was capable of flaws?"

CJ finally smiled. "I guess I was beginning to wonder. But, if being overly passionate is your only flaw, I guess I can manage."

Brad laughed. "Overly passionate and overwhelmed," he said, leaning back against the rock. "When it comes to you, I don't always react the way I should. A man has his limitations. Sometimes my mind drifts off and, well, never mind."

CJ reached out and placed her hand on top of Brad's. "I'm sorry. I should have resisted, but with all of this," she paused, shaking her head, "I just didn't care what happened. I figure if God wants to throw me out here like this, He doesn't care, either."

"That's not true, CJ, and you know it. You've got to end this and let go of your anger."

CJ felt her defenses go up. "For what purpose?" she questioned softly and pulled away. "I've tried it and God rewarded me with this."

Chapter 17

Brad wanted to say something more, but CJ had obviously ended the conversation. He'd never met anyone who held so much anger inside, and it bothered him more than he could say. All he'd wanted to do was help her to recover her life. Now, it was almost as if they were back at step one, and Brad was uncertain he had the strength to go through it all over again.

The storm held on throughout the day, and as the light diminished, Brad pulled out emergency lights he'd brought from the plane.

"We'll only use these if we absolutely need to," he said, giving one to CJ. "There's no telling how long we'll have to wait to be rescued."

The shadowy light inside their shelter made it difficult to make out any features on her face, but Brad knew from her stilted silence that CJ was still upset. All at once, he remembered the breakfast the hotel had packed for them that morning.

"You know, we've been sitting here hungry, and I completely forgot the food we brought from Jackson. I'll go scrounge around the plane and see if I can find it."

"You're going out there?" CJ asked weakly.

"It's only thirty, maybe forty feet away, and you have a light. I'll be right back," Brad answered.

"I could come with you," she offered.

"And have both of us get wet and cold? No, stay here. I'll need your warmth when I get back."

Crossing her arms in frustration, CJ said no more and waited alone while the wind roared across the valley. She shivered, realizing that two bodies together had produced much more heat than one alone. "Please hurry, Brad," she whispered. She started to feel the odd sensations of her claustrophobia return.

"Why are You doing this to me, God? I've tried to do exactly what

I thought You wanted. I've tried to work through the past, and I didn't give in to defeat. What more do You want from me? Why must I suffer again? What is it that I'm not doing that You still expect?"

The wind calmed, and the silence seemed deafening. CJ pulled her knees up and rested her head against them. Why must she always battle against God? For such a wonderful, short time, she'd really thought she had come to terms with her anger and bitterness.

Minutes passed and still Brad hadn't returned with the food. CJ rocked back and forth, trying to comfort herself. She began to hum a song absentmindedly and suddenly realized it was a praise hymn she'd learned at Bible study. Rejecting the solace it offered, CJ took a deep breath and leaned back in the dark.

Without the wind's constant pummeling, she could hear Brad's approach before the blanket was pulled back. He shined the light right into her face as though she were a criminal being confronted in a dark alley.

"Surprise," he said humorously. CJ didn't laugh.

"I was beginning to think you'd hiked out of here," she muttered and hid her face.

"Nah," he answered and hurried to resecure the blanket. "I found some of the food, though. Oh, and look, the thermos of coffee. It's not pilot coffee, but it's pretty good."

He left the light on and poured some of the liquid into the thermos lid. "It's even a little warm. It'd make a great commercial for the thermos company." Donning an announcer's voice, Brad held up the thermos in an advertising manner and began his mock spiel. "This thermos survived a tragic air crash and, after sitting in the snow-covered wreckage for an unbelievable twelve hours, it amazingly managed to keep the coffee warm!"

"Very funny," CJ said, taking a sip.

"Well, I try," Brad replied. "It took some doing, but I managed to find the donuts, although I think they're frozen solid, and look, here's some packets of jelly! I figure there must be toast somewhere in the plane, but I didn't see it."

CJ took one of the offered donuts and wondered silently if they'd starve to death eating packets of jelly without toast before someone had a chance to find them. Brad seemed unconcerned.

"Shouldn't we ration this stuff?" she finally asked, staring at the donut in her hand.

"Sure. Eat half now and the other half after that." CJ frowned at his joke. Brad just shook his head. "Look, I've got a real good feeling about this. I just know that we'll be rescued soon. Where's your faith and trust?"

Indeed, she wondered, *where is my faith?* She munched on the donut without giving him a reply. Before she knew it, the meal was gone and Brad was sharing a cup of coffee with her. Still she said nothing.

The wind picked up again, and CJ shivered. The temperature had dropped dramatically, or at least it felt that way. She was thankful for the wool sweater and T-shirt she wore beneath the coveralls. Opening her bag, the only other thing CJ found that could help stave off the cold was her other sweater, which she pulled on over the coveralls.

Feeling at odds with the world, CJ concentrated on keeping warm. When other thoughts filled her head, she systematically pushed them aside and refused to deal with them. But perhaps the hardest thing to ignore was the man sitting beside her. He stared at her from time to time and then, just when CJ feared he'd want to start a conversation, he eased himself down on the ground, turned off the light, and went to sleep.

CJ stared down at where she knew Brad rested in the dark. A weary feeling washed over her, but she remained fixed to her spot, contemplating the situation. Surviving the cold required them to share their body heat, but CJ wondered what might happen. How could she just casually sleep beside him and not be overcome by her feelings?

Realizing that her emotions frightened her, CJ wondered what she should do. If she stayed where she was, they both might freeze to death, and if she joined him, well she couldn't even put words to mind to tell what she was thinking.

What if they don't find us? CJ suddenly realized that living through this crisis was very important to her. She didn't feel the same apathy she had experienced after her parents' crash. She wanted to survive. Her stomach churned. The darkness frightened her more than she could admit.

"Brad," she whispered, not really wanting to wake him, but hoping he wasn't asleep.

"Umm?" His groggy response made her instantly sorry for the disturbance.

"What if they don't come?" CJ realized her question sounded more like a child's whimper.

"They'll come," he answered more clearly.

"But what if they don't? What if the storm doesn't let up? What if we have to stay here for a long time?"

She could hear him sit up and then she felt his hand touching her arm. "Come here," he ordered, and CJ hesitated.

"I don't think I should," she replied. "I mean, I feel. . .well, I mean. . .remember earlier."

"Hush and come here," he insisted more gently than before. He pulled CJ to him, then touched her face with his. His mouth was up against her ear; his breath was warm.

"Everything is going to work out. You'll see," he whispered. "Now stop fretting and let's get some sleep."

"But, Brad—" she started to protest.

"I'm not going to get carried away, if that's what worries you," Brad replied.

CJ felt her heart pounding harder. She couldn't keep from replying, "What if it isn't you I'm worried about?"

Brad chuckled softly. "Got it bad for me, eh?"

"Ohhh!" CJ nudged him away, but he held her fast.

"Look, I got it just as bad for you, but we know what we have to do, and we know what's right and what's wrong. Now, let's get some sleep, and I promise to be a perfect gentleman and," he whispered against her ear, "I'll make certain you remain a perfect lady."

Still embarrassed at having told Brad her concerns, CJ settled stiffly into his arms, relishing the warmth as he tucked the blanket around them. She lay straight and rigid, every nerve in her body taut.

"You can't sleep like that," Brad said and yawned. He seemed completely unconcerned. Outside, the wind roared over the mountain like a lion, and CJ reflexively nestled her face against Brad's chest.

"That's better," he chuckled. "Sometimes we just need a little motivation."

In moments, Brad's rhythmic breathing told CJ he was asleep, and although she would have thought it impossible, CJ finally managed to do the same.

Curled up next to Brad, she tossed and turned, reliving the crash. The scene changed abruptly and faded into the old nightmare. Falling from the sky, CJ could see her parents' stunned faces.

CJ whimpered in her sleep, rousing Brad. He didn't know if it would be better to let her go on dreaming or wake her up. Before he could make a decision, CJ began to cry out. Brad put a hand out to shake her just as she sat straight up and screamed.

Brad reached out and took hold of her. "CJ, wake up. It's only a nightmare."

"Oh, Brad, God must hate me!" she sobbed and fell against him in the dark.

"CJ, you've got to get ahold of yourself. God doesn't hate you. I've been trying to tell you over and over, God loves you. He sent His Son to die for you. Do you honestly think He'd walk away from you with an investment like that?"

"But I've walked away, or maybe I never even knew Him," CJ moaned. "In my dream I—"

"It's the anger inside," Brad interrupted. "Maybe this is what you've got to see, once and for all. The anger you have toward God is eating you alive. It's driving you away from Him."

"But He killed my parents."

"No, He allowed them to die and go home to heaven."

"It's the same thing," CJ wailed.

"No, it's not. Satan is benefiting by the walls you've erected, not God. Satan wins if you walk away," Brad stressed. "God loves you, CJ. I love you. I want you to marry me and share a future together, but not until you've settled this thing."

"But I'm so afraid," she whispered, choking back her tears.

Brad turned on the light. "We get scared in the dark. You're in the dark, CJ. Move toward God and you move into the light."

"Help me, Brad. Pray with me. I want to be free of this. I need to let go of my parents and truly accept God."

After that, sleep came easily, and CJ had no more dreams. She'd made her peace with God, and this time she knew it was real. She wasn't using God as a crutch or even as a way to get to her parents. She had given herself in full to the love that He offered. Things might get rough from time to time, but this time she kept nothing back to accuse Him of later on.

🙠

Morning came with a calm and stillness that matched CJ's internal peace. She felt energized and alive. Waking up in Brad's arms seemed to be the most natural thing in the world, and she was hesitant to move. Suddenly, she remembered his words the night before. In a strange but significant way, he'd declared his desire to marry her.

CJ traced her fingers lightly upon Brad's stubble-lined jaw, then placed a light kiss upon his cheek. "I think Daddy would have liked you," she whispered. "I know I sure do." She reached up and pushed back brown hair that fell across his forehead in little-boy style. His even breathing continued, prompting CJ to go on. "You are the bravest and most handsome man in the world, and I love you." She placed another kiss on his cheek. "And you're mine. . .all mine."

Slipping silently from Brad's sleeping form, CJ scooted back against the rock and smiled smugly to herself.

"You look like the cat who caught the mouse," Brad whispered. He surveyed her through barely opened eyes.

CJ jumped. "You ought to warn a person when you do that."

"Do what?" he questioned, easing himself up on one elbow.

"Spy on them." She blushed, knowing that he'd heard every word she'd said while thinking he was asleep. When would she ever learn to keep her mouth shut?

"Good spies don't announce their missions," Brad replied, giving her a mischievous wink. His grin made her blush even more.

"That wasn't nice," she said, trying to focus on anything but him.

"Maybe not, but it was certainly satisfying to hear you stake your claim."

CJ couldn't stand it and buried her face in her hands, peeking through her fingers. "I can't believe you let me go on. I'm going to remember this moment."

Brad laughed at her discomfort. "I certainly hope so. I know I intend to." He struggled to sit up and winced at the soreness in his side.

128

CJ immediately lost her self-consciousness and came to help him. "You'd better let me check that out," she said, motioning to his side.

"What? Can't keep your hands off of me now that I'm yours?" Brad teased. He unzipped the coveralls and, with a groan, eased his arm out of the sleeve. CJ helped him with the coat he wore beneath the coveralls and pulled his shirt free from his jeans.

"Now lie down on your side," she ordered, reaching for one of the lights.

"It could just wait," Brad said, sounding less than enthusiastic.

"Just do it, or I'll take back what I said about your being brave."

Brad did as he was told and let CJ poke and prod. Using snow, she cleaned the injured site as well as she could, and when she was convinced she could do no more, she bandaged the wound and allowed Brad to redress.

"I think you'll live," she said, putting things back in the first-aid kit. "You're going to need some stitches when we get back."

"So now you finally believe that we're going to make it?" Brad asked, zipping up the coveralls.

CJ laughed at the way he'd backed her into admitting her hopefulness. "I guess I do."

In glaring white light, Brad crawled out from under the rock and got to his feet. "A rescue team should be able to maneuver now," he declared, "but they'll be hard-pressed to see us. The ELT will narrow it down for them, but we can make spotting our site much easier. Let's dig out and throw a little color around this white."

"What about breakfast?" CJ said, reaching for the thermos. "There's still some coffee."

"Cold coffee and frozen donuts. Yum!" Brad exclaimed and threw her a wink.

"You could always go look for the toast," she offered.

Brad reached in and pulled CJ to her feet. "I've got a better idea. First, you kiss me on the lips instead of the cheek and second. . ." His words fell away as he kissed her. He pulled back just a bit, causing CJ to open her eyes. "Never mind about second." He kissed her again.

CJ pushed him back, nearly sending him into the snow. "Oh no, you don't. Ever since I met you, you've been feeding me. Now when I'm really hungry, you won't let me eat."

Brad chuckled. "You win. You win." He threw up his hands and turned her toward the half-buried plane. "Good thing we camped close, or we might not have found it. Looks like it snowed pretty good last night."

CJ nodded, squinting against brilliant light. The snow had placed a shroud over the face of the mountain, while overhead the sky was an incredible shade of blue. Moving out, she plunged into the powdery drifts with Brad close at her side. They cleared the snow from the plane and laid out all their belongings that contrasted the most with white to form an X on top of the snow.

That job done, CJ was overcome with a sense of mischief. When Brad wasn't looking, she hurriedly rolled a snowball into her hands and hurled it at his smiling face just as he turned to ask her something.

Plop! The snow broke up, mostly in powder, with just enough wetness to cling to his stubbly chin.

"So that's the game you want to play." His words sounded as though he were answering a challenge.

CJ began to back up. "Now, Brad," she said with a laugh, "remember your side. You don't want to start bleeding again."

"Then you'd better make it easy on me," he said, reaching for a handful of snow.

CJ waved her hands to hold him back. "You wouldn't."

"Oh, wouldn't I?" Brad advanced with the snow until he'd backed CJ up against the plane. Glancing down at his hands, he spoke. "It wouldn't be very nice to rub your face in this, would it?"

Feeling reprieved, CJ sighed. "No, it wouldn't."

Brad looked up, and CJ knew by his roguish grin that she'd been had. "But it sure will be fun." The words were no sooner out of his mouth than CJ's face met with a handful of snow.

Batting the wetness out of her eyes, she started to reach down for another handful, but Brad stopped her. He kissed her lightly on the lips, then kissed each of her eyes. "Remember my weakened condition," he teased.

CJ wrapped her arms around his neck. "Be glad I'm compassionate," she murmured.

Brad laughed and, after another brief kiss, released her. "I'm going to melt some snow. We need to drink plenty of water," he said. "You can get dehydrated pretty fast up here."

"I'll see if I can find anything useful in the plane."

CJ searched through the plane for anything that would offer them further help or comfort. With a laugh, she found the toast plastered alongside the radio, bits of frozen paper still clinging to it in shreds. Still laughing, she called Brad to inspect it.

Brad stuck his head inside and saw the mess of bread that had somehow managed to get entwined with the dash controls.

"Well, that confirms it," he said with a grin.

"Confirms what?"

"The radio's toast."

"Oh, Brad," CJ moaned and rolled her eyes. "That's pathetic."

He shrugged his shoulders and reached out to peel off the mess. "Where's that jelly?"

Chapter 18

The day warmed marginally, making it easy to maneuver around the small area that Brad deemed safe. He reminded CJ that they knew very little of the terrain beneath the snow and that it would be easy to fall into a hole or miss a step.

Brad surveyed their meager supplies, while CJ kept watch on the skies and periodically murmured a prayer. Their prayers were answered when search teams flying overhead spotted them. CJ was more than a little anxious about the rescue, but those concerns faded whenever she thought of Brad's proposal. A proposal that hadn't really been issued.

They gathered their things and waited while the rescue teams decided the best course of action. CJ had hoped Brad would bring up the idea of getting married, but so far he'd kept their conversation light and humorous. Had he changed his mind? Were his words only spoken in the heat of the moment?

Finally she could stand it no longer. The thundering sound of a helicopter overhead caused CJ to glance up from where she sat. A man in bright coveralls and helmet was lowering something down from the open door of the helicopter.

"Looks like we're about to be rescued," Brad said, motioning upward as though CJ had missed it.

It took CJ only a moment to note that the man was now being lowered down, as well. He was strapped to the rope in some strange concoction of lines and was motioning Brad and CJ to stay put.

The man landed several feet from them and shouted, "You okay?"

Brad pulled CJ with him and replied. "Minor injuries, nothing else. Sure glad to see you guys."

The man nodded. "I'll take the lady up first, then come back down for you. You can give us the details later."

CJ inwardly panicked as Brad handed her over to the man and

helped him strap her to the line.

"Yes." She stated the word as though he'd just asked her a question, and Brad could only shake his head.

"Yes?" he asked curiously and stepped back. He noted the mischievous grin on CJ's face and raised a brow to emphasize his confusion. "Yes, what?"

"Yes, I'll marry you," CJ stated with a smug expression.

"Oh, really," Brad said, crossing his arms against his chest while the rescuer finished checking the line.

"That's right," she replied, refusing to give up.

"I don't remember asking you," he stated blankly. His pretense at seriousness didn't put CJ off for a minute.

"Then you better get to asking, because I might not say yes after we're rescued, and it looks as though I'm about to leave."

Brad laughed. "You drive a hard bargain."

"I might say the same. Sometimes I think you planned all of this," she said, waving her arms to indicate their predicament, "just so you could have me to yourself."

"We're going up. Put your arms like this and hold tight," the stranger told her, and CJ turned with a shrug to Brad.

Brad quickly knelt in the snow. "CJ, you're my dearest friend. You mean more to me than my own life does. Will you marry me?"

Tears came to CJ's eyes, but she didn't care. Rising above the ground, she smiled down at Brad. "Yes!" she shouted down. "Yes, I'll marry you!"

❧❦

Denver never looked so good, and even though they were forced apart for an observation stay at the hospital, CJ and Brad were clearly bonded for life.

Cheryl arrived to make certain they were both really alive. "The nurse told me you were fine. Is that true?" Cheryl asked in that motherly tone of worry that CJ remembered from long ago.

"I'm great. A little frostbite, but other than that, perfect health. Brad, on the other hand, has twenty stitches in his side. The doctor said it wasn't anything to worry about, though."

"I was so afraid," Cheryl told CJ. "I even insisted Daddy make his friends step up the search. I hassled them so much, I think they thought I was crazy. . .at least Stratton did."

"Stratton?" CJ questioned from the confines of her bed. "Are things any better between you two?"

"I think so," Cheryl said, rather hesitantly. "We've reset the wedding for Valentine's Day."

"You don't sound too thrilled about this," CJ observed suspiciously.

"Well, it's a long story," Cheryl replied. "Let's just say I'm not sure I'm comfortable with everything in our relationship."

"Meaning what?" CJ frowned.

"Meaning," Cheryl hesitated, "that it's a long story. Anyway, I'm glad you and Brad are all right."

"We're more than that," CJ said, forgetting her worry about Cheryl's situation. "We're engaged. He asked me to marry him, and I said yes."

Cheryl's face lit up. "CJ! That's wonderful! Have you set the date?"

"No," CJ replied, "but knowing Brad, he won't give me much time. He likes things to move forward at a steady pace."

Cheryl nodded. "Yes, he's always struck me as rather insistent. When do you leave the hospital?"

"Tomorrow, and not a minute too soon. I thought people were supposed to rest while in the hospital. I've been poked, stuck, questioned, and hassled ever since being assigned a bed."

Cheryl laughed. "Don't worry. I'll keep them all at bay once you're back home. Good thing I moved in, eh?"

"Yeah, I'm glad you did. I just wish I'd been a better roommate."

Cheryl shook her head. "You've been great, CJ. You've had a lot to deal with, and now it's over. Now your life really begins."

❧

The next day, safe in her apartment, CJ was still thinking about Cheryl's words. Sitting next to Brad, CJ sighed and knew the words were true. It was the beginning. Pressing closer, she whispered, "I'm going to like being married to you. You're comfortable in all the right spots."

"Comfortable, eh?" Brad replied against her hair. "I hope that's a good thing."

"The best," she said, pulling back a bit. "At the very least, a very redeeming quality." With a sigh, she fell back. "I'm so happy."

"That reminds me, when are we going to set the date?"

"How about now? You are, after all, a person who likes to get things done."

Brad laughed and pulled her into his arms. "How about the first of December? Will that give you enough time to plan all those important girl things?"

CJ giggled, sounding very much like a little girl. "I suppose. Will it give you enough time to plan those boy things?"

Brad's smile was nearly a leer. "I guarantee you it will. In fact, if you want, we can just tie the knot tomorrow down at the courthouse. We boys don't need much time to plan."

"Oh, no, you don't. I want it all. I want the church wedding. I want you in a long-tailed tuxedo. I want to wear a gorgeous wedding dress, and I want a wonderful reception at Denver's finest resort hotel," CJ announced in a breathless manner.

Brad shook his head with a chuckle. "Now who's the organized planner? I'd say you've been thinking about this for quite some time. Just when did you decide we were getting married?"

CJ looked up at the ceiling with a sheepish grin. "Probably when I found out you could be so helpful when I got sick. You've got to love a man who'll hold your hair out of your face while you lose your breakfast."

"How romantic," Brad replied. "Here I thought you'd say something like how you planned to marry me the first moment you looked into my eyes."

"Well," CJ paused, "that might have influenced my decision."

"Whatever influenced it," Brad whispered against her ear, "I'm most grateful. I love you so much, I can't even remember the time when you weren't a part of my life."

"I can," CJ responded softly. "And I'd just as soon never remember it again."

❧

The following morning, CJ woke up before sunrise and, taking her portable phone, she went out on the balcony with a cup of coffee and dialed her brother's number.

A groggy-voiced Curt answered the phone. "This better be good," he said instead of hello.

CJ laughed. "Well, good morning to you, too. I figured by your time back east, you'd be up and around. Sorry if I misjudged."

"CJ!" He was instantly awake. "I got your message just today. I heard about the crash, too. You okay?" His voice held the same concern Cheryl's had. Perhaps they were both worried that another crash had sent CJ over the proverbial edge.

"I'm fine. In fact, I'm better than that. Curt, I've wanted to talk to you for so long. I've put the past behind me, and I've dealt with the crash. Both of them, in fact," she continued. "God's really been patient with me."

"I'm sorry I wasn't there for you," Curt said, surprising CJ. Then he went on to explain. "After Mom and Dad were killed, I should have stayed with you. I'm really sorry."

"I know," CJ replied softly. "You couldn't deal with it any better than the rest of us. Cheryl told me how hard it was on you, and I guess I just never thought about it, what with my own traumas. It worked out for the best, anyway. God knew just what I needed, or maybe I should say, who I needed. That's the other reason I called. Curt, I'm getting married."

"Brad?" he questioned.

"Yes. He's everything Daddy and Mom would have wanted in a son-in-law, but more importantly, he's everything I want in a husband, and he loves me."

Curt was quiet for several minutes before he finally said, "I'm glad, kiddo. I really am."

"You'll come to the wedding, won't you?"

"Sure, just tell me when and where," Curt replied.

"The first of December at a little church here in Denver."

"I'll be there," Curt promised.

Chapter 19

CJ was a nervous wreck. She had less than two hours to finish running from one end of Denver to the other and still make it to the florist before 4:00 in order to confirm that her bridal bouquet was finally to her specifications.

Grimacing, she could still see the dreadful arrangement that had originally been presented to her. It was nothing like what she had ordered. The florist had pulled out her order ready to do battle but quickly saw her mistake and apologized, promising to have the bouquet redone in time for CJ's last-minute examination.

A quick glance at the car clock caused CJ to step on the accelerator. When her cellular phone rang, she nearly jumped out of her skin. The cell phone had been Brad's idea, and CJ still wasn't used to it.

"Hello?"

"Twenty-six hours, forty-five minutes, thirty-seven seconds, and—"

"I get the idea," CJ laughed. "And you're wrong. It's only forty-two minutes, not forty-five."

Brad laughed. "Okay, I stand corrected and quite happily. Where are you?"

"Headed to the florist."

"Gonna make sure they don't mix in red carnations again?"

CJ shuddered. "It really was hideous."

"I can well imagine. Is there anything I can do to help?"

"No," CJ answered as she pulled into the florist's parking lot. "Not unless you can alter time."

"If I could do that, we'd already be married." Brad's impatience was betrayed in his voice.

"I'm beginning to think we should have eloped," CJ sighed and turned off the engine. "I don't think I have the energy for much more of this wedding stuff."

"Chin up, ol' girl. This time tomorrow—"

"Will be even worse," CJ moaned the words. "Look, I have to run or the florist will close and I'll end up with balloons that say, 'It's a Girl!' floating up from my arrangement."

"Don't let it get you down, CJ. I'll marry you no matter what you end up carrying down the aisle."

"If things get much more difficult, you'll be carrying me down the aisle."

"I can do that, too." Brad was still chuckling as CJ said good-bye.

❧

The hotel's grand ballroom was filled to overflowing with well-wishers, friends, and family. CJ stood beside her new husband and prepared with trembling hand to cut their wedding cake. She looked up at Brad for a moment and smiled.

Brad's eyes met hers, and CJ thought her heart might burst from the happiness she felt. *If only Curt could have been here,* she thought. Something had prevented him from coming at the last minute, however, and though CJ had his promise he'd visit for Christmas, it just wasn't the same. Nevertheless, everything else was perfect, including Cheryl and Stratton, who seemed completely devoted to one another.

CJ felt a deep satisfaction. It was just as she'd planned. The cream-colored satin she'd chosen for her wedding dress was rich and elegant. Styled with a basque waist and sweetheart neckline, the entire bodice was encrusted with tiny seed pearls on lace. The voluminous skirt billowed out around her and ended in a lace inset train that flowed behind her for several feet.

Her thick copper hair had been carefully fashioned with long ringlets cascading down from where the bulk of it was pinned high on top of her head. To this, an exquisite antique lace veil had been attached to trail far behind her like a royal mantle.

Brad, too, cut a dashing figure in his black, long-tailed tuxedo. His cummerbund matched the pale peach gown that Cheryl wore as maid of honor, and the rose in his lapel was the same as the apricot roses in CJ's bouquet. And to her extreme satisfaction and relief, there were no red carnations.

The photographer devoted his attention for the moment to the four-tiered wedding cake. On top was CJ's own special touch—a bride and groom seated in a biplane. Brad thought it especially appropriate and commended her for her ingenuity.

"I didn't know I was getting such a creative wife," he whispered.

"I was going to have the whole cake designed like that mountain you flew into, with us and our little Cessna on top, waiting to be rescued," she teased. Brad started laughing, which drew the attention of everyone.

When the photographer was satisfied that he'd snapped the cake from every angle, he motioned them to go ahead. CJ felt Brad's warm hand cover hers. Together, they drew the knife down through the bottom tier of the wedding cake, while the photographer moved rapidly to capture the moment.

With a grin, Brad raised a piece of cake to CJ's mouth. "Seems I'm always feeding you," he whispered.

"You'd better not get that all over my dress," she replied softly, the smile never leaving her face. "Just remember I get my turn at this."

Brad chuckled and managed to feed her the cake without a single crumb escaping to mar her gown. CJ took her turn, and then they shared glasses of wedding punch. Arms intertwined, bodies touching, CJ and Brad made the perfect couple. After sips of the punch, the crowd around them broke into cheers.

❧

It was two hours later before CJ and Brad could slip away to the penthouse. Knowing the hour would be quite late when the reception concluded, they'd already decided to spend the night at the hotel rather than head out on their honeymoon.

CJ pulled out the pins that held the lace veil and carefully draped the material over the back of a chair. She was married! What a wonder. She'd just committed her life to another human being. It was a responsibility she was only now coming to realize.

She could hear Brad on the phone in his office. Funny how people seemed to know the most inappropriate times to call. CJ walked to the balcony window and pulled back the draperies. All of Denver seemed to be lit up in celebration. *Beautiful,* she thought. Mesmerized by the twinkling lights, she didn't hear Brad come up behind her. Warm hands touched her neck, soon followed by his lips.

"Ummm," she sighed. "I could get used to this."

"You'd better," he replied. "I think it will be one of my favorite pastimes." Brad turned her around and lifted her in his arms.

CJ wrapped her arms around his neck. "No more phone calls?"

"I turned the phone off," Brad replied.

"What about the maid service?" she grinned.

"I hung the 'Do Not Disturb' sign on the door, and I informed the elevator attendant that no one was to be allowed up to the penthouse until I said otherwise."

CJ giggled. "My husband, the planner."

Brad's lips curled upward in a most mischievous way. "These are plans that I definitely don't want interrupted."

"Whatever you say, Mr. Aldersson," she murmured, nuzzling her lips to his neck. "Whatever you say."

❧

The sun was already high in the sky when CJ opened her eyes. For a moment she forgot where she was, but the warmth of the man beside her quickly brought back the wonders of the night.

Snuggling closer to Brad, CJ traced a heart on his chest. His hand shot out and closed over her wrist, surprising her. Bringing her fingers to his lips, Brad greeted her.

"Good morning, wife," he whispered.

"Good morning," she replied and leaned up on one elbow, with her hair falling in disarray around her. "I wonder if I'll ever be able to catch you sleeping."

"How's a guy supposed to sleep with someone so beautiful lying next to him?"

CJ laughed and pulled away. "I've got a surprise for you, but we have to get out to the airstrip—and look," she said, pointing to the window, "we've already wasted half the day."

Brad shook his head. "Are you sure we can't just stay here?"

"Come on," she replied. "I've worked very hard for this surprise."

"Okay," he relented, "but only because I have a surprise out there for you, as well."

❧

The trip to the airport was passed in laughter and conversation of the days to come. They'd decided to fly to a warmer climate for their honeymoon, and because she'd never been there, CJ requested the Bahamas and Brad had readily agreed.

The three-story stone house looked somehow different to CJ. It was her home now. . .hers and Brad's. The very thought filled her with excitement and anticipation.

"I'm so happy," she said, squeezing Brad's arm.

He parked the car and pulled her into his arms. "Me, too," he whispered before giving CJ a long kiss that left her weak in the knees.

CJ melted back against the seat of the Jeep and rolled her eyes. "You sure are good at that."

"Come on," he said with a laugh. "I want to give you your surprise."

They walked hand in hand to a newly built hangar, where Brad came to a stop. "Now, close your eyes," he said firmly.

CJ closed them. "All right, I'm ready," she called.

Brad looked over his shoulder for a moment at his wife. She stood there in a long, navy wool coat, copper hair flowing down behind her, and the most innocent look of anticipation on her face. It was definitely hard to concentrate with her looking like that.

Pulling open the hangar doors, Brad stood back. "Okay, you can open your eyes."

CJ did just that and gasped at the newly acquired biplane. "A Curtiss Jenny!" she exclaimed. Her namesake.

"You like it?" Brad asked.

"You know the answer to that. Of course! I love it!" She went to the plane to inspect it. "Oh, Brad, she's lovely." CJ ran her hand along the wing.

"No more so than you," Brad replied. "She's all yours."

CJ turned around with a look of complete shock. "Mine?" She shook her head and added. "Ours. From now on, we're a partnership. Remember?"

"I'll remember. You just remember how much I love you and that for the rest of our lives, I'm going to work very hard to be a good husband."

CJ walked from the plane and pulled something from her pocket.

She reached up and handed it to Brad.

"My surprise doesn't seem nearly as nice," she said.

Brad looked down and immediately recognized the pilot's license. "You're a pilot again?" It was Brad's turn to be astonished.

"Yes, and this time I can fly all on my own, too," she replied proudly. "Although I'd much rather fly with you."

"How did you manage this and plan a wedding?" he asked curiously.

"You think you're the only planner in this family? We girls can accomplish quite a bit when we put our minds to it. I just thought it would be nice if I could help fly part of the way to the Bahamas."

"I don't know," Brad replied, taking on a doubtful air. "I'm pretty picky about whom I fly with."

CJ laughed and reached her arms up to Brad's neck. Pulling his face down to hers, she whispered, "I bet I can convince you to fly with me." She kissed him long and lovingly, then added, "Does that help?"

"I'm a pretty tough case," he answered. The look in his eyes betrayed his amusement. "I might need a lot of convincing."

CJ laughed and danced away. "Well, I don't," she called back over her shoulder. "I'm flying high and clear. I've married the man I love, and I'm at peace with my God. What more could anyone want out of life?"

Brad easily caught up with her and whirled her around in a circle. "As long as I have you and a wing and a prayer," Brad remarked, holding her close, "I have it all."

"A wing and a prayer," CJ whispered with a nod. "Now I know Daddy would have loved you."

In the distance the familiar drone of an airplane engine crossed the silence to CJ's ears. It was a good sound, and CJ smiled at the bittersweet memory of another day and time. She was finally free of the past and ready to face the future with a wholeness and happiness of which she'd only dreamed.

"A wing and a prayer, Jenny darlin'," she could hear her father say, "are all that you'll ever need."

Wings
Like Eagles

Dedicated to Michael Daugherty:
When autumn leaves blend gold from green, I think of you.
Denver in '97 for sure,
and we can all bring our friends!

Chapter 1

Christy Connors bolted upright in bed. She was drenched in a cold sweat that left her brown hair plastered to her skin as though she'd just stepped from the shower. Panting for breath, she noticed for the first time that it was light outside.

The elegant brocade draperies allowed only the smallest amount of sunlight to filter into the room, but it was enough. Settling her nerves, Christy realized the haunting scene, which had so startled her, was only a nightmare.

Candy! Her little sister, dubbed so because the name Camille seemed much too dramatic for the little squirt of a kid, was in trouble. At least she had been in Christy's dream. She started to reach for the telephone to call Candy and assure herself that it had been nothing more than her wild imagination, but a quick glance at the clock stopped her. Candy needed her sleep now that she was nearly eight months pregnant. The little squirt of a kid was now nineteen, married, and expecting her first child.

Pushing back the covers along with her concern, Christy stretched her legs over the side of the bed. With a yawn that nearly sent her to seeking the comfort of her pillows again, she forced herself to get up.

The pink silk nightgown swirled gracefully around her long legs as Christy crossed the room to pull back the drapes and let in the day. At twenty-five, Christy had experienced more than many people twice her age. She'd modeled for several years, but found the constant race between New York, Paris, and a hundred other points of interest exhausting. When she'd announced her retirement at the mere age of twenty-one, the world had mourned the loss, and her agent still continued to harangue her to return to the spotlight. Christy satisfied her own interests, however, and using the large sums of money she'd made modeling, she re-entered the public eye in an entirely different way.

For nearly four years, Christy Connors had been the proud owner and sole operator of Designs by Christy. Her business was one that catered to the very rich, and Christy was quite choosey about her clientele. Now that she had international recognition and fame for her one-of-a-kind, handcrafted wedding gowns, Christy Connors was rapidly becoming a wealthy woman.

After momentary consideration of the Rocky Mountains in the distant west, Christy's next point of business was to seat herself at an eighteenth-century desk and study her appointment book. The entire world clamored to be part of her agenda. At least it felt that way at times.

Of course, it hadn't always been so. When she was still a senior in high school, a man had spotted Christy in a local shopping mall and asked her if she'd ever thought of modeling. Christy thought the whole thing one of those put-on farces by men who were seeking to lure innocent young women into the dark confines of their vans. She told the man emphatically that she had no interest whatsoever in his proposition. Two days later he showed up with the governor of the state, and her mother had nearly fainted. Within an hour, Christy had an appointment for an interview and photo shoot in New York City.

Boarding a plane and leaving the Mile High City, Christy had been sure that she'd never return. She wasn't leaving with any regrets. In fact, she was more or less running away from home. Only this kind of running had everyone's blessing.

Modeling hadn't been a dream job, however. Anyone who thought it a life of glamor had another thing coming. Glamor was the end result, but it certainly wasn't the life that one led getting there. Christy hadn't even graduated from college. There'd never been time to take more than a few classes in fashion design and marketing before some assignment sent her halfway around the world, disrupting her whole life.

She was up early each morning, working with a professional trainer who saw her through exercise routines and runway moves. Christy worked harder to learn the trade than anything she'd ever put herself into before. It didn't take long for the world to recognize her talent and demand the long-legged beauty grace the covers of their magazines. In one year alone, she had seventeen covers and over a dozen feature stories.

When she finally decided to put modeling behind her and go to school full-time, her agent had been livid. What did she need with an education, when she had a body that brought the world to a standstill? But Christy wasn't naïve enough to believe it would last forever. A woman who depended on her looks to make a living raced against a clock that never slowed down. Wrinkles, weight gains or losses, sagging skin, and blemishes—it was all too much to pay attention to, and Christy tired of worshiping at the altar of her own face.

College was a new and exciting world and, while some people recognized her for her modeling work, most just thought she was a struggling student like everyone else. Christy was honestly happy. Happy, that is, until she made the mistake of falling in love. He was older and wiser, or at least that's what Christy had thought. He was gentle and loving and everything she was looking for. Instead, she got another example of shallowness and infidelity. So Christy left school in order to isolate herself as far as she could from the man who'd broken her heart. Since he was a professor with tenure at the university, she couldn't very well expect him to leave.

Shaking her head to clear the past, Christy tried to focus her attention on the day's appointments. She had two. One was set for 9:00 and would be the first fitting for Mariah DuBane, a wealthy debutante from Dallas. The second appointment was a first interview scheduled at lunchtime and would require that Christy serve more than her routine refreshments.

She made a note to call the caterer and finalize the delivery time for the luncheon. When Christy Connors chose clients, she did it in style. No one could ever complain that they weren't addressed with the utmost respect and genteel refinement.

She scanned the appointment book for notes on the new couple: *Curt Kyle and Debbie Bradford, June 28 wedding. Formal, after six. Bride desires an elaborate gown with imported Belgian lace.* That was the end of her information, and Christy snapped the book shut.

Dropping her slip-styled nightgown from her shoulders, Christy walked into her white marble bathroom and turned on the shower. Another day, just like all the others, was about to begin.

An hour later, Christy descended the oak staircase, looking a masterpiece of perfection. Her shoulder-length, chocolate brown hair had been swept off her face and gathered with two gold clasps on either side. Her heart-shaped face had been carefully accentuated with a delicate blend of powders and shadows that made the most of Christy's natural beauty. She knew she was a beautiful woman, but inside she felt empty and uncertain. Why, she wondered, was it never enough?

An older woman in a black-and-white uniform appeared at the foot of the stairs. "Good morning, Miss Connors."

Christy nodded. "Morning, Aggie. Breakfast ready?"

Aggie laughed. "The same as usual. Your orange juice is on the table, and the coffee will follow as soon as you give the word."

Christy moved through the front room and opened French doors onto a small, glassed-in balcony. "Oh, would you call the overnight people and check on the location of my delivery from France?"

"I'll get to it after I serve your coffee," the older woman replied and took her leave.

Christy smiled to herself. There was a refined, yet friendly relationship between the two women, and Christy knew she'd be lost without the helpful insight of Aggie. More than once Christy had sought the older woman's advice, and more than once Aggie had offered it on her own. It was an amicable companionship.

The balcony resembled a small garden. The entire room had been designed to use year-round, with removable glass over screens. A magnificent view of the snowcapped peaks of the Rocky Mountains glistening against the sun greeted Christy. White wicker furniture graced the retreat and stood out in sharp contrast to the deep greens of house plants in their various colorful pots. It was Christy's favorite room in the house.

After fussing over each plant as though it were a beloved child, Christy finally took a seat at the table and began to read the *Denver Post*. There was comfort for Christy in her routine. It seldom varied and always managed to give her a positive outlook on the day. Checking her watch, she downed the rest of the juice and finished the first section of the paper just as Aggie appeared and poured coffee.

The two women didn't exchange a single word as Aggie went to make the required phone calls, and Christy turned her attention back to the newspaper. Twenty minutes later, Mariah DuBane arrived, and the fragile peace of the day was broken.

"Don't tell me I'm a size six," the bleach-blond screeched at Christy. "I've always worn a four, and I'll always wear a four. I'm certainly not going to be swimming down the aisle to my wedding in a size six gown!"

Christy was used to debutante fits and merely crossed her arms against her cream-colored cashmere suit. "Ms. DuBane, perhaps you would like to go elsewhere to have your gown created. I'm a very busy woman, and I take my designs very seriously. I would not threaten my reputation with an ill-fitting gown. That goes for one which would be too tight, as well as one in which you might swim."

The blond started to speak, then tightened her lips. "I suppose it's just nerves," Mariah finally offered, and the fitting continued.

After Mariah blew out of the house, Christy barely had enough time to receive the caterers and double-check the table. Casting a quick glance around, Christy found everything in order. The entire house was devoted to the charm and elegance of another era, and here was no exception. The dining room table was a delicate Queen Anne, with matching chairs upholstered in a dusty rose fabric. The walls were papered with a floral print of the same shade, with fine gold ribbons running the length of the print to set it off as though a hundred little borders lined the room. Original oak woodwork added the most dramatic touch, framing the room with its elaborate curlicues and scrolling.

Smoothing a slight wrinkle in the cream-colored, Irish linen tablecloth, Christy inspected the place settings of ruby red dinnerware before turning her attention to the food.

The door chime sounded, and Christy glanced down at her watch. *At least they're punctual,* she thought, and grabbed her appointment book on the way to open the door.

"I'm Deborah Bradford," an exotic-looking woman said. She put out her hand and flashed dark eyes in greeting.

Christy extended her hand. "I'm Christy Connors. Won't you come in?" She stepped back to allow the young woman entry.

Christy could tell just by the way the woman moved that it would be a pleasure to work with her. She was exquisite, and Christy stole a moment just to study her. Long black hair fell straight to the middle of Deborah's back, and large dark eyes were framed by the blackest of lashes.

Christy concluded she was nearly the same height and size as Deborah, but there was something almost intimidating about the look of this woman.

Christy was so taken aback by Deborah's beauty that she didn't hear the man who had followed them into the house until he leaned down and whispered in her ear.

"I'm Curt Kyle, just in case you wondered."

Christy's head snapped up in surprise and met the most incredible blue eyes she had ever seen. If Deborah's beauty had stunned Christy, then the strange attraction she instantly felt for Curt was more than a little troubling.

"Christy Connors," she managed to reply and extended her slender hand.

Curt Kyle reached out and took Christy's slender fingers into his warm grip. *It's almost a caress,* Christy thought, wishing she could find the strength to pull away.

"Glad to meet you. I guess you know why we're here," he said in such a nonchalant way that Christy was certain he was in no way affected as she had been.

Christy nodded. "I've arranged lunch for us," she said, trying to steady her nerves. *It is ridiculous,* she thought, *to act so childish.* "If you'll both come this way, we'll eat and discuss your plans."

"You have a beautiful home, Ms. Connors," Deborah said as they made their way to the dining room. "I love the Victorian age, and I see you have decorated with many lovely pieces from that time."

"Thank you," Christy replied. "Miss Bradford, if you'll sit here—"

"Please call me Debbie," the woman interrupted. "I'd be much more at ease if you would."

Christy smiled. "Certainly." She waited for Curt to seat his fiancée before leading him to the seat opposite Debbie. She started to seat herself, only to suddenly find Curt assisting her into her chair. "Thank you, Mr. Kyle."

"Curt," he said with a grin.

Christy felt a tremor run through her as she stared deep into the man's eyes. "Curt," she whispered, almost afraid to use the name. Then, needing to break the spell, she glanced back to Debbie. "And you must both call me Christy."

Chicken salad with grape and almond slices oozed out from between fluffy croissants, forcing each person to slice their sandwich in half. Added to this were bowls of fruit salad and glasses of flavored mineral water and, of course, coffee. Christy wasn't certain, but for herself, she deeply suspected that functioning without coffee would have been impossible.

Setting aside her fork, Christy opened her book to take a few notes. "I understand you have a passion for Belgian lace," she began.

"Yes," Debbie replied. "My family was stationed overseas when my father was in the air force. We visited Brugge and saw several old women hand-making the lace right on the walkways in front of the shops. That's when I fell in love with it. It was incredible the way they took thread and bobbins and created masterpieces. I can't imagine having a gown made with anything else."

Christy nodded. "It will be extremely expensive to import."

"Money's no object," Curt answered before Debbie could. "I want her to have the best."

Christy made the mistake of meeting his eyes. For a moment she was helpless to look away. Curt recognized the attraction, and though his lips remained noncommittal, his eyes lit with amusement. Finally composing herself, Christy nodded and made note of the Belgian lace even though she'd already noted it once before.

I can't look at his eyes, she told herself. *When I speak to him, I'll look elsewhere, but not into his eyes.* Feeling more composed, Christy continued the interview.

"I accept very few clients, as I'm sure you are aware. I hand-make only six gowns a year, and all of my gowns start at five thousand dollars. That amount is for the label and the quality that the name represents.

"I am quite choosey about whom I work with. There must be a bond of sorts, which may sound extremely ridiculous in this day and age of making a buck, but I'm not in this business for the money alone," Christy stated firmly.

"What are you in the business for?" Curt asked.

Christy refused to look at him. "I want to create beautiful things. I want to give brides a glimpse of the fairy tale," she replied. Then turning to Debbie, she asked. "What is your idea of the fairy tale?"

Debbie looked thoughtful for a moment. "I want an incredibly beautiful wedding. Like Curt said, money is not one of our limitations. I intend to have over twelve thousand dollars' worth of flowers and six attendants. The reception alone will be catered to the tune of twenty thousand, and we're inviting more than four hundred people."

Christy nodded. The amounts were not that shocking. Most of the people she dealt with could afford weddings like that, or they certainly would not have come to her for the gown. Most of her gowns ended up costing close to fifteen thousand dollars, so only the very affluent could afford to seek her out.

"What about the gown itself? Have you a particular style in mind?" Christy asked.

Debbie smiled at Curt. "I want one of those romantic ballroom gowns."

"Full skirt, basque waist, that sort of thing?" Christy questioned while writing.

"Yes," Debbie said with a sigh in her voice. "I want it made of silk and Belgian lace. And I want lots of seed pearls and sequins. I want it to stand out as the most beautiful gown ever created."

"For the most beautiful bride," Curt said with a note of appreciation in his voice for his bride-to-be.

Christy had to take a deep breath to steady her nerves before she could continue. "What about the neckline and sleeves?"

"I'm not really sure," Debbie said thoughtfully. "What would you suggest?"

Christy looked at the woman for a moment, then closed her eyes as if seeing the completed gown in her mind. "I think Juliet sleeves—poufed at the top with lace insets and fitted with lace to the wrist."

"Yes, I like that idea," Debbie replied.

"For the bodice, I would definitely suggest a sweetheart neckline. It will set off the basque waist and your natural assets," Christy said, causing Curt to grin.

"She has many natural assets," he couldn't resist throwing in.

Christy ignored the playful tone and continued jotting down descriptions, with notes regarding the materials the bride wanted. Still refusing to look at Curt, Christy asked, "What about your groomsmen?"

Curt's deep velvety voice answered—just as Christy had been afraid he would. "What do you suggest, Christy?" he questioned, forcing Christy to either acknowledge him or appear rude.

Slowly she lifted her face, and instead of meeting his eyes, she focused on his lips. Afterward, Christy would chide herself for the stupidity of this ingenious move.

"Have you a style of tuxedo picked out?" she responded in a deliberately slow, even manner.

Just then the phone rang, and the spell was broken. Christy quickly excused herself, picked up her portable phone, and moved to the balcony where she'd had breakfast.

"Designs By Christy," she announced.

It was another of her clients, only this time the woman was nearly hysterical, and Christy was hard-pressed to understand her.

"You want to cancel the gown then?" Christy asked hesitantly.

The woman assured Christy from the other end of the line that she only wanted to postpone the gown's completion. Christy grimaced. It was the second time Cheryl Fairchild had called to postpone her wedding plans.

"Miss Fairchild, I can postpone the gown for you one more time, but after that, I'm afraid we'll have to discontinue the arrangement. I have other clients, and I can't jeopardize their plans just because yours continue to change."

Christy listened as Cheryl elaborated on her problems for a moment and finally concluded by telling Christy that she would give her a five-thousand-dollar bonus for holding the completion until she was able to put her wedding plans back on track.

Christy finally agreed. After all, five thousand dollars to do nothing but wait was too much money to pass up, and Cheryl Fairchild could well afford it, given the fact that she had recently inherited quite a fortune.

Concluding the call, Christy found herself in a dilemma. Debbie and Curt would expect her decision when she returned. But how could she agree to take them on when Curt had such an effect on her? Still, she liked Debbie's ideas and was already designing the most glorious gown in her mind. Finally Christy convinced herself that Curt wouldn't be a part of the fittings and periodic visits and, therefore, shouldn't even be a factor in her decision.

Returning to the dining room, Christy made her decision. She would demand a hefty down payment, and if that was agreeable, she would take the job. Otherwise, Debbie and Curt could find another designer.

"I've had a postponement," Christy announced to Debbie and Curt. "Because of this, I will take you on as a client, but only if you are willing to pay half the cost up front, in cash. The lace alone will have to be special-ordered, and it may take some doing to locate the pattern you've described. Because of the lavish design, this gown will not be inexpensive, even by my standards."

"That isn't a problem, I assure you," Debbie said with a note of excitement to her voice. "We didn't bring cash with us, but we can drop it off later today, if that meets with your approval. Would ten thousand dollars be enough to start?"

Christy nearly paled at the casual way Debbie mentioned the amount. She was only going to ask for seven. Steadying herself, Christy nodded. "That will be fine."

Christy had no sooner seen Debbie and Curt out when the phone rang again. It was so typical of her daily routine. Rushing to answer it, Christy was relieved to hear the voice of her brother on the other end.

"Erik, it's good to hear from you," Christy said.

"Christy," he began, "there's been an accident."

"Candy?" she whispered. Her nightmare came back to haunt her.

"Yes. She was driving up from Colorado Springs on the interstate. Somehow, she lost control of the car and crashed. They flew her up here about an hour ago. I just now found out."

"How bad is it?"

"It's bad, Christy. She's still in surgery."

"What about the baby?"

"I don't know," Erik answered honestly. "They haven't told me much of anything, but I think you'd better get over here."

"I'm on my way." Christy hung up the phone, still trembling from the shock. Without thought, she grabbed her purse and coat and went to the hospital.

Chapter 2

Erik Connors met his sister in the emergency room and embraced her tightly. "They're still working on her," he whispered against her ear.

When Christy pulled away, there were tears in her eyes. "Won't they tell you anything? For pity's sake, Erik, you work here. Can't you get one of your lab or physical therapy buddies to find out something?"

"I tried, but nobody has the time to talk to them. She's not good; that much I know." Erik's words hung over them like a shroud. "She nearly died on the way here."

Christy felt her knees buckle, but Erik quickly grabbed hold of her. "You'd better sit down," he said and led her to a chair.

"Was anyone else involved?" Christy finally asked.

"No, the highway patrolman said it was a single-car accident. He said it was as though she blacked out or fell asleep and just lost control. There were no skid marks to show she'd applied the brakes or fought to regain control, so they're pretty sure she was unconscious."

"What about Grant?" Christy inquired. Candy's husband was often conspicuously absent, and this time seemed to be no different.

"I couldn't get hold of him," Erik confessed. "I called the law office and their house. I tried everything I could think of, but he seems to be out of town or, at best, out of reach."

"Nothing new about that." Christy's voice told her brother she had no lost love for her brother-in-law.

They waited in near silence for over five hours before the doctor summoned them to a private consultation room. Christy could tell by the look on his face that the news wouldn't be good.

"I am Dr. Edwards," the man stated brusquely when they entered the room. He still wore his bloodstained scrubs beneath the open surgical coat. Christy recoiled at the realization that the blood belonged to

155

her sister. "Have you been able to reach her husband?" the doctor questioned. When Christy and Erik both shook their heads, he continued, "I'm sorry I can't give you good news. Your sister is barely holding onto life at this point. She sustained massive cranial injuries, and that, along with the tumor, doesn't give us much hope for her recovery."

"Tumor?" Erik questioned. The look on Christy's face revealed that she, too, had no idea of any tumor.

The doctor's brows knitted together. "Your sister has a massive, inoperable brain tumor. I presumed you knew."

"No," Christy and Erik replied in unison.

"It is most likely the reason she lost consciousness while driving," Dr. Edwards continued. "I was fortunate enough to reach her doctor in Colorado Springs. It seems she's known about the condition for some time but refused treatment because of the baby. Of course, this type of cancer doesn't have a very high rate of treatment success. I'm sure your sister weighed this all very carefully against the fact that she wanted to keep from harming the fetus."

Christy could not have been more stunned. In one fell swoop, she had been told that not only was her sister barely alive, but even if she recovered from the accident, she would die from cancer.

"What about the baby?" Erik finally managed to ask as he reached out to tightly grip Christy's hand.

"That's the truly amazing thing, and possibly the only good news I can offer. The baby seems to be fine. We've had an obstetrical doctor and a pediatric specialist called in, and both conclude that everything looks good regarding the pregnancy."

"How can that be?" Christy questioned.

"It's hard to say," the doctor replied. "She was wearing her seat belt—that seemed to protect her from being thrown around the car—but she had no air bag and her head hit the steering wheel repeatedly. As I said before, most of her injuries were cranial."

"When can we see her?" Erik asked, taking the words from Christy's mouth.

"Not very soon," Dr. Edwards said with a gravity to his voice that moved Christy to tears. "She'll be in intensive care when she leaves recovery, and I don't want her to have visitors for at least twenty-four hours. If she makes it that long, we'll take it from there."

"But I want to see her!" Christy exclaimed. "If she's going to die anyway, what can it hurt?"

The first real look of sympathy crossed the doctor's face and then was gone. "I'm sorry, but your sister's life and that of her baby are now in my hands, and I think it best that they remain undisturbed. I promise you that I'll allow her visitors at the very first possible moment. Now, I have to get back to her." With that, the doctor rose and left the room.

Erik and Christy sat motionless for several minutes. The news had so paralyzed them that they could hardly conceive what should be done next.

Christy glanced over to find Erik's eyes closed in prayer. She wished she could pray, that she knew God like Erik did, but she didn't.

It was finally decided that Christy would return home and continue to try to locate Grant. Erik had the day off from his work as a laboratory medical technologist, or med tech as they were called, but agreed that he knew the hospital routine best and would stay on and keep Christy posted as to changes in Candy's condition.

Christy tried in vain to locate Grant Burks. She hated him more than ever for not being around in Candy's hour of need. Of course, she reminded herself, he never was there when Candy needed him. Probably because he was busy with some other woman where no one could find him and point an accusing finger. Christy knew all about Grant's other women.

She doubted he had ever been faithful to her sister, but might not have believed him such an evil creature if she had not witnessed his infidelity firsthand. She could still remember the night Grant had come on to her at a birthday party for Candy. His whiskey-laden breath had brushed against her ear as he whispered suggestive things to her while Candy sat across the table, smiling in a loving way.

No, Christy had no love for her brother-in-law. All she felt was a very deep contempt for the man who considered his marriage vows no more binding than the old familiar "check's in the mail" adage.

Finally giving up on locating Grant, Christy took herself outside to her favorite place of repose. The ancient-looking porch swing was the place she often sought comfort and refuge. Positioned on the backside of the house on the three-quarter wraparound porch, Christy knew it was the only place she wanted to be.

The swing creaked and moaned as if in protest or greeting when Christy took her place. Leaning back in the old familiar arms of comfort, Christy let herself cry for the first time since hearing about Candy. The soft cries soon turned to pain-filled sobs, and Christy knew that she was hopelessly lost in her sorrow.

Burying her face in her hands and then bending over to sob against her knees, Christy blocked out the world and the cruelty she knew it capable of. There was no hope. There was no comfort.

Then, as if by magic, Christy felt strong, masculine arms surround her shoulders. The arms pulled her upward, and she started to recoil but had no strength with which to fight. Whoever he was, Christy needed him in the worst way. Rational thought left her mind as she clung to the man's coat and drenched his chest with her tears.

His methodical stroking of her hair caused Christy's pain to ebb. She cried more quietly, and then the tears stopped altogether, followed by several minutes of shuddering gasps as she worked to control her emotions.

The man still said nothing, and Christy was eternally grateful that he had maintained his silence. She knew she would be embarrassed when she learned his identity, but for now, she would take what she could to bolster her strength. When she finally stopped shaking, the man spoke.

"Want to tell me about it?" Curt Kyle's rich, deep voice questioned.

Somehow, Christy was not all that surprised to recognize the voice. "My sister was in an accident this morning. She's not going to make it," Christy managed to whisper. She refused to give up her place of comfort against his chest, and Curt seemed in no hurry to be rid of her as he tightened his arms around her.

"I'm truly sorry. I know what it is to have a tragic accident claim someone you love."

"You do?" Christy seemed surprised that they would share such a bond.

"Yes," he replied. "I lost my parents in an airplane crash. My little sister was nearly killed, as well. She was only sixteen at the time, and it was even harder on her."

"How awful!" After a pause, Christy continued, "I can't find my sister's husband, and she's expecting a baby in another month. She's only nineteen. How can this be happening? She's just a kid." Christy knew she was rambling, but it didn't seem to matter.

"My brother is at the hospital. He's supposed to call me and let me know how she's doing. I was supposed to come back here and find my brother-in-law, but true to form, he's never around when she needs him."

Curt heard the bitterness in Christy's voice and wondered if her anger was directed only at this man or all men. He began to run his hand up and down her arm. Christy had forgotten to wear her coat, and the January cold permeated her skin. "You're going to freeze," Curt said, feeling her begin to tremble again. "Why don't we go inside and talk?"

Christy reluctantly lifted her gaze. The eyes that had so hypnotized her held her fast. Her heart raced at such a pace that it nearly took her breath away.

"Why are you doing this? Why are you here?" she questioned, feeling her guard go up.

"I heard you crying, and you looked like you needed a friend. Do you need a friend, Christy?" he questioned so softly that she had to strain to pick up the words.

"I don't need anyone," she replied in what sounded more like a whimper than anything else.

"Spoken like a truly modern woman," Curt said with a grin. "But, I'm unconvinced. Come inside, and I'll make you coffee."

"You'll make me coffee? In my own house?" Christy questioned.

"Sure," he answered and helped her to her feet. "Because I'm a thoroughly modern man, and I'm not intimidated by modern women and their ways."

Christy shook her head and backed away from the warm hands that still held tightly to hers. "You're engaged to be married. Isn't there any man in this world that recognizes the need for faithfulness?"

Curt surprised her by laughing. "Christy, I just suggested I'd make some coffee. I don't believe that infringes on my fidelity to Debbie."

Christy frowned. "I'm not talking about the coffee. I'm talking about the way you just held me. The way you touched me."

"And how did I hold you?"

"I don't know, it just seemed so. . .well," Christy stammered for words.

"Yes?"

"It was intimate." Yes, that was the word she was looking for. "It was too intimate."

Curt sobered and his eyes narrowed slightly, giving him an almost passionate look. "Has no one ever offered to hold you when you were sad, Christy?"

Christy took another step back at the intensity of his stare. When she met the wall, she wanted to melt into the woodwork. "I don't let people see me when I'm sad."

"Never?"

"I don't want the vulnerability," she finally admitted. "I don't even know why I'm telling you this. I don't usually act this way around strange men."

"I'm not strange, Christy. In fact, I'm probably more normal than most of the men you've known in your life."

"I didn't mean it that way," she countered. "I just meant that I don't know you."

"Would you like to?"

"There you go again. You're about to be married. You should be concentrating your attentions on your fiancée."

"So I can't make new friends, just because I'm engaged?"

Christy sighed and shrugged her shoulders. "I don't know, Curt." Just saying his name caused her to tremble all the more.

"Come on," he said, reaching out to pull her along. "You need to get warm."

Christy refused to move, but Curt was undaunted. Without a word, he lifted her into his arms and laughed at the shocked expression on her face.

"You're heavier than you look," he said with amusement in his voice.

Christy's mouth dropped open. "Put me down, right now."

Curt shook his head. "You aren't that heavy. I was just trying to rile you."

"Put me down!"

"Nope."

"Curt Kyle, I mean it." She started to struggle, but Curt only tightened his grip and pulled her against him even closer.

"The sooner you learn one thing about me, the better off you'll be," Curt said in a completely serious tone.

"Oh? And just what would that one thing be?" Christy asked sarcastically.

"I'm very persistent, and I get what I want," he said, managing to shift her weight just enough to open the front door.

Christy realized what a striking couple they made in the reflection of her vestibule mirror. Her makeup was tear-streaked and her eyes were hopelessly red, but that had nothing to do with the way they seemed to fit together. Almost as though they were designed with each other in mind.

Startled, Christy realized that Curt was watching her. He smiled a knowing smile and put her down. "Fix your face," he said in a teasing way. "I'll go make the coffee."

Chapter 3

C hristy decided the only thing she could do was to wash off all of her makeup and start over. Her face was blotchy from crying, and her eyes were already puffy. After about thirty minutes of cold compresses, she traded the cashmere suit for comfortable jeans and an oversized sweater and went downstairs.

Curt was reclining in the front sitting room, with two cups of coffee steaming on a tray in front of him.

"You seem to have made yourself at home," Christy said and took a seat opposite him on the blue-and-beige-striped, Federal-style sofa.

"You, too," he said motioning to her change of clothes. "I thought for a minute I was going to have to come up and get you."

Christy didn't know why, but his remark made her laugh. "When you end up as much a wreck as I was, it takes a little time to even marginally repair the damage."

"You weren't a wreck, and there's nothing marginal about you."

Christy shifted uncomfortably and accepted the cup of coffee that Curt leaned forward to offer. "Thank you," she replied, realizing as she did that it might sound like she was accepting his compliment. Quickly she added, "For the coffee."

"No problem. You're an extremely well-organized woman, I must say. Everything has a place, and everything is in its place. Have you always been so efficient?" Curt asked curiously.

Christy thought she ought to be offended by the intimacy of his question, but she wasn't. In fact, she couldn't remember the last time she had felt so at ease with a complete stranger. *So long as I don't look into his eyes,* she thought. *If I can just avoid getting lost in his eyes, I'll be fine.*

Taking a sip of coffee, Christy finally answered him. "I started out that way as a child. When I was upset, I cleaned and organized. When I was hurt, I did the same. Anytime there was a major disappointment or the slightest bit of unrest in our home, you could find me picking up and putting away."

"By the looks of your efficiency, I'd say that probably happened quite a bit."

"It did," Christy remembered with a frown. She took a long drink of the strong coffee and glanced at the clock. It was nearly ten. Why hadn't Erik called?

Curt seemed to read her thoughts. "I'm sure you'll hear something soon. In the meantime, why don't we get to know each other better?"

"Better than what? Better than knowing what type of wedding gown you want for your wife? Better than knowing your measurements and the type of tuxedo you intend to be married in?" Christy's voice dripped sarcasm, but she didn't care.

Curt was unmoved by her sudden change of attitude. "Why don't you tell me why you hate men so much?"

Christy's mouth dropped open before she could mask her surprise. "I didn't say I hated men."

"You didn't have to. It's evident."

"No, it's not! I have a brother whom I love quite dearly," Christy protested.

"So you love one man in your life. Why aren't there any others?" Curt pressed for an answer.

"Because they were all jerks," Christy replied dryly.

"Even your father?"

"Especially my father."

"I'll bet your mother didn't feel that way," Curt said, hoping to learn more about Christy's childhood.

"She was a jerk, too," Christy replied, surprising him. "They deserved each other."

"Why do you say that?"

Christy stopped thinking about how terribly personal the conversation was and poured out her heart. "My father had one affair after another. We knew even as children that he had other women. I used to cry for my mother, thinking how terribly tragic it all was. Here was this steadfast, faithful woman, who stood by her man regardless of his affairs."

"What happened to change your mind?" Curt ask softly.

Christy drained her cup and set it down unexpectedly hard. The cup rattled for several seconds before quieting. "I came home early from school one day and found her with someone else. She tried to explain to me then about open marriages."

"What did you do?"

"Threw up," Christy answered honestly. "It made me sick, and I couldn't stand it."

"You can't very well judge all men by the actions of your father or even those who took advantage of your mother's marital arrangements."

"That's not the only reason," Christy said, not realizing that Curt was leading her where she didn't want to go.

"There was someone in your life, someone you cared a great deal about," Curt stated matter-of-factly. "He was unfaithful, too, is that it?"

Christy stared back, as though the complete shock of his words had silenced her.

"Is that what happened, Christy?"

Still, she stared in mute surprise.

"Well?" he pressed.

"Yes!" she answered angrily.

"I'll bet there was more than just a little reorganizing and cleaning on that day. Tell me what happened."

"There's nothing to tell," Christy stated and crossed her arms protectively against her body.

"Let's see," Curt began; "he was probably older. Maybe even a great deal older."

Christy's eyes widened, telling him he was right. "How do you know?" she questioned.

"You were looking for a father figure. Your own father was a lousy example, so it would stand to reason that you'd look for another. How much older was he?"

"Fifteen years," Christy replied, total dejection in her voice.

"And you were how old?"

With a heavy sigh, Christy answered him. "Twenty-one." Before Curt could question her further, Christy openly volunteered the information. "He was a professor at the university I attended. I thought we were madly in love." Her voice was so sad that Curt had to restrain himself from going to her. "He always told me that I mustn't say a word about our relationship because he might lose his job for dating a student. I believed him—it all seemed so logical, even sensible. We went on like that for several months."

"What happened?"

Christy laughed bitterly. "I went to a party that had been set up by the university to mingle faculty and students on behalf of a visiting international designer. I was excited about meeting this designer and never really gave any thought that *he* might be there."

"But he was?" Curt questioned.

"Yes. Not only was he there, but so was his wife. Someone came up to me and said, 'Oh, have you met the professor's wife?' and I suddenly found myself introduced to this frumpy, middle-aged woman with gray in her hair and about fifty excess pounds around her middle."

"What happened then?"

"I wanted to hate her. I wanted to prove to myself that there was a reason why he'd been unfaithful to her, but I couldn't. She gushed about how wonderful he was. The sincerity in her made me feel like a cheap bimbo. When he came into the room and saw us together, I knew from the look in his eyes that our relationship was nothing more than his lust and my naïveté."

"What did you do?"

Christy shifted and pulled a pillow close. "I died." The words were so simply stated that there was nothing to add, and Christy fell silent.

Curt waited for several moments before he asked, "And now you believe all men are incapable of fidelity?"

"I just don't believe anything anymore," she said softly.

"What about all this?" Curt questioned, waving his hand to encompass the room.

She knew what he meant. He wanted to know why she made wedding dresses—why she participated in planning other people's weddings when she didn't believe in it for herself.

Before she could answer, the telephone rang, causing her to jump. "Candy!" she exclaimed, realizing for the first time that Curt had kept her mind completely off her dying sister.

Jumping to her feet, Christy nearly ran to the phone.

"Hello?"

"Christy, it's Erik."

"How is she?"

"There's no change," Erik answered. "She's holding her own, but just barely. Did you find Grant?"

"No," Christy admitted. "I left a voice-mail message at the law office."

"I guess we have no alternative but to wait until he tries to check in with Candy."

"I guess not," Christy responded tiredly.

"Look, it's nearly midnight. You get some sleep, and I'll let you know if anything happens. You can spell me tomorrow morning, okay?"

"I don't think I'll be able to sleep, but I'll try. I'll see you about eight."

"Good," Erik replied and added, "Just remember, Christy. God can take care of everything."

"Yeah, right. Bye, Erik." She hung up the phone, shaking her head. "God can take care of everything."

"What was that?" Curt questioned.

"Oh, just my brother's blind convictions in an all-powerful, all-knowing God who watches tenderly over His children." The skepticism in her voice was clear.

"You don't believe in God?"

"Oh, I believe in God," Christy replied. "I just don't think He believes in me."

Curt got up and crossed the room. "What about your sister?"

"No change. She's still fighting just to stay alive."

"At least that's something. Some people lose that fight early on."

"And what's that supposed to mean?" Christy snapped back.

Curt smiled. "I think you know. Look, I'm going home, but here's my telephone number. I want you to call me if anything goes wrong or if you just need to talk."

Christy would not take the paper, so Curt put it on the table by the phone.

"I mean it, Christy. I want to be your friend."

Christy looked into Curt's eyes, knowing that she had been reduced to the same quivering jelly as before. There was something so powerful about his eyes, however. Something so deep and meaningful that Christy wanted to look inside them. Wanted to know their depths—even plunge herself deep within them.

"Call me if you need to. And, Christy, no cleaning. At least not tonight," he said with a grin and then was gone.

⁂

Curt made his way back to his apartment, completely mystified by the events of the evening. It wasn't until he was unlocking the door and saw the blinking light of his answering machine that he remembered why he had gone to Christy's in the first place. The deposit!

He patted his pocket and felt the thick bundle of bills. Pulling out the envelope, he put the money in the freezer under a three-pound chuck roast. Few thieves would think to look there, even if they could get past him to sack the place for valuables.

Seeing there was only one message, Curt rewound the tape and played it. It was Debbie. Suddenly he felt a twinge of guilt for not letting her know where he was. Glancing at the clock on the wall and seeing that it was nearly one, Curt decided to wait on calling Debbie back. Morning would be soon enough.

Stripping off his clothes, Curt crawled into bed with more than a little bit on his mind. Christy Connors was a complicated matter that commanded his attention. Stretching his arms up, he folded them behind his head and stared at the ceiling.

What was wrong with him? He knew better than to feel the things he was feeling. He had broken all the rules. All he could think about was the way she'd sobbed in his arms. No woman had ever spent herself like that in his presence. He had never seen anyone cry as though all the life was going out with each and every tear. Usually teary-eyed women made Curt want to run in the opposite direction, but this had been entirely different. Christy had needed him, and he'd responded in the only way he could. Did that make him wrong? With a sigh, Curt rolled over and punched the pillow down several times before closing his eyes.

Chapter 4

The days that followed were torturous to Christy. She tore herself away from the hospital only when appointments or exhaustion forced her to go home.

Candy regained consciousness on the fifth day, but she was still in critical condition and barely able to communicate with the doctors. Christy had been allowed one visit every shift change, which constituted seeing her sister first thing in the morning and then again before she went home for the evening. During the time she sat in the intensive care waiting room, Christy sewed lace insets and did tedious pearl and sequin work on a variety of wedding dress pieces.

Other people in the waiting room were fascinated by her work, but Christy wouldn't openly speak to anyone unless forced to do so. All she wanted to do was forget about her sister's condition and forget about the blueness of Curt Kyle's eyes.

Grant finally showed up on the sixth day. He seemed concerned about Candy's condition, but not overly so. Christy was seething when he came bounding into the room as though just returning from the men's room instead of a six-day absence during which no one could reach him.

"Where have you been?" she asked between clenched teeth.

Grant noted the interested audience around them and motioned Christy outside. Christy put her things down and followed Grant into the hall.

When they had moved far enough away to suit Grant's purpose, he turned abruptly. "Where I've been isn't any of your business. How's Candy?"

"Like you care," Christy replied sarcastically. "She's nearly died more than once, and she's barely conscious now."

"Has she said anything?" Grant asked in a rather nervous way that made Christy suspicious.

"No, not of importance. She hasn't asked for you, if that's what you're wondering."

"Where's she at now?" Grant questioned, glancing back down the hall where double-glass doors had the words Intensive Care written in big blue letters.

"She's in there," Christy nodded to the doors.

"I'll bet that's costing a pretty penny," Grant replied offhandedly.

Christy doubled her fist and brought it up as if to strike the smug expression off his face. Realizing what she was about to do, she quickly lowered it and stepped forward instead. Getting nose to nose with the man her sister had married, she barely whispered.

"It can cost you everything you've saved, for all I care. She's dying, or didn't she tell you that, either?"

"What do you mean?"

"She has cancer. An inoperable brain tumor that's eating up the living parts of her mind. The doctor said that even without the crash, she'd be dead in six months. So if you expect me to care about the cost of her hospital stay, you're a bigger fool than even I gave you credit for being."

Grant finally looked shaken. "She's dying?"

"Yes! Yes! Yes!" Christy nearly screeched in his face.

Grant made the mistake of putting his hands on her to calm her down. Christy went wild and gave a full swing with an open hand against his face that nearly sent him reeling back into the wall.

An expression of complete shock covering his face, Grant shook his head. "We haven't got insurance, Christy. No health insurance and no savings. I can't pay these hospital bills, and once they find out, then what? Mortgage the house? It already has two."

Christy silently tried to collect her thoughts and reason out what Grant was saying. She had been so surprised at her reaction that it took all of her reserves to calm her racing heart. "I'll pay her bill," she finally answered.

Grant smiled. "That's good of you, Sis."

Christy's eyes narrowed until they were angry slits of smokey blue. "You sicken me. You don't care about her at all. Your only concern is who's going to pay what. Well, I say good riddance. Why don't you divorce her while you're at it? Yes, I'll pay her bills and the baby's, too, if necessary."

"The baby? You mean she didn't lose it?" Grant questioned suddenly.

"No. By some miracle, the baby is just fine. The doctor said that if Candy can just hang on long enough, they'll deliver the baby before she dies."

"If Candy dies, I want nothing to do with the baby," Grant said matter-of-factly. "I can't raise a child by myself."

Christy was strangely calm. She looked at the man as if seeing him for the first time. "I can't believe you said that."

Grant shrugged his shoulders and straightened his suit jacket. "I'm just being honest, Christy. I'm not cut out for fatherhood. I never wanted to be a father. I was only humoring Candy."

"That's your own flesh and blood that my sister is dying in order to bear. She could have had radiation treatment or chemotherapy for the cancer, but she wouldn't because she didn't want to hurt the baby. Now you have the audacity to tell me the child means nothing to you?"

"I don't want to become attached," Grant replied. "I can't raise a child alone."

Christy could stand no more. She walked quietly back to the intensive care waiting room, gathered her things, and walked past Grant without a word.

All the way home, Christy felt an overwhelming urge to cry. She allowed herself a brief outpouring when the traffic light kept her waiting an unseemly amount of time and was still sniffling back her tears when she pulled onto her street. Slowly maneuvering the car into the driveway, Christy parked and shut off the engine.

She leaned back against the headrest for a moment, wiped her eyes, and took a deep breath. When she reached for the door, she noticed the other car in her drive. Quickly, she racked her brain for some overlooked appointment, but when nothing came to mind, she got out of the car.

Glancing around the winter-dead lawn, Christy couldn't find a trace of another living soul. She didn't recognize the little red sports car as belonging to any of her friends or clients. Making her way around back, Christy nearly screamed in fright when Curt Kyle popped around the corner with a package in hand.

"I wondered if I was going to have to leave this on the porch," he said innocently.

"What are you doing back here?" Christy asked rather coldly.

"I was hoping to find someplace to put this package inside the house. You know, an open window or door. You locked up real tight though, and I was just about to give up. How's your sister?"

"About the same. She is conscious, though. What are you doing here? Why are you carrying that around?" she questioned, motioning to the package. "You could have left it on the porch."

"I guess I could have," Curt admitted. "But I planned to stick around and talk to you, so I figured I'd just look after it as well."

Christy remained aloof, but motioned Curt to the back door. "Very well," she managed to say in an even tone, "bring it inside."

Curt followed her into the house and waited for her to instruct him as to where she wanted the package.

"Just put it anywhere. It doesn't matter," she said, finally realizing that he was still holding the box.

Curt placed the box on the kitchen counter. "You look as though it's been a rough day. Would you like to tell me about it?"

Christy wanted to say no, but in truth, she really did want to talk to someone about Grant's cold indifference to his own child.

As if seeing her inner struggle to decide, Curt pressed the matter home. "Good friends listen to each other's woes," he said softly. "I'm just offering a listening ear."

Christy seemed to heave a sigh of relief, as though Curt's words made the decision for her. "All right. We can talk."

"Have you eaten today?" Curt questioned.

Christy deposited her purse on the counter and began unbuttoning her coat. "No, not really. I haven't been hungry."

Curt came to her and held her coat for her as she removed it. "I'd be happy to fix you something," he offered.

Christy turned back around and reclaimed her coat. "Is that your way of begging a meal?" she asked, forcing herself to sound lighthearted.

"I guess I could force myself to share a meal with you. That is, if you let me fix it."

"I can cook, Mr. Kyle."

Curt frowned. "Don't call me that. We're friends, remember?"

Christy nodded. "All right, friend, what's your choice of eats?" She opened the refrigerator and leaned inside. "I have sliced roast beef, turkey, and chicken. I also have leftover potato salad from a luncheon I did yesterday." Christy continued to name off several things and turned around, only to smack his chin hard with her head.

"Christy!" he exclaimed. "Are you all right?"

Christy shook her head as if to clear the fuzz. "I think so. I'm so sorry. That must have hurt you more than me."

"Naw, I've always been hardheaded. Come sit down and let me take a look and make sure you aren't hurt." He led her to a chair and pushed her gently into it.

Running his hands through her hair, Curt examined her scalp for any wound. Christy forgot all about the pain, however, as his fingers kept methodically sweeping through the layers. His hand was warm against her, and Christy nearly came up off the chair when he touched her cheek.

"Looks like you'll live," he declared.

"Of course I'll live," she said, trying her best to be irritated with his concern. One upward glance was Christy's undoing, however, when she met his eyes and felt her mouth go dry. "I, uh, I. . ." She couldn't find the words. *This has to stop,* she lectured herself. *This man is engaged to be married.*

Curt smiled, ever so gently, and reached out to brush back a bit of brown hair from Christy's forehead. "I see it's knocked you speechless, so I'll fix us a bite to eat. You get no choices. Go sit down and behave and answer my questions when I speak to you and come to the table like a good girl when I call."

Christy stared after him completely flabbergasted. No one had ever thought to order her around in her own house, much less a client. *But,* she reminded herself, *he's more than a client.* She opened her mouth to protest, but about that time, Curt shrugged out of his own coat, tossing it aside. Christy's eyes fixed themselves to his broad back when he reached up to open the cupboards. Muscles strained against the blue material of his denim shirt, and Christy was helpless to look away.

The time slipped by, and soon Christy found herself sitting in front of her fireplace, lap blanket tucked around her wool slacks, and a tray of delicious-looking food on her lap. Curt busily stoked the fire as though they were husband and wife, enjoying the late afternoon alone.

"You'd better eat," Curt said, taking a seat beside her. His own tray of goodies balanced precariously on one leg while he got comfortable.

Christy picked at the food, still not knowing what to think of this man. He barged into her life like nothing and no one she had ever known before.

"So what had you so upset when you came home? I know you were crying."

Christy tried to sound nonchalant. "I had a run-in with my sister's husband."

"A run-in?"

Christy nodded. "We exchanged some rather heated words. Well, I guess I was the main one exchanging them. I also hit him."

Curt nearly spewed out the coffee he was drinking. "You what?"

"I hit him," she said with a "So what?" look to her face. "He was asking for it, and I couldn't help myself. Look, I don't expect you to understand."

Curt laughed. "I didn't say anything about not understanding. I just couldn't imagine you, in all your prim and proper form, hitting anyone."

Christy frowned. "I'm not usually given to violence."

"So what did he do that made you hit him?"

"He touched me."

"I guess I'd better make note of that one for future reference."

Christy scowled. "He's slime, and I wasn't about to let him put his hands on me after what he'd just said."

Curt's expression softened. "What did he say, Christy?"

"He waltzed into the hospital after a six-day hiatus to who knows where, announced that he bet my sister's care was costing a fortune, and then told me he wanted nothing to do with his own child when Candy dies."

"What do you mean, he wants nothing to do with the baby?" Curt probed.

"He told me he couldn't be a single father. He said he had never wanted to be a father in the first place, that he was just humoring my sister." Christy put the tray on the coffee table and pulled the lap blanket around her as though it could offer her protection from Grant's cold words of indifference.

"I'm sorry, Christy. That must have been a terrible thing to bear alone."

She turned and looked at him. Really looked at him. He was incredibly handsome, at least to her way of thinking. His dark brown hair still held reddish glints from days in the sun, and his face bore a tanned, healthy look that Christy was certain hadn't come from Denver living.

"Where are you from?" Christy suddenly asked. She composed her shaken nerves and forced herself to continue looking at him.

"I just moved here from Florida," he replied casually. "Why?"

"You look so healthy, so alive. I just couldn't imagine that you'd gotten that way here."

Curt's eyes sparkled at the compliment. Christy's seeming indifference and hostility were falling away in bits and pieces.

"Denver's not so bad. It can be a really great place if you have the right person to share it with," Curt offered softly.

Christy appraised the man and his words for only a moment before getting to her feet. "Debbie is a lucky woman," she murmured and left the room.

Chapter 5

The next evening, Curt thought of Christy's words regarding Debbie's good fortune all the way to his sister CJ's house. The long drive to the north of Denver gave him plenty of time to remember every detail about Christy Connors. Why did she have to be so beautiful? Why did she have to haunt his every thought?

So she thinks Debbie is lucky, Curt thought smugly. If only he could tell Christy the truth and cut through the walls that separated them. Curt shook his head. There was too much at stake to blow his cover.

CJ Aldersson lived near the Tri-County Airport. Correction—she lived at the airport. The strip had been built to accommodate an unusual housing arrangement where wealthy pilots could taxi from the tarmac right up to their front doors. The houses were beautiful, with the snow-covered Rockies in the background. Curt pulled up to the house, checking the address against the one written on a piece of paper. This was it.

After parking the car, he made his way slowly up a fashionable cobblestone walkway. Before him, the three-story native-stone house rose up to greet him like a welcoming beacon. Lights shown from several of the windows, giving a warm glow of home. Curt stopped for just a moment in order to take it all in.

At the door, he hesitated. He had not seen his sister in nearly five years. It had been a long time since he'd deserted her, and now he felt guilty for the distance he'd placed between them. Of course they'd talked on the phone from time to time, but he knew he had sorely neglected her. CJ was all he had left in the world, and now she was married and living happily with a man he knew very little about.

Finally getting up his nerve, Curt pressed the bell and waited. A tall man with brown hair answered the door and gave Curt a good once-over before a smile broke across his face.

"You're the spitting image of Doug O'Sullivan. I'd say that must make you his son, Curt, the long-lost brother my wife has been frantically searching to get in touch with."

Curt smiled sheepishly. "That'd be me."

The man extended his hand. "I'm Brad Aldersson. It's good to finally meet you."

Curt shook Brad's hand and glanced past his shoulder toward the sound of a feminine voice.

"Who is it, honey?" The voice had to belong to his sister.

Curt put his finger to his lips and motioned Brad to let him surprise CJ. Brad nodded and quickly backed out of the way in order to let Curt pass.

"Brad?" the voice came louder as a redheaded woman appeared in the hall. "Curt!" she exclaimed with a squeal of excitement. "Curt, is it really you?"

She ran to her big brother's open arms and held him as though she'd never let go. "I was so worried. I've tried to call you for days, but the operator said that your number had been disconnected. Why didn't you let me know you were coming? Are you hungry? Is anything wrong? Where are you staying?"

Curt started laughing so hard that CJ pulled away and stared at him for a moment with a quizzical look on her face.

"Maybe if you'd slow down and give the man time to answer one question at a time, you'd get more information," Brad suggested.

CJ laughed in spite of herself. "I'm sorry."

"I expected an enthusiastic reception, but nothing like this," Curt admitted. "I hope I haven't come at a bad time."

"Not at all," CJ replied. "We were just about to eat. You'll stay and have supper with us, won't you?"

"Sounds good to me," Curt replied. Then with a mischievous grin over his shoulder, he asked Brad, "Can she cook?"

"She makes a mean pot of pilot coffee, but her curried beef tips could use some work. I've been helping her along, however, and she's going to make a good wife someday," Brad replied.

"I can cook, Curt. Just ignore this man. He thinks just because we've been married more than a month, he knows it all."

"That's not true," Brad said in his own defense. Then, leaning over, he whispered to Curt, "I knew it all before the month was up."

Curt put back his head and laughed, while CJ jabbed Brad in the ribs with her elbow. "Men!" she exclaimed and left them both to follow her to the kitchen.

Dinner passed much too quickly for Curt. He'd not been a part of a family for longer than he cared to remember. The last time he'd seen CJ, she had been recuperating from the accident that claimed their parents' lives. She had certainly recovered from the sullen, moody child of sixteen who he'd run from in despair.

"Why don't we have coffee in the living room?" CJ suggested as they got up from the table.

Curt took a seat on the couch and the smile suddenly left his face. How could he possibly say what he had come to say?

"You've come here with a purpose," CJ said suddenly. Her statement stunned Curt.

"I guess there's no use putting it off or pretending that you aren't right."

CJ smiled and took a seat beside him. "Go on," she encouraged as Brad joined them.

Curt ran his hand back through his hair and eased back against the plush sofa. "I wanted to talk to you about the crash—about Mom and Dad."

CJ swallowed hard. "Go on," she repeated her words, this time less enthusiastically.

Curt watched as Brad lovingly rubbed CJ's cheek with his fingers. *He seems to adore her,* Curt thought, and suddenly he felt better about what he had to do.

"What do you remember about the crash?" he asked.

CJ frowned. "I remember most everything, I guess. The way the plane rocked and then dropped from the sky. The feeling of falling forever. Daddy fighting the controls to land the plane and Mom praying."

"Did Dad say anything?"

"Daddy told Mom, 'He's done us in.'" CJ trembled, and Brad put his hand on hers. "What's this all about, Curt?"

"Do you remember the air show before the crash?" CJ and Curt had grown up as members of the O'Sullivan Flying Circus. Their father, along with his best friend, Ben Fairchild, had formed O&F Aviation and sponsored air shows all across the country.

"Of course," CJ whispered. "We were all together. Even Ben was there. You left early to get back to school. Yes, I remember it all."

"Dad called me," Curt replied. "I had just gotten back, and the phone was ringing. I picked it up, and it was Dad. He must have been just about to fly out. He was pretty upset, CJ."

"Why? What had happened?"

"He'd found cocaine in one of our planes."

"You mean you've known all this time and said nothing?" CJ's voice was clearly upset.

"You were in no shape to learn that the crash was no accident. How could I tell you that Mom and Dad had most likely been murdered?"

"Murdered?" CJ sounded as though she might faint. "But all this time—all these years, you've never said anything. Murder?"

"I'm sorry. That's why I came tonight," Curt offered apologetically.

"So what do we do about it?"

"*We* don't do anything. You have to stay out of it," Curt replied. He put up his hand at the look that crossed his sister's face. "Don't get started; just listen. What I have to say isn't going to come easy, and you must swear to keep it confidential. My life and the lives of other people depend on my ability to maintain my cover."

"Your cover? What are you talking about?" CJ questioned, easing away just a bit from Brad.

Curt met Brad's eyes before returning his gaze to his sister. "CJ, I know this is going to be difficult for you to accept, but I work with the Drug Enforcement Administration. The DEA. I'm here in Denver undercover to try and break a ring of drug dealers. I believe they are the people responsible for Mom and Dad's deaths, and I believe whoever is in charge is someone inside O&F Aviation."

CJ fell back against Brad in complete shock. The look on her face told Curt he'd expected too much. Her eyes were huge in surprise, and her mouth had dropped open to speak but remained unmoving, in mute dismay.

"Have you been at this very long?" Brad questioned when CJ seemed unable to collect her thoughts.

Curt nodded. "From the moment the plane crashed, I just knew it was related to what Dad had found. I figured someone wanted him quiet and that a plane crash was the best way to take him out. Unfortunately for them, but fortunately for me, they had no idea that Dad had told me about the drugs."

"The FAA investigation had always seemed a little rushed, as far as I was concerned," Brad commented. "It seemed strange for the accident of an international flying hero to be so quickly stamped 'pilot error' and moved over without so much as a single protest."

"I couldn't protest it then," Curt admitted. "Although holding my peace was difficult. I knew I needed proof. Also," Curt said, nodding toward his sister, "CJ was in no shape to take the controversy, and I couldn't risk that whoever was responsible would think she knew something about the drugs and come after her."

CJ shuddered from head to toe, and Brad wrapped his arms around her tightly as Curt reached out to pat her hand. "I'm so sorry, Sis. If I could have found an easier way to tell you, I would have."

"I thought this was over with," she whispered weakly.

"I know." Curt wondered if he'd done the right thing.

"How can we help you?" Brad questioned. "What can we do to make your job easier?"

Curt frowned and dropped CJ's hand. "I don't know. Right now, I just need discretion and sound judgment. I could also use a few prayers," Curt admitted.

"Of course, you'll have that," CJ said, seeming to recover from the shock. "Brad and I will pray continuously for you."

"Good," Curt replied. "That means all the world to me." He glanced at his watch and saw the hour was getting late. "I'd better go, but I'll be in touch."

He got up, and CJ jumped to her feet and nearly flew at him. Throwing her arms around him, she let go of her tears. "Oh, Curt, please be careful."

Curt wrapped his arms around her and buried his face against her auburn hair. "I promise to be especially careful, just for you."

"Honey, why don't you go ahead upstairs and lie down. I'll be right up after I show Curt out," Brad said lovingly.

"But—" she started to protest, but nodded and left the room while Brad retrieved Curt's coat and walked with him to the car.

"You looked like you had something else to say," Brad said sternly.

"I guess I do," Curt confessed. "Look, I'm worried about CJ. I don't think anyone will be suspicious of what she knows or doesn't know—not after all these years. Still, there's always that chance. Keep your eyes open, Brad. Protect her, and don't let her share this information with anyone."

Brad nodded soberly. "I'm grateful for the warning. Don't worry. I'll keep her safe."

"Thanks," Curt said and reached out his hand to shake Brad's. "I can keep my mind on business if I know she's not in danger."

Chapter 6

What have you learned?" Debbie asked, while Curt tried hard to concentrate on the rush hour traffic.

"Not much," he said. It had been several days since he'd seen Christy, and now he and Debbie were on their way to have Debbie measured for the wedding gown.

"How did Christy Connors seem?"

"Huh?"

Debbie shook her head and rolled her eyes. "Where is your mind, Curt? I just asked you about Miss Connors. You know, the woman who's at the center of this investigation?"

Curt glanced over at the attractive woman who was playing the role of his fiancée. "I don't know," he finally answered. "Christy's sister Candy is still not responding very well. She's in and out of consciousness, and Christy is totally devoted to her. It would seem that Grant Burks, Candy's husband, is less than admirable in his commitment to his dying wife. Christy told me that he wants nothing to do with his baby, and that causes her a great deal of anxiety."

"Sounds like she told you quite a bit," Debbie said, her dark eyes sparkling in amusement. "Of course, a ladies' man like you never has too much trouble getting women to talk."

Curt looked over at her and grinned. "Like it's ever gotten me anywhere with you."

Debbie laughed. "If I weren't engaged to Frank, you'd probably have your hands full."

At this, Curt raised an eyebrow and gave her a look before turning his attention back to the road.

"Anyway," Debbie continued, "Pricemeyer said that you used your own money to pay for the wedding gown. Why?"

"I don't know; it just seemed better that way. Besides, won't you need a dress to wear when you marry old Frank?"

"I have my dress, thank you, and what's with this 'old Frank' stuff? 'Old Frank' is only three years your senior. That makes him. . ."

"Nearly thirty," Curt filled in. "I'm about to turn twenty-seven, remember? Frank's going to be thirty, and that's old. At least in this business."

Debbie nodded. "I know," she said soberly.

From the window of the house, Christy watched Curt help Debbie from the car. Their heads were close together as he spoke. *Probably terms of endearment,* she thought. *He's probably telling her how this is the start of their beautiful wedding and how much he loves her.* Christy was defeated before she could even begin.

Working to put her emotions back under control, Christy rechecked her carefully pinned hair and then her makeup. Aggie was greeting the couple at the door and showing them into the fitting room where Christy did most of her work. With one final deep breath, Christy tightened the silver concha belt that complemented her burgundy dress and went to greet her clients.

"Good morning," she said, entering the fitting room.

Debbie smiled warmly. "Good morning, Christy. I'm so excited, I can hardly sit still. Curt had to get after me all the way over here, but I just can't help it."

Christy tried not to show how jealous she felt at the way Debbie chattered about Curt. "It's always exciting to plan this part of your wedding," Christy said in a rather reserved tone.

Curt came from behind Debbie and smiled, although Christy refused to look at him. "Debbie gets excited when the street department resurfaces the roads. Just ignore her."

Christy smiled at his words. She knew he was trying to reduce her obvious discomfort. "We'd better get started. I have a 10:30 appointment after this. Curt, there's coffee and pastries in the front room. You can entertain yourself there while I measure Debbie for the gown."

"The front room?" he questioned innocently.

Without thinking, Christy started to reply, "It's the room where we had. . ." She quickly fell silent. "Debbie, you undress, and I'll show Curt where the food is."

Debbie laughed, but the situation rekindled Christy's nerves. All she'd been able to think about was Curt Kyle, and now that he was here with his bride-to-be, all Christy wanted to do was run away.

Curt followed Christy to the room he well remembered. "How's Candy?" he asked when Christy finally stopped and turned.

Christy still wouldn't look at him and snapped, "The same."

"Then why are you so agitated? That Burks guy getting to you again?"

"No," Christy replied nervously. "I've just got a lot on my mind." She fidgeted with the concha belt, then turned to leave, but Curt reached out and stopped her.

"We're friends, remember? You can talk to me."

Curt's words were low and soft—so alluring to a woman as lonely as Christy was. She pulled away with a shrug. "There's nothing to talk about. She's dying, and that's all there is to it." With that she went back to the fitting room and tried to forget Curt was just down the hall.

The fitting went well, and Christy found herself enjoying Debbie's company. "If you'll go ahead and get dressed," Christy told Debbie, "I'll retrieve those swatches I promised to show you." She pulled the door closed behind her to afford Debbie privacy and moved silently down the hall.

Her storeroom door was open, causing Christy to frown. Aggie must have forgotten to close the door earlier. Entering the room, Christy nearly jumped a foot when Curt popped out in front of her. She had no time to prepare herself, nor to prevent meeting his eyes with her own.

"Curt! What are you doing in here?" she questioned with her heart in her throat.

"Sorry. I didn't mean to scare you."

"Why are you in here?" she asked sternly. Never mind that her heart was pounding like a triphammer. Never mind that his eyes were bluer than any she had ever seen before.

"I was looking for the bathroom," Curt answered.

"Oh," Christy replied. It was logical if she wanted it to be. And she did. "You missed it by a couple doors. It's back that way," she explained, gesturing to her right.

Curt moved his hand up her arm, and Christy felt her legs grow weak. "I really am sorry that I frightened you."

Curt reached up and touched her cheek. His hand was like fire against her icy skin. Christy trembled, unable to take her eyes from his. *I'm losing myself to him,* she thought. She hadn't felt this way about anyone in her entire life. Not even her stupid professor had aroused her emotions this way.

Closing her eyes, Christy felt like she had died and gone to heaven. *Why does he have to belong to someone else?*

Someone else! Debbie! The thoughts jolted her like a lightning strike. Jerking away, Christy's temper flared, and her eyes flashed electrically.

"You're just like every other man," she said angrily. In her eyes there were newly formed tears. "Why can't there be a faithful one among you?"

She turned to storm out of the room, forgetting all about the swatches, but Curt pulled her back. "I'm not your other men, Christy. I'm your friend, and I'm sorry you think otherwise. I just wanted to let you know I care."

Christy tried to pull away, but Curt wouldn't let her. "Save it," she spat the words. "Save it for Debbie. She's the one you're supposed to love and care for."

"Debbie understands that we're friends," Curt stated softly. "I think you're just mad because I scared you and got lost in your storeroom."

Christy finally managed to pull herself away from him. "Rot in here, for all I care," she said and charged from the room, slamming the door behind her.

❧

Curt and Debbie were halfway back to the office when she questioned him about Christy. "Did she seem upset that you were in the storeroom? Did she suspect anything?"

"No," Curt replied gruffly.

Debbie eyed him for a moment before continuing. "Did you see anything? Anything out of the ordinary?"

"No."

"Curt, are you all right? You haven't said much of anything since we left. Did you have a fight with Christy?"

"Yes. No. Well, it's difficult to explain what happened between us," he admitted. "I don't think she's involved, Debbie." He looked at her hard for a moment, before returning his eyes to the traffic around him. "I've spent enough time with her now that I'm sure I would have sensed it or something would have slipped into the conversation. I don't think Christy Connors has a clue about what is happening with her shipments."

"We can't rule her out. She's been under surveillance too long. You know the first rule of the game, Curt. 'Never trust anyone.' "

"Yeah, yeah. Tell me something I don't know."

"Curt, this is serious stuff. This is an international drug operation that has been under observation for three years, and only God knows how long it existed before that. You can't get involved with her." The look Debbie gave him was a cross between sympathetic and worried.

"It's a little late for that," he said heavily.

"Rule number two, Curt."

"I know, 'Never get involved with a suspect.' "

Curt dropped Debbie off with the excuse of needing some time alone. He waved off her concern and promised he'd get himself together, but could he?

Driving down the one-way streets of downtown Denver, Curt wasn't sure he could look at the case objectively. He had fought long and hard to find his parents' killer. There were only a handful of people in the DEA who even knew what his primary motivation was. He kept to himself generally, but over the last year he had formed a bond with Debbie and Frank.

Hitting his fist against the steering wheel, Curt couldn't believe the way he had allowed himself to get attached to Christy Connors. He'd been so careful over the years. He'd even alienated CJ. Of course, that was behind him now, but nevertheless, the facts were still the same.

It had been too easy to slip into a relationship with Christy. She was so needing of friendship and love that Curt had automatically taken advantage of it and jumped in with both feet. He kept telling himself in the beginning that it was the case, that with her trust, he could learn far more about her. But now—now he wasn't just interested in the case. Now he wanted to know Christy for himself.

Debbie was right. He had broken the rules. He couldn't trust just anyone, but he could trust himself and his instincts. Hadn't they kept him alive through more than one sticky situation? *A finely tuned instinct is the kind of thing that lets DEA agents make it to their thirtieth birthday,* he thought to himself. *Or at least to their twenty-seventh.*

Chapter 7

As the week wore on, Christy tried to forget the scene with Curt. What she couldn't forget, however, was the feeling of his hand against her face. Even while she made sketches of Debbie's wedding gown, Christy kept losing her concentration. So lost was she in thoughts of Curt that Christy nearly jumped out of her skin when someone knocked on the front door. Knowing she had no morning appointments, Christy steadied her nerves and wondered if it might be Curt.

Opening the door, she was greatly disappointed to find Grant Burks filling her doorway. His dark black hair had been combed straight back, and with the dark sunglasses he wore, Christy thought he looked a bit sinister.

"What do you want?"

"I came to talk," he said, pushing his way into the house. "You look wonderful in that dress, Christy. You really should wear tight-fitting clothes more often."

"You have a wife, remember?" she asked snidely.

"Of course, but that doesn't mean I can't appreciate beauty. You and I could have a very special relationship, Christy. No one would have to know, and no one would have to get hurt. Candy's dying, after all," he said, stepping toward her.

"What would you tell your mistress?" Christy suddenly snapped back. She obtained the effect she wanted when Grant paled and stopped moving. With a smug look of satisfaction, Christy crossed her arms. "Does Candy know about her? I imagine she'd like to."

Grant shrugged. "I don't think you'll hurt her like that. She can either die peacefully or in grief. If you choose to abuse her with tall tales about my exploits, I can't be bothered. But, please, don't tell me how compassionate you are and how indifferent I am when you share the news with her. Don't tell me how much you love her when you take away the only dream she's ever known."

"You're a hideous excuse for a human being," Christy said, unable to think of anything vile enough to call him.

Grant smiled in a slow leering way that made Christy's skin crawl. He reached out his hand and touched her arm. "You really ought to be nicer to me."

Christy couldn't contain the shudder that rippled through her body. "Take your hands off me. I'm not going to tell Candy anything. I could never hurt her the way you have. Do you really imagine she's that stupid? She may only be nineteen, but she was always an observant person, even as a child. My guess is that Candy already knows about your other woman, or women."

Grant let his hand trail up Christy's arm until it came to rest against the back of her neck and his body was nearly touching hers. "We could have a lot of fun together. You ought to think about it."

"Get out of here," Christy demanded. "Get out and leave me alone. If you never come to see Candy again, it will be fine by me." Grant backed off, surprising Christy, who was fully ready to fight him for all she was worth.

"You let the hospital know today that you're responsible for her bills," Grant said, sliding his sunglasses back on. "I don't want any more of their questions about how I intend to meet the cost of Candy's hospital stay."

"I'll tell them; just leave her alone."

"Don't order me around, Christy. We need to work real close on this one," Grant said with a smile. "Real close." He opened the front door and walked out.

Christy slammed the door as hard as she could, hoping that it made her point clear. She was so shaken that she had to sit down for a moment in order to regain her composure. Grant Burks frightened her in a way she couldn't begin to express.

Curt was just pulling onto Christy's street, when he saw the black Porsche pull out of the driveway. The driver didn't so much as glance Curt's way, and when he passed, Curt quickly made note of the tag number and wrote it down to check out later.

Parking the car, he made his way to the front door of Christy's house and knocked. For several moments he waited, without even a sound being heard from the house to indicate someone was home. But Christy's car was in the drive, and Curt was certain that she was inside. Knocking again, this time a little harder, Curt was almost ready to bust down the door when Christy opened it.

The look on her face was one he had not seen before, and if Curt hadn't known better, he'd have thought she was frightened. The look vanished with recognition and was quickly replaced by anger.

"What do you want?"

"To apologize," Curt replied honestly. "I upset you the other day, and I haven't been able to get it out of my mind. I even told Debbie about it."

"I don't care," Christy said and started to close the door, but Curt put his hand firmly on the frame.

"I'm not going until we talk."

Christy stepped back in exasperation. "Then come inside. I'm getting cold standing here."

Curt needed no further invitation. He stepped into the house and closed the door behind him, then turned to follow Christy, who was already making her way to the sitting room he'd shared with her before.

"How's your sister?" he asked.

"Weaker. The doctors want to give the baby as much time as they can, but the pregnancy is draining Candy of her strength."

"If they take the baby now, will Candy pull through and live a while longer?" Curt asked, tossing his coat to one side.

Christy shook her head and walked to the fireplace mantel where a high school graduation picture of Candy sat. "I don't think anything will help," she whispered.

Curt watched her for several moments. She was far and away the most attractive woman he had ever seen, and the blue dress she wore showed off her shapely figure to perfection. Thinking of that, Curt remembered something in his coat pocket. Pulling out a magazine, Curt held it up.

"I found this," he said proudly.

Christy turned and saw the outdated fashion magazine. A glossy photograph of her in a black miniskirt and white and black polka-dot tank top stared back at her. Beside her in the picture were two Dalmatians and a red fire hydrant.

"You must have looked very hard to find a relic like that," she replied and took a seat on the sofa.

"Relic? If this thing weren't dated, I would have thought it was just done. You haven't aged a bit in six years."

Christy winced. "Six years? Is that how old that thing is?"

Curt laughed and gave the magazine a toss to where Christy sat. "Look for yourself."

Christy did, and it confirmed his statement. "I can't believe it was that long ago. I was barely nineteen," she said and then added sadly, "the same age Candy is now."

Curt came to where she sat and, in spite of the frown she gave him, sat down beside her. "I didn't mean to make you sad. I thought it pretty neat that I could find something like this and even better that I knew the gorgeous model on the front of a popular fashion magazine."

Christy rolled her eyes. "Did Debbie like it?"

"Debbie?"

"Yes, you remember Debbie, don't you? The woman you're supposed to marry and all that wedding stuff?"

"Debbie thought you looked fantastic. She remembered your covers from before, while I didn't have much experience with women's fashion magazines. In fact, I probably had my head in the clouds, literally, when you were posing for those pictures."

"I don't understand." Christy shifted to put a little more distance between herself and Curt. "What are you talking about?"

"I'm a pilot. I used to fly a lot," Curt answered, realizing that he shouldn't say too much. Hoping to change the direction of the conversation, Curt moved the subject back to his visit several days earlier. "Look, I really did come here to apologize. Somehow I gave you the wrong impression the other day, and I just wanted you to know that I'm sorry."

"How gallant of you," Christy murmured sarcastically.

"I try," Curt replied, refusing to be insulted. "I can't help it."

"Huh?" Christy's confusion was evident.

"When I'm around you, I just kind of forget myself. I've never met anyone quite like you, Christy Connors. You aren't mad at me anymore, are you?" Curt asked softly.

Christy sat stiffly, refusing to look at him. "I would never be mad at a client for getting lost in my house while looking for the bathroom."

Curt realized her game. "What about when the client made the mistake of touching you? Would you be mad at him then?" He reached his hand out and turned her face to meet his.

Christy's eyes narrowed slightly. "I'm not mad," she breathed the words.

"Then what's wrong?"

"You. Me," Christy managed to say. "This whole thing between us. It's inappropriate. You're a client, and to let you become anything more places my business at risk."

Curt smiled. "You falling in love with me, Christy?"

Christy's breath caught in her throat. Curt watched her closely, hardly daring to believe what he saw in her eyes. The realization that he may well have touched on the truth was just starting to register when the telephone rang. Christy jumped up so quickly that he could only stare after her in surprise.

"Hello?" Christy answered the phone rather breathlessly. "Yes, I'll be right there." She hung up the phone and turned with a look of complete hopelessness to Curt.

"I'll drive you to the hospital," he said simply.

Chapter 8

The cold sterile hospital halls and the smell of antiseptic cleanliness made Christy nauseous. She hadn't realized until this moment just how much she hated hospitals.

Curt had put his arm around her the minute they'd walked into the building and he hadn't volunteered to remove it, even after riding the elevator up to the intensive care ward. Christy wasn't inclined to ask him to remove it.

Erik greeted Christy and extended his hand to the man who so familiarly held his older sister. "I'm Erik Connors."

"Curt Kyle. How's Candy doing?" he asked, taking the question right out of Christy's mouth.

"She's asking for Christy," Erik admitted. "I think you'd better go right in. Oh, and stop by the nurse's desk. You have to wear a gown and mask now."

"Why?" Christy questioned.

"Infection precautions," Erik replied.

Christy nodded and reluctantly left the solace of Curt's arms and passed through the double-glass doors into the intensive care area.

Christy was greeted by a slim, dark-haired nurse in surgical scrubs. "Here," she said gently, "you'll need to put these on over your street clothes. Your sister is so very weak, and in order to give the baby every advantage, we need to keep Candy from being exposed to possible bacterial and viral infections."

Christy nodded and took the yellow gown, while the nurse pulled a pair of booties from a box and handed them to her also.

"These go over your shoes," the nurse instructed. "And these," she said, pulling a cap and mask from a drawer, "are to cover your hair and face."

Christy donned the articles, feeling like she was about to go into surgery. The final item was a pair of thin, latex gloves. Pulling them on, Christy realized that she'd not even be allowed to touch her sister without this material between them.

Finally garbed in a manner that met with the nurse's approval, Christy slid back the door to Candy's room and entered as quietly as she could.

At first glance, Christy presumed Candy was sleeping. She glanced at the machines that lined both sides at the head of the bed. A heart monitor kept a visual and audible record of Candy's weak heartbeat, while nasal tubes hummed with the rhythmic pulsing of precious oxygen and IV bags dripped bits of life-giving fluids into both of Candy's arms. Toward the end of the bed was a machine that Christy had been told was a fetal monitor.

Reaching out, Christy put her hand on Candy's. Her sister's eyes instantly opened.

"It's me, kid," Christy said, trying to sound lighthearted. "I heard you wanted to talk with me."

"Yeah," Candy answered weakly. "We have to talk about the baby."

Christy nodded. Behind the mask she frowned as she remembered how coldhearted Grant had been about his child.

"You have to save the baby, Christy. No matter what else happens, the baby has to live."

"The doctors are doing everything they can," Christy replied.

"Whatever it takes," Candy said in a pleading voice. "I don't matter in this anymore."

"Of course you do," Christy stated, almost alarmed. "I don't want you to—"

"I know," Candy said softly. "I don't want to die, but there doesn't appear to be much choice in the matter. Erik told me God has it all under control and that I don't have to be afraid of what's to come. You should talk to Erik, and he'll help you understand what he's told me."

"Erik would have all the answers where God is concerned," Christy said a bit more sarcastically than she had intended. "What do you want me to do?"

"I want you to take the baby," Candy answered matter-of-factly. "When I die, I want you to raise my child. Will you do that for me,

Christy? Will you be my baby's mother?"

Christy felt tears come to her eyes—tears that she couldn't hide from Candy. "I'll do whatever I can," she whispered, but just then an image of Grant's face came to mind. "But what about your husband?" Christy asked.

"Grant can't take this baby. He doesn't know the first thing about being a father, and he doesn't deserve to be a father after all he's done."

"What do you mean?" Christy questioned, trying to sound unaware of Grant's exploits.

"Grant can't be trusted," Candy answered simply. Her weak voice reminded Christy of when they'd been children. "He's no good, Christy. He mustn't be allowed to take the baby." Candy gripped Christy's hand tightly. "He can't!"

"Relax, Candy. You shouldn't excite yourself. I'll do whatever I can to see that the baby is protected, but please try to hang on, Candy. Maybe the doctors can do something for you after the baby is born. Maybe chemo or radiation."

"No," Candy whispered, weaker than ever. "There's no course of action. I made that choice a long time ago. The doctor told me there would be no turning back."

Hot tears fell against Christy's mask. "No possibilities?" she questioned, her own voice sounding like a child's.

"No," Candy said with a knowing look. "Christy, please don't hate me for my choice. I wanted this baby more than I wanted to live without it. I knew there'd never be another one because Grant... Well, never mind. This baby is very important to me, and I know I can trust you to raise it the way I would have."

Christy patted her sister's hand, hating the latex gloves that separated them from one another.

Candy offered her a brief smile. "I'm going to rest now," she murmured.

"Yes, you rest. I won't be far." Christy gently brushed back a bit of Candy's hair from her bruised and battered face.

Leaving the room, Christy kept thinking about Grant and how he had acted about the baby. If Candy's wishes were going to be adhered to, Christy knew she would need some legal standing to accomplish it.

A will! Whatever else happened, she needed to get a lawyer to the hospital right away in order to draw up a will for Candy.

Leaving her isolation gown in the trash receptacle, Christy was still deep in thought as she came from intensive care. She would have to find a lawyer, get the papers drawn up, and get Candy to sign, not only before she died, but before the tumor rendered her permanently unconscious. How much time did she have? Where would she find a trustworthy lawyer?

Christy entered the waiting room to find that Curt was alone. "Where's Erik?"

"He had to report to work. Are you doing okay?" Curt asked.

"Do you know the name of a good lawyer?" Then without waiting for him to answer, she shook her head. "Of course you don't. You just moved here."

Curt folded his hands in his lap. "My sister lives here. She and her husband are in business and know a lot of people. I'd trust her to know an honest lawyer. Why do you ask?"

"I need to get a lawyer to come to the hospital and work with Candy. She needs a will."

Curt nodded. "I'll call my sister." He reached across and took hold of her hand. "That is, if you want me to."

Christy's heart pounded so hard that she was sure Curt could hear it. She choked out acceptance of his offer and turned away to steady her nerves.

"I'll be right back," he said and let go of her hand.

Christy nodded but continued to look past him to the wall. *He is an incredible man*, Christy thought. He was good to her, beyond anything she could have ever expected from a friend, and that was what he kept reminding her they were. Friends.

"Just friends," Christy said aloud as if to drive the point home to herself.

Chapter 9

Within twenty-four hours, Christy found herself sitting with Erik in a private hospital consultation room, across from a lawyer who introduced himself as Michael Kesler.

"My sister made the decision to forfeit her own life in order to give birth to her child. The baby means everything to Candy; perhaps it's her way of living on after the cancer," Christy said softly.

Michael Kesler nodded and made notes on a yellow legal pad. "What about the father?" he asked, tapping the pen against the paper.

Erik shook his head. "Most of the time he's nowhere to be found."

"Are they married?" Kesler asked.

"Of course!" Christy snapped, then relaxed, realizing that Kesler had no way of knowing. "Sorry," she apologized. "They've been married about a year."

Kesler wrote it down, then looked up at Christy rather apprehensively. "Your sister wants you to raise her child after she dies, but what about the father? The legalities involved in separating a biological child and father, especially in a situation where there is a legitimate marriage, are complicated, to say the least. The court always desires to keep children with their biological parents in any situation where it won't be detrimental to the child. Have you discussed your sister's desires with your brother-in-law?"

Christy glanced briefly at Erik before replying. "Grant told me he wants nothing to do with the baby if Candy dies. He told me that he never wanted to be a father in the first place. It is my impression that he would find the arrangement most agreeable."

Kesler wrote the information down, but still sounded unconvinced. "What people say when they are facing the death of a loved one and what they do afterward are usually totally different. Once Mr. Burks actually loses his wife, he will probably feel differently. Right now, he might even be using this as a method to convince himself that she won't die. Maybe in his mind he believes that if he tells her and everyone else that he doesn't want the baby, she'll have to live in order to care for their child."

"I don't think that's a consideration of his," Christy blurted out.

"Well, I'm going to see Mrs. Burks to confirm several points, and then I'll prepare the papers. I should be able to have them ready by tomorrow morning, and if we can manage to locate Mr. Burks, I'll confront him with the terms."

Christy stood up as the lawyer did. "Thank you for coming so quickly. I know you're doing this as a favor to your friends, but I just want you to know that I truly appreciate it."

Michael Kesler smiled broadly. "I know you do. I just wish we could have met under better circumstances." He sobered for a moment. "You must realize that this matter creates a very delicate legal situation. If your brother-in-law wants to fight this, there will be little chance of you winning."

"I already imagined that to be the case," Christy admitted.

Erik offered to walk Michael to Candy's room, leaving Christy alone with her thoughts. Would the lawyer manage to put the will together in time? What would happen to the baby if Candy died before signing the papers? What if Grant refused to agree to the terms? Nervously, she paced to the window of the small room and stared out. All of Denver seemed to be going about its paces while her own world was falling apart.

"Did you get everything settled?" Curt's words sounded with the warmth of his breath against her neck. Christy wished that she hadn't pinned up her hair. She felt so vulnerable with his lips nearly against her ear.

Afraid to turn, she continued staring out the window. "The lawyer has gone in to see her. Erik took him."

"Yes, I saw them," Curt replied. "I hope he can help."

Christy realized that she had not thanked Curt for his assistance in locating a lawyer and turned without thinking. They were only inches apart, and Christy couldn't help but wish that Curt would hold her and make the awful things of the world disappear.

"Thank you, Curt," she said in a barely audible whisper. "I really appreciate the way you. . ." She fell silent, losing herself in his eyes.

"I know," Curt answered and started to say something more, but was interrupted by Erik's voice.

"Curt, I'm sure I don't have the right to ask, but I'd like it very much if you'd take Christy home. She's been here since yesterday, and I know she could use a good hot meal and a night's sleep."

Curt turned to face Christy's brother, who had just returned from Candy's bedside. "I'd be happy to help."

"Oh no you two don't," Christy protested. "I'm not going home."

Curt and Erik raised their eyebrows in unison and turned to stare at Christy. Christy blushed at their response. "I don't need to go home," she stated firmly.

Curt looked at Erik, then back to Christy. "Erik, you can count on me. I'll deliver her safe and sound."

"Thanks, Curt. I owe you," Erik replied as though Christy had never said a word. "Get some rest, Sis," he said before turning to leave. "You look awful."

"Thanks a lot, Erik. I appreciate your honesty," Christy replied sarcastically. "But I'm staying. You can both go on without concerning yourselves about me. If I need to go home, I'll drive myself."

Curt put his hand gently on her arm and smiled in a way that told Christy she'd lost the fight. "Come on," he said, "you have to ride with me. Remember? I brought you here yesterday, and you don't have a car."

The drive home nearly put Christy to sleep, but it also doubled her determination not to be pushed around by her brother and client. When Curt turned off the motor, she didn't wait for him to come around and help her out. Instead, Christy reached inside her purse for her keys and quickly got out of the car.

"Now that I have a car of my own," she said, "I'm going back to the hospital."

She reached for the door handle on her car, but found her wrist encircled by Curt's powerful grip. "You're going to bed," he said sternly. "You really do look like you could use some sleep."

Christy's mouth dropped open in surprise, but Curt just grinned. "Don't worry, Princess," he whispered, pulling her along, "you still wear the crown well."

"What?" she questioned in confusion.

Curt laughed and reached out to take the keys from her. "Which one's the house key?" he asked.

Christy pointed it out, then questioned him again. "What did you mean by that remark?"

"Just what I said. You run this place and your family like you're some kind of queen on a throne. You're used to getting your own way and having people do what you tell them. This time, someone told you something other than what you wanted to hear, and you feel slighted. You'll get over it. I think it's about time somebody took care of you."

"And you think you're that someone?" Christy questioned. "What about Debbie?"

"I think Debbie has enough to do without worrying about you," Curt replied, completely putting the issue of Debbie aside.

"I didn't mean it that way," Christy said in complete exasperation, "and you know it."

Curt opened the door and waited for Christy to turn on the lights before speaking. "Sometimes I wonder if you even know what you mean."

Christy stared at him for a moment. "I'm going back to the hospital as soon as you leave, and there's nothing you can do to stop me."

"I kind of figured that would be your attitude. That's why I'm not going to leave," Curt replied and took off his coat.

"What do you mean?"

"Just what I said."

"But you said that you weren't leaving," Christy said, watching him make himself at home.

"I'm not." Curt faced her with a mischievous grin. "I'm staying the night."

"Just like that?" Christy asked, standing with hands on her hips.

"Yup," he replied and went in the direction of the kitchen.

"And what makes you think I won't get in the car and leave as soon as you're asleep?"

Curt held up the keys and gave them a little jingle as he kept walking toward the kitchen. Christy had no choice but to follow him.

"I have more keys."

Curt turned. "Then I'll disable your car, disconnect the phone, and bolt you in your bedroom." His voice was serious, even though his eyes held a glint of amusement.

"You're impossible!" she exclaimed in disgust at his now retreating form.

Christy stomped off to the foyer, removed her coat, and put it in the closet. She noticed Curt's coat where he had draped it across her receiving table. After a moment of deliberation, she picked up the coat, causing the silver calling-card tray to rattle beneath it.

Reaching for a hanger, Christy paused and brought the coat to her face and inhaled deeply. The lingering scent of Curt's cologne filled her senses.

"It's just the cheap stuff," he said from behind her.

Christy was mortified and felt her face grow hot. Without answering, she quickly put the coat on a hanger and placed it in the closet. When she turned around, Curt stood there, grinning. If it was possible, her face reddened even more.

"You really are impossible," she half whispered, half moaned.

"Yeah, I am," he conceded with a roguish laugh, "but you like me anyway."

Christy rolled her eyes and pushed past him. "You can't keep me here," she stated firmly, her confidence returning. "You have to sleep sometime."

"I'll camp at the foot of your bed if you aren't going to be cooperative," Curt said.

Christy stopped in her tracks and turned. She eyed him for a minute, seeing that he was serious. "You really mean that, don't you?"

"I do," he replied. "Your brother and I had a nice talk about you the other day. You know, while you were visiting Candy," he reminded her. "Anyway, he's very worried about you. Said you wouldn't let anyone help you or care for you. He said there wasn't anyone more stubborn in the world, and I told him he was wrong. I'm ten times as stubborn as you are."

"So he turned me over to you as some kind of mountain to conquer? Did you have some kind of ceremony? You know, the passing of the torch? Or maybe it was more like transferring ownership of a car?"

Curt grinned. "However you want to see it."

"I want to see you walking out that door and never coming back," Christy lied, hoping that she sounded convincing. She didn't.

Curt crossed his arms and kept smiling. "I don't believe you. I think you like the fact that I've been helping you. I think you like being taken care of and are just too proud to admit it."

"Aghhh," Christy groaned and turned to climb the stairs. "There's bedding in the closet by the bathroom—if you don't get lost and end up in my storeroom again. I hope you get a stiff neck from the sofa because I'm not letting you have the privilege of any of my guest rooms."

"Good night, Christy," he called after her. "Sweet dreams."

"Don't forget to call Debbie," she said sarcastically. "Let her know that you're spending the night with another woman."

"I'll do that," Curt said, without the effect Christy had hoped for.

Curt waited until he was certain Christy was asleep before he went to work. He cast a cautious glance up the stairs before making his way to the storeroom and flipping on the light. Once inside, he went to work checking the shipping crates, noting weights and markings and comparing them with bills of lading that were still in plastic pouches on the side.

Pulling out a notebook from his pocket, Curt quickly copied the information down, with wary glances at the door from time to time. Feeling satisfied that he had the suspicious makings of something he could investigate, Curt turned off the light and went back to the couch. It was only after several hours of staring at the ceiling and seeing smokey blue eyes stare back that Curt finally faded off to sleep.

Chapter 10

Christy woke up feeling remarkably refreshed. Stretching out in a catlike manner, she forced a glance at the clock. She couldn't even remember what day of the week it was.

Pulling on a white, lacy Victorian-style robe, Christy pushed her hair out of her eyes and made her way downstairs. *No doubt Aggie will be amused to find me like this*, Christy thought. She rarely ever came downstairs without her makeup, hair, and wardrobe in place.

Below, she could hear Aggie moving around the kitchen and raising such a clatter that Christy couldn't imagine what was going on. When she stepped into the room, she wasn't prepared for the sight that greeted her.

"What in the world?" she sputtered the question. She'd totally forgotten that Curt had camped out in her sitting room for the night.

"Do you always look this good in the morning?" Curt asked, putting down the frying pan he had been about to use.

"Why are you still here?" she asked, suddenly self-conscious about her attire. She clutched the robe nervously.

"I'm fixing breakfast."

"Where's Aggie? I have a woman who comes in during the morning. Where is she?" Christy questioned.

"I told her that her services weren't needed this morning," Curt replied, expecting the storm to come.

Christy moaned. "You didn't tell her you'd spent the night, did you?"

Curt grinned. "Of course not. I told her I was helping out and fixing breakfast."

"You had no right," Christy said, coming across the room. "I'm in charge here, remember? This is my house. Aggie is my help, and I pay all the bills."

"So I've heard."

"What's that supposed to mean?" Christy looked at him curiously.

"I heard that you were paying your sister's bill. What happened to her husband?"

"They're broke, as far as I can tell. He never stays in his law office long enough to earn a living. I don't mind paying for Candy, though I wish it weren't quite so convenient and helpful to Grant. He doesn't deserve anything good." Christy shuddered at the memory of him touching her.

Curt's eyes narrowed slightly. "Is Grant bothering you, Christy?"

"It isn't anything I can't take care of myself," she tried to say in a reassuring voice.

After several minutes of awkward silence, Curt finally asked, "You want one egg or two?"

"I don't want anything. I always have orange juice and coffee for breakfast and nothing else. I can get that by myself, so please just get your coat and go home."

"My good-smelling coat?"

Christy rolled her eyes and turned to go back upstairs. Curt caught her around the waist before she made it much farther than the kitchen.

"You really are beautiful," he whispered.

"Don't say that."

"Why not? It's true."

"Because, you know it isn't right for you to say things like that to me. And this," she said, motioning to the way he held her against him, "is definitely off limits. I need to get dressed."

"You're better covered up in this than in that blue number you were wearing the other day." Christy's mouth formed a silent O, and Curt smiled.

"Besides, you're too skinny," he said and released her.

"Once before you told me I was heavier than I looked."

"Well, I can't help that," Curt grinned. "Maybe it was the heavy clothes. Now, answer my question. One egg or two?"

Christy sighed. "Can't I win just one of these arguments?"

"Nope."

She shook her head. "One egg."

"How do you like it?"

"Over medium."

"There," Curt replied with a self-satisfied look on his face, "that wasn't so hard, was it?"

"Go cook. I need to get dressed and put my makeup on."

"Then I have plenty of time." Curt chuckled and walked away. "Maybe I'll even read the paper."

"Why stop there? There's a copy of *War and Peace* in the den."

"Good idea," he called over his shoulder.

When Christy returned to join Curt for breakfast, she was stylishly dressed in an attractive Armani wool-viscose suit. The classy number was not lost on Curt, who had some knowledge of fashion and the price tags that accompanied designer clothes.

"You look. . ." He paused, giving her a complete once-over.

"Yes?" Christy asked, hands on hips.

"Expensive."

Christy laughed. "That's good, because I am."

Curt came around the table and pulled out a chair for her.

Christy shook her head. "Oh no, you don't. I may have relented on breakfast, but I have a special place I like to start my day." She picked up the juice he had poured for her and motioned him toward the enclosed balcony. "Right this way."

Curt followed and nodded at the cozy sight that met his eyes. "I can see why you like it. I'll just bring our food out here." He left Christy to fuss over her plants and returned within a matter of seconds, balancing plates of food.

"You've cooked considerably more than eggs," Christy said, noting bacon, hashbrowns, and toast.

"They looked lonely," Curt said by way of excuse.

He could see that Christy was trying hard not to smile. *She's something else*, Curt thought. Then he noticed again the way she was dressed. Sitting down on the white wicker settee, Christy looked all business and no play.

"You have someplace special you're going today?" Curt questioned, trying to get a conversation going. Remembering his investigation, he wondered if this might break into something he should know about.

"As a matter of fact, I do." Christy offered nothing further, and Curt realized that short of coming out and asking, he wasn't going to find out anything more. He was surprised when, after tasting the egg he'd fixed for her, she looked up and asked him, "What about you? What do you do with your days that allows you to buy an expensive wedding dress for a woman you apparently hardly ever spend time with?"

Curt tensed. How could he explain? He couldn't very well tell her that he was part of a billion-dollar aviation industry. Nor could he admit he was with the DEA. All she knew about him was that he'd just moved here from Florida and he could fly a plane. Just as he prepared to lie and tell her that he flew commercially, the telephone rang.

"You sure get a lot of calls," he mused.

"This is a business phone, you know," Christy reminded him, reaching for the portable phone.

"Hello?" Christy grinned broadly at Curt. He could tell she was up to something. "Yes, Erik, I slept quite well and so did Mr. Kyle. Would you like to talk to him?"

Curt nearly spit out his coffee and Christy started to laugh. Curt waggled a finger at her and said, "You'd better tell him the truth."

"No, Erik, Mr. Kyle slept on the couch," she said and paused. "No, I suppose it wasn't nice, but neither was saddling me with this baby-sitter." The lightheartedness left her voice as Curt heard her ask, "How's Candy?"

There was a long pause, and Curt watched Christy's eyes fill with tears. "Yes, I understand," she said weakly. She struggled with her emotions.

Without a word to Christy, Curt took the phone and talked to Erik. After assuring Christy's brother that he would take care of her, Curt hung up the phone and went to sit beside her. She was crying softly into her hands, and Curt simply pulled her into his arms.

He didn't say a word. He didn't have to. Christy clung to him like she had that night on her porch. How he wished he could bear her pain and somehow relieve her of losing someone she loved. He knew that pain very well. At times it still came back to haunt him. At times it felt like yesterday.

Christy lifted her face and opened her mouth, but Curt put his finger against her lips, then reached up and wiped the tears from her eyes with his handkerchief. This done, he leaned forward and without warning, pulled her forward as he pressed a kiss against her lips.

For a moment Curt felt her melt against him, then without warning she pushed him away and jumped to her feet.

"Get out of my house. You are just like all the rest. I thought there was something special about you, but you're no different." She stormed out of the room and would have run for the haven of her bedroom, but Curt stopped her.

"You've got me all wrong. I'm not like those other men. I believe in faithfulness, and I would never consider having an affair."

"What do you call what just happened? Sure it was just a kiss, but what happens next?" Christy asked angrily.

"I guess that's up to you," Curt said softly.

"I won't be the other woman in Debbie's life," Christy replied a bit sadly. "I've had to deal with too many 'other women' to become one myself. I just can't do it, so don't ask me to."

"I'm not," Curt assured her.

"You're not?" Christy questioned. "Did I read too much into that kiss? Was that intended as a brotherly kiss of friendship? Did I just imagine your heart pounding like it was going to come out of your chest?"

Curt smiled slowly. "No," he answered. "That was no friendship kiss."

Christy nodded. "At least you're being honest about that." She turned to leave him, but Curt put out his hand and held her fast.

"I'm not going to marry Debbie," he said, shocking himself almost as much as Christy.

"You're what?"

"You heard me. I'm not going to marry Debbie. She's got someone else," Curt added, grateful that it was the truth.

"I'm sorry," Christy said, knowing the heartache he must be feeling.

"You are?"

"It's hard to lose someone you love and plan to spend the rest of your life with," Christy replied. "At least that explains your actions."

Curt pulled her with him to the sitting room. "Tell me what you mean," he said, guiding her to a seat on the sofa.

"I just meant that what with your breakup being so fresh and Debbie having someone else, you couldn't help yourself. You were lonely, I was hurting, and you kissed me. Just that simple."

"Really?" Curt questioned with a raised brow. "Was that all it was for you?" He prayed that she wouldn't say yes.

Christy blushed and turned her face. "I don't want to talk about it."

"Well, I do," Curt replied. "I didn't kiss you because I couldn't have Debbie. Yes, your pain might have prompted the start of the kiss, but it certainly had nothing to do with the end of it." Christy started to get up, but he pulled her back down. "Talk to me, Christy. Tell me that kiss meant nothing to you."

"I don't want it to mean anything to me."

"That's not answering my question."

Christy fidgeted with the button on her jacket. She realized there was no other way to deal with the situation than to just be honest. "It meant something," she finally whispered.

Curt reached out and stilled her hand. "Tell me what it meant to you."

"No," Christy said, jerking her head up to meet his eyes. "I can't. I don't want to feel anything for you. Can't you understand that? I've been hurt too many times. My father had his mistresses and was never there for me. My mother was content with her open marriage and lovers. The great love of my life was married to another woman. Even my sister's husband has had one affair after another and tries to force himself on me whenever the notion takes him." She put her hand to her mouth as if realizing that she should never have said anything.

Curt's eyes blazed in anger. "I kind of figured it must be that way. But I assure you, it won't be that way anymore."

She put out a hand. "I don't want to feel anything for you, Curt. I've seen too many relationships sour. I've seen the mockery people have made out of marriage. I can't bear to become a part of that."

"What do you mean, become a part? You are a part of it. You're at the very center of it. You design the wedding dresses that women wear to begin their marriages. You're at the very heart of the entire 'mockery,' as you put it."

Christy shook her head. "No, I'm not. I'm a part of the fairy tale. I'm a part of the dream. I make beautiful wedding gowns that a woman will only wear once, maybe twice if she repeats her vows later in life.

Maybe she'll pass the dress down to her daughters. Whatever else, that gown represents the rose-colored glasses, the perfect picture. That gown is before the madness and the mundane. Before the broken promises." Christy paused and got to her feet. This time Curt didn't attempt to stop her.

"I make a dress as beautiful and as intricate as I can. I sew my own dreams and wishes into every gown and dare to hope that this might be the one couple who will truly love and cherish each other until death separates them."

"But don't you want that for yourself? Don't you want to find that one person with whom you can make those dreams and wishes come true? Don't you want the fairy tale, too?"

Christy turned and looked at Curt for a moment. She blinked back tears before answering. "I'm not Cinderella, and there is no glass slipper."

Chapter 11

Driving down the interstate, Curt tried to fight the memories that flooded his mind. Memories of Christy crying in his arms. She'd said she was no Cinderella, but to Curt she was that and so much more. Curt gave the car dashboard the fury of his fist. Why had he allowed himself to care about her? Determined to rectify the situation, Curt vowed to forget all about Christy Connors except as a suspect in a drug investigation.

"She doesn't want me in her life, and I shouldn't be except as a DEA investigator. I will not care about her anymore."

His resolve lasted all of three minutes—then he suddenly remembered what she had said about her brother-in-law, Grant Burks. Grant was pressuring Christy, and Curt knew that boded trouble. She wouldn't be able to keep him at bay forever, not if he was the determined type.

"Oh God," he murmured, "I've made such a mess of this. Please keep Christy safe and let this whole thing be done with so that I can go to her on an equal footing and be open and honest with her." But even as Curt said the words, he knew approaching Christy with the truth would be difficult. She'd been used before, and now she'd just see this as a bad rerun of the past. She wouldn't understand that he had only lied to stay in line with his job.

Christy's smokey blue eyes haunted him throughout the day, and even when Curt was at his desk looking over the information he had obtained about Christy's shipments, he couldn't help thinking about her.

"You aren't even here, are you?" Debbie stated, not expecting an answer. "I've never seen you like this before, Curt. You've really gotten in over your head this time."

"Stay out of it, Debbie," he fairly growled. "I don't need your advice."

Debbie's eyes registered hurt, then anger. "You need someone's advice, that's for sure. Maybe Frank can talk some sense into you."

"I don't want to talk to Frank, either."

"Well, you don't get a choice," Frank said from the doorway. "I want you in here. Now."

Curt rolled his eyes, and Debbie backed away from the desk. "Thanks, partner," he muttered under his breath before going into Frank's office.

Curt pulled up a chair, knowing that the big man would give him a good lecturing. He deserved it, too, but what he didn't want to hear about was the way he'd jeopardized the investigation, because he didn't believe he had. Not yet, anyway.

Frank eyed Curt with cool, unemotional eyes for just a moment. His towering six-foot, six-inch frame seemed to take up the room. "We've been friends for a while now," he began. "I like you, Curt, I really do. You've been a good friend to Deb and me, and you've made a good member of the team."

"But?" Curt threw in before Frank could continue.

"But—and this is strictly between you and me, friend to friend—" Frank said, leaning down with both hands on his desk. "If you ever talk to Debbie that way again, I'll see to it that you're grounded to paperwork for the rest of your career."

Curt knew the threat was idle, but he also appreciated Frank's protectiveness of the woman he loved. Didn't he feel that same way about Christy? The thought startled him so much that he never even heard what Frank said next. He'd fallen in love with Christy Connors. Why did it seem so surprising?

"You're a million miles away from your job and that could mean your death or Debbie's. I'm pulling you off the Connors's investigation."

"No!" Curt jumped to his feet. "You can't!"

"Give me one good reason why I should keep you on."

"I have Christy's trust, so to speak. I can't explain it to you. There are some things going on that I'm curious about and without me on the inside, you'll spend months just working to get someone that close again."

"What kind of things, Curt?"

"I'm not sure, but there are problems with her shipping invoices. You know about the New York shipments and the fact that 90 percent of her deliveries come from out of the country. She imports a great deal of the material and accessories that she uses in her designer line."

"I know all of that. That doesn't justify keeping you inside." Frank stared hard at Curt, daring him to elaborate.

"I saw some of the cargo papers, as well as other shipments that have come directly to Christy at her home. There are real problems. The weights vary from those listed on the invoices and those on the crates and bills of lading. What few I could match up were off sometimes as much as one hundred pounds."

"Why hasn't she noticed this? One hundred pounds of material would be considerably higher in shipping charges. Doesn't she ever compare the costs?"

"That's just it. She isn't charged for it," Curt said sternly.

"The shipper is involved then?"

"I'd stake my career on it. I'd also guess that the whole thing is networked from start to finish. Christy always uses the same shipper, same import brokers, same ports of entry. It's my belief that whoever is in charge has choreographed this thing from beginning to end. I don't have all the pieces, and I certainly don't have the names of who's responsible, but I'd bet my life that Christy Connors isn't one of them."

"That's the trouble with you, Curt. You'd bet your life in this situation, and it very well may cost you your life. Now you may be willing to risk that, but I'm not. Nor am I willing to risk your partner's life. I love that woman, and I'll protect her just the same way you're protecting Christy." Frank sat down and his face softened. "Look, I realize that you're in love with this Connors woman, and that's exactly why you can't stay on the case."

"I have to, Frank. Christy's life is at stake, and she's got deep problems in her family life that I believe may well be related to the case. She's not going to let anyone else get close to her." Curt wondered silently if she'd even let him remain close. Knowing he had to gamble his all, Curt continued. "There's something else—something I haven't even told Debbie."

Frank eyed him suspiciously. "You'd better tell me, and don't leave any details out."

Curt nodded. "The shipper Christy uses is a subsidiary of O&F Aviation."

Frank looked at him blankly for a moment. "Your company?"

"None other."

"Do you know who's running things?"

"Not a clue, but I will. That's why I have to stay in this thing. It's personal, now more than ever," Curt said determinedly.

Frank stared at him for a moment. "All right. You can stay on it for now."

"Thanks, Frank; you won't be sorry."

❧

Curt pulled into the crowded driveway to his sister's house. CJ and Brad were throwing a small get-together and had insisted that he join them. Reluctantly, Curt had agreed, but only because he wanted to speak with Brad.

"Curt, you made it. Come on in," Brad said, opening the door. He ushered Curt into the house and took his coat. "Looks like it might snow again," he said, hanging the coat in the closet.

"Yeah, I guess," Curt answered, a bit preoccupied.

"Something wrong?" Brad asked.

"I don't know. Can we talk privately?"

"Sure, come on upstairs."

Brad led the way, managing to avoid the small gathering that mingled around his house. Curt followed, hands deep in his pockets, a frown on his face.

Brad opened the door to his private study. "We won't be disturbed in here."

Curt waited until the door was closed behind them before talking. "There may be a bigger threat to CJ than I'd originally thought. I can't explain everything because the truth is, I don't have the answers."

Brad crossed his arms, worry clearly etched in his expression. "What should I do?"

"I don't know. I can't help but wonder if we shouldn't get her out of here. I'm afraid of what I'm going to find, and when I find it, I'm afraid I won't be able to protect those I love." His words were intended for Christy as well as CJ.

"We haven't been back from the honeymoon all that long, but I could suggest a trip related to the hotel business. CJ knows I want to expand. We could go scouting for property to build on."

"That might be good. She wouldn't be suspicious that way."

"Don't kid yourself," Brad laughed. "CJ would be suspicious no matter what. That's just your sister's way. We're already in trouble for being up here alone. I haven't a clue what excuse I'll give her for this one."

Curt smiled and nodded. "Some things never change."

"Come on," Brad said. "We'll think of something."

Curt never knew what excuse Brad used with CJ because the moment they came downstairs, Curt's eyes fell on the vivacious blond who stood at the end of the staircase. Blond curls bobbed back and forth while the woman chattered nonstop to a group of three other people.

Curt paused behind the woman for a moment, causing the man on her right to eye him intently. The group grew quiet, and the woman turned.

"Curt?"

"Hello, Cheryl," Curt said with a smile. Cheryl Fairchild was even more beautiful now than when they'd been engaged over six years ago.

"CJ didn't say anything about you being here," she said softly. Stepping forward a single step, Cheryl's expression grew thoughtful. "You look fantastic."

"You, too," Curt grinned. He looked Cheryl over, appreciating the stylish red dress that showed off her figure. Cheryl had always dressed a bit on the flamboyant side.

"I can't believe you're really here," she whispered. "When did you come to town?"

The man on Cheryl's arm seemed to scowl, and Curt enjoyed his discomfort. Looking past her to the man, Curt's smile broadened. Cheryl followed Curt's gaze and realized she'd totally ignored everyone else.

"Curt, this is my fiancé, Stratton McFarland."

Curt nodded to the dark-headed man and extended his hand. "So you're the lucky man who ended up with this gorgeous lady."

McFarland shook Curt's hand and then took hold of Cheryl in a possessive way. There was something about the man that caused Curt to wonder if they'd met before. As if reading his mind, Cheryl spoke. "Stratton works for O&F Aviation corporate offices."

"How nice," Curt said, having passed the point of enjoying the man's discomfort. "I guess that makes me your boss." Curt immediately wished he'd not mentioned that little fact.

Stratton's eyes narrowed, and Cheryl giggled nervously. "Curt is CJ's brother."

The other people moved away to mingle, leaving Cheryl and Stratton to chat with Curt. "Stratton, would you be a dear and get me a glass of mineral water?"

Stratton seemed annoyed that Cheryl obviously wanted to talk alone with Curt, but he said nothing and left the couple, grumbling under his breath.

"I don't think he likes me," Curt dryly observed.

"No, I don't imagine he does. Curt, I've missed you. CJ tells me you're hard to get in touch with these days. What are you up to?"

"Oh, little bits of this and that," Curt said guardedly. "What does Stratton do for O&F?"

"He's Daddy's right-hand man. Daddy always figured on you having that job, so maybe Stratton's a bit intimidated to know that you're around."

Just then Stratton returned. He thrust the drink into Cheryl's hands and pulled her close. Curt smiled at the man, knowing it further irritated him.

"It was good to visit with you, Cheryl. I'm glad you and CJ are still close. We'll have to get together and discuss old times." At this, Stratton frowned, just as Curt knew he would.

On the way back to his apartment, Curt considered Cheryl's words about her father and Stratton. Maybe it was time to make a visit to Ben Fairchild and feel him out for whatever information he might give. Maybe it was time to try on Doug O'Sullivan's shoes and see if they fit yet.

Chapter 12

Spurred on by the memory of rejecting Curt and thinking about her sister's rising hospital bills, Christy threw herself into her wedding gown creations. She so thoroughly lost herself in work that before she realized it, she was nearly a month ahead of schedule on three different dresses.

The ringing phone tempted her to get an answering service, but knowing it to be a lifeline to the hospital, Christy couldn't bring herself to do it. Just when things seemed to calm a bit, however, she picked up a call and heard the one voice she hoped never to talk to again.

"I understand you want custody of my baby," Grant said without any other introduction.

"Candy wants me to raise the baby, and I told her I would. You'd already made it quite clear to me that you wanted no part of the child's life, so I didn't figure you cared."

"I only care that I get my fair share out of the deal. After all, maybe fatherhood isn't such a bad thing for me to consider."

"What do you want, Grant?"

"Money, of course."

"I'm already paying all the bills," she replied weakly. "What else did you have in mind?"

"I need a great deal of money, and I intend for you to supply it." Grant then named an outrageous figure that nearly made Christy drop the telephone. "And don't tell me you can't get it. I heard about the success of your spring line in Milan."

"All right," Christy replied. "So I get you the money. How do I know that you'll give me legal custody of the baby?"

"When the money is in my hands, I'll give you the signed papers. It's that simple."

"It'll take me a little time to get the money," Christy admitted. "But

I'll get it. You just make certain you hold up your end of the deal."

"Don't worry," Grant replied before issuing her final instructions. "And, Christy, don't mention this to Erik. The fewer people involved, the better."

The call from Grant had been so unnerving that Christy couldn't function in a normal manner for days. She tried to figure out how she was going to arrange everything, but her mind wouldn't cooperate. She really wanted to talk to Curt about it. She needed his advice, but knew she wasn't entitled to it.

Setting her mind to accomplish something more, Christy contemplated a room for the nursery. If things went as planned and she did bring the baby home to live with her, Christy wanted everything just right. She remembered little things Candy had said about planning her own nursery and jotted down notes to herself. She'd use as many of Candy's ideas as possible and augment them with ideas of her own.

Working at the nursery sketch, Christy was startled by the sound of the doorbell. What if it was Grant? What if it was Curt?

The bell sounded again, and Christy felt her heart begin to pound. She both dreaded and hoped it would be Curt. *Just please don't be Grant,* she prayed. Squeezing her eyes shut, Christy took a deep breath and pulled the door open. She flashed her eyes open quickly and prepared to do battle.

"Can we talk?" It was Curt, looking as warm and wonderfully appealing as he always did.

Christy drank in his tanned skin against the variegated brown wool cardigan he wore. Her eyes trailed down his jeans to his boots and back up to his face, where she met his amused grin.

"Finished with the inspection?"

Christy blushed crimson. "I just thought I recognized the sweater." She hurried on to cover her obvious interest. "The designer, I mean."

Curt nodded. "Of course." His eyes still held their bemused twinkle, and Christy fervently wished she hadn't been so obvious.

"So, may I come in?"

"No," Christy said with as much fortitude as she could muster. "I don't think we have anything to say to each other."

"Well, that's where we differ, Christy," Curt said and took hold of her arm. "I think we have a great deal to say to one another."

"Very well," Christy said, knowing she was defeated. Curt once said he was a man used to getting what he wanted. Why should this time be any different?

"I was working in the den," she said. "I have a pot of coffee back there. Do you want a cup?"

"Sounds good."

He followed Christy into the fashionably stylish room. A home entertainment system lined one wall with the stereo softly playing Beethoven. Curt glanced down at the sketches on the drawing table that stood against the opposite wall.

"Are you switching to interior designs?" he asked casually.

Christy came to where he stood and held out a mug of coffee. "Just say what you came to say and then go." She tried very hard to sound firm and unemotional.

Curt appeared unaffected by her words. "I don't want things to be like this between us. I want to be friends again. In fact, I'd like to be more than friends."

Christy moved back a step. "More than friends?" she whispered, knowing full well she shouldn't continue the conversation.

Curt eyed her warmly. "Yes." He put the coffee on the drafting table and stepped toward Christy.

Christy backed up again. "I don't think so, Curt." She hated herself for sounding almost breathless. Her heart pounded harder at each step he took toward her. "I think we need to just walk away from each other and not look back." *There*, she thought, *I said what needed to be said.*

Curt just kept coming at her with a slow, deliberate pace that reminded Christy of a wild animal stalking its prey. She kept backing up, realizing that soon she'd be against the wall and there'd be no place to go.

"I don't want to walk away. I care about you, and I think we should give this a try. There's no one else to stand in our way, so why not?"

Christy was mesmerized, her eyes fixed on his. His voice was soothing—almost hypnotic in its baritone whisper.

"I can't. We can't," she barely mouthed the words. Her voice was shaky, and the color drained from her face as Curt backed her into the corner.

"Why not?" he persisted.

"I. . .I, uh," she struggled to speak. Curt was just inches from her. "I just can't."

Curt leaned forward, but still did not touch her. "Why not?"

"I'm afraid," she finally admitted.

"I haven't given you any reason to be afraid of me."

The scent of Curt's cologne drifted up, and Christy lost herself in a moment of memories. Memories of Curt holding her. Memories of her smelling his coat in order to catch the sweet, musky scent. She shook her head and couldn't speak.

"Christy, what are you afraid of?" Curt questioned and gently reached out to brush back a stray curl from her shoulder.

Christy began to tremble from her head to her toes, and her teeth chattered noticeably as she cowered in the corner.

"What are you afraid of?" he repeated.

Christy swallowed hard. "It would be easier to say what I'm not afraid of." She tried to say the words with a bit of a laugh, but it sounded more like she might break into tears any minute.

"Are you afraid of me?" he asked.

Christy started to say yes, but quickly realized it wasn't true. She'd never felt more secure with anyone in her life. She looked at him for a moment, and her trembling stopped. Without thinking of the consequences, Christy reached her hand up to touch Curt's cheek.

"No," she whispered. "I'm not afraid of you, only of what you represent."

Curt pulled her into his arms, and Christy didn't resist. "I don't represent what the others did, and I'll tell you why."

Christy felt her will collapse. "Why are you different?" she asked, hoping he would have a reason that she could believe in.

"I'm a Christian," he whispered against her ear. "I believe in biblical values, moral purity, and the sanctity of marriage. I hold many things sacred, unlike a great many people in the world who believe there is nothing sacred in this life."

Christy pulled away and looked at him. He didn't seem like any of the religious freaks she'd met in the past. She'd have never pegged him for an all-in-all Bible thumper, but he sounded staunch in his convictions.

"I don't know much about your beliefs," Christy said, almost afraid to admit her ignorance. "Erik believes strongly in the power of God. Candy told me that Erik helped her to understand about eternity, but I don't think I can cozy up to a God who lets nineteen-year-old girls die while fighting to give birth to their own children."

"You have to trust someone, sometime," Curt said, leading her to the love seat in the middle of the room. Pulling her down with him, he held her close and began rocking the chair back and forth. "God has all the reliability you have never been able to find in people. Even I won't pretend that I'll never disappoint you or annoy you," he said with a good-natured smile. "But God is forever the same. He's faithful even when we aren't."

The words sounded good to Christy. But her heart had been so scarred from previous encounters that she resisted considering their hope.

"Give us a chance, Christy. Please."

Christy felt his arms tighten around her. She wanted to say yes. She wanted to accept his love more than anything else in the world, but painful memories haunted her mind and frightened her in such a deep, unyielding way that she pushed him away. Jumping to her feet, Christy ran as fast as she could back down the hall. At the foyer table, she grabbed her purse and car keys and, without getting so much as a jacket, she bolted out the door.

❧

Christy drove in circles around the city before finally ending up at the hospital. Making her way to intensive care, she was surprised when the nurse told her that Candy was awake and had been asking for her. Christy hastily donned isolation garments and went into her sister's room.

"Candy?" she whispered, coming to her bedside.

"Christy, I'm glad you're here." Candy's voice was so weak that Christy had to lean down to hear it.

"The nurse said you were asking for me."

"Yes. Did Grant sign the papers?"

Christy frowned. "I don't know. Grant told me he would sign the papers, if I. . ." She let the words trail off and hoped that Candy wasn't lucid enough to realize what she'd been about to say.

"If you what? Tell me, Christy, what did Grant make you promise?" Candy's voice seemed to take on a bit of strength.

"You answer my question first. Are you and Grant in financial trouble? I mean, before this accident and even before the cancer."

Candy closed her eyes tightly. "Yes."

"Why didn't you come to me? You could have asked for my help. What happened? Why isn't there any money?" Christy seemed to forget her sister's delicate condition.

"Grant's gotten himself involved in some bad deals. He's gone through everything. I didn't know what to do, and that's why I was coming to see you when I had the accident."

"Grant asked me for a great deal of money," Christy admitted in a hushed tone. "He promised to sign the papers giving me the baby if I gave him the money."

Candy nodded. "I thought as much. I'm really sorry, Christy. It's a bad situation, and I can't help you."

"Just tell me why," Christy said, gently stroking Candy's cheek. "Why does Grant need so much money? What has he gotten himself involved in that merits that kind of cash?"

Candy opened her eyes to reveal her tears. "Drugs," she whispered. "Grant is dealing drugs. Something happened to one of his shipments, and he owes a lot of money—they'll kill him if he doesn't deliver. If you don't give him the money, no doubt he'll sell the baby to pay them off."

Christy shuddered. "Don't worry. He won't get the baby."

Candy's expression was one of dire gratitude. "Thank you, Christy. You'll never know. . ."

"Shhh," Christy replied, putting a finger to her sister's lips. With a tender kiss to Candy's forehead, Christy turned to leave. "Get some rest. I've got work to do."

"Christy?" Candy barely mouthed the name. "I love you."

"I love you, too, Sissy."

Christy drove home in silence. Thoughts of Grant and his underhanded dealings consumed her mind. Her sister wouldn't be in the hospital right now if it weren't for him. Maybe none of this would have happened—the cancer, the accidents, the infidelity—had Grant not been involved with drugs.

When Christy pulled into her drive, she wasn't surprised to find Curt's car there. Night had fallen, the temperatures had dropped down into the twenties, and without a coat, Christy was shivering noticeably when she walked through the front door of her house.

"I was worried about you," Curt said, coming to greet her as though it were routine.

"You're still here?" Christy stated, uncertain what else to say.

"I fixed us some dinner," Curt replied with a smile. He took her hand and walked to the dining room, where Christy could see he'd arranged a very intimate table for two.

"I thought you might like this," he said, expertly helping her into a chair.

Taking the seat beside her at the head of the table, Curt stared into Christy's surprised face. "Why don't you tell me where you've been and why you look so angry?"

Chapter 13

Christy started to get up from the table, then changed her mind. On one hand, she resented Curt's invasion of her privacy, and on the other, she was relieved to find someone to come home to.

"You shouldn't have done this," she said stiffly. "You can't just take over my house like it's yours."

Curt smiled. "I was just sharing. I'll restock the fridge—I promise." He handed her a plate of beef Stroganoff. The aroma of the food made Christy's mouth water and her stomach growl. She quickly realized it was the first thing she'd eaten all day.

She started to eat, but noticed that Curt bowed his head to offer a prayer for the food. Quietly, she waited, uncertain what to do and feeling very awkward.

"Father, I thank You for Christy and this food. Amen."

"That's it?" Christy asked in surprise.

Curt laughed. "I could go on and on about how fantastic I think you are, and I could ask God to fix things between us and—"

"I get the point," Christy interrupted. "I didn't mean it that way, and you know it."

Curt shrugged. "Talk to me."

Christy ate silently for several minutes and accepted some warm garlic bread from a very patient and persistent Curt.

Finally Christy knew that she couldn't keep it all inside. She put her fork down and eyed Curt as if trying to figure out how he would react to the idea of one of her own family members being involved with drug trafficking. *Not that drugs are all that unusual in this day and age,* she reminded herself, *but will Curt understand?*

As if reading her mind, Curt reached out to touch her hand. "You can trust me, Christy."

222

"I went to see my sister," she began. "I just drove around and around for a while, but I ended up at the hospital."

"But that's not what has you upset tonight, is it?"

Christy stared at Curt thoughtfully while she chewed. How should she tell him? Did one just blurt out that your brother-in-law was the neighborhood drug dealer?

Picking up her fork again, Christy played with the noodles on her plate. "My brother-in-law has asked me for a great deal of money."

"To pay the hospital bills, right?"

"No, in addition to the hospital bills," Christy replied. "My sister wants me to raise their baby, and Grant has agreed, so long as I give him the money."

"He's selling you his child? How much money did he ask for?" Curt asked suspiciously.

"Let's just say it's a very substantial amount. I asked my sister what possible reason there could be for Grant needing so much money."

"And what did she say?"

Christy looked Curt straight in the eye. "She said he's dealing drugs, and he's in trouble. He needs the money to bail himself out. If I don't provide it, he'll most likely sell the baby to pay off his suppliers."

"Is she sure?"

Christy tried to note whether he sounded shocked or not, but the truth was, he appeared totally unaffected. She took a deep breath and replied, "Yes. That's why she was coming to see me before the accident. Candy said they've lost everything of value and that Grant can't meet his obligations. That's why she was so desperate about the baby."

"And what does Grant say? Does he know that you know about the drugs?"

"Grant told me that as long as I pay Candy's hospital bill and give him the money he's asked for, I can have the baby."

"And you believe him?"

Christy realized it did sound rather stupid to trust a man like Grant to keep his word on a matter. "I don't think I have much of a choice," she said softly. "I didn't know what else to do. I can't let him take the baby, and now that I know he's involved in something like this, well, I probably should call the police. Do you think I should?"

"For now," Curt began slowly, "you should probably keep it to yourself. After all, if Grant gets wind that the police know what he's up to, there's no telling what he'll do once the baby is born."

Christy nodded. It all made sense to her.

"I am curious, though," Curt continued, "have you thought about the responsibilities of raising a baby alone?"

Christy bit at her lower lip and refused to meet his eyes. "I suppose I can't fully understand the responsibility," she confessed. "But I do know that I'll love that baby almost as much as its biological mother would. No one else can give it that." She seemed defensive and almost frightened.

"No one could doubt that you would love the child, Christy. I just wondered if you understood how time-consuming it would be."

"There's no other choice," she whispered, and her eyes were filled with conflict. "I have to do this. There's no one else. Erik certainly can't be responsible for an infant. At least I can stay home and be here with it."

"What about a father?" Curt asked gently. "Every baby deserves two parents."

"What we deserve and what we get in life are usually two different things," Christy said rather bitterly.

"That's true enough, but, Christy, you can't deny that a mother and a father would be better than a single working mom."

"Better? I don't know. More convenient and perhaps easier, yes. But I can't say that two parents are more ideal unless I know who the two parents are. I can give the baby a home and a mother," Christy said as though reasoning with herself. "I am financially secure."

"There's more to offering a good home and security than the financial aspect," Curt reminded her. "You can't be everywhere at once, Christy. You'll wear yourself out, and then what good will you be to the baby or to yourself?"

"If you know a better way, I'm open to suggestions," Christy stated, getting to her feet. "But if that way includes giving the baby over to someone else, then don't bother to tell me about it."

Curt got up slowly and put his napkin on the table. He walked to where Christy stood looking so strong and determined and encircled her with his arms. "We could do it together, Christy. You could marry me."

Christy's mouth dropped open and the shocked expression on her face said more than words ever could. Curt remained undaunted, however.

"I mean it. It's not such a bad idea. You know I've come to care for you. I want us to work through our differences and—"

"Be parents?" she interjected.

"I'd like very much for us to be parents, one day. With kids of our own and all the trappings that go with frumpy old married life. I enjoy your company, Christy, and I think we're good for each other."

Christy pushed at his chest, but Curt held her firmly. "Ah, Christy," he whispered against her ear, "I could take care of you and the baby. You wouldn't have to face this alone, and you wouldn't have to be so afraid."

"You only want to marry me because you can't have Debbie," she said and pulled away. This time Curt let her go.

"You're on the rebound, Curt. You just want to get married. I've seen it before in my friends, and it never works out. I don't think we should see each other anymore because you'll just go on putting your love for Debbie into what you imagine we could have in its place. I won't be the other woman."

Christy walked out of the room and left Curt to contemplate her words.

"I don't love Debbie," he called out, and Christy stopped. "Debbie and I were always meant just to be friends."

Christy felt her heart give a jump. "Curt, I—"

The telephone rang and before Curt could stop her, Christy went to answer it.

"Hello?" Christy waited for a moment. "Yes, this is she." Several seconds passed, and Christy heaved a heavy sigh. "I'll be right there." She hung up the phone and felt her heart break.

"The hospital?" Curt questioned.

"Yes," she murmured, turning to him. "They can't find Grant, and they need me to sign some papers. Candy's on a respirator now, and they have to take the baby by cesarean. They don't expect Candy to live through the surgery."

Chapter 14

Grant was still unavailable when Christy and Curt reached the hospital. Because of this and the lack of time to do otherwise, Christy was given a battery of papers to complete and sign, all while the nurse told her what was about to take place. Candy had already been taken to surgery and was barely holding her own. Her blood pressure had steadily dropped to the point where the doctors knew they had come to the end of waiting. If the baby was to survive, they would have to take it now. With a shaky hand, Christy filled in the appropriate information, glancing from time to time at Curt as though looking for reassurance.

"What about your parents?" Curt questioned after the nurse had left the room.

Christy grimaced. "Dad is in Australia with his latest wife. His job is very demanding, and he can't leave. It's typical for him, and the only reason we called him was to be able to say we did it."

"And your mother?"

"I let Erik call her. She's in Europe."

With nothing more to say about the matter, they sat in the sterile silence of the private waiting room. *This,* Christy thought, *is where they isolate the family who is about to lose someone to death. This is where they keep you so you can't upset everyone else when you get the bad news.*

Christy was grateful when Erik showed up. Refusing to have anything further to do with her brother-in-law, she gave Erik the job of trying to find Grant and took up the duty of pacing the room for herself.

Everything in her life was about to change. How could she prepare herself? Within a short time she would be responsible for a baby. Not her own baby, but her dying sister's baby. What in the world gave her the impression that she could take on such a job? Feeling panic rise like bile in her throat, Christy looked once again to the stalwart man who'd pledged to see her through this ordeal. Curt sat silently nearby, never once trying to force her to sit. He seemed to understand her needs. He nodded at her as if to say, "Yes, I'm still here, and I always will be." It gave her a fragment of peace, and she took a deep breath before she began to walk the confines of the room again.

With Erik spending most of his time down the hall at a pay phone, Christy was very aware of her privacy with Curt. All at once, she stopped, looked at him for a moment, then came to sit on the edge of the sofa beside him.

In her mind were questions. Questions about life after death and Candy and Erik's understanding about what would happen. Suddenly it was very important for Christy to understand as well.

"Curt," she began softly, "you said that you were a Christian." He nodded. "So you know about this eternal life stuff, right?"

Curt smiled. "Yeah, I know about it."

"Candy told me that Erik had helped her to understand and that she wasn't afraid anymore. You know—about what would happen after she died." Christy felt as though she were rambling. "I just wondered, what is it that she understood? How can she not be afraid?"

Curt took hold of Christy's cold hands and rubbed them gently. "She knows where she's going," he offered casually. "Candy no doubt accepted Christ as her Savior. Are you familiar with the plan of salvation?"

"Not really," Christy admitted. "I've heard about getting saved and the fires of hell and all of that, but I don't really understand or know much about it."

Curt wasn't the least bit condemning for her ignorance, and Christy took a genuine interest in what he shared with her next. "God sent His Son, Jesus, into the world. It was a gift that He offered in order to help people reconcile themselves to Him. Jesus' sole purpose was to come and bridge the gap between God and mankind, and it cost Him His life so that it wouldn't cost us ours."

"But everybody dies," Christy said, as though it would be news to Curt.

"Sure," Curt nodded, "everyone dies once. The Bible says that's something that happens because of our physical limitations. But we don't have to die twice."

"I don't understand."

"Spiritually. The Bible was talking about spiritual death. If you accept Christ as your Savior and bridge that gap to God, you don't have to die spiritually and be forever separated from God. People sometimes get all wrapped up in the image of hell as this burning place with the devil and his pitchfork. They shudder in revulsion at that image, yet they miss the bigger picture. Hell isn't just physical suffering and torment; it's separation from God. It's the ultimate realization that you have completely negated your existence in God's eyes."

Christy stared at him for a moment. "If God is so good, why doesn't He just fix things permanently with people so that they won't go to hell?"

"Because He gives us a choice. He doesn't force a relationship on us. He lets us taste of His goodness, His peace, and His love. Then He lets us decide for ourselves."

"But if that's true," Christy said, trying desperately to sort through Curt's statement, "if God is truly offering all this wonderful goodness, why would anyone choose any other way?"

Curt smiled. "Good question. Ask yourself, what keeps me from giving my life to God? Maybe you'll find the answer to your own question."

Just then, Erik returned. "I finally reached Grant on his car phone. He's on his way up."

Christy nodded and moved away from Curt. "I think I'd like to be alone for a few minutes."

"I was just about to suggest some coffee," Erik replied. "Curt, you want to join me?"

"Sure," he answered and looked at Christy. "We'll bring you back some."

"Thanks," she murmured and went to stare out the window into the Denver night.

This God stuff was new to her in many ways, and in other ways it wasn't at all foreign. Erik had tried on more than one occasion to talk to her about Christianity. Christy remembered telling him that she wasn't interested—that he might need God, but she certainly didn't. Now she wasn't so sure.

Minutes ticked by, and Christy wondered silently why God had brought her to this point in her life. She'd been so many places and done so many things, and yet, all in all, this was the hardest.

"So what seems to be the problem now?"

Christy whirled around to find Grant standing there, looking for all the world like he was bored.

"Your wife is about to die, and your baby is about to be born," Christy replied sarcastically. She came to Grant and stood only inches from him. "We just thought you might like to know."

"The only thing I want to know is whether or not you have my money." Grant's statement clarified any possibility that he felt concern about the situation.

"I'm working on it," Christy spat the words. "You could at least pretend you care about them."

"Why? To salve your conscience? To make this easier for you and your brother? I don't think so," Grant said in a heartless manner and looked at his watch. "I just want the matter settled. I haven't got time for games."

"This isn't a game!" Christy exclaimed.

"Keep your voice down," Grant said, taking on a threatening appearance. "I don't need any hassles, Christy. Just get me the money, or you'll never see the baby. It's that simple."

Curt had returned with Christy's coffee, but seeing her with the stranger, he held back in the shadows just outside the waiting room. He could see that Christy was mad. She was ranting at the man, who stood with his back to the door. Curt realized it was probably her brother-in-law and started to go into the room, but something held him back. If it was her brother-in-law, then this was the man he was after. This man, Grant Burks, was possibly the man responsible for his parents' death, and Curt wasn't about to let him get away by blowing his cover.

It looked as though they were about to end their conversation, so Curt moved away from the room and waited out of sight. He watched and nearly dropped the coffee, however, as the man turned to stalk out of the room. It wasn't Grant Burks at all. It was Cheryl Fairchild's fiancé, Stratton McFarland.

Curt started to approach the man, then thought better of it. Turning away as Stratton rushed by, Curt could hardly wait to get back to Christy and find out why she had been arguing with McFarland.

Christy appeared shaken and was even more reserved than before when Curt approached her with the coffee. "Who was that?" he motioned with his head in the direction McFarland had just disappeared.

"That was my brother-in-law, Grant," Christy said, taking the coffee from Curt's hand.

Curt began to put two and two together and didn't like what he came up with. Grant Burks was posing as Stratton McFarland, or vice versa. Either way, he was living two completely different lives, with women at both ends and an uncertain, but obvious, relationship to the drugs that had cost Curt's mother and father their lives.

"Christy," Curt suddenly found himself saying, "what do you really know about him?"

"Grant?"

"Yes," Curt said, his eyes narrowing in concentrated interest. "Have you known him long?"

"Not long, really. About a year I guess. He and Candy met through mutual friends and were married nearly a month later. They eloped and didn't even bother to tell anyone until they were back from their honeymoon. Why?"

"I was just curious," Curt replied.

"Where's Erik?" Christy asked, completely unconcerned with Curt's questions about Grant.

"He said he'd be here shortly. Here he is now," Curt said and nodded toward the door. Erik entered with the doctor, who Curt immediately recognized as the man who was to perform Candy's surgery. Erik had tears on his face.

"Your sister gave birth to a little girl," the doctor said softly. "She appears to be healthy and strong. Erik tells me that Candy wanted to name her Sarah."

"Yes," Christy whispered and felt Curt come to stand beside her.

"Well, they've taken Sarah to the intensive care nursery where she'll be monitored and given all of the attention she needs. You can visit her there every day, and I encourage you to start bonding to her immediately. That is, if you're still going to be the one who adopts her."

"I am," Christy said, hardly able to say the words that followed. "What about my sister?"

The doctor shook his head. "She lasted much longer than any of us expected, but she just wasn't strong enough to last through the surgery."

Christy stood bone stiff, not even breathing.

"I'm sorry, Miss Connors. It's never easy to lose someone you love."

"I want to see her," Christy blurted out. All three men looked at her questioningly.

"The baby will need to be cleaned up and evaluated before I can let you see her," the doctor said.

"No," Christy replied and turned to Curt, "I want to see my sister. I need to say good-bye."

Curt nodded and looked to the doctor. "It's all right. I'll be with her."

"Me, too," Erik chimed in possessively.

The doctor drew a deep breath. "I'll have the O.R. team clear out and then take you back."

Minutes later, Curt led Christy, with Erik following close behind, to the small recovery room where Candy's body had been moved. Thoughtfully, the doctor had already pulled the sheet down to lie just under Candy's serene face. *She looks like she's only sleeping,* Christy thought. She reached out to touch her sister's still warm cheek. Didn't dead people get all cold and stiff?

Christy shook her head mutely. The doctor was saying something, but she couldn't hear it. Her mind was blurred with the images of a little girl dancing around the room, showing off her frilly dress, talking about her new doll. Candy was gone, and all that remained were fuzzy memories and a tiny infant girl who they would call Sarah.

Erik cried openly, but Christy had no tears. She needed to accept this death, but in her heart there were still too many unanswered questions. Erik finally left, unable to deal with the emotions of the moment, but Curt remained by her side.

"I'm here, Sissy," Christy whispered, bending down to Candy's ear. She smoothed Candy's hair back as though she were still alive.

Reaching under the sheet, Christy gripped Candy's hand tightly. There were no words. No words at all. She just stood there, staring into the face of death and a lifetime of love. *Oh, Candy,* she thought, *you can't really be gone!*

After several minutes, Curt gently removed Candy's hand from

Christy's and led her out the door. Christy could barely make her legs walk beside Curt down the long hospital corridor. She just couldn't accept that Candy was dead.

She said nothing as they moved out into the night air. The parking garage where Curt had left his car seemed to take forever to reach. Christy felt her head grow strangely dizzy. Her legs felt as though they were weighted rubber. They'd nearly reached the car when Christy stopped.

"Are you okay?" Curt asked and reached over to lift her face to see her better in the dim parking garage light.

"I think I'm going to be sick," Christy whispered, trying desperately to focus her eyes.

"You mean throw up?"

"No," she said, shaking her head and reaching out to fight the gravity that was pulling her downward. "I think I'm going to faint."

Curt put his hands under her arms and pulled her forward. "Christy, just close your eyes, and it'll be all right. I'll carry you to the car."

"No," she whimpered against his hold. "I can walk. I never do this. I can't stand fainty women. I have to fight it."

"It's okay to be a fainty woman if you have a reason like you do."

"I have to be strong."

Christy was still unable to move, and Curt finally ignored her pleading and lifted her into his arms. "You can be strong tomorrow," he said insistently, "but right now, you'll let me take care of you."

Christy snuggled against him, feeling the blackness lift just a bit. *Yes,* she thought, *I'll let Curt take care of me, just this once.*

Chapter 15

Curt took Christy home and insisted that she go right to bed, refusing to listen to her protests.

"I'll be downstairs on the sofa," he said at the top of the steps by her bedroom door. "If you need me, just call for me. I'll hear you."

Waiting to make sure Christy actually went into her bedroom and closed the door, Curt then made his way quickly to the telephone. He dialed the number absentmindedly and waited for Debbie to answer.

"Hello?"

"Debbie, it's Curt."

"Where in the world have you been?" Her voice was edged with true concern. "I've been trying to locate you for hours."

"I know. Listen, something big has happened, and I need your help. . . ."

Minutes later, Curt dialed the second of two phone calls he knew he'd have to make. It was quite late, but there was no putting it off.

"Hello?" a sleep-filled voice sounded on the other end of the line.

"Brad, it's Curt."

"What is it?" Brad's voice immediately sounded clearer.

"Something's happened tonight, and I think you should be aware of it. I also think the time has come to get CJ out of Denver. Especially away from Cheryl." Curt's voice was a low whisper.

"Why?" Brad asked without hesitation.

"Cheryl's fiancé, Stratton McFarland, is the man at the center of our investigation. He's really a man named Grant Burks, at least I presume that's his real name. My partner is checking it out even as we speak. Look, I don't think Cheryl has any idea about the drug ring, but I can't risk it. I'm going to see Ben tomorrow, and I have no idea how it will go. It's very possible that even Ben is involved in this. We can't risk CJ being with Cheryl when things go sour. I think you'd better get her out of town."

"I understand, and I'll see to everything at this end," Brad replied.

"CJ won't like it," Curt said as if Brad wouldn't already know.

"No, she won't," Brad replied. "But she'll do what she's told—at least this once."

Curt hung up the phone and took a deep breath. If only he knew whether or not Cheryl and Ben were involved. Surely they weren't. Doug O'Sullivan had loved Ben like a brother. The families had always been inseparable. Ben would never have allowed anything bad to happen to Doug if he could have stopped it, of this Curt was certain.

"Oh, God," Curt breathed, "where are the answers?"

ॐ

Upstairs, Christy lay awake in the huge Victorian bed. She thought at first, when she'd crawled between the cool comfort of her sheets, that she'd sleep forever. But that wasn't to be the case. She felt wide awake.

Hours passed as she tossed from one side of the bed to the other, trying without luck to find a comfortable position. Why couldn't she just relax and forget about the events of the night?

Moonlight came through the window, streaking shadows across the room. Christy sat up and hugged her knees to her chest. Curt had said that Candy knew where she was going and that was why she wasn't afraid to die. But Christy didn't know where she was going. Christy felt alone and lost, so helplessly lost. The void inside was eating her alive, and she finally threw off the covers and went to find Curt. She had to settle this thing once and for all. She had to make peace with God and know where she was going.

Silently she crept down the stairs and went to the sitting room, where she knew Curt would be sleeping. She glanced at the small fire he'd built before retiring. It was dying down so that just a flicker of flames danced upward every so often. She came to stand beside the sleeping man and noticed in the dim light that he had the most beautiful eyelashes.

"Curt," she whispered his name.

"Yeah?"

The fact that he was wide awake startled her for only a moment. "I need to talk to you about God. I need. . ." Her words fell away as tears came unbidden to her eyes.

Curt sat up and pushed the covers away. "Come here," he said, patting the couch.

"I'm so lost, Curt. I'm scared and lost and empty. I don't know where I'm going. Do you understand?"

Curt reached out and wiped the tears from her cheeks. "Yes, I understand. You need to have peace in your soul. You want to know that you'll see your sister again and that God will take care of all the details and give you strength to go on."

"Yes," she whispered, nodding her head. "Oh, yes!"

There was no tone of condemnation, nor did Curt offer a pious sermon. He simply took her hand and smiled. "Isaiah 40:30–31 says, 'Even youths grow tired and weary, and young men stumble and fall; but those who hope in the Lord will renew their strength. They will soar on wings like eagles; they will run and not grow weary, they will walk and not be faint.' I always liked that verse because I was a pilot and soaring on wings like eagles was an important part of my life. But just like you, there were times when I couldn't cope and things seemed much too difficult to deal with. My mom showed me this verse when I was quite small and told me that I had a source of strength that would never fail me. All I had to do was put my hope in the Lord, and He would do the rest."

Curt continued to share God's love, and when he asked Christy if she was ready to accept salvation through Christ, she knew she was. It not only felt right, but it was clearly the only choice.

"Then we'll just pray," Curt told her softly, "and ask God to save you. We'll ask Jesus to bring you into His family forever."

Christy bit at her lower lip. "I don't know what to do. I don't know how to say it right."

"Then we'll do it together," Curt said supportively. He pulled her close. "Just repeat after me, and only say it if you really and truly mean it. God already knows your heart, Christy. He just wants you to recognize what He's already seen there."

"All right. I'm ready," she replied.

"Dear Father, I know I'm lost without You," Curt began and Christy repeated the words, knowing them to be truer than anything she'd ever spoken in her life.

"Forgive me of my sins and help me to turn away from evil, so that I might live forever with You in heaven." Again Christy echoed the words.

"I accept what Jesus did for me on the cross, dying to take my place. I ask that You would accept me now as Your child and forever keep me in Your care. In Jesus' name, amen."

Christy finished the prayer and sat silently for several minutes. She thought of Curt's words and her prayer and wondered if she would ever truly feel as though she soared on wings like eagles. Even with the assurance that she had salvation, Christy still ached from the loss of her sibling, and she faced the idea of motherhood with uncertainty.

Gently, Curt turned Christy to face him and cupped her chin in his hand. "I love you. I've loved you for a very long time, and I will always love only you."

Christy felt her heart skip a beat. "I love you, too." The words slipped out before she could guard her thoughts. Feeling almost embarrassed, she tried to turn away, but Curt would have no part of it.

"Trust me, Christy. Just as you are trusting God for your soul and eternity, trust me to love you and be faithful to you," he whispered sincerely.

"It's not easy to trust after a lifetime of hurt."

"I know, but I'm patient and," he paused and grinned broadly, "determined."

"Yes, you certainly are," Christy agreed.

"I want you to understand some things, but now isn't the right time. Please trust me in this, and when the time comes, try to remember that I love you and that you can count on that love."

Christy wondered what Curt could possibly mean. What things? She opened her mouth to ask, but Curt put his finger to her lips.

"Don't worry, sweetheart. Just trust me."

When Christy returned alone to her room, she found that sleep quickly replaced her restlessness. When morning came, she awoke refreshed, and though the memory of Candy's death dimmed her spirits, Christy realized there was hope.

She quickly showered and styled her hair. Christy decided that routine would be the best way to keep from being bogged down in grief.

Going to her desk, she reviewed her appointment book and made plans for the day. Cheryl Fairchild was coming at 9:30, so she would have to finish with her makeup and hurry if she was going to get a chance to read the paper and have her juice.

Nearly floating down the stairs with a heart lighter than she'd ever known, Christy wondered if it was her acceptance of God and His promises that made her feel so free or Curt's declaration of love.

"Good morning, sleepyhead."

Although his clothes were wrinkled, Christy thought she'd never seen a better-looking man in all her life. "Morning. I see you're cooking again." She motioned to the stove.

"Yes, but you'll find that your juice and paper are already in the usual place."

Christy shook her head and laughed. "Are you trying to push Aggie out of a job?"

"Naw, just showing you how useful I am. What's on the agenda for the day? I know you'll want to go see the baby, but what else have you got planned?"

"I have an appointment at 9:30. It's a final fitting, so it shouldn't take long. If you want to stick around and go up to the hospital with me, you're welcome to do so."

"I'd like that, Christy," Curt said, coming to place a light kiss on her forehead. "It's the first time you've ever asked me to take you somewhere."

"It's the first time you've given me a chance to ask. Usually you just jump in and demand," she said with a smile.

"Okay, I'll try to be less demanding," he said, matching her smile. "What else have you planned?"

Christy lost her smile, remembering that she'd no doubt be required to make arrangements for Candy's funeral. "My sister," she stated hesitantly, and Curt nodded. There was no need to continue, so Christy dropped the subject and went to the enclosed balcony where her juice and paper awaited her.

Curt was cleaning up the kitchen while Christy made ready for Cheryl in the fitting room. She was glad this was to be the final fitting. Cheryl Fairchild was very rich, but also very flighty. *At least,* Christy reasoned, *she must be or she wouldn't have cancelled her wedding so many times.* When the doorbell rang, Christy made her way down the hall, but not before Curt answered the door.

"Curt O'Sullivan!" Cheryl exclaimed. "What in the world are you doing here?" Christy froze in place as the perky blond continued. "I would never in a million years expect to see you here. Did CJ tell you I was coming for my final fitting today?"

Curt cast a wary look over his shoulder, and Christy met his gaze.

Cheryl was impervious to the couple's reaction. "Curt O'Sullivan and I are longtime friends," she said to Christy. "We were once engaged, but that's all water under a long, distant bridge."

Christy said nothing, concentrating instead on the fact that Cheryl Fairchild had called him Curt O'Sullivan for the second time. She finally tore her eyes from Cheryl's bubbly face and met Curt's stare. He seemed to be trying to apologize with his expression, but Christy remained unemotionally stiff.

"I have another surprise," Cheryl continued, still not realizing that any problem existed with her declaration of Curt's true identity. "I know I promised no more delays in the wedding and there aren't any, but there is a minor problem." She glanced at Curt. "I'm pregnant. I thought we might need to make sure the gown will still fit in another month."

Christy noted that Curt's face registered shock, and then, a look of almost anger seemed to penetrate his expression. Maybe he didn't like the idea that his onetime fiancée was expecting another man's child. Maybe he'd never gotten over his feelings for her. Maybe. . .

Christy shook her head and dismissed the matter from her mind. First he'd been engaged to Cheryl and then Debbie. How many more women were in his life? Curt had lied to her. He'd said she could trust him, but he'd even lied about who he really was. He wasn't Curt Kyle at all, but some man named O'Sullivan.

"Go on to the fitting room," Christy said mechanically, her eyes refusing to leave Curt's face. "The gown is hanging on the wall. Go ahead and get ready to try it on."

"You aren't miffed with me, are you?" Cheryl questioned as she came to where Christy was standing.

"What?" Christy broke contact with Curt to question Cheryl.

"This pregnancy thing," Cheryl said in explanation. "You aren't mad about it, are you?"

"No," Christy stated. "You're small enough that another month isn't going to matter that much. The dress design is such that you shouldn't have any trouble."

"Oh, good," Cheryl said and turned to Curt. "It was great seeing you again. By the way, Stratton really did enjoy meeting you the other night. He's always had a great interest in CJ and Brad. He wants us all to be close friends. Say, will you be here when I'm done with the fitting?"

Curt said nothing.

"Mr. O'Sullivan," Christy said, with pointed reference to his last name, "was just leaving."

"That's too bad. Call me, Curt. You can get the number from CJ. I want to be sure and have you come to the wedding. You know, for old time's sake."

The minute Cheryl was out of the room, Curt tried to explain. "Remember, I told you there were things I had to talk to you about. Trust me, Christy, please, just trust me."

"No. Get out!" she demanded as quietly as she could.

"You have to let me explain."

"No, I don't." Her words were guarded and low. "I never want to see you again. Now leave." She turned to go assist Cheryl and found Curt's arms pinning her in a steely grip. He pulled her against him, and Christy fought back.

"Just listen to me."

Christy brought her foot down on top of his, but it didn't phase him. She pushed and struggled against his hold, but she was no match for him. Finally, she grew quiet, and Curt released her.

She turned slowly and couldn't keep the tears from forming in her eyes. "Haven't I been through enough? Did you think it was some game you could play with me? Did Debbie even know who you were?"

"I'm sorry, Christy. I told you last night that there were things we needed to discuss, but I wanted to wait until the time was right."

"And when would that have been?" Christy questioned softly. "Maybe when we were filling out the papers for a marriage license? Oh, by the way, you won't be Mrs. Kyle, you'll be Mrs. O'Sullivan."

"Christy. . ."

"No," she shook her head, saying, "please just go. If you truly love me, then go. I can't deal with this now."

Curt reluctantly left Christy's house and had nearly reached the corporate offices of O&F Aviation before realizing where he was. It was time to talk to Ben Fairchild. There was no putting it off, and Curt had enough anger and regret burning inside to fuel the conversation.

Steeled with determination, Curt marched into the building and made his way to Ben's office, mindless of the uproar he caused when he bypassed three secretaries and kept going.

"Sir, do you have an appointment with Mr. Fairchild?" a woman questioned, dogging Curt's heels all the way to the massive door that read, "B. Fairchild, President."

"He'll see me, lady," Curt announced unemotionally. "He'll see me."

"But, sir, I have to let him know. . ."

Curt stopped with his hand on the doorknob. "I'm half-owner of this operation. You don't have to let him know anything." With that, he threw open the door and stared at the white-haired man, who looked back at him in complete shock.

"Curt!" Ben Fairchild declared, getting to his feet. "I'd heard you were in town. Come in." He seemed to look past Curt to the woman and added, "It's okay, Janice. This is Curt O'Sullivan."

The woman and Curt exchanged brief glances before she made her way out of the room and closed the door. Curt studied his father's friend for a moment, wondering silently if this man had given the order to kill his father. *Steady,* he thought. *I have to be cool about this or he'll never talk. Give him enough rope to hang on.*

"Ben, it's been a long time," Curt finally said. "I'm sorry for barging in like this, but I didn't have time to call."

"No problem, son. I've hoped you'd come home for a long time. Sit down and tell me what you've been up to. Are you home for good?"

Curt took the offered leather chair and shook his head. "I'm not sure. I heard about CJ's marriage and wanted to come see for myself that she hadn't married some bum who just wanted her money."

Ben laughed, and Curt thought it sounded a little stilted. "Aldersson has plenty of his own money. You can be sure of that. I checked before CJ married him. I wouldn't have let harm come to her."

"Really?" Curt said without thinking.

Ben's eyes narrowed questioningly. "Why do you say that?"

Curt put his elbows on the armrests and drew his fingertips together. "Ben, there are some things from the past that you and I need to talk over. I'm not real sure how to go about this, but I need some answers, and I think you may well be the one man who has them."

"Me?" Ben questioned, and this time there was no mistaking the tremble in his voice. "What kinds of things are you talking about?"

"Mom and Dad. The crash." Curt watched as the color drained from Ben's face.

"That's not an easy topic."

"I know, but it is one that needs to be settled."

"Settled? What do you mean, settled? The crash is more than five years behind us."

"Yeah, but not everything about it is five years behind us. Some things are still very much current affairs."

"Such as?"

Curt bit at his lip as if thinking of just the right words. What he wanted to do was to unnerve Ben enough that the man would jump into the conversation without Curt having to ask any questions. Waiting a minute more, Ben did just that.

"I can't tell you how hard life has been for me without your father. I loved him like a brother. He and your mother both were like family." Ben paused, shuffled some papers on his desk, then returned his gaze to Curt. "I've done my best by the business, Curt."

"No one said you didn't, Ben."

"I've had some difficulties, but I've done what I could to straighten them out. It hasn't always been easy, but maybe you could come back to work and give me a hand."

"What would Stratton McFarland do for a job then?"

"Stratton?" Ben swallowed hard, and Curt refused to cut him a single inch of space. "He's engaged to Cheryl, you know," Ben said abruptly.

"Yeah, I know. I also know a great deal more about Mr. McFarland than I think you realize."

Ben coughed spasmodically and got to his feet. "Look, Curt, I don't know what you're getting at. I don't know why you're here today, but I've tried to do good by you. I felt I owed it to your mother and father."

"Why, Ben? Because you were the reason for the crash?" Curt hadn't meant it to come out that way, but now it was said and there was nothing more to do.

Ben's breathing quickened, but Curt sat with an unmoving eye on the man.

A look washed over Ben's face that seemed at first to be one of searing pain and then almost relief. "I didn't want them to die." Curt remained silent. "I didn't want them to die!" Ben repeated emphatically. "I told Doug just to keep quiet and let me deal with things, but he was angry and out of control and I couldn't reason with him."

"So you had him killed because of your little cocaine industry?"

Ben grabbed for the desk and Curt wondered if he would fall. "How did you know about that?"

"Dad called me right after he found the shipment."

"That's impossible. He talked to me after finding it. It wasn't long after that, that he took off and. . ."

"And crashed. Dying a painful death, knowing that he had been betrayed by his best friend. Knowing that he couldn't save the life of his wife and daughter because he'd seen too much." Curt's voice was deadly calm. "Only CJ lived. Your people hadn't counted on that."

"No one was supposed to die, Curt. Your father was the best at flying. It was only a warning. They just wanted Doug to keep quiet about the drugs."

"Who wanted him quiet, Ben?"

Ben retook his seat and loosened his necktie. "Look, I'll explain everything, but you have to believe me. I never wanted your family hurt. I've carried this around inside for years, all because I couldn't keep it from happening."

"Go on." Curt still showed no emotion.

"I got O&F into some trouble. I made mistakes in the taxes, and by the time they were brought to my attention, we owed millions in back taxes. Someone came to me and promised to clear it off the books if we would cooperate and help them out in return."

"Who?"

"McFarland," Ben said weakly. "McFarland was an attorney on

staff. He's the one who found the problem with the books, and he's the one who backed me into a corner."

"McFarland? He seems to be too incompetent to accomplish something like that on his own."

"I swear it was him, Curt. He told me that if O&F would help him transport his cocaine throughout the U.S. via the air shows, he would fix the books and make sure we wouldn't be penalized for the mistake. It seemed harmless enough."

"Harmless?" The first hint of emotion came into Curt's voice. "Since when has cocaine been harmless?"

"I know how it sounds, Curt, but I was up against the wall. If we'd been found out by the feds, it would have meant an end to the business."

"Instead, it put an end to my parents' lives and nearly killed my sister. Ben, please don't expect me to be civil about this." Curt rose from the chair and pounded his fists down on the large executive desk. "Please don't tell me how harmless this was."

Ben's eyes welled with tears. "I didn't think they'd kill him. I just thought they were going to scare him. Believe me, I haven't had a peaceful moment since it happened. I even tried to get rid of McFarland, but he has me by the neck. If I fire him now, he'll prove our tax evasion to the feds."

"You're pathetic," Curt said, suddenly knowing all the answers he needed. "I can't believe you sold my father out that way. You killed him and Mother, just as surely as if you'd put a gun to their heads. And I'll tell you something else," Curt paused and straightened. "Dad blamed you. As the plane was going down he said to my mother, 'He's done us in.' CJ remembered it quite vividly. What she didn't know is that you were the 'he' responsible."

"No!" Ben cried out in such agony that Curt almost regretted his words. "I wasn't the one. I didn't make it happen!"

Curt turned to leave, knowing that if he stayed one minute more, he might lose control. "You didn't stop it, either."

Chapter 16

Christy could barely remember getting through Cheryl's fitting. Before 10:15, however, she'd sent the happily expectant Cheryl on her way and locked the house and pulled the drapes. Making her way upstairs, Christy threw herself across the bed and cried.

She had thought he was different. She was sure of it. Curt seemed so sincere, and his love of God had made her feel that he could be trusted. Why, then, had he lied to her? Why had he hidden his true identity from her? Was he in trouble, like Grant?

She heard the telephone ring several times, but certain that it would be Curt, she refused to answer it. Sometime around noon, Christy fell asleep and didn't wake up until nearly three-thirty. Uncertain that she even wanted to get up, Christy rolled over and stared at the ceiling for another fifteen minutes before giving in to her responsibilities.

When she came downstairs to the darkened rooms, she felt like crying all over again. Why couldn't she have found happiness and settled down to a peaceful life with a trustworthy man?

Coming into the darkened sitting room, Christy nearly screamed when Curt appeared in the doorway. "We have to talk."

"No. No; just go away." She tried to flee, but he pulled her back and forced her to sit.

"My name is Curtiss Kyle O'Sullivan. I grew up here in Denver, and I have a younger sister named CJ. I grew up flying because my father was a famous pilot, and he and my mother began an aviation corporation with a longtime friend, Cheryl's father, Ben Fairchild. When I was twenty-one, about six years ago, my parents were killed in an airplane crash that left my sister severely injured. Before my father died, he found drugs on one of his planes and called me to ask if I had any idea who was responsible. I didn't, but figured my father and I would work together and figure it out. But we didn't get a chance to because they sabotaged his plane and killed him."

Christy said nothing and Curt continued. "I'm an officer with the Drug Enforcement Administration, Christy. We traced drugs to your warehouse in New York. We thought you were at the center of the ring, and that's why Debbie and I posed as a couple and came to you for a gown. Debbie has never been more than a good friend and my partner. I was supposed to snoop around and learn what I could while you were fitting her for the dress."

At this Christy raised her face in stunned apprehension. "You thought I was dealing drugs?"

"It pointed to you," Curt said, finally taking a seat in the chair beside her. "But I knew the moment we met that you couldn't possibly know anything about it. I knew when I held you in my arms the night of your sister's accident that you were innocent of any wrongdoings. I also knew that I was falling in love with you."

"Don't say that. You can't possibly mean it. You were just using me to get information. Dear God, how stupid can one woman be?" Christy said with her eyes raised to the ceiling.

"It wasn't like that," Curt replied. "At first I did try to get information from you for the purpose of the investigation, but it wasn't the reason I kept coming back. I fell in love with you. My boss even threatened to take me off the case—that's how bad I was about the whole thing. I spent more time protecting your image than digging for the truth. You have to believe me, Christy."

The pleading tone wasn't lost on her. She nearly cringed at the sadness in his voice. It was almost like he knew he was fighting a final battle, and the outcome would forever change his destiny.

"I can't believe you," she whispered. "I don't even know who you are."

"Yes, you do. Down deep inside, you know the real me. The only important me. Christy, I told them all along that you were innocent. You can ask Debbie. I told her what happened this morning and that we were going to have to let you in on it or totally blow the work we'd accomplished. We have to put Grant away, Christy. He may be the person responsible for my parents' crash."

Christy shook her head. "You're just using all of this to make yourself look better."

"What can I say to convince you? I know things about you that you haven't told me. I know about your shipping schedules and your European brokers. I know that you always use T.D. Express for your shipments. What you might not know is that T.D. Express is a subsidiary of O&F Aviation, the company that I co-own with my sister and Ben Fairchild."

"All of this sounds contrived," Christy said, sniffing back tears. "I mean you start out with this story about airplanes and drugs, and you end up snooping through my house and business affairs. Where's the connection?"

"There are several, although until recently I didn't realize just how many. When I started working on finding my parents' killers, I was on my own. What I knew, I couldn't prove. Then I met up with some people in the DEA, and we became good friends. Next thing I knew, I was part of the force, making it a whole lot easier to investigate. I knew that people in O&F Aviation were involved, but I had to get proof."

"I still don't see how this connects to me. I'm a dress designer, for pity's sake."

"Christy, you have to trust me. I can't give the entire case away because it involves too many people. You have to understand, the biggest problem that's facing us in the case right now—the one that worries me about your safety—is Grant."

"Grant?" Christy questioned. "Why Grant? I mean, I know he's involved in drugs, but how does he figure into your case and why is it any of my concern?"

Curt shifted restlessly in the seat. "Cheryl Fairchild is one of your clients, and she's involved with Grant."

"Grant? Why should I believe you?"

"Because whether you care about the adults involved, the lives of two children depend on you keeping my cover intact."

"Two children?" Christy questioned curiously.

"Yes, and both of them are unfortunately Grant's."

Christy's eyes narrowed and her brows drew together as if she could somehow solve the equation that Curt put before her. "What are you saying?"

"Cheryl Fairchild is carrying Grant's baby. She knows him as Stratton McFarland, however. I met him at a party my sister gave. I thought he looked vaguely familiar, but it wasn't until I saw him arguing with you at the hospital and learned who he was that I was able to place him. I'd seen him leaving your driveway in a black Porsche. I didn't get all that good a look, however, so when I met him at CJ's, I just didn't remember."

Christy felt the blood drain from her face. She thought for a minute she might even faint.

"I'm sorry, Christy. I had to tell you because I fear for your life. I want to protect you, but I can't unless you help me. Sarah is at stake, also. You can't keep her safe by yourself. You need me and I need you, not only for this case, but for each other."

Christy remained silent, contemplating everything Curt had shared with her. It was so much to take in, yet somehow she knew it must be true.

"Cheryl's been engaged to Stratton, or Grant, for nearly a year. He must have met her right after marrying Candy," Curt continued. "He courted Cheryl in great style, but according to my sister, he was strangely absent for long periods of time, and he didn't explain his whereabouts. I presume that's when he was at home with Candy. He and Cheryl set a wedding date, and Cheryl moved back to Denver from Los Angeles—at least I think that's where they originally met—and planned her wedding. One thing after another took place to delay their plans. You should know, too, that it was Grant who insisted that Cheryl use your wedding design business. He told her, right down to the last detail, what he wanted her dress to be composed of."

"Yes, I do remember Cheryl stating on occasion that her fiancé had specified many of the materials we were to use in her gown," Christy said, forgetting that she didn't believe Curt's story.

Curt smiled for the first time since arriving. Refusing to let him have any hope in the situation, Christy immediately covered her mistake.

"Cheryl could have told you that," she replied stiffly.

"In a way, I guess she did. She told my sister, and my sister found it very strange that a man should be so involved in the design and materials of a woman's wedding dress. She even told me that Cheryl had to re-arrange her scheduled appointments with you on more than one occasion because she was trying to get Stratton-Grant to come with her and see the dress. But he knew he couldn't come here because you would recognize him as your brother-in-law."

"But why become involved at all?"

"The drugs. As best as I can figure it, Grant needed something special in a nonroutine shipment. He knew if he could get you to place a specific order, he could have the drugs or whatever it was he needed imported right along with the materials. Christy, this thing is bigger than you can imagine. The proportions for this operation outrank anything even I expected."

Christy got up and walked to the window. Lightly fingering the drapes, her mind raced with unspoken questions. Before she realized it, Curt was at her back, his hands on her arms.

"Please, Christy, please believe my love for you is real. I want to walk away from this entire matter when it's done and know that I still have you. That I haven't lost the one precious thing I have in life."

When she didn't react to his touch or respond to his voice, Curt continued. "I'll give you the money Grant's demanding for Sarah. I'll do whatever I can to prove to you that I love you and the baby. Just help me nail Grant. Help me put him away where he can't hurt anybody ever again."

"How can you be sure that Grant is responsible for the deaths of your parents?" Christy finally asked in a strained voice.

"Because Ben Fairchild told me he was."

"I just don't know," Christy finally said. "I need to think."

Curt dropped his hands. "Don't take too long," he said and added, "we don't have much time."

Christy nodded and waited for him to leave. She heard his footsteps as he went from the room and through the foyer. She heard the front door open and close, then watched as he walked down the sidewalk, not even looking back to where he knew she stood. Then he was gone, and Christy felt the emptiness in her heart fill her being.

Fool! Her mind seemed to scream the word. Her heart pounded harder. What was she supposed to do? Grant was dealing drugs and would most likely take Sarah away from her if Christy didn't do everything he told her to. Curt was involved in some major undercover sting operation, and her designer business was stuck in the middle of everything.

Fool seemed too mild a word.

Chapter 17

Christy stood with her brother at the graveside of their sister. Candy's funeral had been a quiet affair with so few people to mourn her passing that Christy felt even sadder. How could a child of nineteen pass through life and leave so little behind?

Neither her mother nor father had taken the time to come back to the United States for the service. Even Grant hadn't bothered to show up, not that Christy really expected him to. He'd given no recognition of the baby's existence, nor of Candy's passing. Why would it surprise anyone that he hadn't bothered to pay his final respects to a woman he had never respected in the first place?

"Psalm 116 says, 'I love the Lord, for he heard my voice; he heard my cry for mercy,'" the minister stated, but Christy barely heard the words. Her mind was turned back to that moment with Curt when she'd accepted the Lord as her own Savior.

"'Be at rest once more, O my soul,'" the minister recited, "'for the Lord has been good to you. For you, O Lord, have delivered my soul from death, my eyes from tears, my feet from stumbling. . . .'"

Christy thought of Curt's verse in Isaiah. *What was it? Even youths grow tired and weary, and young men stumble and fall.* . . . Christy remembered the words and felt as though a warm arm had come to wrap itself around her.

The minister's compelling voice continued the eulogy, "'I believed; therefore I said, "I am greatly afflicted." And in my dismay I said, "All men are liars."'"

Christy felt the breath go out from her as though someone had punched her in the stomach. *Those could be my own words,* she thought. Hadn't she felt men unworthy of her trust because they always lied? Wasn't it the reason she felt Curt had betrayed her? She had to struggle to pick up the rest of the psalm.

" 'Precious in the sight of the Lord is the death of his saints. O Lord, truly I am your servant; I am your servant, the son of your maid-servant; you have freed me from my chains.' " The minister paused, and Christy waited in a strange sense of anxiety for what he would say. "This young child, Camille Burks, better known to her loved ones as Candy, is now free of her chains. Her brother explained that before she died, Candy found the truth of God's love for her and felt peace in her departure from the life she knew on earth."

Tears came to Christy's eyes. She knew her desires to keep Candy on earth had been selfish, but the loss was so great and her pain so complete.

"Erik, Christy," the minister was saying, and Christy snapped her head up to meet the face of the aging man. She barely heard the words of comfort he offered, however. Curt stood not twenty feet beyond, and Debbie was at his side.

Her eyes locked with Curt's, and Christy knew that she loved him as much as she feared that she couldn't trust him. It was all she could do to remain planted beside Erik and not run to Curt for comfort. But she refused to be made a fool of. She couldn't let Curt know how much she needed him. She couldn't be vulnerable and feel the pain of betrayal again.

The short service concluded, and before Christy could say a word to Erik, he left her side and went to where Curt and Debbie stood. *So much for his support,* Christy thought. Instead of waiting for Erik to return, Christy decided to walk back to the car.

"Curt, it was good of you to come," Erik said and extended his hand.

"I thought Christy might need me, even if she doesn't think so," Curt replied. "By the way, this is Debbie. She's a good friend of mine, and we work together."

Erik smiled with genuine warmth at the exotic-looking woman. "It's a pleasure to meet you."

"Debbie, would you mind waiting at the car? I need to speak with Erik alone."

"Sure," Debbie replied and walked off, leaving the two men to talk.

Curt shifted uncomfortably for a moment, then made his mind known to Erik. "I wonder if I could ask you a favor?"

"What is it?"

"I'd like for you to take Debbie home, so that I can drive Christy home. We have to talk, but I'm not sure she'll do it unless forced to."

"And you expect me to force my sister to do something against her will? You've been a steady support, but, good grief, man, I don't know you at all," Erik stated honestly.

"I know," Curt replied. "I don't blame you for your apprehension, and sometime, when I can, I'll explain in more detail. The bottom line is that I love your sister, and I want to marry her. Right now she's hurting from all of this," Curt said, waving his hand to where Candy's coffin rested. "And she feels that I've wronged her, and in some ways, I guess I have. But, Erik, you have to understand that I want only the best for Christy. I want to love her for all time, and I want to help her raise Sarah."

"Sometimes," Erik said softly, "she can be very stubborn. She often misses what's best for her. Maybe you're exactly what she needs."

Christy, still lost in thought, glanced up to see Erik assisting Debbie into his vehicle. What was he doing?

"Christy." Curt's voice sounded from right behind her.

She whirled around to protest that her brother was deserting her, but quickly realized it was exactly what Curt had planned. How could Erik do this to her? How could he leave her?

Christy glanced back at Erik as he prepared to drive away, then to Curt as if awaiting his explanation.

"I asked him to take Debbie home so that you'd have to accept a ride from me. Christy, I want so much for you to talk to me. I want. . ." He couldn't continue. "Don't look at me like that," he whispered, coming to stand only inches from Christy.

"Look at you like what?" she asked in surprise.

"Like you expect me to hurt you. I've told you the truth—all of it. I even received a severe reprimand from my superiors."

"You did?" Christy's voice seemed to soften for a moment, then she quickly put her walls back in place. "Maybe you could just manipulate them like you did my brother." She started to stalk off, but Curt put his hand out and took hold of her arm.

"Erik realizes that my intentions toward you are honorable. I've honestly never felt this way about anyone else, Christy, and I never will. Like it or not, I'm 100 percent yours."

Christy fought between emotions of pure joy and stubborn denial. Curt always made her feel protected and cared for, but she quickly reasoned that feelings weren't enough.

"I've heard a lot of words in my life," Christy finally said. "I have a hard time putting trust in words."

"Then seek your answer in prayer. Trust God, if you can't trust me. I know you love me, Christy. I can see it in your eyes. I can feel it in your voice. When you looked up from Candy's grave and saw me, what did you feel? What did you think?"

Christy opened her mouth to say something completely untrue, but Curt put his finger to her lips. "Remember how much you hate lies."

Christy blushed, hating the fact that Curt knew her so well. "All right," she said and twisted away from his hold, "you can drive me to the hospital. I'm going to visit Sarah."

"First, answer my question. Tell me what you thought. Better yet, tell me what you wanted to do."

"You think you know me so well," Christy said sarcastically; "you tell me."

"I believe I will." By this time, Christy and Curt were the only ones left in the cemetery. "You wanted to come to me," Curt stated simply. "No. You needed to come to me. You needed me to hold you and tell you that it would be all right. We're two halves of a whole, Christy."

Christy stared at him with more surprise than she'd intended to let him see. Two halves of a whole? Could it really be that way between them?

"I love you, Christy," Curt said, taking her hands in his. "Marry me. Marry me and let me prove to you, day-by-day, just how faithful and true my love is."

Christy shook her head. "I can't." She saw the pain in his eyes and added, "At least not yet. Give me some time."

Several moments of silence filled the air around them. "All right," Curt said with great exasperation, "but I need to talk to you about the case. That I can't wait on. Has Grant contacted you about the money yet?"

Christy shook her head. "No, I haven't heard from him."

"Good. When he calls you or comes to see you, you have to let me know. We figure we can pin him down when you give him the money."

"I won't do anything that puts Sarah's life in jeopardy," Christy stated firmly.

"I wouldn't expect you to."

"If Grant believes he's being set up, he might try to hurt her, and I can't have that."

"I understand, Christy; just don't let the exchange take place without me." His voice was pleading.

"I'll do what I can," Christy replied thoughtfully. "But I won't let anyone put Sarah in the middle of this. No amount of money or retaliation is worth the life of that child."

"Just let me know," Curt said and gently took hold of her once again. "Come on. I'll take you to see her. I want to get to know her, too, you know."

Christy looked up at him and thought to herself that he would make a good father. If only she could work through her anxieties and trust him. If only there weren't so many lies already between them.

The floor of the hospital devoted to nurseries and new mothers was a far cry from the sterility of the intensive care ward. Pink and blue trimmed the halls, and photographs of babies very nearly wallpapered the lobby.

Making their way to the intensive care nursery, Christy felt very maternal. Sarah was completely dependent upon her for the future. The baby girl would one day call her Mommy, and the responsibilities were overwhelming. Almost against her will, Christy lifted her face to meet Curt's eyes.

"It'll be all right, sweetheart," he said softly, and Christy nodded as if that was all she needed to hear.

When they approached the intensive care nursery, Christy learned that Sarah was thriving beyond the anticipations of the doctors. Christy and Curt were given gowns to cover their street clothes, then taken to a private room in the back of the unit. The nurse soon reappeared with the isolette containing Sarah, and Christy found that she had to sit down in order to keep her knees from shaking too hard.

"Isn't she a dolly?" the nurse said with a joyful smile. "And she's our best patient. She's gaining weight consistently. She's up from four pounds, three ounces, to four-six. She's doing so well, in fact, that you can hold her for the first time out of the incubator. The doctor said that her lungs are in excellent shape, and if she continues to grow at this rate, he'll probably release her in a week."

"That soon?" Christy's voice was a squeaky whisper.

"Yes," the nurse replied and began opening the incubator. "Now, who wants to hold her first? You, Dad?"

Christy looked up at Curt, who was staring questioningly down at her. It all seemed so right. When she nodded, Curt eagerly held out his hands for the tiny girl.

"Have a seat, Dad," the nurse instructed. "Now Sarah can only be out of the incubator for five minutes, so you two share her. I'll go get a bottle and let you feed her while you're here. That always helps to bond adoptive parents with the newborns." The nurse waited until Curt was seated beside Christy before placing the well-wrapped baby in his arms.

Neither Curt nor Christy paid any attention to the nurse as she left the room. Their eyes were fixed on the dark-headed, ruddy infant who stared back at them with dark blue eyes.

"Oh, my," Christy whispered and felt her heart skip a beat. "She's so beautiful."

"Just like her first mom and her new mom," Curt replied. "You ready to hold her, Mommy?"

Christy swallowed hard. "I guess so." Curt moved the tiny baby ever so gently into Christy's arms, then lingered with his arm around Christy's shoulder. "I never realized just what I was doing in agreeing to take her on. Oh, Curt," she whispered in despair, "I don't know anything about this. I don't have the slightest idea of how to care for a baby."

Curt smiled lovingly and ran a finger along Christy's cheek. "We'll learn together, just as though we awaited her for nine months. We'll buy the books and read up. We'll ask questions, and since we don't have to worry about money, I'd suggest a good nanny might be in order for at least the early months." Christy nodded with a rather blank stare on her face.

"Here we are," the nurse said, handing Christy a red-nippled bottle. "Sucking is hard for her still, but she gives it all she's worth. Sarah is a fighter, for sure."

Christy smiled. "So was her mother."

"So are you," Curt added.

Chapter 18

C urt awoke on March 31 still encouraged and content from his moments at the hospital with Christy. He remembered the way she trembled when he'd handed Sarah to her. She was so needy in those moments that she hadn't even argued with him when he made suggestions for their future together.

Whistling to himself, Curt drove over to Christy's, intent on making her drop whatever else she had planned to spend the day with him.

"Good morning," he said, when Christy opened the door. *She is absolutely perfect*, he thought while surveying the black pleated skirt that hit just above her knees. She almost looked like a schoolgirl with the black-and-white plaid vest and white oxford blouse.

"Curt! I wasn't expecting you," she said in surprise.

"I know, but whatever else you were expecting to do, I want you to change it. I want you to spend the day with me."

"But. . . ," Christy stammered, "I. . .I was. . ."

"I don't want to hear it. This is a very special day, and you must be extra nice to me," Curt said with a delightful grin.

Christy raised a brow questioningly. "Why?"

"Because it's my birthday," he announced.

Christy's eyes opened wider. "Your birthday?"

"That's right," Curt said, feigning indignation. "I can have a birthday, can't I?"

"I stopped at twenty-five, personally," Christy grimaced.

"Well, today is my twenty-seventh, and I intend for you to spend it with me. How 'bout it?"

Christy sighed. "I need to go shopping for Sarah or I would."

"Shopping for Sarah sounds great!" Curt said with a laugh. "We can even use my credit cards."

"No, I won't have you paying for her things," Christy protested.

Curt crossed his arms and gave Christy a determined stare. "Either I pay or we don't go."

"I'll just go without you then," Christy said and reached back for her purse on the foyer table.

"Nope. I won't let you go without me, and with me, you get my credit cards. Come on, Christy. Let me do this for Sarah. I'm rich, remember?"

Christy shook her head. "You're also very determined, stubborn, and—"

"I get the picture," Curt replied, looping his arm through Christy's. "It means I get to pay for everything." The smile on his face was one of triumph.

"Fine," Christy said, waving her free hand. "You can pay for everything. I have an entire nursery to stock, plus her wardrobe, formula, diapers, and toys. I hope you have an extensive credit line, Mr. O'Sullivan."

"Spend to your heart's delight, Miss Connors, and get used to it."

"Get used to it?"

"That's right," Curt replied, reaching to pull the door closed behind them. "After yesterday, I intend to make myself a part of this family by any means necessary. If I can do it by wooing and charming you, I will. If I have to resort to other methods, well, let's just say, I'll do what I have to. I have friends in high places," he said and looked heavenward.

Christy couldn't help but laugh. "Yeah, I'm sure I'm already outnumbered."

Three hours and ten stores later, Christy and Curt sat in complete exhaustion at a small restaurant. Christy was going over an extensive list, while Curt was studying her.

"We still haven't found a crib," Christy noted. "We should also pick up a. . ." She halted when she realized he was watching her. "What? Did I spend too much already?"

Curt smiled. "I'm just happy." Christy could tell he truly meant it. "This is the first birthday in a very long time that I've truly been free to enjoy myself. I'm certain it has something to do with the company."

Christy flipped her hair over her shoulder and tried not to blush. Curt had a way of making her feel like she was a teenager again.

Curt reached across the table and put his hand over hers. "Thank you, Christy. Thank you for spending the day with me and making my birthday fun."

Just then the waitress returned, bringing their order, and Christy used the opportunity to escape and check her makeup. Coming back to the table, she got a sudden brainstorm and cornered the waitress.

"Today is my friend's birthday," Christy whispered and reached inside her purse to hand the woman some money. "Bring us a cake, and if you can round up any of the staff to sing and make a big fuss over him, I'll throw in an extra big tip."

The waitress giggled and nodded. "I'll get everybody out there; you just say when."

"Wait until we're nearly done, then sneak in from behind him," Christy said and quickly went back to the table.

"I missed you," Curt said lightly, when Christy sat down.

"You don't leave me alone long enough to miss you," Christy joked. The truth of the matter was that she was finding herself quite content with Curt's attentiveness.

"I just don't want you to forget me or get lonely."

"How could I? And now that Sarah will be living with me, I won't have time to get lonely."

"That reminds me," Curt said thoughtfully, "have you given thought to hiring a nanny?"

"I have, and for once, it seems that the demanding Mr. Kyle," she paused and corrected herself, "O'Sullivan has come up with a good idea."

"What do you mean, for once?" Curt questioned in mock dismay. "All of my ideas are good ones."

"That's debatable, but anyway, I intend to put Aggie to full-time, and then I'll start interviewing nannies."

"It won't be easy," Curt said between bites of food. "Sarah's welfare will have to be considered at all cost. Speaking of costs, let's not let that be a factor, all right?"

Christy smiled. "I have to be careful of money, even if you don't."

"Consider it our money," Curt said, leaving no room for discussion as he continued. "Raising a child requires a great deal of thought. There are so many things to decide: philosophies, theologies—"

"Colleges," Christy interrupted with a sarcastic tone to her voice.

"Right," Curt replied seriously. "You have to plan for the future."

"Why can't we just get her home first and then work at it a little at a time? We could decide when things come up how we'll react."

Curt grinned. Christy narrowed her eyes. "What?"

"You said 'we.' I think you're finally coming around to my way of thinking."

Christy's face grew hot. "You are absolutely impossible." She leaned forward and whispered. "Just remember, I haven't said yes to anything."

Curt appeared undaunted. "We shouldn't wait until the horse is out of the barn to decide that closing the door every night is a good idea. After all, we have to consider the other children as well."

"What other children?" Christy said, halting her forkful of French fries halfway to her mouth.

"Why, the children we're going to have together. You don't want Sarah to be an only child, do you? I mean, I always wished I had more than just one sister. You do want us to have more kids, don't you?"

Christy was so flabbergasted by his casual reference to their future parenting that she couldn't speak. Curt stared smug and self-assured at her reaction. He eased back in the chair and crossed his arms against his chest in a most satisfied manner.

"You can't take me by surprise, Christy Connors. I'll always be one step ahead of you."

The waitress's timing couldn't have been more perfect. Christy saw them coming and burst out laughing at Curt's statement.

"You will have to eat those words, Mr. O'Sullivan."

Curt started to respond, but just then a huge chocolate cake was thrust in his face with a lighted taper candle stuck in the middle, awaiting his wish. The entire restaurant staff had turned out to sing "Happy Birthday." Christy didn't know how they managed it, but they had three helium-filled balloons, which they quickly tied to the back of Curt's chair.

When they began to sing, Curt finally looked up at Christy, his mouth open in shock. The song finished, and everyone broke into cheers and laughter. They slapped Curt on the back, wished him a happy birthday once more, and went back to work.

"You were saying?" Christy questioned.

Curt shook his head. "Never mind. I'll get you for this, but never mind."

The rest of the day passed just as pleasantly as the morning. By two o'clock, they had managed to locate a beautiful Jenny Lind canopy crib. Christy fell in love with it, and in spite of the expensive price tag, Curt quickly agreed that it was a bed fit for a princess.

By five o'clock, it was clouding up, the sun was heading for the majestic backdrop of the Rockies, and Curt decided they'd better return to Christy's house. With promised delivery of all the furniture they'd purchased, Curt and Christy hoisted what seemed like hundreds of bags of clothing, diapers, toys, and food into the small sports car.

"I guess I'll need a bigger car," Curt said casually.

"Maybe even a semi for all those kids you have planned," Christy quipped and walked off.

Back at the house, Christy and Curt brought all their purchases inside and deposited them by the front door. Noting Christy's weariness, Curt led her outside to the porch swing where he had first held her.

As the swing eased into a gentle rhythm, Christy let Curt pull her into his arms and lay her head upon his shoulder. She enjoyed the feeling of being cared for, and Curt was more than happy to meet her obvious need. Rocking back and forth in the fading light, Christy couldn't imagine a more perfect ending to the perfect day. For the first time in weeks, she'd forgotten about Candy and Grant. She'd even forgotten Curt's deceptions and why she felt she couldn't trust him.

"You asleep?" Curt asked softly.

"No, but it's a close call," Christy murmured.

"You made my day very special, Christy. I enjoyed sharing it with you more than I'd even imagined."

"Me, too," Christy admitted in the security of his arms. "Happy birthday."

"Christy?"

"Ummm?"

"I love you." The simple statement filled all the loneliness in Christy's heart.

"Yes, I know," she whispered. "And I love you."

Curt smiled. He'd only dreamed that she'd be willing to admit it again. They rocked in silence for several more minutes before he stopped the swing and maneuvered himself from Christy's side.

Christy stretched and moaned in complaint of being disturbed. With her eyes still closed, she waited for Curt to say something more. When he didn't, she opened her eyes and found him kneeling beside her.

"Marry me, Christy," he said in an almost pleading way.

Christy stared at him for a moment.

Curt smiled. "At least promise me that you'll think about it before you give me an answer. Unless, of course, the answer is yes. In that case, I'll take that right now."

Christy sat up, straightened her skirt, and tried to look very controlled and reserved. Curt laughed and got to his feet, pulling her into his arms at the same time.

"You'll never look prim and proper, so stop trying. You're exquisite and unique, and everything about you demands attention. I want to spend my life with you and Sarah. Promise me you'll think about it, please."

"I promise," she managed to whisper.

Curt allowed himself the luxury of a long passionate kiss. Christy melted into his arms, surprising him at her eagerness. He felt his breath quicken when she wrapped her arms around his neck. If ever he doubted her attraction to him, he no longer needed to concern himself with it now.

"I'd better go," he said hoarsely, knowing that if he didn't leave, he'd take her in his arms again. "Don't forget your promise."

After Curt had gone home, Christy carried the sacks of baby clothes out to her laundry room. Other people might clothe their children right away into things they bought, but the thought of doing so made Christy cringe.

Retrieving a pair of scissors, Christy began to cut tags off the outfits and sort them out according to the washing care required for each garment. While she washed the clothes, her mind went back over the day. Curt had spent thousands of dollars on a child who didn't even belong to him. Or did she?

Christy sighed. He wanted to marry her and be a father to Sarah. She tried to make a mental list of the pros and cons, and when her mind wouldn't allow her to concentrate very hard on the negative things, Christy gave up. She had promised Curt that she would consider his proposal. She didn't say how long it might take.

Turning on the television, Christy paused as the scene revealed ambulance attendants pushing a covered gurney away from a high-rise. She turned up the sound and was stunned at the announcement.

"Ben Fairchild, president of O&F Aviation was found dead this morning by members of his staff. Police are calling it a suicide, and no other further information is available to us at this time."

Christy felt her knees weaken. Cheryl's father was dead, and he had somehow been connected to Grant and the drugs. Had it truly been suicide, or was it murder? Swallowing hard, all Christy could think about was Sarah.

A cold chill settled on Christy and she shuddered. What if Grant were responsible? Would he kill his own child in order to get his own way?

"I'll give him whatever he wants," Christy said aloud. Instantly thoughts of Curt came to mind. He would need to know when Grant came for the money in order to capture him and put him in jail. Yet to involve Curt any further might threaten Sarah's safety or Curt's. In her mind she saw Ben Fairchild's sheet-covered body.

"No more death," Christy vowed. "No more."

Chapter 19

Even a week later, Christy's mind kept going back to the scene on the television. She was determined to put it behind her and believe Ben's death to be a suicide, just as the papers were now stating it had been ruled. Surely if she could put it behind her, everything would work out and Grant wouldn't cause her any more trouble.

Moving amid the boxes of newly delivered nursery furnishings, Christy grimaced at the idea of trying to put everything together on her own. She smiled when a thought to call Curt came to mind. *Curt would just love it if I gave him this responsibility,* she thought.

Before she could reconsider and stop herself, Christy picked up the phone and dialed the number she hadn't even realized she'd memorized. After three rings, Christy was just about to hang up when a breathless-sounding Curt finally answered.

"You running a marathon?" Christy questioned lightly.

"Christy? Is that you?" Curt couldn't contain his surprise.

"Yes, I'm afraid so," she said, sounding rather grim.

"Is something wrong?"

"Yes," Christy replied, trying hard not to smile.

"What is it? Is it Sarah? Grant?"

Christy began to giggle. Why did she all of a sudden feel so good inside? "I have a nursery full of boxes that are supposed to be made into cribs and dressers and changing tables and all manner of nifty baby conveniences."

Curt chuckled. "Sounds bad."

"It is," she answered. "I can skillfully design and craft beautiful clothing, but I haven't the foggiest idea what slot A is or where the double brace bolts go."

Curt laughed. "Why, Miss Connors, if I didn't know better, I'd think you were asking for help."

There was silence for several seconds before Christy responded. "I guess I am. Do you suppose Debbie could come over and put together this crib? Sarah's due to come home from the hospital tomorrow, and if it's left to me, I'll still be trying to find the double brace bolts when the sun rises again."

Curt smiled to himself. "Debbie's busy. Something about an important dinner date with her real fiancé."

"Pity. I really would have liked to talk over several things with her."

"Oh? And just what kind of things did you have in mind?"

"Why, double brace bolts, of course," Christy laughed.

"Of course." Curt waited, saying nothing more.

"You aren't going to make this easy on me, are you?" Christy finally muttered.

"Nope." Curt's simple reply filled her ears.

"Very well," she said with a sigh. "Would you come over and help me put this crib together?"

"I'd be delighted," Curt said in a formal tone that left Christy smiling. "I'll be over in a few minutes."

"Thanks. You know the way over, and I'll do like that motel chain and leave the downstairs light on for you. I'm afraid I shall be upstairs sorting through bags of important metallic discs and little nut things and—"

"Just leave them in their little sacks and wait for me," Curt quickly interrupted. "I'll be right there."

Christy didn't have long to wait. As Curt's sports car roared into the drive, Christy wondered whether a DEA agent could get speeding tickets fixed. Maybe if the police stopped him, Curt would just tell them he was on a case.

Waiting to open the door until he knocked, Christy suddenly felt self-conscious. Things had changed between her and Curt, and while she didn't feel the same sense of betrayal that she once had, her feelings frightened her.

Curt knocked and without even waiting to look as though she was doing something other than standing with her hand on the doorknob, Christy opened the door in welcome.

"Hello," Christy said rather shyly.

"Hello." His voice was soft and warm, and Christy immediately felt her heart beat faster. Curt came into the house, and when Christy did nothing but stand there, he asked, "So where's the nursery?"

"At the head of the stairs," she announced and led the way.

Opening the door opposite her bedroom, she went to where the instructions for the crib lay, with four bags of bolts, nuts, and other pieces that she couldn't name. Picking them up, she thrust them into Curt's hands.

"I defy you to find the double brace bolts," she said with as much reserve as she could.

Curt laughed, glanced for a moment at the instructions, then at the bag, and finally held up the smallest of the four. "These, my dear Christy, are double brace bolts."

Christy looked at the drawing on the instruction page, then back to the bag, and returned her gaze to Curt's amused face. "Dumb luck," she replied and went in the direction of the door. "You create the crib. I'll go get us some refreshments."

"You sure you can cook?" Curt teased.

Christy popped her head back around the door. "You mean to tell me that you plan to spend the rest of your life with me, and you still don't believe I can cook?" She hadn't really meant to refer to his marriage proposal, but the words spilled out before she could check them.

Curt's eyes twinkled mischievously as he dropped the bags of bolts and instructions and came to the doorway. "I figured it wasn't as important as other things I already knew you were good at."

"Such as?"

"I already know that you can sew like a dream," he smiled. "And you can handle a caterer with the greatest of ease, and you wear expensive clothes better than anyone I know."

Christy feigned a look of disgust. "You're hopeless. You know nothing about me except for what your DEA dossier tells you." She started to walk away, but Curt quickly pulled her back.

"My files didn't tell me what a great kisser you are," he said and lowered his lips quickly to hers before she could protest.

Christy melted against him and sighed. She wanted to forget all her fears. She wanted to give in and tell Curt that she would marry him.

Curt pulled away, and Christy opened her eyes to find him staring down thoughtfully at her expression. "I can always hire a cook."

Christy smiled and pushed him away playfully. "And I can hire a crib builder, and I will if you don't get back to work."

The evening passed in a state of near perfection, as far as Christy was concerned. Curt continued to tease and joke about her kitchen skills, but when he tried her almond cheesecake, he stopped laughing and had seconds.

They worked well together, putting not only the crib into sturdy order, but the dressing table, baby swing, and bassinet, as well. Curt finally noticed that it was nearly eleven o'clock and held up his hands to halt their operation.

"Enough for tonight. What we haven't finished, we can do tomorrow after we bring her home."

Christy yawned and agreed, making her way to the door. Arm in arm, they walked down the staircase, enjoying the quiet moment together. Curt started to kiss Christy, when the telephone rang.

Christy made her way to the sitting room to pick it up. "Hello?"

"Christy, it's Grant." The color drained from Christy's face, and she hoped that Curt wouldn't pick up on her sudden trembling. She turned away, praying that Curt would just ignore her and think the call was something private, which of course it was.

"Yes," she finally managed. "What can I do for you?"

"Do you have my money?"

"I think so," she answered carefully.

"Sarah is being released tomorrow, you know. I have the lawyer's papers right here in front of me, and I'll be happy to sign them, but not before I see the money. I'll come over in the morning and—"

"No!" Christy exclaimed a bit more harshly than she'd intended. "I mean, that wouldn't work for me."

"Then where?" Grant questioned irritably.

"I'm not sure," she answered softly. "Why don't you call me in the morning?"

"All right, but don't think about pulling anything stupid, or I'll take Sarah."

"Of course, I'll talk to you tomorrow. Good-bye." Christy replaced the phone with trembling hands. She bolstered her courage and turned to face Curt, who was admiring a Victorian vase.

"Planning another wedding dress?" Curt questioned without looking up from the ornate rosebud vase.

"Something like that," Christy replied. "It's late, Curt. I think you'd better go." The playfulness was gone from her voice.

"I was thinking the same thing." He replaced the vase on the Queen Anne table and walked to the door with Christy close behind him.

Pausing, Curt surprised Christy by turning to take her in his arms. Christy closed her eyes, anticipating a kiss, but Curt did nothing until she opened her eyes. Then just as suddenly as he'd held her, he released her and walked out the door.

Christy followed him outside and stood at the top of the porch stairs. At the bottom step, with something between sorrow and anger in his eyes, Curt spoke. "Sooner or later," he said stiffly, "you're going to learn to trust me. I'm not a fool, Christy. People don't call at this hour of the night to arrange for a wedding dress." With that, he walked to his car and drove away, leaving Christy feeling as though she were a small child who had just received a reprimand.

Aching to explain, Christy sighed deeply and went back inside. *Dear God,* she prayed silently, locking the door and turning off the downstairs lights, *how can I tell him? How can I allow Curt to get in the middle of this thing?*

After a restless night, Christy awoke to the telephone ringing. Her house might as well be Grand Central Station for all the endless interruptions. Certain that it would be Grant, Christy was stunned when one of the nurses she'd become well-acquainted with at the hospital spoke from the other end.

"Christy, I just wanted to call and let you know that Sarah's father picked her up a few minutes ago."

Christy felt as though she was going to be ill. Had she truly heard the woman correctly? "Are you sure?"

"Yes, I'm sure. I was so surprised, but he had all the correct identification. I figured he must have changed his mind about raising her. I just wanted to call and make sure you were all right. I know how much you were looking forward to taking Sarah home."

"Thanks," Christy whispered, trying to wipe away tears and sleep from her eyes. She hung up the phone without waiting for the woman to say anything more. Grant had Sarah! Now the real waiting game would begin.

Christy flew into action. She got dressed as fast as she could and hurriedly put her makeup on before rushing downstairs to get her bankbook. She had to get Grant's money before he called and expected the exchange. She was nearly out the door when Curt appeared.

"Going somewhere?" he asked casually, then continued, "Of course you are. Sarah's coming home today. Come on, I'll drive you."

"No, that won't be necessary," Christy said rather abruptly.

"You aren't going to punish me because I forced your hand last night, are you?"

Christy felt her breath quicken. If she didn't hurry and get to the bank, Grant might call while she was out, and she would miss knowing where they were to meet. "I'm not upset with you!"

"You sound upset," Curt replied softly. "What's wrong, Christy?"

Christy wanted so badly to break down and tell Curt everything. But fear won out, and she shook her head.

"I have to go somewhere, and I need to do it quickly. I can't pick up Sarah until later," she lied, while telling herself it wasn't a lie because she didn't know when Grant would allow her to exchange Sarah for the money.

"I could drive you," Curt insisted.

"No, I—" The phone rang and broke Christy's train of thought as she jumped. Hurrying back into the house, she picked up the phone.

"Do you have it?" Grant questioned.

"Yes," she said, "at least I will. I have to stop by the bank." She didn't realize until she felt Curt's hands on her shoulders that he had followed her into the house.

"I'll expect you at ten," Grant told her and gave her instructions to a nearby shopping mall.

"I understand," Christy replied and hung the phone up. Curt's hands felt like heavy weights. Weights of truth and trust that threatened to unnerve her reasoning.

Relying on old modeling skills, Christy turned with a smile fixed on her face. "I really have to go, Curt. I'll see you later and then maybe you can help me get Sarah." Her hands were shaking, so she held them together tightly, hoping that Curt wouldn't notice.

"All right, Christy. I'll come back later."

Christy nodded, not trusting herself to speak, and waited until Curt's car was well down the road before heading out to her own car. Then, just as she started to back up, a delivery truck pulled up to the end of her driveway and blocked her exit.

"You Ms. Connors?" the deliveryman questioned.

"Yes," Christy replied, getting out of the car. "Look, I'm in a bit of a hurry. Can I help you?"

"I have a delivery here for you. Just sign on the line," he said, handing her a small computerized tablet and marking pen.

Christy signed and handed the machine back to the man, shaking her head. "I don't remember any shipment being due in. Can you tell me what it is?"

The man punched something into the computer. "Looks like material from Ireland."

"But that should have been shipped to New York, not here," Christy protested. "I have a warehouse waiting for this."

"I can't help that, ma'am. I have to leave it here with you. Just show me where."

Christy threw up her hands in exasperation. "All right," she said, fumbling for her house key. "Bring it inside, but please hurry."

Chapter 20

Christy barely made it to the designated place by the appointed time. She glanced nervously up and down the corridor of the busy shopping mall. Where was Grant? It only took a moment before he appeared, and when he did, Christy's chest constricted in fear. Sarah was not with him.

"Did you get my money?" he questioned.

"Yes, but where's Sarah?"

"She's safe. For now that's all you need to know." Grant casually toyed with his sunglasses.

"That's not good enough," Christy protested and hugged the briefcase of money close. "You can't have this money without giving me Sarah and the paperwork that gives her to me legally."

Grant considered his sister-in-law for a moment, then stuffed the sunglasses into his pocket and took hold of Christy's upper arm.

"You will listen to me and do just as I tell you; otherwise, you will never see Sarah."

Christy cringed at Grant's touch and words, but nevertheless let him lead her to a small bench.

"What do you want? I brought the money, and I've already paid for all of the hospital and funeral expenses," Christy said in an exasperated whisper.

"You have a shipment that I need," Grant began to explain. "I don't know what all Candy told you, but if I knew my little wife the way I think I did, then I'm certain she told you everything about me. Is that true?"

Christy nodded. "I know about the drugs, if that's what you mean."

Grant's face tightened uncomfortably for a moment. "That's exactly what I mean." He glanced around as if expecting someone to be watching them. Grant returned his stare to Christy's nervous face. "You haven't told anyone else about me, have you?"

270

Christy knew that Sarah's safety would depend on her answer. She could feel her palms grow damp with sweat. Slowly, with as much confidence as she could muster, Christy faced Grant. "Who would I tell? Erik? Like he isn't devastated enough with losing Candy. They were quite close, you know. This won't be something he gets over quickly. I couldn't burden him with the fact that you're the local drug czar."

Grant laughed softly, and he put his arm around Christy as though they were lovers, not mortal enemies. When Christy tried to pull away, Grant pressed his hand painfully against her shoulder. "Stay put and listen. I don't want this to appear to anyone else as anything less than an intimate moment."

Christy settled down. *This is for Sarah,* she reminded herself.

"Good," he murmured against her ear. "Now listen carefully. Have you received a shipment that you weren't expecting?"

Christy nodded, unable to speak. Her throat felt as though it were about to swell shut. She fought to control her emotions, but fear was quickly edging out all other thoughts and feelings.

Grant was running his hand down her arm in a much-too-familiar manner. "The shipment was intended for your warehouse in New York, correct?" Again, Christy nodded. "That's what I thought. Somewhere along the way, this particular crate was accidently rerouted to you here. It contains a great deal of high-grade cocaine, and it belongs to me."

Christy felt as though she couldn't breathe. A priceless shipment of cocaine was sitting in her storeroom, a DEA agent was looking at every turn for some way he could lay his hand on the killer of his parents, and a tiny helpless infant was the only bargaining chip offered.

"I want my goods, Christy. Until I get them, you can't have Sarah."

"I certainly don't want your drugs. Come get them and bring me Sarah!" Christy exclaimed.

"No, you could easily arrange for someone to be there. You go home and get the stuff loaded into your car. I'll call you just before we're to meet, and if you dare to try and cross me up, you'll never see Sarah again. Understand?"

Christy felt angrier than she'd ever been, but she clenched her jaw tightly and nodded.

"Good, now hand over the money and—"

"Oh, no," Christy said, clutching the case closer. "You'll get the money and the drugs when I get my niece safely and legally delivered. You'd better make sure those papers are in order," Christy added and got to her feet before Grant could protest. "Because if they aren't, I'll torch your shipment bit by bit, until I get what I want."

Grant looked stunned, and Christy felt better just knowing she had something of importance to hold over his head.

"And I want you out of my business affairs," she snapped, not caring who heard her in the passing mall traffic. "You know what I mean, and I'll expect results immediately." She turned to leave, but Grant caught her arm and turned her back around.

"You may think you're a brave little girl, Christy, but I'm the one with the real power. Power, money, and enough dangerous friends that you could be killed before you ever knew what happened."

Christy nodded. "I know all of that Grant, and I'm not at all brave," she admitted. "I do, however, love Sarah, and I want to make a good life for her. You can't possibly hate her so much that you don't care where she ends up or with whom, do you?"

Grant shrugged. "It's immaterial to me. I never wanted a child, and I told Candy that. Now I'm telling you. It really doesn't matter if she ends up with you or with someone else. I just want my shipment and money. Be a good girl and do what I say, and I'll be cooperative and let you have Sarah. Otherwise. . ." He let the word trail into oblivion, but Christy fully understood his meaning.

The drive home seemed to take forever, but once there, Christy quickly raced through the house to the storeroom, never taking time to close the front door.

She eyed the crate suspiciously, then took a crowbar to it and pried off the lid. The first few layers were devoted to packing materials and Irish lace. Beneath that, however, were neatly placed rows of brown paper-wrapped packages the size of bricks. Christy picked one up and tore the paper away to reveal her worst fears. Slamming the package back in the crate, Christy steadied herself against a nearby chair. What was she going to do? This was even worse than giving Grant the money, because now he was making her a part of his drug trafficking.

"The door was open, and I thought maybe something was wrong,"

Curt said from the doorway.

Christy shrieked, calmed herself, then quickly pulled the lid to the crate back in place.

Curt came forward with a frown. "I didn't mean to startle you. Are you okay?"

"I. . .I'm. . .it's just that. . ." Christy gave up and tried to settle her nerves.

Curt reached out and took Christy's face in his hands. "What's wrong, Christy?"

"Nothing." She looked away.

"You're lying to me," he said softly. "Trust me, Christy. I love you, remember?"

Christy felt a lifetime of regret wash over her. If she couldn't trust Curt, then how could she love him? And she did love him. She loved him so much it broke her heart to think of losing him.

"Where's Sarah?"

"Huh?" Christy questioned dumbly. She was standing between a DEA officer and millions of dollars' worth of cocaine. How could she possibly think of Sarah?

"You remember, Sarah?" Curt said in low even tones. His calm was driving Christy crazy. She couldn't tell him about Grant's demands. She couldn't tell him about the drugs. Weren't DEA officers required to turn over such evidence? And if he did, she wouldn't have what Grant wanted, and he would take Sarah away.

"Sarah's at the hospital," Christy lied and saw something akin to sorrow wash over Curt's expression. She began to tremble in earnest as his hands slid down from her face to her shoulders.

"No, she's not," Curt replied. "Grant has her."

"Wha. . .what? How did you. . .I mean. . ." Christy paused as if waiting for an answer and saw that none was coming. "How did you find out?" she finally managed to question.

Curt refused to release her. "The phone is tapped. It has been for some time." His words were matter-of-fact but couldn't have stunned Christy more. *Of course!* she thought. How foolish of her not to realize that Curt would have taken such a measure. She wanted to be angry at him for the intrusion but instead felt relieved that he knew. What he didn't know about were the drugs because she'd never talked about the drugs over the telephone.

Curt watched the color drain from her face. "I just want to help you. Can't you believe me? Can't you trust me just a little, Christy?" His voice was pleading, and Christy couldn't take the pressure anymore.

"I'm so sorry, Curt." She began to cry, and Curt pulled her into his arms.

"It's all right. I guess I'd have done the same thing if I thought someone I loved was in danger. Caring for someone and seeing them hurt makes you do strange things. I'm proof of that."

"I didn't know until this morning," Christy whispered between sobs. "I wanted to tell you, but. . ." She stopped and pulled away. "Curt, I'm so scared."

"I know, sweetheart, but I'm here to help. I want to put Grant away permanently, and then you'll never need to worry about Sarah again. We can work this out together, but you have to help me. Have you given Grant the money yet?"

"No," Christy said, shaking her head.

"But you did meet him?"

"Yes," Christy admitted hesitantly, "but he did not have Sarah with him."

"Where was she?"

"I don't know. Curt, please," she said, reaching out to take hold of his muscular arms. "I'm afraid if you interfere with this, he'll leave the country and take her away. He might even hurt her; he might hurt you. Please, Curt. Please don't interfere. I'll do anything you want. Anything!"

Curt eyed her carefully. "Anything?"

Christy nodded. "Yes. Anything! I don't want you to get killed. I'll marry you or whatever else you say, but please. . ." She began crying so hard she couldn't speak.

Curt pulled her close and waited for her to calm down before he spoke again.

"There is only one way this can work out, Christy," Curt said softly against her ear. "And that is if you love me enough to trust me with your life and Sarah's. I know it won't be easy, but I've come to love that little girl, too, and I won't see her hurt. As for my own well-being, I kind of like the idea of sticking around to marry you, but not because you don't have a choice in the matter. I want you to marry me because you can't imagine life any other way. I want you to marry me because it fulfills all your dreams and needs and desires."

Christy gripped him tightly, almost afraid to let go for fear he'd never again hold her. Grant would kill him; she just knew it.

As if reading her mind, Curt spoke again, "I'm good at my job, Christy. I've been at it for a long time. I can handle Grant and anyone else who comes between us. God has destined me to find my parents' killers, but He's also destined me to love you."

Christy drew a ragged breath. "I don't know enough about God to understand what He wants me to do."

"Then pray about it and trust your heart to do the right thing. God is righteous and good. There is no lie or deception in Him. He wants us to emulate Him, so there can be no lie or deception in His will for us."

Christy looked up into Curt's face and knew he was right. She had to take the plunge and step out in faith. She had to trust God and trust the man she loved.

"All right," she said, struggling to gain confidence. "What do you want me to do?"

Curt sighed in satisfaction. "Tell me what Grant wants you to do. Tell me where you're to meet him and when."

Chapter 21

Christy began to shake so hard that Curt pulled her back over to the chair, sat himself down in it, and pulled her to his lap.

"I'm supposed to wait for his phone call," Christy said between chattering teeth.

Curt nodded, acting as though they had all the time in the world.

Christy continued, "I have his money, and I've already paid all the hospital and funeral bills."

"Were those also part of his demands?"

Christy nodded. "He wanted the money so he could leave and start over."

"Did he want anything else?" Curt asked, never taking his eyes from Christy's tear-streaked face.

Christy thought for a moment, realizing that she needed to explain the drugs to Curt. She and Grant had only discussed them at the mall, not over the telephone. Curt might have monitored every single call she'd received, but he couldn't possibly know about her conversation at the mall. She hesitated, wanting to tell him, but knowing that if she did and he didn't allow her to meet Grant, Sarah would be lost to her forever.

She searched his face for a moment, looking for something that would tell her what she should do. Curt's eyes were filled with love and patience, and Christy wanted to wrap her arms around him and forget all about Grant and Sarah.

"Christy," Curt spoke her name in a low, hypnotic way. "You can't trust a man like Grant to live by his word. Whatever he's promised you, whatever he's demanded, you have to realize that he's dangerous and evil. Men like him never play by our kind of rules. Chances are better than not you'll show up with his money, and he'll leave you with nothing."

Christy started to protest, but Curt put a finger to her lips.

276

"I've dealt with Grant's kind before. He'll use Sarah as long as he can benefit by it. What's to keep him from returning from time to time to demand more money from you? This isn't the end of anything," Curt said in a voice betraying weariness. "It's only the beginning."

"But he promised," Christy finally remarked.

"Sure he did, honey," Curt said gently. "Look, I know you want to believe him, but ask yourself why you should. I know I've deceived you in the past, Christy, but everything is on the level now. I only did what I did because of the investigation. I didn't know you then—even if I was falling in love with you. I'm not lying to you anymore. I risked it all to confide in you, to solicit your help. Please, Christy, tell me everything. Did Grant demand anything else?"

Christy realized the moment she'd dreaded had finally come. To continue, she would either have to lie to Curt and betray her love for him, or she'd have to tell him about the drugs and hope that he'd help her. *Dear God,* she prayed silently, *please show me what to do.*

Christy got to her feet and walked over to the crate. Struggling with her emotions, she paused. Taking a deep breath, she pushed aside the lid and looked back at Curt.

"He wants this, too," she whispered. "It seems there's a great deal of cocaine in here, and Grant says it belongs to him."

Curt got to his feet, his eyes penetrating Christy's heart with their warmth and admiration. "I know," he said with a bit of a smile.

"You knew?"

"Yeah," Curt nodded. "In fact, I arranged it." He reached out and touched her face with his fingers. "Thank you for trusting me, Christy. I love you so much, and now I know you really love me, too."

Christy threw her arms around his neck. "Of course I really love you, but what are we going to do?" she questioned fearfully. "Grant says I'm to pack the drugs in my car and meet him later. He's going to call me, and if I don't do everything he says, Sarah could get hurt."

"Christy, I want you to listen to me," Curt began. "The DEA is going to work with you on this exchange, and maybe, if we all do exactly as we've planned it out, nobody will get hurt, and Grant will go to prison for a very long time. Are you with me on this?"

Christy refused to lift her head from his shoulder, but she nodded.

"Then I want to go over every detail of this with you. There will be a lot of lives at stake, not just Sarah's. I'm not at all happy about letting you participate in this exchange," Curt said, and Christy jerked away from him at this.

She opened her mouth to speak, but Curt quickly hushed her. "I know you have to be involved. I don't have to like it, though. Just as you're feeling rather protective of my life, I feel five hundred times more protective of yours. I've had training, and I know how ruthless these people can be. You haven't, and you don't know the ropes the way I do."

Christy realized that Curt was right. She would have to listen and learn, right down to the most minute detail, in order to keep blood from being shed. Blood that could be Curt's.

"Tell me what I need to do," she said softly. "I'll do whatever you say."

Curt smiled and gave her a wink. "Just keep thinking that way, and when this is all over, I'm going to cash in on those promises." Then taking her hand, he led her from the room. "The plan goes like this. . ."

❧

Christy had just finished loading her car with the drugs in just the way Curt had instructed her when the ominous ring of the telephone signaled Grant's call.

"Do you have my stuff?" Grant asked, not even bothering to identify himself.

"Yes," Christy said nervously.

"Good. Meet me back at the mall, south side. Be there at four sharp." Before Christy could respond, Grant disconnected.

Christy turned back to Curt, who sat on the sofa, calmly waiting for her to tell him everything Grant had said. "I'm to meet him at the mall at four."

"Same mall? Same place?" Curt questioned.

Christy looked surprised for a moment and Curt smiled. "I heard the first arrangement on tape, and I wasn't about to let you meet that man without protection. I was only about fifty feet away when Grant made you sit with him on the bench." He frowned at the memory. "I nearly blew my cover when he pulled you into his arms."

Christy laughed out loud, a nervous laugh that betrayed her fear and anxiety, but helped to relieve her tension. "I should have known.

You and God," she mused. "Neither one of you will let me wander far, will you?"

Curt got up and closed the space between them. "Not on your life, Christy." He kissed her soundly, then pointed Christy in the direction of the old railroad wall clock. "We have an hour and forty-five minutes. Wanna cuddle on the porch swing?"

Christy laughed and pushed away. "No!" she stated emphatically. "I want to wash all this mess off my face and start over with fresh makeup. Seems like I've spent the last few weeks crying day and night." She wiped under her eyes, knowing she probably looked a mess. "Then I want to eat something, because I feel like I might get sick if I don't. Then, if there's still time, I might sit with you on the swing, Mr. O'Sullivan."

Curt grinned. "I'll make lunch."

"I thought I proved to you that I could cook."

"You did, but I figure if I fix lunch while you fix your makeup, we'll have more time on the swing."

Christy rolled her eyes, but Curt noticed that she wasted very little time scurrying up the stairs.

As soon as she was gone from sight, Curt's grin faded and a look of worry crossed his features. Quickly he picked up the phone and dialed his team members.

"Debbie, it's Curt. I take it you heard Burks's call," he said when his partner answered the phone.

"I heard. What about Christy? Is she with us on this?"

"Yes. She showed me the drugs and told me everything Grant had demanded of her. She's going to be okay," Curt replied. "She loves me, Debbie."

"I never would have guessed," Debbie said in mock sarcasm. Curt could imagine her smiling face as she continued. "A woman would have to be made of granite not to give in to a man who pursued her as hard as you have, Curt."

"Well, I suppose I was rather enthusiastic. Anyway, the plan goes as scheduled. I'll instruct Christy where to park. You know her car; the drugs will be in the trunk. Better get our hospitality team to update Denver P.D. while this goes down."

"You got it," Debbie answered confidently. "Oh, Curt," she added hesitantly, "be careful."

"I'll most certainly do that. I've made it to twenty-seven, and now I have a woman who loves me and a baby who needs me. I've got too much at stake."

Curt hung up the phone and went to the kitchen. After putting the coffee maker to work, he pulled out wheat bread and mustard and put together roast beef and swiss sandwiches, just the way he'd once seen Christy do for herself. He was cutting a cantaloupe into slices when Christy walked into the room.

"I feel famished," she admitted and plopped down on the kitchen bar stool. "I suppose you're used to all this and it doesn't phase you much anymore, but this sneaking around detective work, isn't for me. I'd gain forty pounds in a month."

Curt laughed and put a plate of food in front of her. "You could stand a little meat on your bones." He grabbed his own plate and joined her. "The coffee will be done in just a minute. Why don't we pray?"

Christy nodded and bowed her head, waiting for Curt to speak. "Would you mind saying the blessing, Christy?"

She lifted her face for just a moment and met Curt's eyes. "I'm not sure I know what to say."

"Just speak your heart. God honors that kind of prayer over all the rhetoric and memorized poetry in the world," Curt replied and closed his eyes.

Christy bowed her head again and opened her heart. "Dear God," she whispered, "I ask You to bless the food, but even more I ask You to bless the people who are trying to help me. I ask that You guard them and protect them from Grant and his evil ways. I want so much for everything to work out. God, please don't let Sarah be harmed. And God," she paused, "please keep Curt safe. Don't let Grant hurt him, because I love him, and I intend to see to it that he marries me like he keeps asking me to do. Amen."

Curt coughed, trying to cover his amusement with Christy's statement. "I take it that was a yes," he mused.

Christy looked at him for a moment. "Yes."

"You're really going to marry me when this is all said and done?"

"Yes." She didn't even blink.

"And you're going to love me forever and give me lots of beautiful children who look just like you?" he grinned.

"Yes," she sighed.

"Good," he replied in a rather clipped, smug way. "Just so we have that straight." He had his sandwich halfway to his mouth when he glanced over and met Christy's determined stare.

"You are going to be careful, aren't you? You aren't going to play the hero and try for this to be movie-of-the-week material, are you?"

Curt put the sandwich down and reached out to take Christy's hand. "I'm going to be more careful than I ever have been in my life. Because until now, I really didn't care if I stayed on this earth or went on to live with God in heaven. But now I do, and I want to get old with you."

Christy let out a sigh of relief and glanced at her watch. Then with a mischievous smile, she began wolfing down her sandwich. She wasn't about to spend time worrying, not when the porch swing awaited them.

The calm and peace passed much too quickly, and soon Christy found herself waiting at the south mall entrance for Grant to appear. She fidgeted with her briefcase and wondered how she would ever manage to remain calm. Curt had wired her with a minimum of audio equipment so that he and the other team members could keep track of what was going on. It was imperative that she act as if nothing were amiss.

"You're right on time," Grant said, sneaking in behind her.

Christy nearly jumped a foot. She turned with an angry retort on her lips, but found Grant's arms once again empty.

"Where's Sarah?"

"She's outside in the car with a friend," Grant replied.

"I want to see her," Christy insisted. "And I want those papers."

Grant patted his pocket and pulled the papers out. "They're all signed, nice and legal. I told you, I don't want the brat. I just want the money and my drugs. You did bring both, I presume?"

"Yes," Christy replied. "I have the money here, but the drugs, of course, are in the trunk of my car."

"Good. Let's go get them," he suggested and put his hand on Christy's arm.

"No. Not until I have Sarah," she demanded. "You may have the money now, and I'll take those papers. Then when you produce Sarah,

I'll take you to my car and turn over the keys."

Grant frowned at her forceful attitude. "It isn't wise to try my patience, Christy."

"Nor is it wise to play me for a fool, Grant. I'm done playing games." She stared at him hard. "Now do we do this my way, or do I drive that shipment of coke to the nearest police station?"

"It's of little consequence to me that you have Sarah first, last, or never. But my friend knows nothing about this deal. She's innocent of everything, and you'd better not say a word to make it seem that we are doing anything out of the ordinary. I told her we were baby-sitting."

Christy nodded and extended the briefcase. "Give me the papers. I want to look at them before we leave the mall."

Grant did as Christy demanded, but glared at her severely. "You are testing me sorely, Christy. If I didn't know better, I'd think you were stalling. You did bring the drugs, didn't you?"

Christy reviewed the papers and smiled. Grant's signature was in place, and all the copies had been properly notarized. Sarah would soon belong to her.

"I'm ready to go," Christy replied. "As soon as I have Sarah, I will take you to my car. And," she added with a strained smile, "I won't let your friend know that anything out of the ordinary is taking place."

Chapter 22

Christy had never been more afraid in her life. Her hands were trembling and sweat beaded up on her temples. Somewhere in the parking lot were a tiny, innocent baby and the man she loved. Glancing up at Grant, Christy grimaced. Here was the one person who could take both of them away from her.

Grant approached the black Porsche with determined strides. "Remember what I said, Christy," he murmured. "She doesn't know anything about this."

Christy bit her tongue to keep from making a nasty remark. She had to keep peace until Sarah was safe and Curt had his chance to capture Grant. Silently she walked just behind Grant, keeping pace and watching for his slightest move.

Grant reached for the door just as it opened, and Christy was stunned to find Cheryl Fairchild sitting in the passenger seat, holding Sarah. The baby was sleeping soundly, oblivious to the dangerous scene that she was a vital part of.

"Christy!" Cheryl exclaimed. "What in the world are you doing here?"

Grant raised a silencing brow over Cheryl's head and Christy swallowed hard. "I'm here for Sarah," she said in a slow, deliberate way.

Cheryl looked down at the baby and back up to her wedding dress designer. "Do you know Stratton's sister-in-law?" she questioned.

"I beg your pardon?" Christy was momentarily stunned at Cheryl's reference to Grant as Stratton. What was it Curt had told her?

"I, uh," Christy stammered, while all reasonable thought left her mind. She looked down at Cheryl's petite face and felt instant pity for the woman. She knew Cheryl obviously loved Grant by the way she was looking up at him with those huge, trusting eyes.

"Stratton?" Cheryl questioned. "What's going on? I thought you said we were watching the baby for your sister-in-law."

Grant reached down and pulled the baby from Cheryl's arms. "We are," he replied, taking the blanket that Cheryl held out. He wrapped it haphazardly around Sarah, while she slept on.

"But, what about this?" Cheryl questioned. The confusion was clearly etched in her features, and Christy wished she could somehow ease Cheryl's worry. "I know Christy doesn't have any children, so whose baby is Sarah?"

"It isn't anything you need to worry about, Cheryl," Grant said rather brusquely. "Stay here. I have to go with Christy to her car."

Cheryl was obviously hurt by Grant's indifference to her concern. She started to say something, but Grant slammed the car door in her face and nudged Christy forward.

"Where are you parked?" he asked, holding Sarah away from Christy's reaching hands.

"Over there," Christy motioned. "Please give me the baby."

"In due time," Grant said with a sneer on his face. "I wouldn't want you getting jumpy and running out on me. Not with so much at stake." He paused for a moment, looking down at Christy rather intently. "You know, you really are the most beautiful woman I've ever known. We could still have a good time together, Christy." His leering eyes made Christy shudder, and Grant only laughed. "What's the matter, Christy? Not good enough for you?"

"Never!" Christy hissed. "You'll never be anything but trouble to any woman who is stupid enough to care for you. Look what you've done to Candy and now Cheryl. Even poor Sarah has been wounded by you."

Grant looked hard at Christy for a moment, then shrugged. "It's just the way things are," he said without emotion. "Now move out. I want to make certain you fulfilled your part of the bargain."

Christy moved across the rows of cars, wishing that she had Sarah in her arms. Before Grant opened the trunk of her car, she'd have to insist on the transfer, otherwise it would ruin Curt's plans.

They approached her vehicle slowly, and Christy had to force herself not to look around for Curt's reassuring face. Stopping at the rear of her car, Christy turned and held up her keys.

"It's in the trunk. You can have the keys, but I'll take Sarah."

Grant considered the situation, then handed the baby over to Christy and snatched the keys. Christy was almost stupefied that it had all happened so smoothly. Inching her way back along the side of the car, all Christy could think of was how she had to put some distance between her and Grant.

"Which key is it?" Grant questioned.

Christy froze in place. "The round one," she whispered.

"You're going to have to help me transfer this stuff," he said, searching for the right key.

"Why don't you just take my car?" Christy more stated than questioned. "I promise to wait at least twenty-four hours before I report it missing. In fact, if you'll just call and tell me where it's at, I won't even call it in." Christy knew she was rambling, but she had to restore some semblance of order to her mind. The chattering seemed to almost calm her into sensibility again.

Grant inserted the key and the trunk lid lifted smoothly. "Ah, yes!" he exclaimed and reached inside to inspect the cocaine. Picking up one of the wrapped packages, Grant tore off the end, played with the contents for a moment, then slipped the package into his coat pocket.

Christy was finally able to think and, as planned, moved rapidly away from the car and disappeared behind a nearby trash dumpster. Trembling from head to toe, Christy got down on the ground and covered Sarah with her body, just as Curt had instructed her.

She heard Grant call her name, and then Curt's voice rang out loud and clear.

"Drug Enforcement—you're under arrest! Put up your hands and back away from the car!"

Christy cowered in desperate fear. All she could do was pray. There was no way of knowing what else was happening. She couldn't see anything, and the not knowing was driving her insane.

Silence engulfed the parking lot. Christy could very nearly hear her own breathing above the routine noise that she knew must be taking place. Thankfully, Sarah continued to sleep.

Christy stared down at the slumbering form of her niece. *No,* she thought to herself, *Sarah is my daughter now.* Curt's voice brought her back to what was happening.

"Burks, I'm not going to tell you again. Back away from that car and put up your hands."

Curt's voice sounded louder, and Christy could only imagine that he had come out from wherever he'd been hiding. *Dear God,* she prayed, *keep him safe. Don't let him get careless in his desire to avenge his parents' death.*

೫ঌ

Curt eyed the back of Grant Burks intently. He held a 9 mm pistol at eye level and moved cautiously forward. This man was the reason CJ had suffered so much. This man had killed his parents and threatened the woman he loved. This man was scum and deserved to die. All reasoning left Curt as he felt his finger tighten on the trigger.

Without warning, Grant turned quickly and in doing so brought a small caliber revolver up and pointed it at Curt. Just then a woman screamed and Curt glanced aside briefly, fearing it was Christy. Cheryl Fairchild was running across the parking lot.

"No! No!" she screamed over and over.

"Cheryl?" Curt said, taking his concentration from Burks. Grant took the moment of Curt's surprise to fire a shot.

Curt instantly reacted and fired, as did several of the other agents. Bullets hit Grant's body, leaving tiny red stains across his midsection. He stood in shock for several moments, then raised the gun at Curt again, only this time Cheryl was in the way. She looked torn between the two men, then seeing that her fiancé was bleeding, she moved toward him just as he fired the gun twice.

Curt rushed at Cheryl like a linebacker in a critical play. Shots rang out over their heads, and Grant fell to the ground as Curt rolled with Cheryl, taking the full impact of both bodies as they hit the pavement.

Cheryl moaned once, then grew silent and still. Curt heard Debbie declare Grant disarmed. He eased Cheryl away from him. She was bleeding badly from an abdominal wound, while a thin but steady stream of blood poured from a shot she'd taken in the head.

"I need help here," Curt declared, pulling Cheryl onto her back. He straightened her body out before pushing up the bloodstained sweater.

Debbie was at his side instantly. "Ambulance is on its way. They were just on the other side of the parking lot, waiting for our signal."

Curt nodded. "She's pregnant," he said and glanced up at Debbie with serious eyes. "This shouldn't have happened."

"It's not your fault," she whispered. Sirens in the background brought Curt to his feet.

"Christy!" he said and glanced around. She was nowhere in sight.

Debbie put her hand on Curt. "You're wounded!" she said, realizing for the first time that he'd taken a bullet in the arm.

Grant was writhing and crying out from his wounds, catching Curt's attention. How could he still be alive? Ignoring Debbie's concern for his welfare, Curt moved to where other members of the DEA were working to save Grant's life.

Curt knelt down and caught Grant's eye. "I'm putting an end to this," Curt said with only a moderate amount of satisfaction. Frank had once told him that revenge was a poor substitute for the loss of someone you loved. Frank was right.

Grant stared at Curt with blank eyes. "An end to what?" He barely breathed the question.

Curt's face held a tight register of anger and sadness. "You and the O&F Aviation drug ring. You killed my parents—or maybe you don't remember Doug and Jan O'Sullivan and the plane you or your people sabotaged. They were my parents, and my little sister was on the plane as well."

"I remember," Grant replied, then laughed a hoarse, dying laugh. "Fairchild said to just shake them up. I guess I did more than shake, aghhh." Grant grabbed at his bleeding abdomen. "Too bad you weren't in that plane, too," he gasped, and then grew still. Grant Burks was dead.

"You'd better go to Christy," Debbie stated. "She needs you, Curt."

Curt sobered for a moment, then looked at Debbie. She was beautiful even with her dark hair tied back into a tight ponytail and her DEA ball cap snugly concealing even the tiniest wisps. Slowly he nodded, seeing in her eyes all that he needed to remember. Christy and the baby!

"Where are they?" he questioned.

"Over there," Debbie pointed, and Curt glanced across the parking lot to see Christy being comforted by two women team members.

Christy seemed to sense his eyes on her as he started walking toward her. One of the women accepted Sarah's sleeping form, while Christy ran to close the distance to Curt.

"Oh, Curt, my dearest love," she cried and threw herself into his arms.

Curt held her so tightly that Christy thought he would break every single one of her ribs, but she didn't care. She never wanted him to let her go, and she tightened her grip around his neck.

"It's okay, honey," he whispered. "It's okay. God was watching over us all."

"Is he," Christy tried to speak. "Is Grant. . ."

"Yes, he's dead."

Christy pulled away. "God forgive me, but I'm glad. If ever anyone deserved what he got—"

"Shhh," Curt said and put his finger to her lips. "It's over."

Christy reached out and lifted Curt's hand to her lips, then gasped in horror. Blood stained his fingers and hand. Tracing the blood up his arm, Christy cried anew at the sight of the torn material. "You're shot! You've got to get help! Debbie!" she called for the only other person she recognized.

"It's okay," Curt tried to assure her, but Christy would have no part of it.

Debbie came up with a medic. "Your turn, Curt," Debbie said and motioned Curt to the ambulance.

"How's Cheryl?" he asked, and Christy glanced past him for the first time to see the paramedics working on the blond woman.

"She's losing a lot of blood," Debbie stated. "They're doing all they can to stabilize her."

"And the baby?" Curt asked, reminding Christy of Cheryl's condition.

Debbie shook her head. "I don't know. What I do know is that you're going to go with this man right now and have that arm looked at. I can't have you going into shock here in the parking lot."

Curt grinned and drawled casually, "Yes, ma'am. I surely wouldn't want you ladies to faint at the sight of a little blood."

Debbie rolled her eyes.

"Will you take Christy and Sarah home for me?" Curt asked before turning to leave with the medic.

"Of course I will," Debbie replied.

"I want to stay with you," Christy protested.

"Sarah needs you," Curt reminded her. "Get her out of here. The press will be here any minute, and you don't want this all over the newspapers. Take her home, and I'll be there as soon as I can get away."

"But—"

Curt crossed his arms adamantly. "I won't go with them at all until you agree to go with Debbie," he stated.

"You!" Christy exclaimed in exasperation. "You are the most infuriating man. Always ordering me around, telling me where to go and with whom. Don't you think it might be nice if just once you'd let me make up my own mind about how I want to handle things?"

Curt raised a single brow as though humoring her outburst. "Look around you, sweetheart. This is what happens when I leave you to plan for yourself."

Christy opened her mouth, then closed it again. For a heartbeat, she said nothing, then turned to Debbie. "Take us home, Debbie." Then to the paramedic at Curt's side, she leaned over and whispered with a touch of a smile, "Use the stuff that stings a lot, and maybe you could sew him up with a blunt needle. If you don't have one, I do."

Curt burst out laughing. "I think I'm going to like being married to you. At least I won't be bored!"

Epilogue

Christy woke up slowly. Somewhere in the back of her subconscious, she realized that someone was kissing her. She sighed and relished the passionate lips that ran the length of her neck before capturing her mouth for a warm inviting kiss. Opening her eyes, she found Curt's steely blue ones staring down intently at her.

"Ummm," she murmured and reached up her arms to embrace his neck. "Good morning, Mr. O'Sullivan."

"Good morning, indeed, Mrs. O'Sullivan," he whispered against her mouth before reclaiming it.

Christy snuggled down against her husband of two days and smiled. "It seems strange that everything is so quiet. Sarah would normally have had us up for an hour or more by now. I'm glad CJ agreed to keep her at their place while we honeymooned."

Curt laughed. "She's got quite a set of lungs on her—I have to say that. Never realized babies could be so demanding."

"You should hear her in the middle of the night when she thinks she's starving to death and nobody's going to come feed her." Christy suddenly sobered. "You aren't sorry you married us, are you?"

"You trying to get rid of me?"

Christy pushed Curt aside and rolled up on one elbow. "I mean it," she said completely serious. "I just don't want you to regret—"

He reached up and put his hand across her mouth. "You should know by now that I rarely do anything against my will. I'm a determined man, Christy. Especially when I'm convinced that God is leading me in a particular direction. You were one of those directions in which He led me. Understand?"

Christy nodded, and Curt lowered his hand with a grin. "Besides," he continued, "I seem to recall a promise you made to do anything if I got Sarah back to you safely."

"I married you, didn't I?" she teased and flopped back against the pillows. Curt followed her and pulled her close against him.

"You don't regret it, do you?" he said, reflecting her question back at her.

"Why would I regret it?" Christy questioned innocently.

"Well, I'm not your regular guy," Curt admitted.

"No, you certainly aren't!" declared Christy with a smile. "You are most unusual. Unique, in fact."

"Unique, eh?" Curt got a mischievous look on his face. "I think I like that. One-of-a-kind. Like some of the other little treasures in your massive Victorian museum-of-a-house. Maybe you're just collecting rare priceless pieces."

"Or little bits of junk that nobody else will have," Christy teased.

"What a thing to say!" Curt exclaimed and began tickling Christy until she was laughing so hard, she begged him to stop.

Curt reached up and brushed back a strand of chocolate brown hair. His finger trailed down her cheek to her neck, then rested on her soft, white shoulder.

Christy stared back at her husband, no longer afraid of the stirring impact. She remembered the times she'd fought to keep from looking at his face—to keep her eyes from meeting his and feeling the power he held over her. Now she relished that feeling and sought it eagerly. Now she belonged to him in full, and nothing would ever separate them. At least she prayed nothing would. A slight frown crossed her face as Christy remembered all the infidelity in her life. Surely Curt would remain faithful. His values were different, and Christy was sure that would make all the difference.

"What are you thinking about?" Curt asked softly.

Christy shook her head. "Nothing."

"You're lying," he said firmly. "After all we've been through, is it possible that you still don't trust me?"

"Of course not!" Christy declared, but she knew there was an element of truth in his question.

"Then what made you look so sad just now?"

Christy took a deep breath and looked away. "I just don't want what we have to end."

Curt pulled her face back to his. "And you're worried that it will?"

"I can't explain it."

"Yes, you can, although I'm not sure you need to. I think I already understand," Curt said and kissed her lightly on the lips. "You're wondering when I'm going to treat you as badly as every other man in your life. Isn't that it?"

Christy's eyes widened at Curt's words. They hit their mark.

"I thought so," he said, without waiting for her to confirm his suspicions. He pulled her against him tightly and held her for several minutes without saying a word. When he did speak, he was close to tears.

"Christy, I have never cared for anyone in my life the way I care for you. I love you with all my heart, almost as though you were an extension of my soul. I know I'll make mistakes, but we'll take it one day at a time—together."

"Together," she murmured.

"Together, with God," he added. "Leave it in God's hands, Christy. Things might get difficult from time to time. That's just life. Remember that verse in Isaiah?"

"About youths getting tired and weary?"

"Not just that part. Do you remember the rest of it?"

"I don't know. I guess I kind of remember it."

" 'But those who hope in the Lord will renew their strength. They will soar on wings like eagles; they will run and not grow weary, they will walk and not be faint,' " Curt recited and added, "That's us, Christy. We've put our hope in the Lord. When the times get rough and things look impossible, God will renew our strength. He'll give us wings like eagles to fly high above and beyond the tribulation that threatens to destroy us. We can count on Him, Christy. You believe that, don't you?"

"Yes," she nodded, "more than I ever thought possible."

Sometime later, Christy stood on the deck outside the rustic cabin that she and Curt shared for their honeymoon. The log-framed hideaway was nestled amid tall ponderosa pines overlooking a small mountain lake.

Catching the crisp May breeze, Christy lifted her face to the sun's warmth and sighed. A movement overhead caught her attention, just as Curt came from inside the cabin to stand behind her.

"Look," she whispered. A solitary eagle rose on graceful wings against the rich blue of the mountain sky. His wide, powerful wings took him higher and higher until finally he achieved the heights he sought. Then the eagle sailed downward, gliding silently. Never once did he beat his wings against the wind. He simply soared across the skies, catching warm pockets of air that lifted him higher and higher, until he once again turned to drift down toward the earth.

"Wings like eagles," Christy whispered. *A perfect design,* she thought. *A design only God could create and that He offered His children in return for their hope placed in Him.*

"Wings like eagles," Curt murmured against her ear. "Wings that will take us home to Him."

Wings
of the Dawn

With thanks to Steve DeWolf,
who took me flying in his Stearman biplane
one beautiful Dallas morning and
who inadvertently taught me that often in life
you only get to answer yes or no.

Chapter 1

Everything remained unchanged. And yet nothing was the same. Cheryl Fairchild put down her small suitcase and stared at the familiar walls of her father's house. Nestled against a mountainous backdrop on one side and the Denver skyline on another, this place had been their home off and on for the last ten years. But now Ben Fairchild was dead. Dead by his own hand. Cheryl still found it impossible to believe. Any minute now he would surely call out from his office wanting to know what outlandish way Cheryl had spent money that day. Any minute now. . .

But of course, Ben Fairchild didn't call out, and Cheryl grimaced at the stuffiness of the closed-up house. For nearly four months she'd been in either the hospital or the private convalescent center, and during that time, the housekeeper had only come on Saturdays in order to keep the dust at bay. *It's evident that she never bothered to air the place or check the thermostat*, Cheryl thought, sweltering in the heat of the July afternoon.

Switching on the central air, Cheryl listened for the familiar hum of cool air blowing through the vents. When it came, it was like an old friend. Familiar. Comforting. Consistent. Forgetting the suitcase, Cheryl wandered aimlessly through the house, touching first one thing and then another, almost as if she had to force some memory from each article before she could move on to the next.

Daddy and I bought this vase in France, she remembered, idly fingering the elegant Lalique crystal. *We found it at that wonderful shop near our hotel. Daddy said, "If your mother were alive, she'd pick this one." And so we did.*

A bevy of other objects received just as much attention until Cheryl had walked completely through the spacious first floor and found herself once again standing beside her suitcase. Her side ached a little. A constant reminder of the bullet that had been surgically removed some four months earlier. The scar was still there, while the one that had marred her forehead had been expensively removed with plastic surgery. For the first time in weeks, Cheryl let herself think about the shooting. . .and Stratton.

No, she reminded herself, *his name is Grant Burks*. He wasn't Stratton McFarland as he had told her when they first met. Nor was he really Stratton McFarland when he had proposed marriage and she had accepted. And he wasn't Stratton McFarland when he had deceived her into believing that it didn't matter what you did with your life—so long as it made you happy.

She picked up the suitcase and made her way upstairs to her bedroom. Here, the heat was worse, and Cheryl thought only of a cool shower and lightweight clothes. She stripped down, leaving her designer jeans and flashy pullover on the carpet, and stepped into her private bathroom. The reflection of her hollow-eyed expression stunned Cheryl momentarily. Months before, she wouldn't have been caught dead looking so unkempt and dowdy. Her blond, curly hair looked more askew than normal, and her collarbone and ribs stuck out in an anorexic way that was most unflattering. But she didn't care anymore. There was no reason to care, because there was no one left to care for.

She showered and dressed in an oversized T-shirt that had once belonged to her father. Long ago she had claimed it for her own and used it as her favorite nightgown. Now it was just one more reminder of her father, and for the present time, she needed it to help her through the loneliness that threatened to consume her soul.

With a sigh, she sat down on her bed and noticed for the first time that a stack of mail lay there awaiting her inspection. There was something else there as well. A black book, an album of sorts, had been neatly placed beneath the mail, and it was this that drew Cheryl's attention. Cautiously, almost reverently, she opened the book and found cutout headlines representing the last six months or so of her life.

Mary must have done this, she thought. The housekeeper was fond of cutting out any public announcements of her employer and saving them for his consideration. Now, perhaps, she felt Cheryl should take over that job as well.

It seemed odd to hold the pages of one's life in a single book. The headline announcing her father's suicide opened the chapter and Cheryl forced herself to read the details aloud.

"Ben Fairchild, cofounder of O&F Aviation Corporation, was found shot to death in his downtown office today. Police are ruling the death a suicide. Fairchild was the focus of an intense Drug Enforcement Administration investigation, and it is rumored that charges were soon to be leveled in connection with a national drug smuggling ring."

Cheryl fell silent. There was no way they would ever convince her that her father had been corrupt. Ben Fairchild had been a paragon of virtue. He had given liberally to charities, had received multiple community action awards, and had never failed to make certain Cheryl had everything she needed. *He was a good father and citizen,* she assured herself. He couldn't possibly do the things they accused him of.

She turned the pages and saw articles that laid out the foundation for the DEA's suspicions toward her father. Those suspicions were only heightened when it was discovered that Ben had transferred everything he'd owned into Cheryl's name some two years prior to the investigation. Cheryl had known nothing about this. The house, the cars, stock, money markets, bank accounts, even the businesses her father had built were all officially the property of Cheryl Fairchild. It was almost too much to consider.

Toward the end of the book, Cheryl came across an article that told of her own misfortune. "DEA Drug Bust Claims Victims," the headline read. Cheryl held her breath for a moment, then let it out slowly. This was where her life had ended. This was where the love of her life had been killed and the baby she'd hoped to give him had miscarried.

"DEA Officer Curtiss O'Sullivan. . ." She couldn't read past the name. Curt had been an intricate part of her life. His father had been her father's partner in O&F Aviation. They had wooed the country with aerial barnstorming shows and biplane exhibitions. Her father had maintained the business dealings, while Curt and his father had performed the actual flying feats. Cheryl and Curt's sister, CJ, had become fast friends, while Cheryl had lost her heart completely to CJ's gangly adolescent brother.

They had grown up as one family, or very nearly. The O'Sullivans and Fairchilds were quite inseparable. They worked together, vacationed together, raised children together. *And now,* Cheryl thought, *they are dead together.*

Cheryl's mother had passed away many years earlier from cancer, and CJ and Curt's parents had died in an airplane crash. It was that same crash that had left a sixteen-year-old CJ horribly injured. Cheryl had been engaged to Curt at the time, but he'd rapidly changed after the death of his parents, and now Cheryl knew why. The night of the plane crash, Curt's father had telephoned him to say that he'd discovered cocaine on board one of the planes, and Curt immediately picked up the banner of what would become his private crusade. Their breakup had hurt, but not nearly as badly as knowing that Curt was responsible for the death of Grant, and in some ways, her baby as well.

Cheryl put her hands to her flat stomach, and a shudder ran through her from head to toe. She'd known it was wrong to give in to Grant's desires, but she'd been so confident that nothing bad could come of it. CJ had tried to warn her—to convince her that God had a better way in mind—but Cheryl wanted nothing of religion and rules. Grant showed her a side of life that said rules were unimportant so long as you had plenty of money. With plenty of money, you could buy new rules or make up your own as you went along. And Cheryl found that it worked. At least for a while.

She tried hard not to think of the child who would never be born. She tried hard not to think of the emptiness inside her when she knew the baby was gone for good. She slammed the book shut and dropped it as though it had grown red hot. She couldn't let herself think about the past anymore.

"Ha," she said sarcastically, "as if I could ever forget."

She shuffled downstairs, the T-shirt bobbing at her knees, her bare feet sinking deep into the plush, supple carpet. She had no idea what she was going to do with herself for the rest of the day, but even this seemed taken from her control at the sound of the doorbell.

She pushed back damp curls and stared at the door for several moments. *Who could it possibly be?* The bell rang again.

"Who. . .who is it?" Cheryl called out nervously.

"It's CJ, Cheryl. Come on and open up."

Cheryl slowly opened the door and stared at the petite red-haired woman. "I'm not up for visitors, CJ," she said flatly.

"I was worried about you," CJ said, seeming to ignore Cheryl's tone. "I thought you were going to let me bring you home."

"I never agreed to that." Cheryl noted the hurt expression on CJ's face but continued. "I told you before, I can't deal with you just now."

"I don't understand."

"It isn't that hard," Cheryl replied. "Your brother ruined my life."

"That's not really true, Cheryl, and you know it," CJ countered.

Cheryl's anger erupted without warning. "What would you know of the truth? You've lived in a shell most of your life. First with your picture-perfect family, then hidden away from the world in the misery you felt after the death of your parents." CJ paled, but Cheryl was unrelenting. "You have your husband and your wonderful life, so please don't feel like you need to show pity on me. I don't want it, nor do I need it."

"I wasn't offering you pity, Cheryl. I thought we were friends."

"Were friends," Cheryl repeated. "We were friends."

"But not now, is that it?" CJ's eyes filled with tears. "You're going to throw away a lifetime of friendship because of what has happened?"

"You say that as though nothing of great importance has transpired. As though you put a scratch on my car or a hole in my favorite sweater." Cheryl looked hard at CJ for a moment and tried to feel something other than rage. It was impossible, however. She couldn't stop the flow of words that came.

"I have lost everything that mattered to me. My father is dead. Stratton—" She paused and shook her head. "Grant is dead. My baby is dead. Do you suppose I care very much that your feelings are hurt because I don't want your friendship? Do you suppose I care at all whether I ever see you again, knowing that just seeing your face reminds me of the man who murdered my loved ones?"

CJ was now openly weeping. "Don't be like this. Curt was only doing his job." She struggled to keep control of her voice. "Curt didn't want to kill him, but Grant pulled a gun and started shooting. Those were Grant's bullets that struck you; did you forget that? He was trying to kill my brother."

Cheryl refused to be moved by the display of sorrow or by CJ's words. "Curt didn't have to start the whole thing."

"You mean let the murder of my parents go unpunished?" CJ questioned, sobering a bit. "That's it, isn't it? You'd rather my parents' murder be swept under the rug so that the business could go on as usual. Ben could have kept his little drug-ring secrets, and Grant or Stratton or whatever other name he used could go on deceiving you."

"If it meant bringing back my loved ones, then yes," Cheryl answered coldly. "Now I'd like for you to leave. I told you before that I haven't the energy to deal with this."

"But I care about you," CJ said, wiping her eyes. "I know that you're just using your anger to camouflage the pain. I want you to know that you aren't alone. I still care and so does God."

"Don't give me that religious song and dance you're so fond of. God didn't care enough to keep my baby from dying or protect my father from your brother's slanderous accusations. And God certainly didn't care about Grant."

"But you're wrong," CJ replied. "God cared for each of them. Is it His fault that Grant and Ben wanted nothing to do with Him?"

"Get out." Cheryl's voice was deadly calm. "Get out and take your God with you. I don't have to listen to this now or ever."

CJ turned to leave but hesitated for just a moment. "Cheryl, I want you to know that when you are ready for a friend, I'm here for you. I won't stop caring about you just because you say mean things, so if you're using that to push me away, it won't work."

A strange sensation coursed through Cheryl. Looking into CJ's eyes, Cheryl could read the sincerity and love her friend held for her. But just as quickly as she recognized this truth, Cheryl pushed it away. To see the truth of CJ's concern meant that her own beliefs of needing to endure injustice and suffering alone were invalid.

"There's nothing more to be said, CJ, unless it's to make clear to that brother of yours that if he ever sets foot on my property, I'll personally even the score."

CJ's eyes widened in shock at the threat, but it mattered little to Cheryl. She watched CJ go and slammed the door hard. Closed doors were all she would ever give CJ from this moment on. It was a promise she made herself, and for reasons beyond her understanding, it gave her a moment of peace.

Chapter 2

But you don't understand," Erik Connors told his sister and her husband. "Cheryl Fairchild is, in my opinion, suicidal. No doctor in his right mind should have released her, even if her physical wounds were healed."

"Erik, it isn't your concern," his sister Christy offered. "If the doctors okayed her release, then you can't interfere with that. Besides, Cheryl allowed herself to be mixed up with Grant Burks, and now she's paying the piper. Don't forget, she was the 'other woman' in our little sister's short married life."

Erik nodded, knowing full well that their sister had suffered greatly because of Grant's infidelity. Candy had barely been old enough to marry when she'd fallen in love with Grant Burks, and in spite of both Christy and Erik's misgivings, she had married him and found herself almost immediately pregnant.

"But, Christy, Cheryl didn't know he was married to Candy. She had no way of knowing that he had a wife and baby on the way. To my way of thinking, she was just as duped as Candy was."

Curt O'Sullivan nodded. "I think that's true in many senses." He exchanged a brief apologetic smile with his wife. "I don't think that it makes what happened justified or right, however. Cheryl has always lived life in the fast lane. Her father taught her that, and he lived the example right up until the end. It was one of the biggest reasons I had to cut off my engagement with Cheryl."

"Good thing, too," Christy said with a loving smile.

"Well, despite her fast-lane approach to life," Erik said seriously, "she deserves forgiveness for her mistakes. God isn't going to hold a grudge against her, and I don't see where we have the right to, if God Himself doesn't plan to."

"She has to want to be forgiven," Curt interrupted. "She has to seek repentance, recognizing that she was wrong in the first place. So far, I don't see that Cheryl feels she has anything to confess."

"But given all that she's just come through, she's got to be doing a great deal of soul-searching."

"Erik, that is a matter of opinion, and not only that," Curt added, "but what makes you think Cheryl's brand of soul-searching includes wanting to hear about God from a complete stranger?"

"Who better? I don't hold anything against her, so it isn't like you or CJ going to see her. Cheryl has no past with me through which she might just feel even more ashamed, and she knows me from the hospital."

"I can't help but think she's going to feel a very strong past with you," Christy interjected, "even if you don't want her to feel that way. Once you explain the connection and she realizes that you're Candy's brother, she won't want anything else to do with you."

"Christy's probably right," Curt replied.

From upstairs came the cry of a baby. "Well, that will be Sarah expecting to be fed," said Christy, getting to her feet. Sarah, the baby Candy had given birth to shortly before succumbing to a brain tumor, had come into Christy's life much in the same way her husband Curt had. Most unexpectedly, yet most welcomed. Erik knew his sister held a deep abiding love for both of them, and he'd never seen her happier.

"Does she pack it away like her daddy?" Erik asked, noting Curt's second helping of barbecued ribs.

"She's worse," Curt said, grinning. "At least I don't cry at the top of my lungs."

Christy laughed. "I'd say it's debatable as to who makes more noise. It just depends on the day."

Erik smiled, while Curt ignored this comment and dug into his food. With Christy gone, Erik felt like he could get more personal about Cheryl.

"Look, Curt, I know Cheryl Fairchild is a sore subject, but I'm hoping that at least you will try to understand my thinking in this. I feel led to go to her. I've prayed all of this through, and count it a 'holy mission' or whatever else you want to call it, but I feel somehow responsible to extend Christian charity and love to that woman."

"Cheryl will never take it," Curt replied. "Mark my words. She'll have you thrown from the house faster than you can say, 'Jesus saves.' "

"But she talked to me in the hospital. I used to have to draw blood from her on my morning collection rounds. I sympathized with her situation and commented on her recovery, and she always seemed to respond."

"Throwing a pitcher of water at you can hardly be deemed a positive response."

Erik laughed. "Yes, but it was only that one time. After that, I made sure things were kept out of reach when I came into the room. Besides, she threw things at everybody."

Curt leaned forward and put down his fork. "Look, Erik, I know you have a big heart, and I'm certainly not trying to tell you to disregard something God has directed you to do—if, indeed, God has directed you to minister to Cheryl. I'm simply saying that once Cheryl finds out how you are related to Grant, she'll have nothing more to do with you."

"But like I said, Curt," Erik began again, "she was duped by Grant, and she has to know that we don't hate her for it. She must be feeling fifteen kinds of fool for her involvement with him. Just imagine all the rhetoric and lies he must have told her to get her to surrender to his charms. Even you said that Cheryl wasn't the kind of person to go from man to man and that she was most likely pure when she came to Grant."

"But what if she doesn't feel like a fool? You are presuming that Cheryl sees the error of her ways, and I'm telling you that the Cheryl Fairchild I know may well think herself completely in the right. She probably believes that she and Grant were the victims in this mess and that the rest of us are unfeeling liars who planted evidence and strung up the wrong man."

"But you said that once everything sunk in—"

"I remember what I said." Curt sighed. "Once she *allows* everything to sink in, she'll see the truth of the matter for herself. And when she does that, she's going to feel worse yet. Seeing how stupid you were and being smacked in the face with your mistaken judgment and actions is not something that anyone handles well. Cheryl will be especially hard to deal with in this area, mainly because as far as she's concerned, she's never been wrong about anything."

"So you think I should stay away from her because she'll never believe me, is that it?" Erik questioned honestly.

"That and the fact that I also don't want my investigation messed up because you interfered in a matter you should have stayed completely out of."

Erik looked at his brother-in-law and tried to figure out how to present his case in such a way that Curt might better respect his plan. Ever since he'd learned of Cheryl Fairchild's plight and misguided involvement with Grant Burks, Erik had felt a strange concern for her. The more he learned about her, the more he found himself wanting to help.

"She's gone through so much." Erik tried another approach. "The surgeries, losing the baby, recovering from severe intestinal damage—all of it took its toll. She was lucky to only have to endure a temporary colostomy instead of a permanent one, 'cause I can tell you from first-hand knowledge, the initial opinions on her condition weren't that great. The surgeon thought that *if* she lived through the operation, she'd be permanently disabled in one way or another."

"I know all of this, Erik. And now that her physical injuries are healed and she's nearly the same old Cheryl in body that she was before, she's more messed up inside than a simple visit and 'Hey, I'm praying for you, kid,' is going to fix."

Erik felt suddenly put off by Curt's attitude. "I'm not suggesting that I'm going to drop in and perform a miracle. You make it sound like I think that I alone can put her on the road to spiritual healing. Like I expect to walk on water. It isn't that at all."

"Then what is it?" Curt asked, eyeing him seriously.

"I'm the only one who's offering to help," he answered matter-of-factly. "I don't see anyone else going the distance with her."

"My sister tried," Curt said softly. "That's why I know Cheryl won't take kindly to any kind of spiritual lecturing or pat, formula responses. I know this lady well enough to say this." He paused as if trying to word what he would say in a precise and exact manner. "If Cheryl is determined to kill herself, you won't stop her. She doesn't do things by halves, and she doesn't care what anyone else thinks about her. The only person in the world she really cared about was her father, and he's dead. Next in line was probably Grant Burks, and he's dead, too. So you see, I have very serious doubts that anything you say or do will be the slightest bit positive."

"I have to try, Curt," Erik said, getting up from the table.

"Try what?" Christy asked as she returned to the room, balancing five-month-old Sarah against her shoulder.

"Your brother believes he has a mission to witness to Cheryl Fairchild, and even though I've tried to dissuade him, Erik feels he has to reach her."

Christy frowned. "To what purpose, Erik?"

"To the purpose of helping her find salvation," Erik replied. "You may not think her reachable, but I believe there is a great need inside that woman. I don't intend for her to slip away without at least offering her the means to find her way back to God."

He left the room, feeling for all the world as though a huge weight had fallen upon his shoulders. For all his time working in the hospital and on the mission field during his summer vacations, Erik had never before had a case present itself in such a way that it demanded his complete attention. But Cheryl Fairchild had stirred up a consciousness inside him that he couldn't ignore. She was needy and hurting, but then, so were many others he'd seen in his twenty-five years. What exactly made Cheryl different was a mystery to Erik.

Sliding into his aged Chevy pickup, Erik turned the key and listened to the engine roar to life. She might not be much to look at, but even when the windchill registered twenty below zero, this truck would start as smooth and easy as if it were a summer's day. And with a four-speed transmission and a four-bolt main for an engine, Erik could compete with the newest four-wheelers in exploring the mountainous back roads.

"They just don't understand," he said as though the truck were a living companion. "If I don't at least try to reach her, I'll never be able to live with myself."

Chapter 3

Cheryl stared at the flamboyant clothes hanging in her huge walk-in closet. These were the clothes of a very confident woman. These were the clothes of a woman who knew what she wanted and wasn't afraid to go after it. She pulled a red, sequined number from the hanger and studied it for a moment. The halter-style bodice left little to the imagination either on the hanger or off. Tossing it to the middle of her bedroom floor, Cheryl reached for another. This time a silky black sheath slipped from the satin-covered hanger. She had been wearing this dress the first time she'd met Grant.

Grant. It was still so hard to get used to calling him that, and yet Cheryl knew that it was his real name. Still, it had been the name Stratton that she'd whispered in tender "I love you's," and Stratton was the name signed to all her love letters and cards.

The black sheath joined the red gown on the floor, and after those first few moments of deep consideration, Cheryl rapidly eliminated nearly every article of clothing from her closet. She finished by tossing aside the maid of honor dress she'd worn at CJ's wedding. Standing back, she stared at the massive pile.

What should she do with it all? She couldn't very well set it on fire, although that was her first thought. These clothes represented a large portion of her adult life. So much time and care had gone into shopping for just the right outfit, for just the right affair. She'd rather enjoyed the attention it had brought her, and while she knew people thought her overly extravagant and flashy, Cheryl thought it very important to dress her role.

But what's my role now? she wondered, still staring at the mess she'd made.

She picked up the telephone and dialed directory assistance.

"Yes, I need the number for one of those charity organizations who handle secondhand clothes." Pause. "Yes, Goodwill, Salvation Army, any one of those is fine." She listened as the number was given, then hung up the phone and redialed.

"This is Cheryl Fairchild. I have a large number of next-to-new clothing items that I would like to donate to your organization." She listened as a woman rattled on about the type of clothing they were interested in before interrupting. "Look, can someone just come get these things?"

The woman objected and began to give a list of reasons for why Cheryl should bring them in herself. "Ma'am, I just got out of the hospital, and I'm unable to bring myself to your address. I have clothing here worth hundreds of thousands of dollars. Do you want them or not?"

This seemed to bring the woman to life, and with little more said, Cheryl gave her the address and promised to be waiting that afternoon for their man to arrive.

With that taken care of, Cheryl went to her father's closet and pulled on one of his white oxford shirts. It had been freshly laundered and pressed and still hung inside the dry cleaner's plastic wrapping, but nevertheless, it made her feel closer to her dad. She accompanied the shirt with an old pair of baggy black sweats and padded down the stairs barefoot to see what else the day might offer her.

Passing the mirror in the hall, Cheryl hardly recognized her own reflection. She looked like a bag lady with her unkempt hair and mismatched clothes. But she didn't care. She never intended to step foot outside the house again, so what did it matter if she looked a fright?

The morning passed by painfully slowly, and Cheryl found that the only way to keep her mind occupied was to keep her body busy. She made one trip after the other up and down the stairs to deliver her clothes to a growing pile in the living room. The tenderness of her left side made her think about taking a break, but she was too fearful of what might happen if she gave in and rested. *No sense in having a pity party in the middle of the day,* she reasoned. *Better to save that for the night.*

She had made the last trip downstairs and had just deposited the last of the clothes into a pile nearly as tall as herself, when the doorbell signaled the arrival of the deliveryman. At least, that was who she'd presumed would greet her from the other side of the door. Instead, she found the familiar face of a man who'd worked in the hospital where she'd convalesced.

"Hi," Erik Connors said. Smiling rather sheepishly, he added, "How are you feeling?"

Cheryl was taken aback by the handsome young man. He was tanned from the summer sun, and his jogging shorts and T-shirt made it clear that his lifestyle lent itself to a great deal of physical activity.

"I'm fine. What are you doing here? Is this a part of that home-care service I told them to forget about?"

Erik shook his head. "No. I didn't come here on hospital business."

"What then?"

"I was kind of. . ." He paused and actually grew red in the face. "I was worried about you."

Cheryl found his words disconcerting. "I don't understand. Why would you be worried about me?"

"Well, it's just that—" Erik paused, looked at the ground, and seemed to struggle to continue. "Look, could I just come in for a few minutes? I want to talk to you."

"I hardly think that would be appropriate," Cheryl answered in a no-nonsense manner that she hoped would put him off.

"Appropriate or not," Erik countered, seeming to regain his self-assurance, "I need to talk to you."

"Why?"

"Because I care about you."

Cheryl looked at him for a moment and read nothing but genuine sincerity in his expression. "You have no reason to concern yourself with me. I'm no longer a patient, and the doctors have given me a complete release from medical care."

"Look, I know all about that, but this is different."

"How is it different?" she asked suspiciously.

"This is personal. You don't understand, but there are things that connect us to each other's lives and I, well—"

"Look, if you're thinking of asking me out, forget it," Cheryl said, backing up in order to close the front door in his face.

"No!" Erik exclaimed and put his hand out to halt her progress. "I didn't come for a date. I came because I know you're hurting. I know that you were deceived, and I know that you believe no one in this world cares for you."

Cheryl pulled the door back very slowly. She stared at the handsome face, noting laugh lines at the corners of his blue eyes. "And just how do you know all this? Surely the blood you drew from me didn't reveal this information."

"No, it didn't," Erik admitted. "The truth is, Cheryl, I'm Erik Connors."

Cheryl shook her head. "Should that mean something to me?"

"My sister Christy is married to Curt O'Sullivan. My little sister Candy was married to Grant Burks."

Cheryl felt the blood drain from her face. Her breathing came in tight, strained gasps. "Get out! Get off my property, and leave me alone!"

"I want to help you," Erik insisted. "Look, I know you must feel pretty bad after all you've gone through, but I want you to know that I don't hold you responsible for Grant's actions. You were as much a victim of his deception as my sister was."

Cheryl gave a strained little laugh. "Victim? I was no victim. I loved the man, and I can't help it if. . .if. . ." She strained for air and began wheezing and gasping. "Can't. . .breathe."

Cheryl felt herself in complete panic. Putting her hand to her throat, she tried desperately to calm her rapid breathing. It was as if air was going in, but nothing was coming back out.

Erik took hold of her. "Breath in through your nose and out through your mouth. You're hyperventilating."

Cheryl shook her head and pushed him away. She wasn't going to listen to this man. He was her enemy. He could offer her nothing but pain and misery. Still gasping, she felt the room begin to spin, and her vision tunneled down with blackness creeping in from every side.

Let me die, she thought, feeling her knees begin to buckle.

Erik half carried, half dragged her to the couch. He forced her to sit down, then pushed her head forward until her face was on her knees. "Breathe in through your nose and out through your mouth. Come on, Cheryl. Long, deep breaths. Force yourself to listen."

Cheryl found herself responding almost against her will. It was as if Erik were breathing for her. In. . .out. . .in. . .out. Over and over she forced the calming breaths deeper into her lungs until the blackness faded and the dizziness passed. She felt helpless and weak, and her side ached terribly from the position in which she was bent.

"Better?" he asked most compassionately.

She nodded, afraid to speak. Gently, he eased her back against the couch and eyed her with a look of consuming attention. "I'm going to get you a glass of water and a cool cloth. You stay right here, and I mean right here. Understand?"

She nodded again, but remained silent. She watched him as he glanced first one way and then the other, searching for some sign of the kitchen or bathroom. She wanted to be angry with him for his interference, but for some reason, she felt sorry for him, and this emotion seemed to calm her further.

He was back in a matter of minutes with the promised items. Cheryl obediently drank sips of cool water and allowed Erik to place the cold cloth on the back of her neck.

"I'm really sorry," he apologized. "I never meant to cause you further harm. Curt and Christy warned me that you might not take too well to my company, and I guess I pushed too hard."

Cheryl took another sip of water and securely put up her defenses. "You have no reason to be here. I'm not your concern."

"I know that, but in another way, I know just as well that you are my concern."

"That makes no sense whatsoever, Mr. Connors."

"I know, but if you would just give me a chance to explain."

"Hello!" called a voice from the still-open front door.

Cheryl sat up abruptly, fearful of who this latest visitor might be. "Yes?" she called out apprehensively.

"I'm here to pick up some clothes," a man called back.

Erik eyed the multicolored pile in the middle of the living room. "Doing all your dry cleaning at once?" he asked with a smile.

Cheryl ignored the humor. "More like early fall cleaning or late spring cleaning," she replied, then raised her voice. "In here!"

The man, dressed in brown work clothes, entered from the hall foyer and dropped his mouth open in surprise at the huge mound of clothes. "Wow! I've never seen that many—" He paused and looked at Cheryl, as if trying to rethink his thoughts. "I mean, you sure you want to get rid of all these, lady?"

"Absolutely sure," Cheryl replied and, ignoring Erik's concerned expression, got to her feet. "If you want to be helpful, Mr. Connors, why don't you assist this gentleman in removing these things from my house?"

Erik looked as though he wanted to say something important, but instead he nodded and turned to the workman. "Well, what say we get at it? I wouldn't be at all surprised to find some lost civilization buried beneath that mess."

The man grinned good-naturedly, and Cheryl found the entire matter uncomfortable. She didn't want to smile or laugh. She didn't want to feel good for even a single minute. Feeling good meant that there was a reason to go on living, and she didn't want there to be a reason to go on. She wanted to end her life, and the sooner she arranged for all her affairs to be properly in order, the better.

Leaving the men to make short work of her affairs, Cheryl took herself into the family room and switched on the television. Two children danced and giggled while their mother snapped pictures of them and advertised the quality of her particular film. Cheryl watched the little girls, their faces beaming smiles at the camera, their eyes lit up in anticipation of the moment.

"I might have had a daughter," she murmured to the empty room.

The commercial passed and another came on advertising, "What to do when those morning aches and pains got you down." Cheryl flipped the switch off and went to the window. Staring out over the backyard, she noticed the sorry state of things for the first time. Weeds grew around the fountain and fishpond. This had been the centerpiece of her father's landscaping, and Cheryl couldn't let it be consumed by neglect.

But if you're dead, what will it matter? a voice seemed to question inside her head.

"Cheryl?" Erik called out.

Cheryl swallowed back an angry retort and returned to the living room. "Why are you still here?"

"I didn't want to just leave without saying good-bye," Erik said with a smile.

"Good-bye, then," she replied and turned to go.

"No, wait," Erik called after her.

"I have nothing more to say, Mr. Connors. Please show yourself out."

She refused to look back, and only after she was out of sight, did Cheryl pause to listen for the sounds that would signal Erik's departure. His footsteps sounded on the marble in the foyer, and then the closing of the door echoed in the stillness around her.

Good, she thought. *Let that be the end of it.*

Chapter 4

So how's the investigation going?" Erik asked.

Curt looked up from his newspaper and shrugged. "Okay, I guess. There's a great deal that remains a mystery. Maybe Cheryl will be able to shed some light on it for me."

"Cheryl? You mean *you* plan to interview her?" Erik grew hopeful. This would be the perfect way to see Cheryl again. He'd actually be there for a reason.

". . .Later today," Curt finished and resumed reading his paper.

"Wait. What did you say?"

Curt gave up on the paper and folded it back together. "I said that Cheryl may have information that will be key to our investigation, and I'm going to her house later today."

"Can I come along?" Erik asked.

"No way. This is DEA business."

"But Cheryl's in a fragile state of mind. I told you what happened the other day and how she hyperventilated. You know from your own sister that she blames you for Grant's death and that she never wants to see you again."

Curt frowned. "It doesn't matter. I have to go. I can read Cheryl like a book, and no one else has that advantage. And although it sounds rather cruel, I can also use her dislike of me to get the answers I want. People under stress often blurt out things they'd never consider speaking of in calmer times."

"That is rather cruel," Erik agreed. "Especially when it's a friend."

Curt sighed and pushed out of the overstuffed chair. "Look, drugs are dirty business and people get hurt. You know from what Christy has told you that even when she was suspected of aiding that same drug ring, I couldn't just drop her off the list of suspects. Even though I'd fallen in love with her and was certain she had no knowledge of what

315

was going on, I still had to investigate her, and I still have to investigate Cheryl."

"But it's so soon," Erik protested. "Don't you care about her recovery?"

"It's been four months," Curt replied. "She was left alone as much as possible during the last few months because I stuck my neck out for her. And because I'm one of the owners of O&F Aviation and have worked from the beginning to keep the feds in the middle of the organization, they were a little more sympathetic to my suggestion. That's not going to carry her the rest of her life, however. She's going to have to answer some very detailed questions. After all, our records show that Ben Fairchild transferred all of his business interests to Cheryl some time ago. That makes her as much a part of this as it does me or CJ or even Grant. Ignorance isn't going to carry a great deal of weight in a court of law, and I, for one, hate to see O&F property remain under seizure for much longer."

Erik realized his mistake in suggesting that Curt might not care about Cheryl. "Hey, I'm sorry. I should have known." He quickly moved the conversation forward. "So you're going there this afternoon?"

Curt glanced at his watch and headed over to his desk to pick up some papers. "Yeah, in fact, I need to put in about two hours over at the office before I see Cheryl, so if you don't mind, I'm going to leave you to lock up."

"That's okay. I'll just leave now."

"You want me to drop you somewhere? Home?" Curt asked.

Erik glanced down at his jogging clothes and shook his head. "No, I need to run. I should never have weakened and stopped by. It's just that I saw your car here and wanted to know about Cheryl."

"No problem."

They parted company, and Erik considered his brother-in-law's words all the way back to his apartment. He might not be able to accompany Curt in a professional way, but what if he just happened to be at Cheryl's house when Curt showed up? A plan began to formulate in his mind. Curt had said that he'd be at the office for a couple of hours. That would give Erik time enough to clean up and get over to Cheryl's before Curt arrived. He picked up speed with each passing thought. *She might not want my company,* he thought, *but once she finds out that Curt is on the way, she's going to need the extra support.* He smiled to himself and, without even feeling winded, jogged up his apartment stairs. His plan would work.

鸷

Erik rang the doorbell and waited for Cheryl to appear. When she did, he had to hide his surprise at her appearance. She didn't look like she'd had a bath all week, and her hair was matted and lifeless. Her face registered only mild disgust at seeing him, and Erik played upon her surprise.

"Hey, how are you doing?" he said enthusiastically. "I thought I'd stop by and see if you felt like some company."

"I told you to stay away from me," Cheryl responded. "What do I have to do—get a restraining order?"

Erik laughed and tried to keep matters lighthearted. "I'm not stalking you, if that's what you think. I just wanted to offer you a day of sunshine." He waved behind him and added, "And a pleasant companion."

Cheryl's expression remained the same. "I'm not interested in seeing you or anyone else for any reason at all." She began to close the door.

"Then you'd better rethink your plans because Curt O'Sullivan is on his way over here right now. I thought you could use some moral support."

Cheryl threw open the door. The color had drained from her face and her blue eyes were wide in fear. "Curt is coming here?"

Erik nodded. "I asked him if I could come along, and he refused. Said it was all business and I should keep out of it. But you know already how persistent I am. I just didn't want you to have to face the DEA's questions alone."

Cheryl's gaze darted back and forth, and she craned her neck forward to see if Curt might already be there before she yanked on Erik's shirt to drag him inside the house. "I can't deal with him," she said flatly. "Will you take me away from here?"

"Take you away to where?" Erik asked, so stunned by this sudden change of events that he didn't know what to do.

"Anywhere! It doesn't matter." She glanced down at her clothes—cutoff jeans and a baggy black T-shirt. "I need shoes. Wait here."

Erik stared after her without quite knowing what to do. As she ran upstairs, his mind raced with the implications of what he'd just done. He'd blown Curt's surprise visit, and he'd inadvertently interfered with a DEA investigation. It wasn't something he relished admitting to.

Cheryl returned quickly, socks and blue hiking shoes in hand. "Hurry, he'll be here any minute."

"There's no way of knowing that—" Erik began.

Cheryl interrupted him, flailing the socks for emphasis. "Then you don't know Curt like I do. I feel it in my bones. Come on."

"But Cheryl, he's with the DEA. You can't just walk away from them. You and your father have a great deal to answer for."

Cheryl gave him a stunned look of disbelief. "You think I had something to do with this?"

Erik felt in his heart that she couldn't possibly have known about her father's dirty deeds. He smiled. "No, I don't believe you did. But," he tried to give her what he hoped was his most sympathetic expression, "it doesn't matter what I think. The DEA has their own idea about things and—"

"Will you stop talking? Are you going to take me away from here, or am I going to have to take myself?"

Erik felt that in some way he owed her. "All right." He motioned to her shoes and socks. "Get those on and we'll go."

"I'll put them on *as* we go," she insisted.

She started to push him forward, but Erik was still torn. "Look, Curt understands your situation. He kept the feds pretty much at bay while you were sick these last months."

Cheryl laughed, and the sound was hollow and bitter. "If you call plaguing me day after day about my relationship to Grant Burks and whether my father had any hidden assets at bay, then, yes, I suppose they were most congenial."

"But they have to know the truth."

Cheryl's expression grew angry, almost hateful. "The truth has never mattered as much as making themselves look good and my father look bad. Now come on."

With Cheryl pulling him to the truck, there was little he could do but flat-out refuse. But he didn't want to refuse her. She was reaching out to him, even if it was for all the wrong reasons, and he wanted to help calm her and make her realize that he cared greatly for her well-being.

He opened the pickup door, noting that she didn't think twice about scrambling up into the cab. A lot of women frowned upon realizing that they were going to be expected to ride in what he called "Ole Blue." But not Cheryl Fairchild. At that moment, Erik realized that he could have been driving a garbage truck and her response would have been the same.

He jumped into the driver's seat and fired up the engine, cautiously keeping an eye out for Curt's arrival. If they managed to make their escape before Curt pulled into the drive, Erik knew he'd have a great deal to explain later. Throwing the truck into gear and praying at the same time that God would somehow intervene and keep his actions from causing too much trouble, Erik pulled out onto the street.

"Where to?"

"It doesn't matter, so long as you get me away from here," Cheryl said, forcing her foot into the shoe. She glanced up to give the neighborhood a quick once-over before resuming her task. "Can't this thing go any faster?"

"This is a residential district," Erik replied, pushing the speed as much as he dared. "I wouldn't want to break the law any more than I already have."

"What do you mean?"

"I mean that I'm sure to be breaking multiple laws by helping you escape DEA questioning." He pulled up to a stop sign and turned to catch her doubtful expression.

"I hadn't thought of it that way," she answered softly. "I'm sorry. I never meant for this to happen. I shouldn't have asked you to take me away."

"No, I suppose you shouldn't have." Erik grinned. "But I'm glad you did."

"You are? Why?"

"Because now maybe you'll believe that I'm really on your side and that I care about you and what you've been through."

Cheryl nodded but turned away to look out her window. Erik smiled to himself and set the truck in motion. *Just don't let me mess this up, God*, he prayed. *I only want Cheryl to see that someone cares enough about her to be there for her. I only want to help her.*

❧

Cheryl barely noticed the passing scenery. She saw places in Denver that she'd never before ventured into and probably never would again. And before long, Erik had wound through the city and was headed up into the mountains via a small, gravel back road.

He's a strange man, she thought, still not knowing quite what to make of him. He just waltzed into her life and with no more than a few well-placed words had somehow assigned himself her guardian angel. In this case, however, she was grateful. The last person in the world she wanted to have to deal with was Curt O'Sullivan. Just thinking about him made her boil. She balled her hands into tight fists and silently wished she could plant each one squarely into his face.

It seemed far easier to hate Curt than to deal with her loss. So long as she focused on the anger she felt for him and the revenge that she one day hoped to have against him, Cheryl could make her way through the day and night with some semblance of order. Curt was the reason she was alone. Curt was the one who should pay.

"Look, now that you're my captive audience, so to speak, I'm hoping to say a few things."

Cheryl glanced up and noted the determined set of Erik's jaw. Even though his face almost always seemed to be on the verge of an impish grin, this time there was something more serious about his expression.

"Well, say what you want. I suppose I owe you for getting me out of there," Cheryl replied.

"I was serious when I told you that I cared. My family has suffered a great deal in this, too. There's a baby without her parents because of this."

"A baby?" This was the first Cheryl had heard of it.

"You remember the baby Grant had you watch for him at the mall? The day of the shooting?"

Cheryl remembered quite well. She wrapped her arms around her waist and hugged them close. "Yes."

"That little girl is my niece Sarah. She was my sister's baby. My sister and Grant's."

Cheryl swallowed hard, remembering that Grant had told her they were watching the baby for his sister-in-law. Curiosity got the better of her. "Why was she there?"

"Sarah? Grant was using her as a trading piece. Christy, my older sister. . ." He paused and smiled. "I forgot that you know Christy."

"She was making my wedding dress," Cheryl replied offhandedly.

"Yeah, well, Christy was supposed to adopt Sarah. Just before she died, Candy begged Christy to keep Sarah from Grant. She knew that he would only use the baby to get whatever he wanted, and Candy had given her life for that child."

"What do you mean, she'd given her life?"

"Candy had an inoperable brain tumor. The doctors could have given her chemo or other treatment, but she refused because she was pregnant. Candy wanted nothing to interfere in the life of that unborn baby, and she was willing to take the chance that she'd not give birth in time to receive treatment for the cancer. I thought at first she was crazy, but the more I thought about it, the more I understood, and I think you can, too. A child is a sacred gift from God."

"Then He seems to be quite contradictory in His giving," she muttered.

"I know you lost a baby, Cheryl," Erik said, lowering his voice almost reverently. "And while I'm a man and can't possibly know what it is to carry life inside me, I grieve for you and your loss."

Cheryl's eyes filled with tears. No one had ever said such a kind thing to her before. CJ had said that God had a purpose in everything, and the doctor had assured her that she could have other children, as though she'd lost her choice of a new automobile, instead of the life of her baby. But Erik said he grieved with her. Erik offered to bear the burden alongside of her, instead of relegating her to a hidden corner where unwed mothers should bury their faces in shame.

"So you don't think God killed my baby because I was evil?" Cheryl said sarcastically.

"No, I don't think God killed your baby. I think Grant did. Frankly, I think it's possible he knew exactly what he was doing."

"How dare you!" Cheryl exclaimed.

"I dare because Curt told me the details of the shoot-out. You threw yourself between Grant and Curt. Grant had plenty of time to recognize that you were there. Maybe too much. After all, if you think about it, he had to redirect his line of fire in order to hit you in the abdomen. He'd already grazed Curt's arm, so shooting you in the head could have been explained away as accidental. Your head was in the line of fire from which Grant was already shooting. But if you're honest about it, you'll realize the truth in what I'm saying. Grant had to deliberately lower his aim to hit you low enough to end his baby's life."

"Stop it!" Cheryl cried out, putting her hands to her ears. What he said made startling, ugly sense, and she couldn't deal with the thought that Grant had purposely tried to kill not only her, but their baby as well.

Erik pulled into a short dirt turnaround beside a rushing stream. He turned off the engine and rolled down his window. Then shifting to better look at Cheryl, he suggested she do the same thing in order to enjoy the fresh air. Reluctantly, she did as she was told.

"Please listen to what I want to say. Then, I promise if it absolutely makes no sense, not even one thread of sense, I'll drop it. But I won't stop caring about you, and I won't just go away as easily as you put everyone else off."

Cheryl shook her head. "Why not? No one else needs to be told twice. Why are you such a hard case? Are you some kind of nut, or what?"

Erik laughed. "I suppose in a way. When I was a teenager, there was a popular saying in our youth group. 'I'm a fool for Jesus, whose fool are you?' I thought it made a lot of sense. You sold out to one thing or another in life. What mattered was which thing you chose. But I suppose the biggest reason I'm determined to stick this out with you is that I feel a sense of responsibility for you."

"Why? I'm nothing to you. You never knew I existed before the shooting."

"I knew someone existed."

"I don't understand."

"I knew Grant was deceiving someone, if not a great many someones. I was praying for you even back then."

Cheryl looked away and noticed the stream for the first time. With the window down, it was easy to be caught up in the sounds of the water as it traveled over the rocks. "CJ was always praying for me," she murmured.

"I know. Curt told me how worried she was about you. See, Cheryl, you can try to shut out the rest of the world and even believe that you've accomplished just that, but somehow things are far more complicated than we give them credit for. Did you know that not only is CJ praying for you, but her husband prays for you as well? Then there's my sister Christy, and Curt."

"Please don't mention his name," Cheryl said, turning to face Erik's compassionate gaze. "I don't want to talk about him. I can't talk about him."

"Sooner or later you're going to have to talk about him. And not only *about* him, but *to* him. He's not the kind to stand back, and he won't leave you alone forever. Just because we've thwarted his efforts this time is no indication we can do it again."

"But if Curt hadn't started all of this. . ." She fell silent and bit her lower lip.

"Curt didn't start this, and the sooner you accept that, the better you'll feel. But that's not what I wanted to say to you just now. I want you to know that God really does love you, Cheryl. He does listen to the prayers of His children, and with so many people praying for you just now, He's getting an earful."

She said nothing, and he continued. "God tells us in His Word that He will never forsake us, and, Cheryl, I believe He will be faithful to that promise. Even when we are disobedient, I don't believe God stands idle. I believe God uses the Holy Spirit to prick our consciences and teach us that some things are unacceptable, even when they seem our only way out.

"You gave in to Grant's demands," he paused, picking his words carefully. "You gave yourself to Grant in a way that went against what God had in mind, but it doesn't mean you can't be forgiven. You trusted a man who was evil and whose actions proved it, but still you can be forgiven. You lived a lifestyle that had no room for God, but He never left—never stopped loving you. He still stands with open arms, waiting for you to see that planning out things your own way will only lead to this kind of misery."

"So now all of this is my fault?" Cheryl questioned, struggling with the strange sensation Erik's words caused within her heart.

"You are partially to blame, aren't you? Weren't you the one who went willingly into the relationship with Grant? Weren't you the one who gave in to Grant, even when you didn't want to—even when you knew it was wrong?"

"CJ's told me all this mumbo jumbo before. I didn't buy into it then, and I don't see a reason to buy into it now. God can't possibly care about me now, anyway. I'm the scum of the earth, as you so eloquently pointed out."

"I said nothing of the kind! I only tried to say that we all make mistakes, and God is willing to forgive us—when we are willing to repent."

"I can't live in a little box," Cheryl said and then easily recognized that this was exactly how she was living. She shrugged and noted the time. "Don't you think Curt will have given up on me by now?"

"Possibly. Do you want me to take you back?"

"Yes, please."

They stopped for fast food on the way back to her house, and Erik insisted that she eat it under his supervision. He drove around Denver until she had managed to finish the cheeseburger and fries. She hadn't believed herself hungry, but by the time she was halfway through, she felt quite ravenous.

Erik pulled into her drive, but when he reached for the keys, Cheryl put her hand over his and stopped him. "Don't."

"I thought maybe—"

"Look," she began, "I appreciate what you did today, but I don't want you to worry about me or see me as some pet project of yours. I'm beyond saving, and you needn't waste your time with me."

"I don't think I'm wasting my time," he replied.

"It doesn't matter what you think," Cheryl said, rather stiffly. "I'm not interested in buying what you're selling, and I think it would be best if you don't come back here again."

She got out of the truck without waiting for his reaction or response. A part of her wished he would come after her and convince her that she was wrong, but an even bigger part wanted to run as fast as she could. Away from Erik Connors and his kindness. Away from Erik Connors and his God.

Chapter 5

One day blended into another, and for Cheryl, very little happened to mark the passing weeks. She spent a great deal of time in her father's study and bedroom. Sometimes she'd lie down on his bed and try to imagine happier days when she'd been a little girl and her mother had still been alive. The memories, dimmed from the years, were the only thing that gave her the slightest comfort. They were probably the only reason Cheryl hadn't taken the drastic way out and ended her life.

She looked around her father's room, feeling so alone and sad that she had to do something in order to rally herself. Opening first one drawer and then another, Cheryl pulled out clean clothes, undershirts, sweats, and pullovers for working outside. She rubbed the material with her hand, thinking all the while of Ben Fairchild and what his absence meant to her. Her entire world had turned around him, and now he was gone.

She pulled out the drawer containing his socks and other personal articles and dumped the contents on his bed. Suddenly she noticed that a lockbox had been taped to the outside of the back of the drawer. She peered into the hole where the dresser drawer had resided and found a hollowed-out indentation that matched the size of the box. Her father had intended to hide this box from any casual search, and suddenly it seemed quite valuable to Cheryl.

Pulling the strips of duct tape off, she held the box at eye level. It was a simple gray metal box, no bigger than five by eight, with a small locking mechanism to secure the lid. She tried to open it and found it was locked tight.

Setting the lockbox aside, Cheryl searched through her father's things for a key and came up empty-handed. *There must be some way to get that box open,* she thought and finally retrieved a screwdriver and pried the lock apart. When the lid flew back, Cheryl could only gasp in surprise.

On top, a stack of thousand-dollar bills greeted her like a flag of warning. Carefully she picked up the money and counted out fifty thousand dollars. She shuddered. *What was Daddy ever thinking to keep this much money in the house?*

She set the money aside and pulled out two computer diskettes, a set of keys, and several pieces of paper that had been folded neatly together and placed on the bottom. She opened the papers, wondering even as she did if this was the information Curt wanted so desperately. Was this the final shred of incriminating evidence that would forever brand her father a drug trafficker?

The first page read like a Chinese-encrypted menu. There were symbols and numbers, dollar signs and totals, all given in neat, orderly columns. The second paper gave a list of street addresses, usually followed by some brief, abbreviated set of directions.

"Third row, second shelf, back. Black/telephone-direct. See J.M.," she read from one line. *What in the world does it mean?*

The more she read, the worse the feeling she got in the pit of her stomach. Surely this information proved more than she was ready to accept. Her father had obviously been involved in something he wanted to keep hidden. After all, he'd gone to all this trouble to put the box into hiding behind the dresser drawer.

With a sensation that someone might be watching her, yet knowing it was impossible, Cheryl thrust the contents back inside the lockbox and resecured the lid. It was an awkward fit after her work with the screwdriver, but she forced it to close and tucked the box under her arm. She would have to hide it away. Hide it where no one could find it. Not Curt and his friends nor anyone else who might have need of what was inside.

She hurried to her room and looked around for a proper hiding place. She thought first of her closet where the striking emptiness was sure to draw immediate attention to any object left inside. That would never do. Next she thought of burying it in a box of personal items that she'd planned to give to Goodwill. But that, too, seemed a likely place for someone to look. She sat down on the bed and rubbed her hands back and forth across the lid as she thought. It would have to be somewhere where it wouldn't seem likely to be. But where?

Then an idea hit her, and Cheryl jumped off the bed and ran to her private bathroom. Her combination shower/tub had a wonderful ledge that had been designed to hold her toiletry items, and for years one end of the tiling had been loose. Her father had put off having it repaired because he wanted to redo the bathroom in imported marble. Now it seemed that his negligence would go one step farther in preserving his reputation.

Cheryl stepped into the tub and pushed aside her shampoos and bath oils. She studied the situation for a moment, determined to make certain that whatever she did, she wouldn't draw attention to the ledge. She put the lockbox on the floor of the bathtub and played around with the loose corner of the tile. With a little work it loosened even more, and before long the white caulking came apart altogether and the tile was free. Underneath, Cheryl could see that the entire ledge was nothing more than a boxed framed with waterproof tiling. This suited her purpose exactly.

Unable to tell how far down the boxing frame went, Cheryl quickly retrieved one of her belts and tied it around the lockbox. It was a tight fit getting the box past the small opening, but once this was done, the box floated freely for several inches before settling with a hollow "thunk" against the bathtub base.

Cheryl reached her arm through the opening and realized she could easily touch the box, so she let the belt drop into the hole and quickly put the tile back in place.

Stepping away, she frowned. It was quite noticeable that the tile wasn't in the same order as the rest of the ledge. The white caulking was shattered, with pieces in the tub and intermingled with her bath articles. She sat down on the tub and considered the situation for a moment. Then a revelation struck her, and Cheryl swung her legs over the edge so quickly she put a stitch in her side.

Toothpaste! She thought. Years ago when she'd lived in an apartment in California, the landlord had patched holes in her wall with toothpaste. It blended right in with the spackling and looked as though there had never been a nail to mar the purity of the wall.

Pulling out her toothpaste, Cheryl breathed a sigh of relief to find that the contents were white, just like the caulking around the tiles. She pulled a nail file from one of the drawers and went to work. First she smoothed off the remainders of the old caulking, and then she liberally applied the toothpaste and worked it into the seams of the tile until it matched perfectly with the rest of the shelf.

Feeling rather proud of her ingenuity, Cheryl replaced her shampoos and bath oils on top of the tile and stepped back to survey her work. Except for the crumbs of caulking in the tub, there didn't appear to be anything out of order. Cheryl smiled, completely satisfied with the results. Her last order of business was to turn on the faucet and wash the caulking down the drain.

She'd just walked from the bedroom when the telephone rang. She seldom ever answered it, but from time to time it was one of her doctors or some other matter that refused to be put to rest, and so she was in the habit of letting the answering machine pick up the call while she listened in.

"You've reached the Fairchild residence," her father's voice boomed on the machine. "Leave a message at the tone." That was it. A simple, no-nonsense message. The machine beeped, and Cheryl waited in anticipation for the message that might be left.

"Yes, Ms. Fairchild, this is Anthony Zirth with the *Denver Post*. I'm doing a feature to honor your father and to award him the posthumous honor of—"

Cheryl picked up the telephone. "Hello, Mr. Zirth? This is Cheryl Fairchild."

"Ah. . .Ms. Fairchild," he said in a hesitant voice, "I didn't think you were in."

"I screen my calls very carefully," she replied rather coolly.

"I can well understand. You must surely receive a great many calls. May I say, first of all, how sorry I was to hear of your father's death?"

"Thank you. That's kind of you to say."

"He was a great man, and we here at the *Post* have planned to name him our man of the year. I was hoping to interview you and get your perspective on what it was like to be the daughter of such a man."

"I'm sorry," Cheryl said, trying hard to soften her voice. "I don't do interviews. I've been through too much of late."

"Of course, that's understandable." The man positively oozed sympathetic concern. "I can do the story without your insight, but of course, it would make it much better with some type of personal touch. Say a photograph or some other bit of information you'd like the world to know about him?"

Cheryl thought for a moment. Mary's scrapbooks came to mind. Not the most recent one with all the black details of their lives, but earlier ones. Albums with comments about the awards he'd been given and copies of programs from gatherings given in Ben Fairchild's honor.

"I might be able to provide some of those things," she finally answered.

"If you could, I want you to know it will make this story truly great."

"Well then, Mr. Zirth, I realize tomorrow is Saturday, but if you can come by then, I'll have a few things put together for you."

"Tomorrow would be just fine. Would one o'clock suit you?"

"Yes, that's good for me."

She hung up the phone feeling another bit of elation. Someone wanted to honor her father. Someone still thought of him as a good man and not an evil drug-ring master.

She went to her father's study and found the albums she wanted. Next, she pulled down a family photo album and took out a picture of her father. It was her favorite one. He looked young and dashing in his three-piece suit. The photo had been taken for his company literature, but Cheryl thought it captured his personality better than any family photo they'd ever posed for. His look was determined, intelligent, and driven, and all of those things were the things she loved most about her father. He had taught her to be self-sufficient and confident. He had taught her to stare adversity in the face and come out swinging.

"Oh, Daddy," she murmured and tears filled her eyes, "what a disappointment I must be to you now." She continued talking to the photograph as if her father might really be listening. "I tried to be strong about all of this, but I just can't. I can't be *that strong*. There's nothing left. You're gone. Grant's gone. I just can't go on without you. There's nothing left. Nothing worth living for."

She broke down and cried with great painful sobs that wracked her body. From deep inside came a stark, hard hurt that would not be released with the simple deluge of tears. She pushed away from the desk and the photograph and thrust her father's office chair across the room as best she could. Next she picked up the trash can and threw it, too. Before long, nothing was safe. She threw books, bric-a-brac, awards, trophies. Nothing mattered. Nothing was sacred.

When her anger was spent and the rage calmed within her, Cheryl surveyed the mess she'd made. It would take some doing to clean it all up, but at least it would give her a sense of purpose. Picking up the trash can, she sighed. *At least this will keep me from thinking.*

Chapter 6

Guilt hung over Erik like a shroud, and he knew that he had to come clean with Curt about his outing with Cheryl. The O'Sullivan family barbecue at his sister's house hardly seemed the appropriate time or place, but Erik hoped that the setting and the fact that CJ and her husband were present would keep Curt from going ballistic.

"You did what!" Curt yelled when Erik tried to explain having gone to Cheryl that day.

"Just listen for a minute, Curt," Erik said, trying to explain his actions. "I only went there to offer her moral support. I thought if I came in on my own, she'd see that I was on her side and that I only wanted to help."

Curt was seething, and Erik could tell by the flushed color of his face that this was no minor issue that would be passed over with a brief justification. By this time, everyone else had stopped to see what the matter was. Christy was just approaching the two when Curt spoke.

"Inside, now!" he told Erik between clenched teeth.

"Curt? What's wrong?" Christy asked, stopping short of touching his arm.

"Your brother and I need to talk. Please try to understand, and explain to CJ and Brad that we'll be back in a few minutes."

"Is something wrong?" she asked again.

"You could say that," Curt said and stormed off toward the house. Erik shrugged and added, "It's all my fault. I'll explain it later."

He followed Curt into the stately Victorian house and made his way to the one room he knew Curt would seek refuge in, his own private study. Coming through the door, Erik could easily see that Curt was trying to get his emotions under control. He paced in front of the window and glanced up at Erik when he entered the room, but he clenched his

331

teeth together even tighter and turned to look out the window rather than speak.

Erik felt terrible. He knew it was no more than he deserved, but he hated the fact that Curt was angry at him, and he hated even more that he deserved that anger.

"Before you start in on me," Erik said, "I want you to know that I take full responsibility for my actions. I know I was wrong, Curt, and I'm asking you to forgive me. It won't happen again."

Curt's shoulders seemed to relax a bit, but without turning around he asked, "Why should I believe that? I asked you to stay out of it in the first place. You didn't respect that request, so why would you respect any other?"

"Because I don't want this coming between us." Erik sat down and put his head in his hands. "I didn't want to do what I did. I knew it would mess up your plans, and yet she was so needy and so. . .well. . . helpless."

Curt turned on this. "Cheryl has never been helpless."

Erik looked up and met his expression. "Then you don't know her as well as you think you do. She's very vulnerable and not at all the pillar of strength that you seem to believe her. A strong woman wouldn't have given in to Grant Burks. Christy didn't."

Curt frowned. "She very nearly did. Oh, not on his suggestions that she become his mistress or anything like that. But she very nearly kept his cocaine activities to herself in order to protect Sarah and, to some extent, to protect me."

Erik laughed. "Christy isn't a good example of a strong person, either. I think we both know the charade she plays when she's worried someone is going to get too close."

Curt smiled tightly at this, but his face instantly sobered. "That was no reason to interfere."

"No, it wasn't. I have no justifiable reason. It wasn't life or death, except maybe in Cheryl's own mind. But it was a matter of earning her trust, and Curt, I wanted that trust very badly."

"Apparently so. It must have meant a great deal if you were willing to threaten our relationship."

"Has it?"

"Has it what?"

"Threatened our relationship?"

Curt sat down behind his desk and shook his head. "Of course not. But honestly, Erik, you can't go around putting yourself in the middle of DEA business. Cheryl might be able to put this whole thing to rest, but she can't relay that information to me if I can't get to her in person. I don't want to hurt her. I've always cared deeply about her, and a part of me will always love her like a sister." Curt blew out an exasperated breath. "I'm tied to her in more ways than one, and there is a great deal of excess baggage that we both need to rid ourselves of. Some of it has nothing to do with the DEA."

"Like you killing Grant?" Erik asked seriously.

"It wasn't my idea. I've searched my heart in this matter, and I didn't instigate the shooting. Grant did. Furthermore, I didn't want to kill him. I only wanted him brought to justice."

"I can't say that I'm not glad he's dead," Erik responded, easing back in the chair and crossing his arms against his chest. "I wish I could be sorry that he died, but I'm not."

"I didn't say I was sorry he was dead, either. I am sorry I had to be the one to pull the trigger."

"As I recall from the paper and Christy's story, there were plenty of people shooting that day. In fact, when Grant was killed, you were busy rescuing Cheryl."

Curt nodded. "Yes, but as far as Cheryl is concerned, it might as well have just been me alone firing the gun."

Erik could well imagine that the sad-faced blond would hold that very opinion. "She feels like you took everything away from her. Your investigation caused her father to come under unbearable pressure, and your organized DEA rendezvous put an end to her happily-ever-after plans with Grant and her baby."

"You aren't telling me anything I haven't already gone over a million times in my own mind. The investigation started out as a need for revenge, but it turned around to be a search for justice and something that would bring about good. I just didn't want my parents to have died in vain."

"But Cheryl can't understand that. In honoring your parents, you dishonored hers. Leastwise her father. She wouldn't even let me speak your name."

Curt winced. "I'm way too personally involved for my own good. I've argued for my position with the DEA in this case because I knew things that would take years to teach someone else. I also knew Cheryl, or thought I knew Cheryl, and I felt that it would afford me an edge that no one else could have. I'd proven over and over that I could remove myself from the personal aspect, but maybe that's no longer possible."

"Are you saying that you're going to remove yourself from the case?"

"I don't know. Maybe." He sighed. "Even if I do, I have to resolve this matter with Cheryl."

"I guess I understand that," Erik answered. He let the silence remain between them for a few minutes before adding, "I intend to tell Cheryl that I've come clean with you. I won't interfere again, but I want you to know that neither will I abandon Cheryl. I feel like I made real progress with her the other day, and I want to play on that and see where it can go from there."

"I don't think that's wise," Curt said flatly. "I think you should stay out of her life altogether."

"I respect your opinion, Curt, but I'm not going to do that."

Curt slammed his hands down on the desk. "You are going to cause more problems, and I'm not going to sit back and let it happen."

"You have no right to tell me who I can befriend. Get real, Curt. You may be an officer of the law, deep into investigating this woman, but you aren't going to boss me around like one of your subordinates." Erik felt his own anger piqued for the first time that day. He had come to Curt in apologetic humility, but now he felt only wounded pride.

"I'm telling you, Erik, it's only going to hurt her more."

Erik got to his feet. "You don't know that. You want to pretend that you have some inside track to the woman just because six or seven years ago you shared marriage plans. Well, I'm telling you that you know nothing of the Cheryl Fairchild who exists today. She's hurt, vulnerable, and very, very angry. I'm not going to let her bear that alone while you and your buddies rip her apart in hopes of exposing the truth about her father."

He stormed out of the house, mindless of the fact that Curt called after him. He paid no attention to Christy's pleading that he come tell her what was going on and instead jumped into Ole Blue and ripped out of the drive.

Erik drove aimlessly through town until he found himself suddenly turning down Cheryl's street. In his heart he might have known all along that it was to Cheryl he was driving, but in his mind he argued the futility of it. Nevertheless, he turned into the drive and shut off the engine before he could change his mind.

He rang the bell and waited, watching and wondering if she would open the door to him. He thrust his hands deep into his jeans pockets and tried to force himself to remain calm. Soon, the door handle rattled and turned, and Cheryl appeared with a look of expectation on her face.

"Erik," she said and her expression fell.

Erik found her notably changed, although still quite dowdy from the Cheryl Fairchild he'd heard so much about. She wore a simple cotton skirt, which flowed down to her ankles in a pastel flower print, and a plain white cotton top. She looked airy and summery and better than he'd seen her since she'd entered the hospital. Maybe, just maybe, she was finally recovering emotionally.

"You look great!" Erik exclaimed. "What's the occasion?"

"Look, Erik, I asked you not to come around anymore." She glanced past him to the drive as if anticipating someone.

"You gonna have company?"

She nodded stiffly. "Yes, and I'd rather you go."

"Who's coming?"

"What?" she questioned, obviously distracted.

"Cheryl?"

She looked back to him and frowned. "A man from the *Denver Post* is coming to pick up some information and photographs."

"What information?"

Cheryl glanced down, seeming embarrassed. "I got a call yesterday from a man who is doing a feature on my father. The *Post* is naming my father Denver's man of the year."

"Did you confirm that?"

Cheryl's head snapped up, and she appeared quite hurt. "Why? Don't you think my dad deserves such a title?"

"I just think something like that ought to be checked out before handing personal items over. Did he ask you for a statement?" Erik asked suspiciously.

"He wanted a full interview, but I told him no."

"And did he accept that for an answer?"

"Look, stop giving me the third degree. You aren't my brother or the law, so stop asking so many questions." She was clearly agitated, and Erik didn't want to further alarm her. In his mind a million possibilities were playing themselves out. Who was this stranger, and was he acting on the up-and-up with Cheryl?

"Well," Erik said, taking hold of her arm and leading her back into the house, "I refuse to leave until after he comes and I feel certain he intends no harm."

Cheryl stared up at him in stunned surprise. "What are you doing? Let me go!" She jerked away, and Erik shrugged.

"Have it your way, but I stay."

"Fine!" she declared and crossed her arms against her chest.

Erik grinned. "Glad you're seeing it my way. Now, how about I fix us some lunch? I was supposed to have barbecue with my family, but I had to leave rather abruptly."

"I'm not hungry," she answered flatly and went to the front window to lift the curtain just enough to look out.

"Too bad," Erik replied. "I'm fixing us something anyway. I'll just be in the kitchen if you need me."

She said nothing, so he went off on his search. Something about the entire matter set his teeth on edge, and he had just reached the kitchen when the doorbell sounded. Turning on his heel, he started to head back to the living room when Cheryl's screams rent the air and made his blood run cold.

Chapter 7

Erik ran the final steps to the foyer, where a strange man held a small microphone in one hand and clicked away with a camera with his other. Cheryl held her hands up to her face, screaming with every click and whir of the 35mm.

"I just want to interview you!" the man declared over and over. "What was your involvement with Grant Burks? Were you involved in trafficking drugs with your father and Mr. Burks?"

Erik pushed his way between Cheryl and the man and grabbed the camera.

"Hey, you can't do that!" the man exclaimed.

"Oh, yeah? Watch me!" Erik pulled the back open and exposed the film, tearing it from the safety of the camera and throwing it to the floor. He handed the stunned man his camera, then reached out for the mike. "Give me that tape recorder."

"Look, I just want an interview. She owes the public an explanation."

"She doesn't owe anyone anything!"

Cheryl was still screaming and crying, and Erik's only thought was to remove the man and shelter her from further humiliation. Taking hold of the man by his shirt collar, Erik dragged him to his car.

"Give me the tape," he demanded, and the man finally gave up his fight and handed it over.

"You can't keep the world from learning the truth," the man said as he got into his car. "Sooner or later, someone is going to get her to talk. I figured it might as well be me as to be someone else."

"Well, you figured wrong, all the way around. If you ever show up here again, I'll personally take care of the problem." He knew he was angry and figured that the rage was evident on his face. He hoped he looked imposing. Apparently he did, for the man quickly nodded and started the car.

Erik hurried back into the house to find Cheryl still crying. Her hands were still protecting her face from view, and his heart went out to her. Closing the door, he took her in his arms and held her close. Her first response was to fight him, but he soothed her with soft words and gentle strokes.

"I won't let them hurt you," he whispered over and over. "You're safe now. I'm here, and I won't go until you feel better."

She grew still in his arms and, sobbing, put her head upon his shoulder. "He didn't even care about my father," she said.

"I know." Erik led her to the sofa and helped her to sit.

Cheryl gripped his arm tightly, and he had no other choice but to sit closely beside her. "He said he wanted to give Daddy an award. How could he be so cruel as to use my father to get to me like that?"

"People can be cruel."

She sobbed into her hands, and Erik pulled her against him and held her until her tears were spent. While she cried, he asked God to give her peace. He prayed, too, that God would use the tenderness he felt for her to bring her a better understanding of Jesus Christ.

"Nobody believes that my father was a good man. CJ thinks he killed her parents. Curt believes he headed up a drug ring. But Erik, they're wrong. My dad was a loving, generous man. He wouldn't have hurt anyone, especially not Doug O'Sullivan. He loved that man like a brother, and he would have given his life in Doug's place if that would have been possible." She looked up at Erik, seeming to need assurance that he believed her words were true.

"I'll bet he was a great dad."

She dried her tears and nodded. "Yes, he was. I could always count on him to be there for me. No matter how much I messed up. Now there's no one."

"That's not true, Cheryl. I'm here."

She looked at him, narrowing her eyes as if considering the validity of his words. "But you don't even know me."

Erik smiled. "Perhaps I know you better than you give me credit for."

"Why? How? I was a stranger to you and your family until last year."

"I don't think there has to be a lot of history between people in order to care for someone. I fly down to Mexico and South America almost every spring or summer with a group of Christian doctors. I help with the lab work and physical therapy, and I find I lose my heart to the people I work with. They need someone to care, and I guess God just gave me the ability to be that person."

Cheryl sat back and folded her hands. "Don't lose your heart to me, Erik Connors. I'm no good, and I know that. The only man who ever really loved me was my father, and apparently I wasn't enough to keep him here."

"Don't say that," Erik said softly. He turned to read the expression on her face and found such sadness that without thinking he pulled her back against him. "Everyone is deserving of love, and if I want to lose my heart to you, that's my business."

But even as he said it, Erik felt something stir inside. He was losing his heart to Cheryl. Maybe not falling in love, but in a deep abiding compassion that made him want to protect her from the world and its hurts.

Cheryl said nothing, seeming content to lean against him. Erik wondered how he could persuade her to let him be her friend. Even if friends were all they could ever be, Erik knew that he wanted it more than anything else. "Tell me about your father," he said without thinking.

"He wasn't involved—"

Erik stilled her. "I didn't ask you to defend his position in this mess. I asked you to tell me about him. Tell me what it was like growing up the daughter of Ben Fairchild. Tell me what you loved the most about him."

Cheryl pushed away, and Erik was surprised by the smile on her face. "That's easy. He always believed in me no matter how badly I goofed things up. He was never condemning—oh, maybe now and then. I had some trouble when I moved back here from Los Angeles. He wasn't too happy about my engagement. It was kind of sudden, and I didn't have a good track record with men. So I stayed in one of the downtown hotels and even lived a while with CJ O'Sullivan. I mean Aldersson."

"But you reconciled with your father?"

"Of course," she replied matter-of-factly. "He could never stay upset for long. Pretty soon he was calling me and saying that if I wanted to marry this man, he would have to respect my opinion of him."

"Sounds like he trusted you to be smart."

"Oh, I don't know. Maybe it was just that he loved to indulge me," she said rather sadly. "When my mother died, he had to fill the emptiness with something, and I was just as handy as anything else. He spoiled me and pampered me with all kinds of good things. We traveled and went on shopping sprees, and we always confided our deepest dreams and secrets to each other."

"How was it you ever found the need to leave home?"

Erik realized he'd asked a very personal question and quickly added, "I'm sorry. You don't have to answer that."

"It's all right," Cheryl said. She finally appeared calm and collected. "I guess with Daddy's spoiling came his overprotectiveness as well. He was smothering me, and yet, I couldn't bear the idea of hurting him. I told him I was desperate to see the world and try my wings and that I had to leave Denver and get away from the painful memories."

"What memories?"

"CJ and her parents," she said without thinking. "They were in a terrible plane crash, but of course, Curt—" She paused at the name. Drawing a deep breath, she continued, "You, no doubt, know all about that."

"Yes."

"Well, CJ became a recluse and withdrew from everyone and everything. Curt and I had broken up. He'd left Denver for parts unknown, and CJ wanted nothing to do with me. Daddy seemed so distraught over Doug and Jan O'Sullivan's deaths that he sort of withdrew as well. He wasn't himself for many years after that.

"Anyway, I convinced him that I needed space to grow up and a different setting in which to have fun. He was so consumed by the business and how to deal with all the problems that he gladly let me go. Well, maybe not gladly. But he gave me an unlimited bank account and access to company jets and housing throughout the world. What girl could have asked for more?"

"It must have seemed quite a fairy tale."

"For a time," Cheryl answered. She looked at him quite seriously and gave him the briefest hint of a smile. "But all good things come to an end, right?"

"Oh, I wouldn't say that. I think some good things go on and on."

"Like your God?"

Erik smiled. "Yes, for one."

Cheryl frowned and looked away. Erik didn't want to do anything to cause her to put up her walls again, and so he directed the conversation back to her childhood. "What do you remember about your dad from when you were small?"

The tension seemed to leave her face. "He was a very busy man, but he always took time out for me. He wasn't perfect. I'm not one of those people who can only remember the good things about a person who's died. He was often absent and often under a great deal of stress, but he was a good man, and I always knew that if I needed him, he would fly from the far corners of the world to be at my side." She smiled. "Mother said he loved us best, but that we weren't as demanding as a new business venture."

Erik chuckled. "I'm sure that's true."

Cheryl went on. "He would make most of my school programs and dance recitals, and when the flying circus really took off and we started doing more and more air shows, Daddy would just pack us along and take us with him. That's how I got to be such good friends with CJ and Curt."

She spoke his name again, only this time she didn't stumble over it, and Erik thought perhaps it was losing its power to haunt her.

They spent most of the afternoon in discussion, and only after noting that the clock was nearing five, did Erik suggest they call for some Chinese takeout and spend the evening together. Cheryl seemed to find this idea acceptable, and with that acceptance came Erik's first real hope. She had opened up to him in a way that he'd only dared to pray for. When she got up to go wash her face, Erik found himself in immediate prayer. *God, please help me to do the right thing. I care about this woman in a way that I hadn't really expected, but now I know it's true. I'm not in love with her, but I could easily find myself there. She doesn't know You, however, and because of that I can't give her the false illusion that such a thing could ever happen. I know it's wrong to be unequally yoked, and I know from other people just how painful those relationships can be. Please guard us both in this, and don't let us use the other for personal gain or glory.*

"Do you like sweet-and-sour chicken?"

Erik looked up to find that Cheryl had returned with a cordless phone.

"Sounds good. How about some cashew chicken as well?"

"That would be fine," she said softly, almost shyly. "I'll go look up the number and call it in."

And with that, she was gone again, and Erik could only sit back and contemplate his next move. *Don't lose sight of what you intended to do from the start,* he reminded himself. *Show her the way to God. Show her the love of Jesus.*

Chapter 8

Cheryl suddenly knew what it was to be truly paranoid about people and motives. Whenever the doorbell rang, she found herself cringing and seeking shelter in some remote part of the house where no one would see her. She'd admonished Mary, who now came three times a week, to let no one in and to leave the door unanswered.

She also ignored the telephone except when Erik called. She'd allow the answering machine to pick up the calls, and whenever Erik's voice sounded, a feeling of peace seemed to course through her. But the other calls left her frantic and worried. Multiple people called wanting information about her father. Others pretending to be some old friend of her father's called on the pretense of making sure she was all right.

Once, she'd thought the voice of an elderly man sounded familiar and picked up the call only to find that he was actually with one of the rag-mags, those paper tabloids sold in supermarkets everywhere. The man immediately offered her ten thousand dollars for her story, and Cheryl had crashed the receiver down, hoping that the sound had communicated her anger to the man.

From the day of her encounter with the man from the *Denver Post*, Cheryl kept the heavy drapes drawn in every room and the door securely locked. She saw the way her home had turned into a prison of sorts, but it was better than being exposed to prying eyes and the heartlessness of journalists.

Fridays were one of Mary's days off, and with them came a kind of gloom that Cheryl dreaded. Saturday and Sunday were days she'd always spent with her father, and even when she'd been engaged to Grant, she'd tried to keep those days open to catch up with what her father was doing or learn what new adventure he'd involved himself in.

But now he was gone, and Saturday and Sunday were just haunting reminders of his death. Because of this, Friday merely became a prelude to the coming weekend. Sitting in front of the television, Cheryl found herself watching a commercial for baby formula. Tears slid down her cheeks. Once again she remembered what she'd lost.

The only light that had been allowed into the room came by the way of the television, and with each changing scene, the shadows on the wall played tricks with Cheryl's imagination. She thought the rocking chair had begun to move, almost as if a ghostly image had taken up residence to keep her company.

"Daddy," she whispered, then the television lighting changed again, and she could see that the chair was quite empty.

Pressing her hands to her head, Cheryl thought perhaps she was going crazy. The sound of children laughing on the television made her stop up her ears and cry even harder. The sound of her heart pounded in her closed ears.

Ba-boom. . .ba-boom. . .ba-boom.

She imagined it slowing, weakening, growing steadily silent. She pictured it stopping altogether and of herself laying dead on the couch. There was no sense in existing when all she felt was pain. The misery threatened her by the minute anyway, so why not give in to it and end her life? Then they'd all be sorry they'd made her suffer.

Cheryl sobered and switched off the television. It wasn't like she hadn't considered suicide before. Her father had taken that way out, so it seemed only appropriate that she do the same. After all, if she was expected to forgive him his choice, surely he would forgive her choosing the same.

"Don't hate me, Daddy," she whispered, looking upward. "Don't hate me because I'm weak. You were the strongest man I knew, and you couldn't stand up under the pressure of life, so why should I have to?"

"Cheryl!" a masculine voice called out.

She started, not expecting to hear her own name being called. It was only then that she realized someone was pounding on the front door. The doorbell sounded, echoing through the silent house. This was followed again with the calling of her name. She strained to hear without leaving her sanctuary. The voice sounded vaguely familiar, yet she knew it wasn't Erik.

"Cheryl, open up. It's Curt!"

Her heart raced. Curt? Curt was here?

She moved toward the threshold and gripped the wall for extra support. She felt her knees grow weak, and her legs felt all rubbery. Curt was here, and he wouldn't leave until she opened the door and allowed him and his painful reminders to enter her privacy.

The pounding sounded again.

"Cheryl, I'll break this door down if I have to. You know me well enough to know that I'm speaking the truth."

She found herself actually smiling at this. Curt would do just what he'd said. She had little doubt about it. Curt could get blood out of turnips, as the old saying was so fond of pointing out.

Swallowing hard, she moved silently toward the door and put her hand out to touch the heavy oak. Curt pounded against it again, and Cheryl allowed the vibrations to shake through her. When it stopped, she turned the lock and knew that he would realize that once again he had won. She tried to imagine the look of sheer satisfaction on his face as they met eye-to-eye.

Turning the dead bolt, she glanced down momentarily to find that she was a mess, as usual. She'd thrown on her father's old, worn sweats and one of his T-shirts. The sweats had been cinched with their drawstring in order to keep them from falling off Cheryl's slender frame, and they ballooned out in a bulky fashion. She hadn't even bothered to brush her hair or put on makeup, and the thought of facing Curt in such a state seemed awkward. Not that she cared what he thought, but he knew how good she could look when she wanted to.

With one last deep breath, she opened the door and squinted against the brilliance of the noontime sun.

"What do you want?" she asked in a harsh monotone.

"Good grief, Cheryl," Curt said, without seeming the least bit concerned for her feelings. "What have you done to yourself? Or maybe I should ask, what have you neglected to do for yourself?"

Cheryl looked at him hard and tried to put aside her rage. If she lost control, Curt would only use it against her. Of this, she was certain.

"You aren't welcome here," she replied. "I think you know that, too."

Curt shrugged. "I'm on DEA business, and whether you like it or not, you have to deal with me." He glanced behind him for a moment, then faced her again. "Unless of course, you have my nosey brother-in-law hiding out in the house, ready to whisk you away from this confrontation."

Cheryl stepped back from the door and walked away. "Do what you have to," she called over her shoulder.

Curt followed her into the living room, and the first thing he did was throw open the drapes.

"Don't do that," Cheryl protested. "I don't need to have people spying on me."

"It's as dark as a tomb in here," Curt answered, allowing light to pour through yet another window.

"That's the way I want it." She plopped down into a wing-backed chair, giving him no chance to sit close to her. "My house. My tomb."

"There, that's better," he said, seeming to ignore her.

Cheryl noticed for the first time that he was dressed in navy slacks and a beige and navy pullover shirt. *He looks rather nice,* she thought. Just like he always did. Not at all like a murderer.

He caught her staring at him and smiled. "I'm still the same old Curt, if that's what you're wondering. I didn't suddenly grow horns and a tail, just because of what happened." He sat in another of the wing-backed chairs and leaned forward. "I want you to know how sorry I am that things have to be the way they are."

Her defenses went securely into place. "No, you aren't," she barely whispered. "You are on a personal vendetta, and I can only hope that your series of killings will eventually include me."

Curt's mouth dropped open, but no words came out. *Good,* Cheryl thought, *let him think on that one for a while.*

"Did you never happen to think about the pain you were inflicting? Didn't you ever wonder what the results of your meddling might be?" she questioned, looking at him with an unemotional expression. "Poor Curtiss O'Sullivan. He had to be a big man and prove to the world that his father was still a great flyer. No pilot error could be attributed to the great Douglas O'Sullivan's crash. No, better to make up a story about cocaine and corrupt business partners. Better to push old men into death and eliminate anyone else who got in the way, including unborn infants. No telling what that baby might have grown up to do for his or

346

her own method of revenge against the O'Sullivan family."

She fell silent and crossed her arms against her chest. She watched Curt, with a need to memorize everything about him. Her anger needed to be fed with the vision of the man who had caused her misery.

"Are you done?" he asked softly.

"Are you?" she countered without missing a beat.

Curt shifted uncomfortably and shook his head. "Not until this is completely resolved."

"What's the matter? Your list of victims still too short?" Her voice was heavily laden with sarcasm. The anger was surfacing against her will. "Hey, did you bring your gun? Maybe you could just go ahead and do me in right now. You want me to run? I could run," she said, getting to her feet. "That way it will look just as justifiable as the other killings."

"Sit down, Cheryl, and knock it off." Curt's voice was demanding, and his expression had changed to one of determined purpose.

"Oh," she said, sitting back down, "do you need a more steady target? That's right, Grant wasn't running when you killed him. Hey, neither was I. I just happened to get in the way. It really is a shame that you had the paramedics so close on hand. You killed my baby, but just didn't have enough luck to take us both out at the same time. Now you have to waste another bullet. Pity. Do they cost a lot? Maybe I could reimburse you."

"Stop it!" he exclaimed, getting to his feet. He crossed the small space between them and leaned over her, putting his hands on the armrests on either side of her. "Stop it now! I'm not going to listen to this anymore. I'm here to do my job and investigate you like I would any other suspect."

"So I'm a suspect now?" she said, staring him in the eye. Blink for blink, she kept her expression fixed.

Curt calmed a bit and straightened. "Yes."

Cheryl could see the anguish in his eyes. She'd really hurt him and it was easy to see that it had taken its toll on his composure. *Good. I hope it hurts a lot,* she thought. *I hope it hurts you like it hurts me.*

Curt retook his seat before continuing. "There are things that I hope you can clarify for me. Things that actually might take the heat off your father's involvement."

"What, and put it on Grant?" she asked angrily. "Of course, both men are dead so you might as well blame one as blame the other. Neither one can defend himself."

Curt sighed heavily. "I'm not trying to assign blame. I'm looking for the truth."

"Your truth," she replied, this time lowering her voice. "The kind of truth that wipes out the innocent and destroys all hope."

"Cheryl, I never meant for you or your unborn baby to get hurt. I never meant for Ben to die. I won't apologize for Grant, however. He pulled the gun first and shot first, and he put your life in danger, as well as Christy's and his own daughter's. Why is it so impossible for you to see that he didn't care who he killed or hurt, so long as he protected his shipment of cocaine?"

Cheryl remembered what Erik had pointed out about Grant deliberately shooting her in the stomach. She felt some of the fight go out from her as she noted the sincerity in Curt's eyes. This was Curt, the man she'd once loved. A man she knew better than many. She shook her head. No, she didn't know him at all. He was a killer, and he had ruined her life.

"Cheryl, I'm not without feeling, and if you'll recall, the first deaths related to this case were my own mother and father. You can deny that possiblity all you want, but the evidence was there and in place. Ben managed to get the matter swept under the rug in order to protect himself."

"Stop bad-mouthing my father," she said coolly. Forcing a calm to counter Curt's sympathetic speech, she continued, "You know very well that I cared greatly what happened to your parents. You are the one who shut me out and left for parts unknown after breaking our engagement. You were the one who deserted CJ when she needed you most, so please don't tell me how much you care."

Curt ran a hand through his hair. "Yes, I did desert you both when you needed me, but I couldn't deal with the situation, and I had to find a way to expose the truth. In my own youthful exuberance, I thought it might honestly be the only way to make things right again. I know now that it doesn't matter how people hate or how much anger they allow to control their actions. It doesn't bring dead bodies back to life. It didn't for me, and it won't for you, either."

Cheryl felt her breath catch at the truth in his words. She didn't want to listen to any more. She didn't want to believe Curt really cared.

"So why are you here? What is it you expect from me? If it's a confession, I hate to disappoint you, but I don't have one."

"I'm here to ask you about what you do have. You have memories of things your father might have said or done. You may even know where he's left vital information. We both need this matter settled, Cheryl. In case you didn't know it, the assets for O&F Aviation are frozen, and it's only a matter of time until you find yourself without any means of support."

Cheryl instantly thought of the fifty thousand dollars hidden in the lockbox. The lockbox! Eyeing Curt suspiciously, she questioned, "What kind of information do you mean?"

Curt seemed to relax a bit. "We're hoping there's paperwork. You know, something that might list buyers, sellers, drug exchange locations. Do you have any idea where such information might be kept?"

"Why should I?"

"I thought maybe Ben might have a special place in the house for keeping things he didn't want anyone else to get ahold of."

"You're that certain my father was the mastermind of your little drug ring?"

Curt shook his head. "I'm not certain of anything except what Ben told me."

"Which was?"

"That Grant forced him into the situation. It seems Grant found problems in the accounting department and threatened to expose O&F Aviation to the Internal Revenue Service if Ben didn't cooperate."

"I don't believe you," Cheryl said flatly.

"I don't much care. I know what Ben said, and I know, too, that he had a part in the plane crash that killed my parents. He told me so."

"No way!" she yelled, getting to her feet. "There is no way my father had anything to do with that. He wouldn't have been able to live with himself all these years."

Curt, too, got to his feet. "Cheryl, didn't it ever dawn on you that it was that which caused your father to act so strangely after the crash? By your own admission, Ben changed after my parents died. He took the crash very hard, you said. Isn't it possible that it wasn't just because friends had died, but because he had a hand in their death?"

"How dare you! Get out of my house!"

"You have to listen to reason, Cheryl, or you may find yourself behind bars. I'm having this house searched from top to bottom, and there's nothing you can do about it."

"Did you forget your buddies already took care of that while I was in the hospital?"

"It doesn't matter. We'll do it again. We'll do it over and over if it means that there is even the most remote possibility of finding the truth."

Cheryl turned away from him and crossed the room. "Until you show up with a search warrant, you can get out of my house. You've done me enough damage, Curt. I hardly think it fair that I should have to be confronted by my baby's killer. Why don't you send someone else next time?"

"Someone else might not be as generous as me," Curt said seriously. He came to stand beside her, and his expression softened in a way that Cheryl would just as soon forget. "Cheryl, I know you're hurting. I didn't stop caring about you just because I became a DEA officer and married Christy. You're like a part of the family to me. Don't shut me out."

Cheryl shook her head. "I'm nothing to you, and you're nothing to me. If you want to care, that's your problem, but maybe a better way of showing it would be to just stay away from me."

Curt sighed. "I'll go for now, but I'll be back later. Don't even think of not answering the door. I think you know me well enough to know that a locked door won't keep me out."

"Yes, I'm sure you'll plow right through any obstacle in order to get what you want," she answered, barely able to keep her anger in check.

She walked to the door and opened it for him. The sunlight didn't blind her as before, but the heat of the day hit her like a blast from a hot furnace. Stepping back, she let Curt pass. Curt turned to face her as if to say something more, but Cheryl read an instant sorrow in his expression that forced her to see his feelings were genuine. *I don't care,* she reasoned. *I don't care how sorry he is.*

"Cheryl," he began, "I hope that somehow, one day, you will forgive me my part in this. I hope that one day you'll understand my need for the truth."

"The truth is that you have ended my life in every way but one. I don't know how you live with what you've done. I don't know how you sleep nights or look at yourself in the mirror without wanting to put a gun to your head for the things you, alone, are responsible for." She saw his shoulders slump a bit and noted that his eyes grew moist. She hated him for making her feel like an ogre, but she pressed home her final point. "I'll never forgive you for killing the people I loved most, and I'll never forgive you for putting me through this misery."

Chapter 9

"Mary," Cheryl began, coming into the kitchen, "I need for you to do an errand for me. Do you mind?"

The older woman straightened from where she was bent over the dishwasher, stacking dirty dishes. "Not at all, Cheryl. What do you need?"

"I want you to go to the bank for me and see about cashing this check. I have no idea if this account is frozen or not, and I certainly don't want to call up and ask. I'm afraid that would only lead to them becoming suspicious if it's not."

Mary nodded. "What should I do?"

"Just take it to a teller and ask to cash it. Since it's drawn on that bank, they'll be able to access the account immediately, and there should not be any problem. Unless," she paused, biting at her lower lip, "unless the account is frozen to my use."

Mary closed the dishwasher and pulled off her apron. "And if they will cash it?"

Cheryl handed her the check. "If they will cash it, there's enough there to stock up on groceries, pay your salary, and keep a little cash in the house."

"Do you want me to go ahead and stop by the store on my way back?"

Cheryl nodded. "That would be great."

Mary gathered her things up and let herself out the back door. "There's an omelette on the warming tray," she said nonchalantly. "Don't forget to eat it."

Cheryl knew Mary would only make a big deal of things if she didn't eat, so rather than argue, she went immediately to the tray and pulled out the plate. "Looks good, Mary. I'll eat it right now." The old woman nodded approvingly and closed the door.

Cheryl picked up a fork and began to eat. At first she just picked around the edges, but soon the aroma and the taste made her hungry for more, and she polished it off in record time. In the old days before her father's death, worry had always given her a ravenous appetite. That, in turn, had given her more than a little bit of a battle to keep her rather voluptuous figure neat and trim. Now she was downright skinny, and the look was not good on her.

She paced the kitchen for a few minutes before deciding on a glass of orange juice. Would Mary be able to cash the check? Curt had warned her that sooner or later her money would be tight due to the feds putting a hold on her financial affairs. *Thank goodness he didn't know about the fifty grand,* she thought. That would be her salvation, thanks to her father's foresight. Still, she would have to be careful. Fifty thousand was a mere drop in the bucket compared to what she was used to having at her disposal. She immediately set her mind to ways of economizing and had just headed to her father's study when she heard the unmistakable roar of Erik's truck.

Going to the window, she pulled back the curtain enough to assure herself that it was him, and him alone, before opening the door.

"Erik, what a surprise." And for once, it seemed quite nice to have him show up unexpectedly.

"I tried to call, but they said your number had been disconnected. Is everything okay?"

"Not disconnected, just changed and unlisted," she said and motioned him inside. "Might as well come in since you're already here."

Erik grinned. "I'm not imposing?"

"Would it matter?" she asked with the slightest hint of good-natured teasing to her voice.

"Nope, not a bit."

"I didn't think so," she answered, and this time there followed a smile. "Come on in."

Cheryl led him to the family room and offered him a seat. "I suppose you heard about Curt's interview with me last week?"

Erik shook his head. "Curt's not telling me anything. I think I've been branded a traitor in the camp. After I came clean with him about sneaking you off that first time, he hasn't been too inclined to include me in his moves."

Cheryl curled up on the sofa and considered this for a moment. "I was pretty hard on him, but he deserved it. He has to know that his little game has hurt a great many people. I just didn't want to be bothered any more by it, and yet he storms into my house and demands that I remember the very things I'd gone out of my way to forget."

"Is that why you changed your telephone number?"

"That and the twenty to thirty calls I was getting from complete strangers. Most wanted to do an interview with me and just came right out and left a message on the machine. Others were more subtle. I've had calls from so many so-called 'friends of the family' that I was ready to scream. I've had calls from doctors, lawyers, politicians, security people, and a dozen others, all who professed to be deeply concerned, old friends of Dad who wanted to lend me support in my hour of need."

"Maybe they were legitimate," Erik suggested.

"Not a chance. Daddy didn't have that many friends. He was too cautious after losing Doug and Jan O'Sullivan and. . . ," she paused to take a long drink of the juice before adding, "my mother."

"But surely there were some of those who actually thought themselves to be friends," Erik replied. "Maybe they really were concerned about your well-being."

"Maybe," she said with a shrug, "but they were nowhere around when he killed himself four months ago. It wasn't until the DEA case was revealed and the shoot-out took place that any of this sudden interest in my well-being started up."

Erik nodded. "I guess I can see where you'd be skeptical."

Cheryl found herself relaxing in Erik's presence. It was strange, she thought, but he made her feel as though no one else in the world cared quite as much as he did. He made her realize that she didn't have to be alone, and yet, he was also mixed up in the whole affair.

"So how did your interview with Curt go?" Erik suddenly asked.

"Miserably, as I knew it would. Curt only wants to believe the worst about my father."

"Whereas you only want to believe the best?" he asked with a hesitant smile.

She nodded. "I suppose that's one way of putting it. And why not? I loved my father and will always love him. I don't want to see his memory dragged through the mud while Curt gets his revenge for something that might have been a total accident."

"But you can't be sure that what he suspects isn't dead to rights. Didn't he admit that your father told him of his involvement with the drug ring?"

Cheryl bristled at this. She wanted Erik to be a friend, not another adversary. "Those are Curt's words. I don't believe them for one minute."

"Then why would your father kill himself? He seemed for all purposes to have the world by the tail. Why would death all of a sudden be preferable to life? Then, too, you have to admit there was something going on between him and Grant. After all, Grant was working for your father under an assumed name."

Cheryl gulped down the remaining orange juice and tried to steady her nerves. "I know it looks bad." She fell silent for a few moments, then surprised both herself and Erik by asking, "What was Grant really like? I mean the Grant who was married to your sister?"

Erik's eyes widened for a moment. "He was the king of deception. I doubt seriously that he was ever faithful to Candy, and I still have a hard time figuring out why he even involved himself with her. Curt thinks it might have been as simple as the fact that he wanted to stay close to Christy's dress design business so that he could continue to import drugs through her warehouses. I'd like to believe that at one point he really did love Candy, for whatever reason. But I don't think he did. He was a user, Cheryl. He made Christy pay for Candy's hospital bills, and he insisted on money from Christy in order to 'buy' Sarah's adoption from him."

Cheryl tried to imagine that it was all true. Erik had no reason to lie to her, and yet she wanted so much for the entire matter to be a terrible mistake.

"He didn't want Sarah?" Cheryl asked, hesitantly.

"No. He told Candy that children were a complication to life that he didn't need. He was angry when she told him that she was already pregnant. I know, because I was there when she broke the news to all of us."

"He wasn't happy about our baby, either," she said in a whisper. She could remember only too well what he'd been like when he found out. He'd accused her of trying to step up the wedding before he was ready.

He'd said she had set a trap for him, and he didn't necessarily have to fall into it.

"It all figures," Erik said, seeming to sense her turmoil. "Grant had too many other irons in the fire. Children would have just interfered with his plans for quick breaks and easy getaways."

"But he married your sister," she replied flatly. "For some reason, it was important enough for him to tie himself that much."

"But what's a wife? It isn't like he'd have to arrange for her care if he should suddenly need to flee the country. He could just as easily divorce her from far away, as to stay here and be married. A child, however, would be an entirely different matter."

"Even if that was the real way Grant operated," she said, trying hard to put the pieces together, "my father was an honorable man. He was good and kind, and I know he could never have been capable of the things Curt has accused him of."

"Fathers don't always turn out the way we'd like them to be."

Cheryl frowned. "What's that supposed to mean?"

Erik shrugged. "We'd all like to believe the best about our parents, but sometimes it just isn't possible. Sometimes, our parents are the first ones to dispel the myths surrounding them."

"Is that how your parents were?" she asked. Suddenly she realized that she knew nothing about Erik and his childhood.

Erik's face contorted as if the pain of answering such a question had become too much. "My parents definitely dispelled any myths I had formulated in my mind."

"How?"

"My father, in particular, was a ruthless man. He did whatever he had to do, walked over whoever he had to walk over, all in order to get things his own way. He was unfaithful in every single relationship I ever saw him have. And that included those with my mother and sisters."

"What about your relationship with him?"

"Especially mine," he said and took a deep breath. "The man's corrupt, and he corrupts everything he touches. He uses people to get what he wants, and then he throws them away as though they were nothing more than wrappings on Christmas presents."

Cheryl frowned. Hadn't she done much the same in life? She knew that she could be ruthless when the situation presented itself. She had been heartless where Curt was concerned and had gone out of her way to say the most hurtful, mean-spirited things she could think of. She felt hot tears form in her eyes, but Erik didn't seem to notice them.

"I hated him for a long time. It took coming to God and begging Him to take the anger and rage from within me. I still can't say that I miss him or have any desire to see him, but I no longer hate him like I did."

Cheryl sniffed back tears, and Erik seemed to notice for the first time that she was crying. "I'm sorry," he said very softly. "I didn't mean to upset you."

His kindness only made matters worse. Cheryl began to cry in earnest. "I'm just as bad," she finally managed to say. "I've used people and walked over them on my way to the top. Grant was the only man I couldn't wrap around my finger and manipulate in the manner to which I was accustomed. He became a challenge and I took the bait without considering the cost. I threw myself into harm's way over and over again, and all in order to have my own way." Her voice was ragged with sorrow. "You must hate me. I sound just like your father."

Erik got up from his chair and came to sit beside her on the couch. "There's a great difference between you and my father," he said, putting his arm around her shoulder. With great tenderness, he lifted her face to meet his.

"There is?" she said, wishing against all odds that he was speaking the truth.

"Absolutely. My father has never once been repentant of his actions," Erik said quite seriously. "Where as with you, I see nothing but regret and the desire to be free from the part you once played. That woman doesn't live inside you anymore."

"How can you be so sure?" she asked, choking back a sob.

Erik smiled, and it gave her such warmth and hope that she wanted to throw herself against him and hang onto him as though he alone could show her the way to peace.

"I see it in your eyes," he replied. "I see it in your face, even though you try to keep your mask in place. I even see it in your actions. You've rid yourself of the clothes that once represented your lifestyle. Your clothes and hair and all that goes with them were visual symbols of what existed in the past. When you finally realize that they don't truly make the wo-man, you won't be so afraid to go back to wearing nice things.

"But I also know that you won't return to the lifestyle you lived back then. You've seen too much, and you know too much to go back and pretend that it doesn't hurt anyone—that it doesn't hurt you." He paused and let go of her face. "I think if you give it some thought, Cheryl, you'll see for yourself that it's true."

She continued to look at him for several moments before speaking. "There's nothing back there for me. That woman is dead, or should be."

"No," Erik replied and his voice held unmistakable tenderness. "That woman needs to live again, but not in the old way. She needs to repent and find peace with God and to realize that she isn't alone. The Bible says that when we come to accept God, we become new creatures and the old is cast off. Wouldn't you like that assurance for yourself?"

Cheryl felt goose bumps form on her arms. Erik had opened a door that she'd thought forever closed to her. The only question now was whether she'd ever have the courage to cross the threshold.

Chapter 10

I'm really glad you agreed to talk to me," CJ Aldersson said, taking a seat in the living room.

Cheryl attempted a smile and took a place on the sofa. "I figured you weren't going to give up."

"You didn't give up on me."

"Yes, I did," Cheryl stated quite seriously. "When I grew tired of being unable to help you after the plane crash, I took off for Europe. Then when I came back to Denver and made plans for marriage to Strat—Grant, well I could see that you needed a great deal of help, and again I didn't know what to do."

"But you didn't stop caring about me, did you?"

Cheryl studied CJ for a moment and considered her question in earnest. For far too long she'd given flippant answers and generalized speeches. Always, she kept in mind what people wanted to hear, and somehow she managed to play the game and tell them what they needed her to say. But no more. She was determined to be honest and straightforward.

"No, I didn't stop caring," she admitted, "but I replaced the importance of our friendship with other things."

"What about now?" CJ asked, pushing back her shoulder-length, copper hair.

Cheryl shook her head. "I don't know, and that's the honest truth. I'm afraid to care about anyone, and I can't let go of my anger at Curt."

"But you loved him once. Can't you draw on that for the moment and remember the good things about him? Can't you try to realize how important it is for him to resolve this situation?"

"But at what cost, CJ? Where do you stop? Curt's need to resolve the situation, as you put it, has taken its toll of victims."

"Why can't you see that Curt never created the victims to start

359

with?" CJ's voice took on a hard edge. "Cheryl, I'm going to tell you something that I never thought I would."

Cheryl watched her friend twist her hands together as if seeking some kind of inner strength.

"When the plane went down the night of the crash, my father turned to my mother. With sadness that was born out of the reality of what was about to happen, he said, 'He's done us in.' My mother's response was rather muffled, and for years I thought she'd replied, 'In?' Now I know that she wasn't saying 'in,' but rather 'Ben.' My father nodded in affirmation. You see, he knew Ben had some part in it because he'd just talked to him before leaving the airport. He'd found cocaine on one of the O&F planes and Ben had told him to mind his own business, or threatened him, or whatever else you want to imagine. We'll never know because my father carried it to the grave, and your father didn't say a whole lot about it."

Cheryl refrained from demanding that CJ leave the house. She felt confused by her friend's statement. It was as if forces were joining together to show her a side of her father that she'd never believed existed.

"I don't want you to feel bad or hate anyone, Cheryl," CJ continued. "I really don't. I no longer feel angry with Ben or, for that matter, Grant. To hate either one or to allow the bitterness of the past to take hold would be to give in to the evil of this entire situation. God doesn't want that for me, and He doesn't want that for you."

"I don't know what to think anymore," Cheryl finally said, laying her head back to stare at the ceiling. "Everyone keeps coming to me to show me these things about my father. Things that I can't believe, yet things that are hard to deny. I just know how he felt about us. How much he loved me and my mother, and how much he loved your father. I can't see him jeopardizing that respect and love for a few extra dollars in drug money."

"But Curt says that Ben explained his predicament, and while it doesn't justify his actions, it certainly shows that your father wasn't just in it for the money."

"And how is that?"

"Ben accidentally fell behind in some bookkeeping, and when it was discovered, O&F owed the IRS over a million dollars in back taxes. The IRS didn't know this, however, and when Grant found out the mistake had been made, he went to Ben and proposed a deal. Ben had little choice. Either he would bury the company in a financial crisis that would probably result in him having to file bankruptcy, or he could go along with Grant's request. My thoughts are that he didn't want to lose my father's respect, nor did he want the public shame and humiliation that would be brought down on them. You know for yourself that appearance was everything to Ben."

Cheryl slowly looked back at CJ and nodded. "He wanted to make a statement to the world. I guess he's done just that."

CJ crossed her legs and relaxed against the back of the chair. "Cheryl, please don't shut me out anymore. I'm not the enemy, and neither is Curt. Don't you want to know the truth? Wouldn't you rather have all slates be wiped clean?"

"Even if it means that my father's name is forever tarnished?"

"Do you think if you don't cooperate and remain bitterly hateful that you will stop the progress of this investigation? Don't you realize that with or without you, they will come to the truth?"

Cheryl shrugged. "At least without me, I won't be a traitor to Dad."

"How does being truthful make you a traitor?" CJ questioned softly.

Tucking her jean-clad legs under her, Cheryl released a heavy sigh. "I don't know. I don't know much of anything anymore."

"Then know this. I'm your friend, and I care about you. I will always be here for you."

Cheryl felt her eyes grow moist. *I will not cry*, she admonished herself. "I'm not worthy of your friendship," she told CJ quite honestly. "The things I've done—the person I am. I don't deserve friends or love."

"Nonsense," CJ replied, shaking her head. "That simply isn't true. There is no one whom God can't forgive, and if we are to follow His example, then we must forgive each other and ourselves, as well."

Cheryl regained her composure before answering. CJ's words so clearly mirrored the things Erik had told her that deep within she found herself actually hoping against the odds that they were true.

"I don't know if I can forgive," Cheryl replied. "I don't know if I want to forgive."

CJ nodded. "I think I can understand, maybe not in full, but at least enough to know that what you say is born of pain and loss. Just promise me that you'll think about what I've said and that you'll give God a chance to reveal Himself to you."

"That much I can do," Cheryl answered.

Just then the doorbell sounded and both women jumped in surprise. Cheryl went to the window and saw that a dark-headed man in a business suit stood outside her door.

"I don't know who it is," she said, coming back to where CJ sat. "I get pretty weird people from time to time. They want interviews or exclusive information about the case, and so most of the time, I don't even open the door."

"Would you like me to answer it?" CJ asked, getting to her feet.

"Would you?"

"Sure." CJ went to the door while Cheryl waited in hiding around the foyer wall. "Can I help you?" she heard CJ question.

"I'm with the DEA," the man said. "Damon Brooks is my name, and I'm here to speak with Ms. Fairchild. Is that you?"

"No, I'm CJ Aldersson, her friend."

"I'm Cheryl Fairchild," Cheryl said, coming into the foyer. "What do you want?"

"I need to ask you some information."

"I just talked to Curt O'Sullivan last week."

The man seemed not in the least bit fazed by this information. "As I said, ma'am, I need to talk to you."

"Then I suppose you should come in," Cheryl replied and turned to CJ. "Can you stay?"

"Absolutely."

The three made their way into the living room, where CJ and Cheryl sat together on the couch, while Damon Brooks took a seat in one of the wing-backed chairs. He took out a pad of paper and a pen before turning a glaring look on Cheryl.

"We need your father's list of contacts," he said abruptly.

It was exactly what Curt had asked for when he'd been there, and Cheryl shook her head. "I don't know about any list of contacts."

"Come now, Ms. Fairchild." The man's irritation grew quite apparent.

"Withholding evidence is only going to dig you in deeper."

Cheryl felt her face flush. "I'm not in this thing, no matter how much you want to put me there."

"You can't expect us to believe that. You were the mistress of Grant Burks, one of the key players, and you were the daughter of Ben Fairchild. We have enough information to see you sent to prison for a very long time."

"But I haven't done anything, except perhaps—" she stopped and glanced momentarily at CJ "—except love the wrong people."

"I'm not playing games with you, lady. You may have thought you could get away with this kind of thing with O'Sullivan, but you are dealing with a completely different man now."

"Is that any reason to be rude and uncivil?" CJ interjected, eyeing the man with a look of severity.

"You related to this case?" Brooks asked angrily.

"Yes, as a matter of fact, I am. I'm CJ Aldersson, and my brother is Curt O'Sullivan. We are co-owners in O&F Aviation with Miss Fairchild."

The man noted this on paper, while posing yet another question. "Do you know anything about a list of contacts and exchange locations?"

"No," CJ replied flatly.

Cheryl felt relief that the pressure was off her even for a few moments. She thought of the papers in the lockbox and realized that they had to be exactly what the DEA was looking for. She thought about producing the goods, then decided against it. What if the papers showed her father to truly have been the mastermind behind the entire drug operation? Could she bear up under that kind of truth? Could she stand by and see his memory forever scarred?

"I don't think you're listening to me, Ms Fairchild." The man leaned forward aggressively.

His action caused Cheryl to grow quite angry. No one came into her house and made threatening motions and got away with it. Standing up, she proclaimed, "As I told Curt, I have nothing to say or to show or to share. You aren't welcome in this house, and the sooner you get it through your heads, the better."

The man jumped to his feet and pushed Cheryl backward, shocking both women. He reached out as if to take hold of her, and Cheryl fought back by slapping the man's arms until finally he stilled her with a vicious hold. His ironclad grip threatened to break her bones. Cheryl winced in pain, and he yanked her to her feet.

"You'd better get it through your head that we mean business. You have something we want, and we aren't going to lie down and play dead just because you tell us to."

"Leave her alone!" CJ declared. "You have no right to handle her in that fashion."

"This is nothing compared to what I'm going to do if she doesn't come clean."

Now Cheryl was truly sorry she'd demanded Curt to send someone else in his stead. She was frightened by the dark eyes of the stranger. There was an underlying hatred in his expression, and he seemed to take great joy in hurting her.

Twisting her wrists outward, Cheryl screamed in pain while CJ, unable to stand any more of it, got up from her chair and went to the phone.

"What do you think you're doing?" the man demanded.

"I'm calling my brother. Your actions are unacceptable, and no DEA agent has the right to treat another person this way."

The man laughed in stilted amusement. "If you don't want me to break your friend's arms, you'll put the phone down and sit yourself back on the couch."

CJ held the phone for a moment. She seemed to weigh the validity of his threat before returning the receiver to its cradle. "Very well. But you won't get away with this, Mr. Brooks. I'll see you brought up on charges of harassment and conduct unbefitting an officer of the law."

The man suddenly pushed Cheryl backward. She fought to regain her balance, but it was useless. She fell against the sofa and struggled to compose herself. Terror gripped her like an iron binding. She could hardly breathe for fear of what the man might do next.

"I'm going to search this house, and there's nothing you can do to stop me."

"Without a search warrant," Cheryl said, suddenly allowing her anger to make her brave, "you aren't going to do anything of the kind."

Just then Mary could be heard coming into the house through the kitchen door. "Cheryl!" she called, "I'm here." She entered the room and frowned at the sight. "Am I interrupting?"

"Mary, call the police!" Cheryl declared, and the man seemed to realize he was suddenly dealing with more than he had asked for.

"There's no need for that," Damon Brooks said. "I will return with your precious search warrant. Until then, don't even think of removing evidence from this house. You're being watched, and it would give me extreme pleasure to apprehend you for failure to disclose criminal evidence."

With that he left, slamming the door behind him, leaving the three women to stare after him as if they'd just witnessed some unbelievable apparition. Cheryl began to tremble, and her teeth rattled together noisily.

"I'm going to have a few words with Curt about this," CJ said, getting to her feet. "If the DEA thinks they can come in and break people's bones in order to conjure up confessions, they have another thing coming."

Mary stared at both women in complete confusion.

"What happened?"

"I. . .I. . .don't wa. . .want to talk about it," Cheryl stammered.

"Suffice it to say, Mary," CJ said, moving to the foyer, "the DEA got a little out of hand. Cheryl, I'd keep the door locked if I were you. I know you have to deal with these investigations, but I'd make sure someone was here to protect you."

Cheryl immediately thought of Erik, but there was no way she was going to call him and ask him to camp out on her doorstep. No matter how appealing the thought might be.

Chapter 11

B^{oom!} Cheryl awoke just before dawn to a late summer thunderstorm in full progress. The flashes of lightning lit the room up as though it were daylight, and with each flash came an earsplitting crash of thunder. The windowpane rattled mercilessly and barely had time to stop vibrating before the next strike came.

Sitting up and hugging her knees to her chest, Cheryl remembered how frightened she'd been of storms as a child. "Think of something pleasant," her mother would say. But for Cheryl there were so many unpleasant things to dwell upon that the pleasant ones didn't stand a chance.

Glancing at the clock on her nightstand, she saw the red illuminated numbers and read 5:45. *It will soon be light,* she thought and decided to go ahead and start the day. The storm would surely seem less menacing if she dressed and busied herself. She went to find her standard wardrobe, T-shirts and jeans, but suddenly felt compelled to do something with her hair. She studied it in the mirror for a moment. The golden ash of her blond hair seemed dingy against her pale skin. When had she last washed it? She couldn't remember.

That determined her first order of business, and despite the fact that the thunderstorm raged on around her, Cheryl stepped into a steaming shower.

The water ran down over her head, penetrating the layers of dirty blond curls, saturating her dry, abused skin. It felt better than Cheryl could ever remember a shower feeling. She lathered her hair and scrubbed until her head ached from the attention. She rinsed this out and lathered again—determined to wash away even the remotest particle of dirt. With this accomplished, she poured on expensive conditioner and massaged her hair the way her hairdresser Michelle had told her to do. *Good grief,* she thought, *Michelle must think I fell off the face of the earth.*

"I guess in a way, I did," she mused aloud. Some people sang in the shower, but Cheryl had always been given to having full conversations with herself.

"I should make an appointment to have my hair cut." She held up the limp lengthy curls and sighed. There had been a time when she'd been a regular every week at the beauty salon.

"What have I done to myself?" she questioned, knowing full well the answer. She'd given up on life, but slowly through the efforts of her friends, and even her enemies, Cheryl realized that just because she wanted life to end was no sure sign that it would. She picked up a plush washcloth and soap and began to wash her body, thinking as she did that she needed to somehow find her way back among the living.

"But I don't feel alive," she said and passed the cloth over her stomach. She remembered the baby, something that happened at the strangest moments. As usual, tears came unbidden to her eyes. Why was this so hard to get past? It was just a baby. An unborn fetus without a name or, for all she knew, sex.

But wait, didn't her obstetrician tell her that the sex of the baby could be determined early on? She had been well into her fourth month when the shooting took place. Why had she never thought to ask about the sex of her miscarried child? Beyond that, what had happened to her baby? She shuddered to think of it joining a pile of aborted fetuses. Those babies had also been murdered, as far as she considered it, but they hadn't been wanted, and hers had been.

So many questions came to mind, and her thoughts blocked out any fear of the storm. She would call her doctor as soon as the office was open and see if the records showed what the sex of her baby had been. It seemed to comfort her to imagine that within hours she would know if she'd lost a son or daughter. These thoughts made a normal progression to the desire to name her unborn child and maybe even erect a memorial stone beside her father's grave in honor of the baby no one would ever know.

Cheryl finished the shower with a new, determined purpose. It wasn't until she'd stepped out and was toweling herself off that she noticed the tile that safely hid her father's lockbox. She pulled on her robe and went to pry open the tile. The need to review the contents of the box was strong. Mary had been able to cash her check, but Cheryl wondered how long those funds would hold out. She couldn't have more than six or seven thousand dollars in that account, and there was no way of knowing whether she could access money from any of the other accounts.

She pulled out the lockbox and took it to the bathroom vanity. Since she'd pried the lock once before, it now wanted to stick and refuse her admission. She opened the drawer and found a pair of styling scissors, which she immediately lodged between the metal frame of the box in order to force it open once again.

Pop! The noise startled her as the lid sprang back and slapped against the countertop.

The money stared up at her like a faithful reminder of her father. Maybe he had known all along that she'd have need of this money. Maybe he'd figured he might need it himself. She fingered it gently, reassuring herself that she'd not be destitute if the bank refused her more withdrawals. Next she took up the paper lists and this time began to read them more carefully. The one with symbols and abbreviations still made little sense, but the one with addresses made Cheryl feel suddenly self-conscious.

Her skin felt prickly, and the hair on her neck stood on end. She felt her heart pounding within her chest and knew that this had to be what the DEA so badly coveted. She licked her lips nervously and tried to decide what to do. From the sounds of it, the storm had died out or at least moved off in a direction away from the city. She looked at the first address and realized that she was quite familiar with the location. Getting there would be a breeze.

Getting there.

Since the shooting she'd not been out on her own even once. Now she was contemplating getting into her car and driving to a location where she had no idea what she'd come up against.

It can't be helped, she thought. She stuffed the list in her robe pocket and had started to replace the lockbox, when it dawned on her that she might need the keys. She reopened the lid and took out the keys as well. Replacing the box, she carefully used the toothpaste once again and secured the tile in place. Satisfied that it looked identical to the others, she hurried to get dressed.

It was only a little after seven when she pulled the car from the garage. She was relieved to find nearly a full tank of gas, and after one quick glance at the list, she mustered up her courage and pulled the car into the street.

Her nerves were stretched taut like radio-tower guy wires. Everything seemed to startle her. The traffic was heavy. She'd forgotten it was Monday morning. Rush hour began early in Denver, and this day was no exception. She maneuvered the car onto Interstate 25 and merged with the oncoming traffic. Beads of sweat formed on her brow, and her hands began to shake uncontrollably. Gripping the steering wheel tightly, she watched for her exit with an apprehensive eye.

Splash! A semi roared past her, spraying up water against her windshield. Cheryl let out a cry and swerved away, almost hitting the line of cars in the next lane. Fighting her fears, she steadied the wheel and signaled to move into the right-hand lane. Two more miles, she noted. Just two more miles and she would be at the appropriate exit. She tried to think about days gone by when she'd whip up and down the interstate like it was her own private drive. She'd been brave then. Brave and certain that nothing bad could ever happen to her. Well, that theory had certainly been blown apart.

She exited the freeway and made her way to the address on the list. The streets were waterlogged, and everything around her looked saturated from the early morning storm. The sky remained gray, lifeless, as though it couldn't decide if it wanted to rain again or not. She hated days like this. She always had. They seemed to drag on in indifference to everyone, not really threatening, but neither did they signal comfort. It was rather a harsh reminder of her own life. She was on permanent hold, or so it seemed. Neither living nor dead. Just existing.

She turned off the paved roads and found herself on a gravel road heading even farther south of town. The houses and businesses were fewer here, although there were still enough to give her a sense of security. She hadn't thought about anyone trying to harm her or approach her for an interview before leaving the house. What if someone had followed her? Someone from the paper or television! They might try to photograph her.

She glanced around, checking her side and rearview mirrors. There didn't appear to be any ominous vehicle behind her, and no one seemed to give her the slightest attention as she drove past. *Good,* she thought and rested a bit easier.

Pulling up to a mailbox that marked a muddy drive, Cheryl noted that this was the first address on the list. A chain-link fence kept intruders from going any farther than pulling in off the street, and Cheryl decided to park and give the ring of keys a try.

Hesitantly, she got out and glanced around. No one seemed at all interested in what she was doing, and there didn't appear to be any other traffic on the road. She played at the padlock, trying first one key and then another, and had nearly given up when the mechanism released and the lock sprang open. Her mouth went dry. So far, so good. She swung the gate open and hurried back to the car.

Pulling down the muddy drive, Cheryl came face-to-face with a metal structure. It appeared to be some kind of storage building or small warehouse. Cheryl had the distinct feeling that she was about to unlock a great many secrets as she pulled the car around to the back. Wondering what she should do, she sat for several minutes in the silence of the morning. It would seem, she reasoned, that maybe Curt hadn't been so far out of line to believe that her father had played a much bigger role in the operation than anyone had imagined. After all, she was here, and the place looked deserted and seemed a very reasonable location for the exchange of drugs.

She got out of the car and walked around to the side of the building where a single door and window were located. She tried the handle and found it locked. Remembering the keys, she started back for the car just as she caught the sound of another car coming down the main gravel road. She froze. What if someone had followed her here? She ran for her car and watched from its safety as the other vehicle passed down the road. It had slowed just enough to make Cheryl aware that whether they were there for her benefit or not, they were definitely interested in what was going on. As soon as they were well out of sight, Cheryl flooded the gas, spinning mud everywhere as she made her escape.

Not even bothering to relock the fence gate, Cheryl hurried back into the city. Her heart was still racing when she made the street corner where her beauty salon was located. *Perhaps it wouldn't be wise to go home just yet,* she thought. *Maybe I should stop and talk to Michelle.*

Pulling into the parking lot, Cheryl suddenly realized it wasn't even nine o'clock yet. The salon wouldn't be open for at least two hours. Feeling rather foolish for her fears, she headed home and decided that she knew enough. She wasn't going to make any more amateur sleuthing trips. She hit the garage opener remote and pulled the car inside.

For several minutes she sat behind the wheel and forced herself to calm down. Whatever the list represented, there was no way she wanted it to fall into the hands of the DEA. It was hard enough to realize that her father had been involved with the drugs, but the list seemed to make it clear—that, along with the money and the fact that Curt had spoken of her father's confession. She'd never known Curt to lie, even when it caused someone else discomfort.

That, perhaps, was the hardest thing of all to realize. Curt probably had every reason to suspect her father, and he was probably right about Grant as well. Suddenly she felt very alone, and the image of Erik Connors came to mind. She wished he were there to offer her his impish smile and soft-spoken words of comfort. Maybe she should call him.

"Maybe I will," she murmured. "There's no reason I shouldn't."

Chapter 12

E rik wanted to sing all the way to Cheryl's house. She'd called him. She'd actually asked him to come to her house. Uncertain exactly what it meant, Erik tried hard not to get his hopes up. It could be anything. She might want to tell him to stay away from her. On the other hand. . . He smiled. It could be that she was healing enough that she desired companionship.

He wheeled Ole Blue into the circular drive and shut off the engine. "Lord," he whispered before getting out of the truck, "please don't let me say the wrong thing. This looks like a good thing here, and maybe Cheryl's ready to accept that You really do care about her." He glanced at the house and felt a twinge of emotion as he continued. "Maybe she's ready to accept that I care about her, too." He sighed and opened the door. "Just don't let my feelings get in the way of helping her see that she can be forgiven. In Jesus' name, amen."

In the fading light, he noticed muddy tire tracks on the wet pavement of the driveway. It had drizzled rain off and on throughout the day, but not enough to wash away the evidence that someone had come to visit. Apprehensive, he wondered who was pestering Cheryl now. He ambled up the walkway and reached out to knock on the door just as Cheryl opened it and greeted him.

"I'm glad you could come over," she said rather nervously.

Erik noticed that she was straining to look behind him, so he, too, turned to look around. "You expecting someone?" His heart took a bit of a nosedive, fearing that the only reason she had called was in order to have him strong-arm another unwanted visitor.

"No, just you," she admitted softly.

Erik turned back around and smiled. "Good. I like the sound of that."

She gave a shot at smiling and opened the door wider. "Come on in."

He followed her into the house just as the grandfather clock chimed seven. "So what did you do all day?"

"Nothing. At least nothing worth talking about," Cheryl said, directing them to the family room in the back of the house.

"I saw muddy tire tracks in the drive. Did you have visitors?"

Cheryl stopped abruptly. Her face seemed quite pale. "Ah, well, CJ stopped by for just a few minutes. She wanted to make sure I was okay after my last encounter with the DEA. She still hasn't managed to talk to Curt about it, but she intends to."

"What happened?" Erik asked, noting the agitation in her voice.

"It doesn't matter now," she said, waving him to take a seat. "Are you sure that you didn't already have plans for the evening?"

The evening? Erik wondered to himself. She'd said nothing about spending the evening with her. He decided to play it cool and not let on how surprised he was by this turn of events. "No, I didn't have anything planned. I had to work overtime. You called just as I got home from the hospital. It was absolutely perfect timing."

"I tried calling earlier," she admitted. "I didn't know what your schedule was."

"Well, it's fairly simple—at least usually it's fairly simple. I go to work at five-thirty in the morning. Actually my shift starts at six o'clock, but I have to change into scrubs, so I need extra time. Then I work until two-thirty, shower and change back into my street clothes, and home I go. Today was extrabusy so they asked me to work over."

Cheryl nodded. "What all do you do at the hospital?"

Erik laughed. "It'd be easier to tell you what I don't do. Lab technicians hardly lead the glamorous life." He plopped down on the couch, hoping she'd do the same. When she did, he continued. "I draw blood from patients, and then I take it back to the lab and analyze it. Sometimes, the vampires do all the sticks, that is to say the lab assistants do all the blood collections." He grinned. "We have our own language at the lab."

"So you work with a microscope and decide what's wrong with people?"

"Sometimes, but a lot of times I run the blood through a series of machines. We have great computerized testing these days, and it's a wonder what you can learn about a person from blood. Your blood tells the story of your life." He thought of how this might make a great way to steer the conversation toward Christ, but before he could speak, Cheryl was asking him another question.

"Do you have a. . .well. . .someone in your life?" She lowered her gaze, seeming quite shy about asking.

"You mean like a girlfriend?" She barely glanced up and nodded. Erik shook his head. "No, there's no one at all."

"Why not?" she asked, seeming less embarrassed.

Erik tried to keep the conversation very casual. He didn't want to alarm her by bringing his new feelings for her into the picture. "I guess I just never found the right woman. For a long time I concentrated on school. I became a physical therapist before going back to college to become a lab tech. Everyone thought I was crazy because physical therapy pays a whole lot better, but I wanted to have a broad scope of training."

"Why's that?"

"I'd kind of like to go into missions work," he answered. He wondered what she'd think of this.

"You mean like to Africa or India?" She seemed horrified.

"No, probably more like South or Central America. There's a large number of destitute people down there, and they need a great many things. It also allows me to get in some extra flying time. That way I can keep up my license."

Cheryl rolled her eyes. "Another pilot."

Erik grinned. "Do you have a lot of us in your life?"

She seemed to grow sad. "Used to."

Erik didn't want to see her withdraw into the past, so he hurried forward with the conversation. "Anyway, enough about me. What about you? What are you going to do with yourself now that you've nearly recovered from the shooting?"

She shook her head and looked away. "I don't know. Daddy always figured I'd come into the business. O&F Aviation business, that is. I guess he figured I'd make a good ornamental executive or something like that."

"You didn't see it that way?"

"Not really. I'm not cut out for much. I don't have skills or schooling or training, and I certainly don't have the interest."

"What would you like to do? What are you good at?"

"Nothing," she answered flatly. "Nothing but causing trouble. . . apparently."

"I don't believe that for a minute," Erik said. "But I didn't come over here for a pity party." Cheryl's head snapped up at this. "I figure you have enough time by yourself to wallow in sorrow." He smiled. "Am I right?"

Reluctantly she nodded in agreement. "I didn't call you over for that reason, either."

"Good. Why don't you tell me why you did call?"

"I just thought some company would be nice."

Erik thought she seemed to be hiding something, but he didn't push her. Maybe once she relaxed and realized he was willing to go the distance with her, she'd open up and trust him to understand her fears. "Do you want to go out?" he asked softly.

"No!" she exclaimed so quickly that Erik was certain something was wrong.

"Might I ask why?"

She looked at him, her blue eyes wide with fear. "I'm not ready for that."

"Okay. You want me to go rent some movies, maybe pick up some Chinese food again?"

"No!" She rubbed her arms as if chilled in spite of her long-sleeved blouse.

The desperation in her voice made Erik unable to remain silent. "Are you afraid of something in particular or just everything in general?"

"It's just a bad day for me, okay? First the storm and then. . ." She fell silent.

"Then?" He reached out to touch her arm. "Then what?"

"Nothing. It's not important."

Erik was beginning to get a little frustrated. He wasn't about to sit around all evening trying to pull conversation out of Cheryl. On the other hand, he didn't want to hurt her feelings or to cause her more grief. He didn't know what to do. Something was really bothering her, and he wanted to help. Then it dawned on him that maybe she'd changed her mind about having him over. Maybe she regretted it and just didn't know how to tell him to go.

"Do you want me to leave?"

"No! Why would you think that?" She seemed very upset with his question.

"I don't know. I guess because you're acting a bit strange. You're obviously upset about something, but you won't talk to me, and I thought maybe you were beginning to regret calling me over."

"Not at all." Cheryl let out a heavy sigh and seemed to search for words. "It's my father's birthday."

Erik relaxed. That explained a great deal. Of course she was having difficulty with the day. "Why didn't you just tell me that in the first place? I would have understood."

"I didn't want to be a baby about it all. It isn't the only thing that has me down, but it's one of the biggest reasons."

"So what do we do about it?"

Cheryl shrugged. "I'm not sure. Mary left some things to eat, and I could warm them up."

"That sounds good." He motioned to the television and video machine. "Do you have any movies you'd like to watch?"

"I don't know. We have a whole cabinet of movies over there," she said, pointing to a huge mahogany cabinet. "You could pick out something. Only. . ."

"Only?"

"Don't make it sad. I don't think I could take sad."

"Okay. You go fix us up something to eat, and I'll look for a non-sad movie."

Cheryl smiled weakly, and Erik noticed that for the first time since he'd seen her in the hospital, she was wearing the lightest touch of makeup. *She's pretty,* he thought. No, she was beautiful, and he knew that he was losing his heart to her. In spite of the fact that she'd warned him not to.

"Are you sure you don't mind staying?"

Erik wanted to go to her and pull her into his arms. He wanted to reassure her over and over that he didn't mind, but he was afraid that such a display of open emotion would send her running. So he played it as nonchalant as he possibly could. "I didn't have anything better to do."

She seemed satisfied with this and took herself off in the direction of the kitchen. After she'd gone, Erik let out his breath. His heart was pounding at ninety miles a minute. There was such a delicate balance to maintain, and he wasn't sure he could keep up his appearance of disinterest for much longer. He really liked her, and he wanted to know her better—wanted to take her out and bring her into the world of the living. Knowing the kind of man Grant had been, he wanted to show her that some men were honorable and true. He wanted to prove to her that she could fall in love with a man and not get hurt.

And he wanted to be that man.

Walking over to the movie cabinet, Erik felt a burden on him like he'd never known before. *This started out as a holy mission,* he reminded himself. He wasn't supposed to fall in love or have feelings other than those of a Christian brother for a lost soul. He opened the mahogany doors and stared in wonder at the vast selection of videos. There were old movies as well as new releases, and he had an endless supply of topics to choose from.

"Don't make it sad," she had said, and he could still see the pleading in her sapphire-blue eyes.

"Nothing sad," he said, running a finger over each of the listed features.

He tried desperately to remember the plots and incidents of each and every movie. A love story might upset her because of what she'd lost. A movie with children, especially babies, might depress her because of the miscarriage. He reached for one, then remembered it had a shooting scene and bypassed it for the obvious reasons.

Comedy! That's what we need. We need something funny. Something slapstick and nonthreatening. His fingers had just touched a tape marked "Three Stooges Marathon" when Cheryl's bloodcurdling scream tore through the silence.

Erik thought his heart had stopped. He rushed to the kitchen and found her trembling as she pointed to the window with one hand and covered her mouth with the other.

"What was it?" he asked, rushing to the window. He looked out into the darkness, but saw nothing.

"I saw. . ."

"What? What did you see?"

She shook her head. "I thought I saw someone out there. I thought I saw my father."

Erik turned away from the window and went to her. He wrapped her in his arms as he had wanted to do from the first moment he'd stepped foot in the house. "It's okay. Sometimes that happens when you lose someone you love."

"I think I'm going crazy," she sobbed and gripped his upper arms as if to steady herself.

"You aren't going crazy, Cheryl. It's a natural process of mourning. A lot of people think they see loved ones after they've died. It's just that we want so much for them to be alive that our mind plays tricks on us."

"See, I told you I was going crazy. My mind isn't working right anymore."

Erik pulled her tighter. "That's not true. Hey, I thought I saw Candy after she'd died."

"You did?" Cheryl looked up at him as if seeking the truth of the matter in his eyes.

"Yes. It happened one morning when I was walking into the intensive care unit at the hospital. See, that's the last place I saw her alive, and it must have just stuck in my mind. Anyway, I was talking to this one nurse, and I looked down the hall and there she was. I was so shocked I had to look away, and when I looked back, I could see that it was just another nurse. It wasn't Candy at all, but in my heart I guess I wished it could have been. I really wanted her to be alive and well."

Cheryl nodded. "Sometimes I wake up hearing a baby crying. I thought maybe it meant I was crazy. I don't want to be crazy, Erik." She put her head on his shoulder and said nothing more.

For several minutes they held each other. Erik wanted to give her strength and peace, but at the moment, he wasn't sure how much he had to share. She'd managed to shake him up in a way that he couldn't explain or ignore. If he said much more, he was certain that he'd declare his love for her. And he couldn't do that. Not yet. Not when she was so vulnerable to the past.

He stroked her hair, breathing in the scent of what could only be described as a garden of wildflowers. He liked the way her curls slipped like silk through his fingers and the way her head seemed to fit just right against his neck. He wanted the moment to go on forever.

Suddenly Cheryl pulled back. "Stay with me tonight," she pleaded.

Erik said nothing, but he knew his expression relayed his surprise.

"I don't mean anything by it," she continued, in a tone of desperation. "Not in a sexual sort of way or anything like that. I'm not like that. . .not really. I just can't stand another night alone in this house."

Erik regained control and shook his head. "I know you aren't like that," he whispered. He saw gratitude in her eyes as she realized he meant every word. "But I can't stay here with you."

Her expression fell. "Why not? Are you afraid of what people will think because of me?"

He shook his head. He couldn't tell her the truth; it might drive her away from him for good. "No, I'm not afraid of what people will think. It's just that I know it wouldn't be good for either one of us. But I have an idea."

She looked at him warily. "What?"

"Why don't you stay the night with CJ? I know you two are good friends, and I know from what she told Curt and Christy that she'd wanted you to come recuperate at her house anyway."

"I'd hate to impose," Cheryl said, barely whispering the words.

"I don't believe for one minute that CJ would find it an imposition. Why don't I call and make the arrangements while you go upstairs and pack what you need?"

"I just don't know."

"It'll be the best thing. You'll see. Staying with CJ will keep you out of the public eye and give you a time of peace and quiet while someone else worries about the details."

"I guess we can try, but what if she says no?"

He thought her very much like a little child who needed desperately to know that the monsters in the closet wouldn't get her. "She won't say no. She loves you," he answered. *I think I love you, too.*

"I guess that would be okay."

"Great. Now you go get your things, and I'll call CJ."

He watched her reluctantly leave. She seemed to war within herself about the decision. He went to the telephone and then realized he didn't know CJ and Brad's number. Dialing directory assistance, he memorized the number they gave, then hung up the phone and redialed.

"Hello?" a sweet feminine voice sounded.

"CJ? It's Erik Connors."

"Hi, Erik. What's up?"

"I'm at Cheryl's and wondered if I could ask you a favor."

"Sure. What is it?"

"Well, Cheryl's a little upset. She thought she saw her father outside the window, you know, just her mind playing tricks and whatnot. I figured, given the fact that today's his birthday, it's probably extrahard on her." When CJ said nothing, Erik continued. "Anyway, I wondered if she could come spend a couple days with you. She's at the point where she doesn't want to be alone, and I think it would be a good idea if we rallied round her and made sure that she didn't have to be alone."

"Of course she can come. Brad and I will be right down."

"No, that isn't necessary. I'll bring her up. I think I remember the way. Look, I really appreciate this. She seems so scared, and even before she thought she saw Ben, she was obviously agitated and upset about something."

"Did she tell you about her encounter with the DEA?"

"She mentioned it, but wouldn't go into detail. What happened?"

"Why don't I tell you when you get here? I'm certain it has more to do with her fears than anything else right now."

"Why do you say that?" Erik asked, suddenly sensing that CJ was keeping something from him.

"Because," CJ replied, "today isn't Ben's birthday. His birthday is sometime around Christmas."

"I see what you mean. Okay, well, I'll have her out there shortly."

"Erik?" CJ called to him. "Don't be mad at her for lying. If I were going through half of what she's been through, I'd probably try to cover up my feelings, too."

"I'm not mad," Erik answered. "Just disappointed. I wish she'd learn that she can trust me."

"Apparently, if she's letting you bring her to me, she's already learned that lesson. Just give her time. I think she's greatly embarrassed by what she's done in the past, and how it's taking its toll now is anybody's guess."

"I suppose you're right." Erik bolstered his courage once again. "I'll see you soon."

He hung up the phone and looked back at the window for a moment. If today wasn't her father's birthday, maybe it was no ghostly apparition she'd seen at the window. Maybe someone was stalking her for information or for some other reason. He had just determined to go outside and check for footprints when Cheryl reappeared, travel bag in hand.

"I'm ready," she whispered.

Erik forced aside his doubts and worries. "Great. Tell you what. We'll stop for fast food on the way. How's that sound?"

Cheryl gave him a tight smile. "Sounds fine."

Chapter 13

Cheryl felt a sense of peace wash over her as CJ and Brad's three-story, native-stone home came into view. She'd remained awkwardly silent throughout the ride, wondering whether she should play it straight with Erik and explain about the list. He'd already proven himself loyal to her in their friendship, but he was Curt's brother-in-law, and she couldn't take the chance that he might even accidentally tell the DEA about the list.

"Are you still okay with this?" Erik asked, pulling into CJ's drive and parking the truck.

"Yes, I think so." She tried hard not to think about how much she'd come to trust him. Would she tell him too much? Would she give too much of herself to him? She pushed these fears aside and reached for the door handle. "Thank you for bringing me out here."

"Hey, I'm not running off until I know for sure that you feel comfortable. I even told CJ that I planned to come in with you."

Cheryl smiled. Once again he'd put her comfort in front of his own. He could be spending the evening out with friends or relaxing at home after a hard day's work. Instead he was chauffeuring her and making sure she was safe and happy.

They walked in silence up to the door where CJ stood waiting for them. "I've watched for you for about the last ten minutes."

"We'd have been here sooner, but I had to feed her," Erik offered good-naturedly. "She can't cook, you know."

Cheryl looked up and shrugged. "I suppose there's no sense in defending myself. Everybody here knows that's true."

CJ laughed. "I was never much of a cook, either, but Brad is so demanding. . . ."

"Hey, did I hear my name mentioned?" Brad questioned, striding into the foyer.

"Hi, Brad," Erik said, pushing Cheryl forward. "CJ was just telling us how you forced her to learn to cook."

Brad put his arm around CJ's shoulder and hugged her close. "Yes, well, if she'd been any less proficient with airplanes, I probably wouldn't have married her at all."

CJ elbowed him sharply, while Cheryl and Erik exchanged a smile. Cheryl knew the truth of this love match. She'd been with CJ when Brad had first come into her life. "Did you ever hear the story of how they met?" Cheryl surprised them all by asking Erik.

"No, I can't say that I have."

"Well, before you get started on that story," CJ said, "why don't you come in and make yourselves comfortable."

"Sounds good to me," Erik said and followed Brad's example by putting his arm around Cheryl. "Lead the way."

If anyone was surprised by his actions, no one said anything, and Cheryl relaxed, allowing him to take her to a plush gold-colored sofa. He sat down, almost in unison with her and seemed not the least bit hesitant about remaining close at her side. Cheryl thought at first that his nearness would make her feel awkward, but instead it had just the opposite effect, and she turned to him with an enthusiasm she'd not felt in months.

"CJ used to be quite claustrophobic, and she got herself locked into the bathroom of one of Brad's hotel rooms. I went for help and thought Brad was one of the hotel maintenance people."

"She nearly pulled my arm out of its socket to get me upstairs with her," Brad commented.

"Well, after he got her out of that bathroom, he didn't have to be forced to remain at her side," Cheryl added.

"Yes, but that was only after I'd thrown up and totally humiliated myself in front of him," CJ said with a laugh. "You know it has to be true love when a man forms a relationship with a woman after he's held her head over the toilet."

They laughed, and Cheryl felt a certain comfort that she'd so long missed in her life. She felt safe here and knew that no one would come to hunt her down and demand answers that she couldn't give. There was always the possibility that Curt would show up to see CJ, but Cheryl knew that CJ would protect her.

"Let me get us something to drink," Brad offered. "We have all kinds of soda, iced tea, juice—so what'll it be?"

Erik looked at Cheryl. "Tea sounds great for me," Cheryl said, trying hard not to notice how blue Erik's eyes were.

"Make it two," Erik told Brad. "You need any help?"

"No, you go ahead and visit. This will only take a second."

CJ lost little time in striking up the conversation. "Cheryl, Erik said you were feeling pretty spooked this evening. Are you feeling better now?"

Cheryl nodded. It was easy to remember her earlier discomfort, but in this house she knew it was far from her. "It was kind of a hard day," she said. Then remembering that she'd told Erik it was her father's birthday, Cheryl had a pang of conscience. "I lied to you, Erik," she said, suddenly needing to confess the truth. "Today isn't Dad's birthday."

Erik exchanged a quick glance with CJ before asking, "What was it then?"

Cheryl took a deep breath. "It was a lot of little things. Everything just catching up with me, I guess. Ever since that Damon Brooks guy tried to break my wrists, I just haven't been the same."

"Damon Brooks? Who is he, and why didn't you say something about his trying to hurt you?" Erik asked, extremely agitated by this news.

"He was the DEA agent who came over the other day when CJ was there. I wasn't sure I wanted to talk about it," Cheryl admitted. "I suppose I have to accept that this kind of thing is just going to be my lot."

"They have no right to hurt you. What happened?" He looked first to Cheryl and then to CJ.

CJ took a seat just as Brad returned with the drinks.

"Well, this guy showed up as I was leaving, and Cheryl asked me to stay while he questioned her."

"Thank goodness I did," Cheryl said softly.

"No, thank God you did," CJ corrected. "I think God divinely oversaw that entire episode. If I hadn't been there, there's no telling what he might have done."

Erik was now very upset. "Just what *did* he do?"

"He got really ugly with Cheryl, demanding that she produce a list of her father's contacts and drug drop-off locations. It was the same information Curt had already asked her about, but Mr. Brooks certainly didn't use Curt's manner." CJ took a glass of iced tea from her husband before continuing. "He pushed Cheryl around and finally grabbed her by the wrists and yanked her up off the sofa. He twisted her arms so that she was in a lot of pain."

Cheryl pushed up the sleeves of her lightweight cotton blouse. Her wrists were encircled with bruises, and Erik's normally jovial expression turned markedly angry. "Why didn't you tell me earlier about this?"

Cheryl shrugged. "What could you have done?"

"I know what I intend to do," Erik replied, gently touching her wrist. "I'm going to Curt on this. I'm surprised you haven't already talked to him, CJ."

"I've tried," CJ admitted. "But he hasn't been around, and I didn't want to talk to Christy about it. Plus, it didn't seem like the kind of thing I could discuss with just anybody down at the DEA office."

"Well, I'll get ahold of him. There's no call for this kind of thing."

Erik was gently massaging her wrist, and Cheryl very nearly lost all thought of her earlier concerns. His touch was mesmerizing. What was happening to her?

"Well, someone definitely needs to get to the bottom of it," CJ said without trying to camouflage her own anger. "I was terrified. He threatened to break her arms when I started to call the DEA."

"What kept him from doing it, anyway?" Erik said.

"Mary showed up," Cheryl answered. "I guess he figured three women were too many to deal with."

"It's uncalled for, and I wish I had been there to keep it from happening."

He let go of her, and Cheryl almost wished she could brazenly bring his hand back to hers. But she didn't. She steadied her nerves and took a long drink of the tea. Everyone was upset because of what had happened to her. The tension in the room made her uncomfortable. She'd come here for her own peace of mind, and now it seemed that she'd caused problems for everyone else. It suddenly seemed necessary to apologize for her part in their discomfort.

"Look, I want to say something, and I'm not exactly sure how to begin," she finally spoke.

She drew another deep breath and tried to start again. "I loved my father a great deal, and I don't want to think badly of him. Still, I know there are things I probably ignored and problems I never knew about. I don't want Dad's memory put through the mill, grinding it up into grubby little bits, all the good along with the bad. He wasn't really as bad as some people want to make him out, but I guess I'm ready to admit he was no saint." She held up her hand when CJ started to speak. "I guess love overlooks a lot of mistakes."

"That's what the Bible says," Erik interjected.

"Well, then," Cheryl said, considering this for a moment, "you can see where it's true. Anyway, I guess what I want to say is that I'm sorry for the way each of you has been dragged into this. CJ, you know I loved your mom and dad. They were like an extra set of parents, and they were fun-loving and kind, and I'll always mourn their passing."

CJ wiped tears from her eyes, and Brad moved in to sit on the edge of her chair and put an arm around her. Cheryl felt a twinge of jealousy that constricted her speaking for a moment. CJ had found true love— love in such a rare and pure form. Cheryl looked away quickly, afraid that her expression would betray her own longing.

"And, Erik, I know I've been particularly hard on you. You've offered me nothing but human kindness and encouragement. I'm really sorry that your sister suffered because of me. . . ." Her words trailed off. She didn't know what else to say. She was able to admit that she was sorry that she'd ever met Grant Burks, but not to this crowd. They hated him enough, and to add to that seemed like it would be throwing gasoline on a fire already out of control.

"You can't blame yourself, Cheryl," CJ said. "You were deceived. We all understand that."

"Curt doesn't. He thinks I'm knee-deep into whatever Grant and Dad had going on. And, frankly, I still don't believe that Dad knew everything that was happening."

"He probably didn't," Brad agreed.

"But whether he did or not," CJ continued, "you have to understand that we don't hold you accountable for something your father did or didn't do, for that matter. As for Grant, well, you are no different than hundreds—no, thousands—of other women who fall for men who woo and wow them, only to use them for information and material benefit. Grant was good at what he did."

"And I was very much in need of being loved," Cheryl said softly.

"You were just naïve," CJ added.

"Well, I don't intend to ever be that naïve again. I'm through worrying about being loved."

"Don't give up on love," CJ said, looking up at her husband with such an expression of contentment that Cheryl felt like running away. "It'll come at you when you least expect it."

"I can vouch for that," Brad said, laughing. "Maybe you should develop a good case of claustrophobia."

Cheryl had to smile. "Those bathroom doors in your hotel still sticking?"

They all laughed, and Cheryl felt the acceptance that she so longed for. Maybe her healing was finally beginning. Maybe CJ and Erik had been right. Maybe harboring bitterness and anger kept a body from healing.

"Look, I'm going to have to get back," Erik said, glancing at his watch. "I have to be to work quite early."

"Well, don't worry about a thing," CJ assured him. "Cheryl will be fine here, and she can stay as long as she wants to."

"Good. I'll rest easy knowing she won't have any more encounters with the DEA. I intend to talk to Curt first chance I get."

He got up, and without thinking, Cheryl followed him to the door. With CJ and Brad awaiting her in the other room, she felt compelled to express her thanks once again. "Erik, I just want you to know that I appreciate what you did for me tonight. I don't know when any of this will be over, but I appreciate your friendship, in spite of what I might have said in the beginning."

Erik's impish smile returned, and without warning, he leaned down and kissed her cheek. "Well, maybe someday you'll be ready for something more than friendship."

At that he turned and left. She touched her hand to her cheek and stared after him in stunned silence. He knew all her secrets. He knew about Grant, and the baby, and her father, and still he suggested the possibility of something more than a friendship.

Cheryl closed the door as soon as Erik fired up the truck. She leaned against the wall and marveled that anyone could know the truth about her and still care. God cared, too, Erik had told her. Dared she believe it, too, might be true?

Later, that night, Cheryl lay awake in CJ's guest room. She thought a lot about how CJ and Brad had welcomed her with open arms. *They love me*, she thought, and instantly she knew beyond a shadow of a doubt that it was true. CJ cared for her. After all they'd come through together. After the desertions and reunions and conflicts and resolutions, CJ still cared for and loved Cheryl as much or more than she had when they were children.

"It's me," Cheryl whispered to herself. "I'm the one who rejected her love. I'm the one who put Erik at arm's length." She thought of Erik and his parting words. Cheryl knew from experience exactly what he'd meant by those words. She might be naïve when it came to giving her heart to the wrong man, but she knew the possibilities of what Erik had in mind.

Maybe someday you'll be ready for something more than friendship. His words hung in the air as though he'd just spoken them.

Cheryl thought of the past and what she'd done and how far she'd strayed from what she knew to be right. "I've disappointed so many people," she said sadly. "But most of all, I've disappointed myself. I've been stupid and very foolish. Now I have a chance to make it all right, and what do I do? I run away. I leave Curt needing vital information—information which I have. I put everyone's life in danger, and I selfishly cower behind the protection of the only friend I've ever really known."

The silence of the night weighed heavily on her. She couldn't deny the truth anymore. She needed to go home and retrieve the papers for Curt. She needed to swallow her pride, admit her mistakes, and go on from there. *Grant is dead. Dad is dead.* And no amount of mourning would bring them back, nor would it make them into the people she had believed them to be.

Rolling onto her side, Cheryl began to formulate a plan. Her future depended on coming to terms with the past. And her past could only be concluded when she turned over all the evidence of her father's involvement with the drug ring.

Chapter 14

Erik knew he wouldn't be able to concentrate on anything until he'd spoken to Curt about Cheryl's encounter with the DEA, and yet he had his obligation to the hospital. All through the day, however, he barely kept his mind on work, and it wasn't until he'd nearly thrown out the wrong specimens that his supervisor pulled him aside.

"You got a problem, Erik?"

"Look, Joe, I'm sorry. I've got some family troubles, and I guess my mind is just a wee bit preoccupied."

"Just a wee bit," Joe said with a laugh. "Look, why don't you clear out of here?" He glanced at his watch. "There's less than two hours left on the shift, and who knows what kind of damage you could do in that time?"

"It's okay, I'll stay. I mean, I'm off tomorrow and the next day anyway."

"No, I insist. You're making me a nervous wreck. Now go shower and get out of here."

Erik didn't argue further. He knew he wouldn't relax until he had some answers from Curt. It worried him that Cheryl would continue to be subjected to DEA strong-arm tactics, and if he had even the remotest chance of protecting her from such a thing, Erik was ready to go to battle for her.

He arrived at Curt and Christy's around one-thirty in the afternoon, and to his pleasant surprise he found Curt's car in the drive, while Christy's was nowhere to be seen. With any luck at all, he'd have Curt to himself and not have to explain to his big sister what was going on. Ringing the bell, he was greeted by a stern-faced Curt.

"We need to talk. It's very important." Erik paused before adding, "It's about Cheryl."

"Okay," Curt said, sounding rather hesitant.

"Are we alone?" Erik questioned, glancing around as Curt led them to the kitchen.

Curt threw his suit coat onto a chair in the hall before replying. "Yeah, matter of fact, I was just stopping in for lunch. You want something?"

"No. I'd rather get this off my chest first." Erik couldn't help remembering how angry he'd made Curt when he'd interfered with his investigation. Would he see this as yet another interference? What if Curt thought the DEA had handled things exactly right? Feeling a frustration born of anxiety, Erik blurted out the first thing on his mind. "I don't like the way your people are treating Cheryl."

Curt had just opened the refrigerator and turned to stare blankly at Erik. "What are you talking about now?"

"Look, I took Cheryl out to spend some time with CJ. She was so upset and spooked that she thought she'd seen someone at the kitchen window last night."

"And had she?"

Erik shrugged. "I don't know. I was going to go outside and check, but she didn't seem to want me to leave her. At first she lied and told me it was her father's birthday. Later, at CJ's, she came clean and told me it was just everything getting to her, including the DEA's rather ugly visit a few days ago."

"I don't have any idea what you're talking about," Curt said and returned to the refrigerator to rummage around for his lunch. "Why don't you sit down and tell me everything from the beginning? I'm just going to make a sandwich. You want one?"

"No." Erik tried to explain what he knew about Damon Brooks's visit. It seemed an inadequate portrayal of what had taken place, but since he hadn't been there to witness the situation himself, he tried to stick to the facts supplied him by CJ and Cheryl. Curt brought his sandwich and drink to the table and ate in silence as Erik continued.

"So when CJ said that he'd threatened to break Cheryl's arms if CJ called you at the DEA office, I figured enough was enough. You guys have no right to treat her like that. Her wrists are black and blue!"

Curt stared back with a dumbfounded look on his face. "I didn't know anything about this. When did you say this took place?"

"I'm not sure. Several days ago," Erik offered, trying to remember if CJ or Cheryl had indicated an exact date.

"And the man's name again?"

"Damon Brooks. Do you know him?"

Curt shook his head. "I've never heard of him. But that doesn't necessarily mean anything. Look," he glanced at his watch and got up, "I'm going to call in to the office and see what's going on. We'll get to the bottom of this."

Erik sat back and waited for what seemed an eternity. He was naturally concerned about keeping Cheryl safe, but he was also quite unnaturally overwhelmed with the feelings he had that went far beyond concern for her safekeeping. When had he come to care so much about her? Had it been in the hospital when she'd lingered between life and death and Erik had wondered if Grant Burks would claim yet another life? Maybe he'd really fallen in love with her when she'd pleaded with him to take her away from Curt. It was impossible to say, but what counted was that Erik knew now, more than ever, that he had fallen in love with Cheryl Fairchild.

Erik could hear Curt in the other room. His voice was lowered, but the anger came across nevertheless. He caught bits and pieces of the one-sided protest.

". . .should have been consulted. . ."

". . .my investigation. . ."

Then Curt's voice raised. "Look, do we have a Damon Brooks or not?"

Silence followed, and Erik found himself growing more and more uncomfortable. The only real peace he had in this situation was knowing that Cheryl was safely with CJ and Brad. He didn't like to think of her at the Fairchild house with no one around to protect her. Of course, she had a security system, but it wasn't foolproof. If someone wanted to get to her, they'd have little difficulty in doing just that.

He heard Curt slam down the receiver and stomp off down the hall. Erik got to his feet and came out into the hallway, just as Curt returned, strapping on his shoulder holster and gun.

"What's going on?"

"The DEA has never employed a man named Damon Brooks'. They didn't send anyone out to speak with Cheryl." He eyed Erik quite seriously. "That means someone else wants the same information we are after. And the only other people who know that such a list exists and who would have any need for it—"

"Are the drug traffickers!" Erik interjected.

"Exactly."

"Tell me more about this Damon Brooks," Curt demanded.

"I don't know anything more than I've already told you," Erik answered honestly. "But CJ and Cheryl could tell you everything. Why don't you call your sister?"

Curt nodded and reached for the telephone. "I'll do that." He dialed the number, talking to Erik the whole time. "If it was one of the drug people, we need to put some round-the-clock protection on Cheryl." He waved Erik's reply into silence. "CJ, it's Curt."

Pause. "I'm okay, but I need to talk to Cheryl."

Erik waited anxiously while Curt listened to CJ. "So how long ago was that?" Curt asked. "Okay. Did she say why?"

What is she saying? Erik wondered.

"Okay, CJ. I'll reach her there." Curt replaced the telephone receiver and turned to Erik. "She says that she took Cheryl home a couple of hours ago. It seems Cheryl had something important to do. Something that involved giving me a call."

"Do you suppose she found the information you had asked for?"

"I think she's probably always had it," Curt replied. He ran his hands through his hair and sighed. "I just wish I could have convinced her to give it to me a long time ago. We could have avoided a great many problems if she had."

"But maybe she doesn't have it at all. Maybe she just wants to talk to you about the investigation and let you look around the house."

"There's no way of knowing unless I ask her. I'm going to give her a call." He picked up the receiver again. "Hopefully we can get to the bottom of this in short order and I can find out who Damon Brooks is."

Erik gave Curt Cheryl's new unlisted number and waited anxiously as Curt punched in the number. After a long pause, Curt hung up.

"No answer," he said in frustration.

"That's strange," Erik said. "She always leaves the machine on to pick up the calls."

"I'm going over there." Curt grabbed his suit coat and put it on, hiding his holster and gun.

"I'm going, too," Erik said, giving Curt a fixed and determined stare. "And you aren't going to stop me."

"Look, Erik—"

"No, you look. I've come to care more about her—more than I should, perhaps—and I'm not going to bow out of this gracefully. She's in trouble, and I want to be there for her. Maybe she has the information you need, maybe not, but either way, I intend to be there for her."

Curt considered his words before nodding. "Fair enough, but you do things my way."

"I owe you that much," Erik replied, already heading for the front door.

They made their way to the driveway, where Erik started to get into Curt's car. "You follow me," Curt said. "I think it's better that way."

Erik did as he was told, even though he had little desire to be set off on his own. He feared that somehow Curt would keep him from following or that through some strange twist of fate, Ole Blue would fail him and he'd never make it to Cheryl's house. But none of his fears came true. Blue started as smoothly as ever, and Curt drove at a steady pace in order to allow Erik to keep up with him.

At Cheryl's house, there was no response to Curt's pounding knock, nor to his multiple rings of the doorbell. The entire place was as quiet as a cemetery, and Erik began to feel fear gnaw holes in his resolve.

Curt went to one of the living-room windows and stared through the tiny opening where the drapes didn't quite meet. "It's too dark to see inside," he told Erik and went back to the door. He tried to force it open, but to no avail.

"I'll go around back," Erik offered.

"I'll come with you."

Together they made their way around the side of the house, checking along the way for the footprints Erik had wondered about. "If there was someone here," he suggested, "he would have made tracks right over there." He pointed beneath the kitchen windows, and Curt made his way over to check the grass.

"It looks pretty trampled," Curt said, kneeling down. "I'd say there was something more substantial than ghostly images out here last night."

Erik shuddered. "Glad I took her to CJ's."

Curt nodded and got back up. "I just wish she'd stayed there." He went to the back door and tried it, but it, too, was locked. He tried to look through the door's curtained window, but again he was thwarted.

"I don't suppose she gave you a key?" he asked Erik.

"No, we aren't exactly that close. Not yet."

Curt raised an eyebrow but said nothing. Instead he studied the back door. Then, without a word of warning, he took up a small yard statuette and bashed in the back door window.

The sound of glass breaking made Erik's blood run cold. It haunted him in a way that he couldn't explain. He watched as Curt reached a hand inside and unlocked the door, and still he couldn't explain his apprehension. What if they were too late? What if the person who had watched Cheryl last night had returned?

Curt pulled his gun, and Erik felt his mouth go dry.

"What is it? Did you hear something?"

"No, it's what I'm not hearing that makes me wary."

Erik frowned. "I don't understand."

"There ought to be all kinds of alarms going off," Curt replied, cautiously moving into the house. "Ben had this place wired to the max. Someone has obviously disabled the system."

Erik followed his brother-in-law into the house. Immediately, he could see that the place had been torn apart. Dishes and pans had been pulled from the cupboards, and cans of food and box mixes were strewn about the floor.

"I'll wager the rest of the house looks the same," Curt said, moving toward the kitchen door. "Why don't you stay here?"

"Not on your life," Erik replied. "She might need me."

Curt nodded and motioned him back. "Then stay down and far enough behind me so that I can maneuver."

They moved out into the hallway and found the house ransacked just as Curt had figured. Nothing had been left untouched. The cushions of the couch and chairs had been cut apart. Even the drapery linings had been cut away from the drapes. Erik felt a tightness in his chest and throat. Where was Cheryl when all of this was going on? Where was she now? Would they find her upstairs, dead?

As if reading Erik's mind, Curt spoke. "She might have found this mess when CJ dropped her off. Maybe she hightailed it out of here and went back to CJ's."

They moved together up the stairs. Erik felt the tension mount. He'd like to believe that Cheryl was safe with Curt's sister, but it didn't seem likely. He felt bad. Very, very bad. His stomach hurt, and his breathing came so rapidly that he was certain he'd soon be hyperventilating. Forcing himself to breathe more slowly, he let his gaze travel over the ravages of the intruder's attack. In the bedrooms, the mattresses had been cut up and searched, while the drawers and closets had been emptied and clothes had been left precariously around the room.

"They were very thorough," Curt commented, and after searching all of the upstairs rooms, he holstered his gun and turned to Erik. "My guess, however, is that Cheryl had whatever they wanted hidden away. Apparently they never found it, and my guess is that Cheryl interrupted their search."

Curt went to the telephone, then shook his head and motioned Erik to follow him. He went outside the same way they'd entered, then went to his car to use his cellular phone.

"CJ, it's Curt again. Look, did Cheryl come back to your place?" Pause. "No, she's not at her house. I'm here with Erik, and the place has been torn apart."

Erik waited helplessly as Curt calmed his sister. "Look, we'll find her, but if she shows up there, make sure she stays put and gives me a call. Okay?" He pressed the disconnect button and instantly redialed. He looked at Erik while waiting for the call to go through. "I'm bringing in help. This one's bigger than we can handle alone."

Erik nodded, and he knew by the grave expression on Curt's face that he suspected the worst.

"It's O'Sullivan. Look, get a team over to the Fairchild house. The place has been ransacked and Ms. Fairchild is, at this point, missing. My guess is that she's been taken hostage."

Erik felt as though Curt had dealt him a blow below the belt. He sucked in air and tried to force his lungs to accept the offering, but his head was spinning from the realization that they were too late. He hadn't been able to save her from harm, and now she might well be dead.

Leaning back against his truck for support, Erik's only recourse was to offer up a prayer. "Oh, God," he whispered, as Curt continued to talk with his people, "please keep her safe from harm. Don't let them hurt her. Please, God, don't let her be dead."

Chapter 15

Cheryl's hip ached from the brutal way she'd been thrown into the back of the utility van. Ropes bound her hands behind her and prevented her from steadying herself as the van bounced mercilessly through a series of twists and turns.

Her mind blurred with images of the house being destroyed by the two thugs who now held her captive. Tears filled her eyes as she thought of all her treasures being broken to shards. So many years of memories now lay in ruin, and the thought of her loss was the only thing that drew her mind from her current predicament.

They'd wanted the contents of the lockbox. At least she knew from their demands that they wanted the list and the keys. No mention was made of the money, so perhaps the money had belonged solely to her father. She'd lied and told the men she had no idea where such a list might be. They'd slapped her, knocking her off her feet, so rather than fight, Cheryl remained complaisantly seated on the floor until their curiosity had been satisfied.

Now, in the darkness of the van, Cheryl choked back a sob and bolstered her resolve not to cry. *I won't give them the satisfaction of seeing me fall apart,* she determined. Yet even as she thought this, fear gripped her body and held it as captive as the men who'd placed her in the van.

She tried to focus on Erik, forcing herself to remember his face. She outlined in her mind his sandy-colored hair and blue eyes. She mentally drew a picture of his impish grin and the way his face always suggested an inner joy and happiness. He said it was the peace of God acting in his heart. He had said on more than one occasion that the joy God gave him just bubbled out from the center of his being and flooded everything in its path. Cheryl couldn't imagine having that kind of joy.

Oh, Erik, where are you now? Why didn't I listen to you and stay with CJ?

But she already knew the answer to that question. She'd returned to the house with every intention of calling Curt and turning over the list that she'd safely replaced in the lockbox before going to CJ's. Instead, she found herself taken hostage by two rather nasty-looking characters, and reconciling the past with Curt was instantly made impossible.

Remembering Curt and how she'd treated him, Cheryl found herself wishing she could at least set the record straight before dying. She didn't really hate him anymore. The pieces of the puzzle had slowly come together, and in spite of her desire to believe her loved ones free of guilt, the truth was hard to ignore. She could now accept that Grant had brought this trouble down around him. Little things popped into memory. Things that had transpired between her and Grant. Things that had seemed odd at the time but Cheryl had chosen to ignore in hopes that they were mere coincidence.

But neither coincidence nor chance had landed her in the back of this van on the way to an unknown destination. Struggling to sit up, Cheryl found herself unable to make out any detail of her surroundings. The van's cargo hold was completely separated from the driver's position. There wasn't a single shred of light to give her even a hint of an image. She struggled against the ropes that bound her hands. They were too well tied to work loose, and each movement only managed to cause her more discomfort.

The van turned sharply, and Cheryl barely managed to balance herself by throwing her right leg out to the side. She came in contact with something metallic and maneuvered her leg across the top in order to get a better idea of what it might be. It seemed to be some sort of toolbox. The cool metal surface was evident even to her jean-clad leg, and in the center, a handle of some sort disturbed the smooth lines of the box.

She brought her right leg back and gingerly put out her left leg in the opposite direction. A soft mound of material easily gave way to her prodding limb before her foot made contact with the van wall. The van moved from the paved road to one of gravel. Instantly Cheryl lost her balance and fell back against the floor. She could hear the gravel striking the undercarriage of the van and felt as though her teeth would be jarred right out of her head by the sudden roughness of the road. *Where are they taking me?*

The van seemed to slow, and Cheryl felt her heartbeat pick up speed. Her mind began to race with thoughts of how she would handle herself. Could she talk her way out of the situation? Could she plot out a method by which she could dupe her captors? *There has to be an answer,* she thought. *After all, I still have the list and the keys.* She smiled to herself in the darkness. Maybe they were her trump card in all of this. Maybe she could face her captors with the same aloof toughness she'd given most everyone else for the past five months. *It might work.*

The van launched itself down an even rougher road, and Cheryl moaned painfully as her head slammed against the metal floor again and again. She struggled back into a sitting position but found this only marginally better. The ride seemed endless, and what little hope she'd managed to bolster within her heart died out when the van finally came to a screeching halt and slammed her against the cold steel walls.

This is it, she thought and waited for someone to open the door to the cargo area. But they never came. They left her alone and went off arguing between themselves. She heard the voices fade into the distance, and a sinking feeling came over her.

What if they never intended to give her a chance to come up with the materials? What if they were only bringing her out to some deserted place in order to kill her? Cheryl began to panic. She fought against the ropes with a vigor born of desperation. It was useless.

Cheryl began to pray. Fear and hopelessness made it seem the only thing left to do.

"God, I know I'm a mess. I know I don't deserve any kind of consideration on this," she began, "but I need a way out. I need help." She swallowed hard, trying to keep her voice steady and her thoughts centered. "CJ and Erik have both tried to help me see the need for having You in my life, but until this moment I guess I figured I was quite capable of taking care of myself." She lowered her voice to a whisper. "Guess I was wrong."

Cheryl tried to remember what it was CJ had said about salvation. What was it she was supposed to do in order to be forgiven? Surely there was more to it than being sorry and asking for God's mercy. It couldn't be that clear-cut. Could it?

"God, I don't know all the right words," Cheryl admitted. "I am

398

sorry for what I've done, and I certainly don't intend to do anything like it in the future. Is that enough? Is being sorry and determined never to do wrong again enough to have Your forgiveness?"

Her heart was in turmoil. What if God couldn't forgive her? What if the things she'd done were too bad to be forgiven? But CJ and Erik had both said that God loved her and that He wanted her to find the truth. *What truth?* Cheryl wondered. Maybe it was the truth of her own stupidity. If that were the case, she'd already learned that lesson.

Find the truth.

She pondered that for a moment. She remembered a verse from the Bible that spoke of the truth setting you free. Could the truth set her free now?

"God, I just don't know what to do. I'm sorry for my life, and I ask You to forgive me. I want to be saved from this mess." Then she remembered CJ speaking of God's salvation. Salvation from Satan's deceptions. Salvation from self-destruction. Salvation from eternal death.

"Yes, that's it," she murmured. "I want to be saved. I want You to save me, God. If I'm not too bad to save, then show me. Show me by saving me out of this physical mess, and then I'll know that You are able to save me from my spiritual mess as well."

For reasons beyond her understanding, Cheryl felt comforted. It wasn't as if the doors had magically opened or her bonds had instantly fallen away. But a small portion of her anxiety had lifted, and in that, she found an understanding of peace. It wasn't an emotional thing, because God knew her emotions were well out of control. The thought almost hit her as a settled matter. God not only could save her—He would save her.

Voices sounded outside the van, and Cheryl braced herself for what was to come. Could she hold onto that tiny slip of faith? The doors opened, and Cheryl blinked rapidly against the light of day.

"Come on," the larger of the two men said and gave her legs a yank. He dragged her to the end of the cargo area and pulled her out by the shoulders. "The boss is ready to see you."

Cheryl faced the man as bravely as she could. "Who is he, and why does he want to see me?"

Offering no explanation, the man grabbed her tightly around the upper arm and pushed her forward. The smaller of the two men glanced around nervously, and Cheryl followed his gaze. They were leading her toward a metal building. It looked like an old airplane hangar with two large doors slid back to leave the interior exposed. Looking beyond the building, Cheryl could see nothing but open space. She realized they were facing east. The mountains had to be behind her, and she tried to twist enough to look over her shoulders to assure herself of this fact.

"Stop gawking around," her captor told her and roughly pushed her forward.

Cheryl would have fallen except for the man's continued hold. She tried to think of where they might be. There were several old airfields in the area, but which one was this one? Could it belong to O&F Aviation? She tried to find some shred of evidence that might confirm or deny the possibility.

"I told you to knock it off," the man said, growling out his displeasure. "It ain't gonna do you any good, anyhow."

Cheryl remained silent as they passed inside the hangar. She looked around and saw nothing but old oil drums, crates, and filthy workbenches. She'd focused on a rusted-out sign, when the man who held her pushed her forward and this time released his hold. She fell to the oil-stained cement and found, as she tried to get back to her feet, that another man had joined them.

"Help her up," a deep, husky voice commanded.

Both men took hold of her and brought her back to her feet. Cheryl steadied herself before allowing her eyes to meet the face of the man who controlled her captors. With a gasp, she felt the strength drain from her body, and once again, she sank to her knees.

Looking up again, still unwilling to believe what she was seeing, Cheryl found the man's amused expression. His dark complexion and dark eyes might have made him a handsome man in his younger days, but a thick ugly scar marred the left side of his face. That feature alone kept him from being an older version of Grant Burks.

❧

"I'm telling you everything I can think of," Erik said impatiently.

"I'm sorry, Erik," Curt said. "It's just that any detail might help us in figuring out what's happened."

Erik nodded. "I know that, and I want more than anything to help you get Cheryl back, safe and sound. It's just that I don't know what's helpful and what's not. I can tell you that there were what seemed hundreds of telephone calls daily. That's why she changed her number. Some of them were legitimate enough, but Cheryl did mention that a great many calls were from people who claimed to be friends of the family and clearly weren't."

"Did she have any idea who the people really were?"

Erik tried to ignore the DEA agents working around him. It was distracting to see strangers going through Cheryl's personal belongings, but he knew it was necessary. "Not really. I think she felt pretty certain that a lot of them were reporters wanting information on the drug situation and her father. When she had her number changed, the calls stopped."

"What about last night? Did she say what she saw outside the window?"

Erik shook his head. "She only said that she'd thought she'd seen her father. But honestly, Curt, I think she only said that to throw me off. She didn't want to admit at that point that she was upset about anything other than her father's death and the fact that she missed him."

Curt ran a hand through his hair. "Okay, start from the beginning. Why did you come over in the first place?"

"She called me. It was the first time she'd ever invited me over. She seemed pretty agitated, you know, kind of nervous and uptight." Curt nodded, and Erik continued. "Anyway, when I got here, she opened the door and seemed pretty glad to see me. She was looking around like maybe she was expecting someone else, and I even asked her about it."

"What did she say?"

"Only that there wasn't anybody else coming."

"Is there anything else that sticks out as unusual?" Curt questioned, his voice edged with desperation.

Erik started to shake his head, but then stopped. "I do remember asking her about the muddy tire tracks in her drive. Remember it rained early yesterday morning? Anyway, there were these muddy tracks in the drive, and I asked her where they'd come from."

"What'd she say?"

"Only that CJ stopped by to check up on her."

"But that isn't true," Curt said, suddenly seeming very interested in the matter. "I just talked to CJ to get the details on that Damon Brooks character, and she said she'd not seen Cheryl since that incident. She'd only talked to her on the telephone."

"Then the tracks belonged to someone else," Erik said flatly.

"Exactly where were they positioned?"

"Right in front of the garage."

"Debbie, come here for a minute," Curt called to an exotic-looking young woman.

Erik smiled as the woman approached. She was dressed smartly in a navy blue suit, with her black hair swept fashionably into a French twist. Erik recognized her as one of Curt's DEA partners. She had been the one working with Curt when he'd first met Christy.

"What is it, Curt?"

"I want you to go to the garage and check the vehicles there for any signs of mud or recent usage."

"Sure thing."

She took off, and Erik looked back at Curt. "What are you thinking?"

Curt shrugged. "Maybe nothing. Maybe everything. What if Cheryl, herself, made those muddy tracks?"

"But Cheryl hadn't left the house since coming home from the hospital. Well," Erik paused, feeling rather embarrassed to bring up his mistake of the past, "except for the time she went with me."

"But what if she did leave the house? What if she went in search of something or someone?"

"But who or what? I know how upset she was about facing the public. It would have had to be something big in order to make her leave."

Debbie returned just then. "There's dried mud all over the tires of the green Volvo."

"That is Cheryl's car," Curt said flatly. "She must have gone somewhere."

"I can take a sample of the dirt and try to analyze where it came from," Debbie suggested.

"She couldn't have gone all that far," Curt murmured, obviously thinking through the situation. "It would have had to be sometime either during or after the storm because everything was pretty dried up until then."

"And as scared as she was of everything," Erik offered, "I doubt she would have driven anywhere very far out of Denver."

"I'll get a sample and see what I can turn up. Maybe it will give us something to go on."

"Thanks, Deb," Curt replied, still deep in thought. "Someone figured out that Cheryl knew about the list. There's evidence of that just in the fact that Damon Brooks or whoever he was came to question her about it. What if Cheryl knew where the list was and tried to do some exploring on her own?"

"To what purpose?" Erik asked, seeing immediately the direction Curt's thoughts were taking.

"Clearing her father," he answered flatly. "It's the only thing I know that she would have felt strongly enough about to put aside her own fears and leave the house."

"But even if she had the list, chances are she doesn't have it now," Erik reminded him.

Curt shook his head. "I don't think that's necessarily true." He looked around the room as if seeing it for the first time. "Either they got what they wanted and Cheryl surprised them, and they felt they had to take her with them to keep her quiet, or they didn't find what they wanted and they took Cheryl with them to force her to help them."

"Either way, it doesn't look good for her," Erik commented grimly. Things were definitely not shaping up the way he'd hoped they would.

Chapter 16

My name is Severon Burks," the man told Cheryl. He maintained a regal bearing and an attitude of aristocratic disinterest. "As you may have already surmised, I am Grant's father."

Cheryl nodded, knowing beyond any doubt that the man was speaking the truth. Looking into his eyes was like looking into the ghostly image of the man she'd once loved.

"Why am I here?"

He smiled tolerantly and motioned to the two thugs. "Bring a chair and some rope. Ms. Fairchild looks a bit spent."

"I'm fine," Cheryl protested, not wanting to be any further confined than she already was.

Burks ignored her and waited until the men had tied her securely to the chair before continuing. "My son was a bit remiss in his duties. There is a list of information that I need to complete certain business transactions. I believe you have that list, and I want it now."

"I don't know what you're talking about," Cheryl replied, meeting his eyes. She knew she had to make this convincing. "For the last five months, people have nagged me to death about a list, and I'm going to tell you the same thing I've told everyone else. I don't know about any list." She drew a deep breath and held it, hoping that her trembling wouldn't be so noticeable.

"You aren't a very convincing liar," Burks said, brushing bits of lint off his otherwise immaculate black suit coat. His jaw appeared to tighten, and his eyes narrowed in a menacing way. "You don't seem to understand how this game is played." He leaned down until his face was only inches from her own. "I don't care what happens to you. Dead or alive, I will have my information."

Cheryl thought of the lockbox securely hidden in her bathroom. It gave her a sense of control to know that it wouldn't be easily discovered.

Surely if she maintained her calm, collected appearance and held her ground, Grant's father would have to let her go.

Severon eyed her suspiciously for several moments. "I knew that Grant had lost his mind when he deemed it necessary to involve himself with you. I warned him about the complications, and now he's dead. You're to blame for that. You and that Curtiss O'Sullivan character. Do you suppose I would stop at anything to get back what is mine?"

Cheryl felt a shudder tear through her and tried to cover it by coughing and twisting in the chair. "I don't have anything that belongs to you. I don't know what list you're talking about and. . . ," she paused, trying to muster her courage, "I'm not to blame for Grant's stupidity."

Severon seemed taken aback by this, so Cheryl pushed her point home. "You let my father's reputation be ruined and all because of some father-and-son drug business. Why do you suppose I would help you even if I could? I made the mistake of falling in love with your son. It doesn't mean I'm inclined to make further mistakes by aiding the enemy."

Severon snapped his fingers, and one of the men who'd taken her hostage appeared with a small suitcase. The man held the case flat while Burks undid the clasps and opened the lid. He thrust the man forward until the case was clearly level with Cheryl's eyes.

"This is why I know you are lying."

Cheryl looked at the rows of neatly wrapped one hundred dollar bills. "I don't understand," she said flatly and forced herself to look at Burks.

He motioned the man away. "My men retrieved this money from the warehouse you so easily led us to yesterday morning. The warehouse was only one of a great many exchange locations on your list and had you not gotten spooked, no doubt you would have led us to other locations."

True panic gripped Cheryl. She had to think fast. She had to offer up some logical reason for going to the warehouse. "I still don't know what you're talking about. The warehouse was property owned by my father. I thought perhaps he used it for storage, and since I'm in the process of trying to settle his affairs, I went there to see what might be housed inside."

Burks shook his head. "No, you didn't."

Cheryl could see that he didn't believe her. His rigidly fixed features frightened her to the core of her being, but there was absolutely nothing she could do. To tell him about the list would mean her certain death, and suddenly Cheryl didn't feel so inclined to give up her life. She tried to muster up anger in order to counter her terror. There had to be some way to fight this. *Please, God*, she prayed, *give me some way out*.

"I'm growing impatient with you, Ms. Fairchild. We both know that the list exists, and we both know that you have the list, as well as the keys that go to each of the locations on that list. I expect for you to turn both over to me, and I'm going to tell you exactly how it's going to be handled."

Cheryl tried hard to face her adversary without emotion. "By all means, please tell me how I'm to perform this magic feat for you."

Burks gave her a leering grin, and it was so like the ones Grant used to offer that Cheryl felt her blood run cold. What had seemed attractive on Grant now struck her as hateful and evil.

"You are going to make a telephone call," he said simply. "You are going to call my son's killer and tell him where he can find the list and the keys and have him bring them here to me."

"You. . .want me. . .to call Curt?" she asked hesitantly.

He crossed his arms and nodded very slowly. "Oh, yes, indeed. I intend not only to reclaim what is mine, but also to avenge the death of my child. You see, it really doesn't matter to me that the operation has been compromised. There are other operations and other ways to bring cocaine into the U.S. It was great using O&F Aviation while it worked, but nothing is foolproof, and in this case, the fool is one Curt O'Sullivan."

"He'll never come here just because I call," Cheryl said, trying to think her way out of the situation. "He hates me now. I blamed him for Grant's death and for the death of our unborn child." She paused to see what kind of effect her statement might have on Burks. His expression never changed. "He won't come to my rescue if that's what you'd hoped for."

"He'll come."

"I'm telling you—"

"He'll come," Burks said angrily. "He'll come because of his need to clear his father's name. After all, isn't that what has driven *you?*" She couldn't hide her surprise, and this made Burks laugh. "You aren't dealing with a simpleton, Ms. Fairchild. I've been in business for the past twenty years, and frankly, I've gotten quite good at it. Now, you'll make the call, and you'll be very convincing. You'll instruct Mr. O'Sullivan as to where he can retrieve the goods, and then we'll relay the directions to this hangar."

Cheryl knew time was running out, yet still she protested.

"I can't help you."

Without warning, Burks yanked her head back and put a gun to her throat. "You will either make the call, or I'll kill you and make the call myself. It really doesn't matter. I'd prefer to watch O'Sullivan suffer as he watches you die, but either way, I'll have my list. You see, that list represents millions of dollars of hidden drugs and laundered money. You aren't going to convince me with your sugary sweet innocence, and you aren't going to rob me of the pleasure of seeing you and your murderous friend die."

He pressed the barrel of the gun harder against her throat. "I'm going to give you a countdown. If you don't agree to make the call by the time I get to 'one,' then I'll blow your head off and resolve the matter without you."

Cheryl swallowed hard and felt the gun press even tighter against her windpipe.

"Five. . .four. . ."

What could she do? What should she do? She didn't want to die, but neither did she want to be responsible for Curt's death.

"Three. . ."

But she was afraid, and her fear won out.

"Two. . ."

"All right. I'll make the call," she whispered, barely able to force the words from her mouth.

Severon smiled and pocketed the gun. He released her hair and ran his fingers lightly down the side of her face. "I knew you'd come to see things my way."

❧

Erik followed Curt into his house, determined to convince him to let him somehow help find Cheryl.

"You don't understand," Erik protested as his sister joined them.

Christy's face betrayed her confusion, and Curt instantly sought her help. "You have to convince your brother that I know what I'm doing and that he doesn't. He needs to stay out of my business." Christy looked first to Curt and then to Erik for some further explanation. "You aren't making any sense," she said. "Convince him of what?"

Erik shook his head before Curt could explain. "Don't bother to tell me that it isn't my business. I'm in love with her."

Christy's eyes widened at this, and Curt threw up his arms dramatically. "If you love her, then let the professionals take care of the situation."

"What is going on?" Christy suddenly demanded.

"Cheryl Fairchild has been taken hostage. At least, we think she has. If not, then she's on the run from someone," Curt finally offered.

"And *he*," Erik said, waving an arm at Curt, "doesn't understand why I want to help find her."

"I didn't say that I didn't understand it. I simply said that you aren't qualified to throw yourself into the middle of a DEA sting operation."

Christy paled. "Erik, he's right. You have to stay out of whatever Curt is doing. I know from experience that it can only lead to innocent people being killed or hurt."

"That's why I want to help. Cheryl's life is in danger, and whether you think she deserves saving or not, I love her and intend to help her."

Christy exchanged a glance with Curt. "You love Cheryl?"

Erik's shoulders sagged, and he let out a heavy sigh. "Yes. I've fallen in love with Cheryl Fairchild. So before you go into some kind of lecture about her history and the fact that she's not good enough for me or whatever else you might conjure up, keep in mind that we all make mistakes. Even you."

Christy nodded. "I wasn't going to lecture you. I'm just surprised."

"Why, because you don't think she deserves love?"

"Stop taking the defensive with me, Erik. I don't like the part she played in Candy's misery, but I'm willing to let the past go," Christy said, sounding rather angry. "Furthermore, I remember my own mistakes very well, and I'd be the last one to say that Cheryl can't be forgiven for the past. I would question, however, whether she wants to be forgiven of the past."

"I think she does. I think she's only just come to realize how much harm she's done herself in believing in people who didn't deserve her devotion. She let herself be used and manipulated. You know how that feels, Chris," Erik said, remembering a time when Christy had fallen prey to a deceptive college professor. The man had tried unsuccessfully to press Christy into an intimate relationship, and he might have succeeded had Christy not found out that he was married.

Christy's expression softened, and Curt put his arm around her rather protectively. "I remember very well how it feels," Christy said. "Feelings aren't what matters here, however." She looked at her husband and gave him the briefest of smiles. "You can't jeopardize Cheryl or yourself by sticking your nose into a situation that's way out of your league. Would you want Curt coming into the lab and telling you how to run things there?"

Erik felt totally defeated. "Of course not. But you don't understand." His heart ached with the thought of what Cheryl might be going through. "She's out there somewhere, and she's alone."

"She's not alone, Erik," Curt said, his voice taking on the first real hint of compassion. "God's watching over her, and we have to pray and trust Him to take care of her in this. She can't be held accountable for the sins of her father, but those sins have obviously revisited themselves upon her. We can't wish her out of this, and you can't go running wild in hopes of locating her. You can, however, stay here and pray. And not only for her, but also for me and my team."

Christy reached out to touch Erik's arm. "He's right. You know he is."

"I suppose so."

Just then the telephone rang, and all eyes turned in unison as if anticipating what the call would reveal. Curt left Christy's side and went to answer it.

"Hello."

There was a long pause. Erik watched Curt's face for some sign of the news, but the only thing he noted for sure was the way his brother-in-law's face had grown pale.

"I understand. Are you okay?"

Now Erik was certain the caller had to be Cheryl. He moved toward the phone, but Curt held out his hand to ward him off.

"Do what you're told. I'll be there as soon as I can." Curt hung up the telephone and turned to face Christy and Erik.

"It was Cheryl, wasn't it?" Erik asked, almost fearful of the answer.

"Yes."

"Is she. . .was she. . ."

"She's being held just outside of town. She told me where the list is, and I'm to bring it to her captors."

"I'm going with you."

"You can't, Erik," Curt said quite seriously. "And if you fight me on this, I'll have you arrested."

"But I love her."

"Yes, and they'll kill her if they see anyone but me."

Christy moved away from the men and sat down hard on a nearby chair. Erik noted her frightened expression. It seemed to match his own fear.

"Do *you* have to take it to them?" she asked weakly.

"I was specifically named," Curt replied.

He didn't say anything more. He didn't have to. Erik knew beyond all doubt that such a declaration meant only one thing. Someone had a grudge against Curt and intended to resolve the matter by having him deliver the goods.

"I could stay out of sight. You know, hide in the back of the car or even the trunk," Erik offered.

"No."

"But, Curt, you can't just walk into a trap."

"I know what I'm doing, Erik." He looked at his wife and then at Erik and added, "I need you to watch out for Christy. She's going to need you more than I will."

Erik could see that he was right, but he didn't want to give in. Cheryl needed him, too, and he longed to be the knight in shining armor that she could depend on.

As if sensing Erik's inner battle, Curt spoke once again. "You can come to Cheryl's house with me and help me retrieve the list. But after that, I want you to come back here and stay with Christy. Will you do that for me?"

Erik drew a deep breath and nodded. There was no other choice.

&

They found the Fairchild estate swarming with DEA agents when they arrived. Curt immediately led the way upstairs to Cheryl's bathroom and began throwing shampoo and conditioner off the ledge that lined the bathtub.

Debbie called to them from the doorway. "Frank passed along your cellular-call message. I've got everything set up here."

"Good. Thanks, Deb," Curt said, prying the toothpaste caulking away from the tile. "Cheryl is one smart girl. I can't believe she dreamed this up on her own. It's brilliant. Who would ever have thought to look here?"

"Obviously no one did," Erik said, leaning back against the vanity, while Curt stood in the tub.

The tile snapped off, and Curt quickly cast it to one side. He pulled a penlight from his pocket and flashed it into the dark hole. "Bingo!" He reached his hand inside. "Well, it's a tight fit. . .but I think. . ." He fell silent and pulled the lockbox from the hole. "I've got it!"

Debbie leaned her head around the door. "Is that it?"

"Yes," Curt said with a certainty that Erik envied. "She said everything we needed was inside." He scrambled out of the bathtub and put the box on the vanity. "Let's see what we have." He tried to release the clasp, but it stuck. Taking out a ballpoint pen, he maneuvered it between the lid and the box and finally managed to pry the thing loose.

"Wow!" Erik exclaimed at the sight of the thousand-dollar bills. "That's some piggy bank."

"Tag it," Curt said, handing it to Debbie. "These, too." He put the diskettes into her hands. "Well, here's the cause of all our troubles." He held up the keys in one hand and the papers in the other.

Erik considered the objects for a moment, then grimaced. The cold, hard reality of what was actually happening had finally begun to sink in. "They're going to kill her, aren't they?"

Curt met his stare and shook his head. "Not if I can help it."

"But maybe you can't. Maybe she's already dead."

"Thinking like that won't help anything," Curt said sympathetically. "You have to trust God on this one, Erik. Illegal activities and concealing evidence is what stirred this into a real hornets' nest, and it won't be easily resolved. But with God, well, I believe we're on the side of right and truth. God will honor that, and I trust Him to watch over us in the process."

"But Cheryl is alienated from God," Erik said sadly. "I wasn't able to convince her of His love for her."

"Don't be so sure," Curt said quite seriously.

"Why do you say that?" Erik looked to his brother-in-law for a hope that might carry him through this nightmare.

"Because she told me she was sorry," Curt answered softly. "She told me she was wrong."

"I hope that's enough."

"I feel confident that it is. Now, listen to me, Erik. The DEA isn't going to take this thing lightly. We have the full cooperation of the Denver police, and together, they'll have all the possibilities figured out before I even go in there. You have to help Christy stay calm. She needs to be there for Sarah, and you need to be there for her. You know how she worries, and you know how stubborn she can be. Please go back to the house and wait for me there. When it's all over, I'll come there first."

"And Cheryl?"

Curt grinned in his cocky, self-assured way. "I'll bring her with me."

Erik wanted to believe him. "Would you do me one favor?"

Curt sobered. "If I can."

"Tell her that I love her. You know, just in case—"

Curt's smile was back in place. "You don't have much faith in me, do you?" He turned to leave. Calling over his shoulder, he said, "You tell her yourself when we get back."

Erik wanted to run after him and demand to be allowed to go with him, but he knew it was no good. Going after Curt would only put Curt in danger. Sneaking around behind his back might even get Curt and Cheryl both killed. Fighting the urge to handle things on his own, Erik sat down hard on the edge of the tub. For the first time since Candy's death, he felt like breaking into tears.

"It isn't manly to cry," he could remember his father saying without the slightest regard for his son's pain.

It might not be manly, Erik said to himself, *but it certainly is human.* He sat there for several minutes before deciding there was nothing more to be done.

Walking through the house, he ignored the tight gathering of agents as they listened to Curt. Outside, the light was fading from the sky as the sun melted into a puddle of orange and gold behind the Rocky Mountains.

Erik climbed into Ole Blue, feeling so lost and discomforted that he didn't know what to do. Where was God in all of this?

I'm with you always, an inner voice seemed to speak.

Erik pounded the steering wheel with his fists. "But I need assurance. I need to know that she'll be okay."

Calming a bit, Erik fell back against the seat and shook his head. "God, I know You care, and I know You have everything under control, but I'm afraid. I don't want anything bad to happen to Cheryl. I don't even know where she is, but You do. She's alone and scared, and I just want You to stay with her."

Then surprisingly the words of a psalm came to mind, and Erik murmured them aloud. " 'Where can I go from your Spirit? Where can I flee from your presence? If I go up to the heavens, you are there; if I make my bed in the depths, you are there. If I rise on the wings of the dawn, if I settle on the far side of the sea, even there your hand will guide me, your right hand will hold me fast.' "

Erik breathed a sigh of relief and felt a peace wash over him that he'd not believed possible under the circumstances. God wouldn't desert them. He wouldn't desert Cheryl. Even in the depths of this hideous situation, God was there.

"I have to keep my focus," Erik said and started the truck. "I have to remember that God loves Cheryl even more than I do."

Chapter 17

Cheryl gagged at the taste of the oily rag in her mouth. Severon didn't want her screaming to warn Curt away, yet he wanted Curt to clearly see that Cheryl's life depended upon his actions. Therefore, Burks left her tied and gagged in the middle of the hangar with both doors open and a single light shining from nearby. As shadows fell across the ground and the skies darkened, Cheryl felt desperation build within her soul.

I'm the bait they're using to capture Curt, she thought. *I'm the reason he's going to die.*

She tried not to think about it. She tried not to think of how she and Curt had come full circle. She'd loved him once. She had planned her life around a future that would see him as her husband and lifetime mate. Those memories were bittersweet. The Curt and Cheryl of those yesteryears no longer existed. Yet the affection had been very real.

But she had hated him as well.

Someone had once told her that love and hate were opposite sides of a single coin. She didn't know if she found that such feelings were far more internalized than she'd originally believed. Instead of hating Curt, she found that she really hated herself. Hated her vulnerability. Hated her neediness. Hated her mistakes. Hating Curt for injustices, real or imagined, came easily. Already steeped in hatred, Cheryl had little ability to love anyone.

But now Curt would face death because of her hatred and her love. It was all her fault, and now all she wanted to do was protect him. She thought of Christy and of Grant's baby. What was her name? Oh, yes, Sarah.

They loved Curt and needed him. How could she ever explain that her stupidity and stubborn refusal to assist Curt had cost them a husband and father? Tears welled in her eyes as she watched and waited for the telltale signs of car headlights.

Then another face came to mind. Erik. She tried to concentrate on her memories of him. His boyish grin. His blue eyes, so bold and bright. He could gaze at her with a look that seemed to go right through to her soul. Just thinking of him caused her stomach to do a flip.

I suppose, she admitted, *that since I'm about to die it can't possibly hurt anything to say I've come to care for him.* She wanted to laugh at her own noncommittal thoughts.

Care for him? The man who'd forced himself into her life and beaten down the walls of hatred she'd built? The man who bore her painful reminders of the past? The man who knew all her dirty little secrets and held no condemnation for her?

She pulled restlessly at the rope that bound her to the chair. Erik was also the man who'd comforted her when she was afraid. He'd been the man who'd refused to be put off, the one who'd gone the distance with her and remained true to her needs.

Maybe someday you'll be ready for something more than friendship. His words came back to haunt her.

I am ready for something more, she agonized. Only now, there might not be a "someday" to count on. She might never have a chance to tell Erik that she'd fallen in love with him.

I've fallen in love with him? she questioned. Her heart knew that it was true. It wasn't the teenage love she'd had for Curt; a love born out of familiarity and adolescent vision. It wasn't the adventurous emotion she'd felt with Grant. No, this was a quiet, saturating kind of love. The kind of love a woman knew she could count on for the rest of her life. The kind of love that would see her through the thick and thin of things and come through stronger than ever.

Headlights flashed before her eyes, and Cheryl instantly forgot her thoughts. Curt had come, and no doubt with him came her only hope of surviving Severon's revenge. She tried to glance around to where she'd seen Severon take his hiding place. The darkness prevented her from seeing him there, however. She looked overhead where the two thugs were calmly waiting in the shadows, no doubt with guns drawn.

If there were only some way to save Curt's life! Cheryl knew she would offer herself up in his place. He didn't deserve to die for this.

He'd only been after the truth. And with that thought, Cheryl knew that she could completely forgive Curt for the imagined wrongs she'd held against him.

Curt's car stopped just outside of the hangar. She could see him now. His expression was quite serious, and for several moments all he did was look at her.

Don't come in here, she thought, and then she prayed, *God, don't let him be killed.*

Curt got out of the car slowly. In his right hand he held the lock-box. Raising both hands aloft, he moved toward her with an ease that made Cheryl want to scream. She struggled against the ropes and made as much protesting noise as her gag would allow. Curt only smiled and winked at her with a cocky self-assurance that made Cheryl want to slug him. This was life and death. Didn't he understand the jeopardy?

If we die now, Cheryl thought, *then everything has been in vain. Daddy will have died in vain. The O'Sullivans' deaths will mean nothing. Even my baby's death will be forgotten and meaningless in the wake of Severon Burks's victory.*

Curt advanced, and Cheryl could see his eyes dart from side to side, even though his face remained fixed on her. "I'm here, Cheryl. I've done exactly as you instructed me."

She moaned against the rag, wishing that he would magically disappear from the line of fire. She suddenly remembered in vivid detail the way it felt to have a bullet pierce her body. At first it had just been a stunning sensation of being hit hard in a very small space. Then it had seemed a warmth spread through her body until it became a white-hot fire. Her breath caught in her throat, and her chest tightened. She shook her head, refusing to allow the memory to take her captive. If there was even the remotest possibility that she could help Curt, then she had to stay clearheaded and focused.

"I've brought your precious list," Curt announced to the air. "So why don't you stop playing this game of hide-and-seek and come out and inspect it for yourself?"

"I believe I'll do just that," came the voice of Severon Burks. He stepped into the light, gun leveled at Curt's midsection. "I suppose introductions are unnecessary."

"I know very well who you are," Curt said, slowly lowering his hands. "Severon Burks, age fifty-eight, Columbian-born native mother and American father. Raised in Columbia until the age of twelve. When your mother died, your father relocated to the U.S. in order to see you receive an American education. You stayed on after the death of your father, married, and raised a son named Grant. When Grant turned eight, you moved your family back to Columbia and joined your mother's family in the cocaine business."

"You've done your homework, Mr. O'Sullivan."

"Just as I'm sure," Curt said with a smile, "you've done yours."

Severon smiled. "You're quite right, of course. We probably know each other better than we know ourselves."

"I don't know that I would go that far, but I suppose we're knowledgeable enough to respect the deadliness of our opponents."

"Exactly."

Cheryl watched the showdown with growing agitation. She couldn't move. She couldn't speak. She could hardly breathe.

"I've brought what you want; now why don't you let Ms. Fairchild go so we can get down to business?"

"Not so fast." Severon waved the gun at Curt and motioned toward a small workbench. "Put it over there, and then go stand beside her."

Curt toyed with the lid's handle. "I would imagine you'd like to review the contents and make certain this is what you've been waiting for. After all, I could have an empty box here, and then you would be back at square one. Wouldn't you like to see?" He looked up with a questioning expression.

"You wouldn't be stupid enough to remove—" Burks fell silent, and his eyes narrowed.

Cheryl drew in a sharp breath, and Severon stepped toward Curt. "Yes, I suppose you would be stupid enough to believe that removing the contents would buy yourself more time."

Curt shrugged and gave the man a good-natured smile. He rolled his head back just a bit and gazed upward as though considering the nature of their conversation. Cheryl watched him and suddenly realized that Curt was studying the surroundings. He was looking for something or. . .someone!

417

Would Severon notice? She began to make a noise, hoping that if he did, he'd forget about it and focus on her.

He looked at her with an unyielding expression of anger. "Be silent." He waved the gun in her direction. "Or I'll silence you myself."

Cheryl cowered down against the back of the chair and nodded. *It was enough,* she thought. Curt had been able to give the area a good once-over. *At least I've helped that much.*

"All right, Mr. O'Sullivan. On the chance that you think you can mastermind some form of heroics in this matter, I'll review the contents of the lockbox first. I will add, however, that if the box contains less than I expect it to contain, I'll put a bullet through the kneecap of your friend over there. You can watch her suffer in pain while we figure out what to do about your inability to follow directions."

"I didn't say that I'd neglected to bring what you asked for," Curt responded quite seriously. "You're just like your son. Grant also had a penchant for using women to buffer himself from harm. Why don't you stop hiding behind Cheryl's presence and look it over? I want to get home, and I want this matter to be settled. You win. You have your list, and you have your drugs. That should make you a very happy man."

"It might, but you neglect to remember one simple fact." Severon's expression turned to a look of pure hatred. The scar on his face grew tight and pale. "You killed my son. That isn't something I'm going to forgive you for. You're going to pay for what you've done, and she can pay as well."

"I didn't kill Grant," Curt replied frankly. "Forensics proved that much. My bullet didn't kill him. I was busy getting his fiancée out of the line of fire. My only concern was to keep my friend from dying."

Cheryl blinked back tears. He had risked his life for her. It was a simple fact she had been quite willing to forget, yet here was history repeating itself.

"You're to blame for the double cross. That makes you responsible for his death."

Curt shrugged. "Have it your way, but Grant brought it all on himself. He didn't even stop at endangering the life of his child. Sarah was just another pawn in this stupid game of yours."

"The child is of no concern to me. Put the box down and move over there." Severon was clearly through playing games. "You people operate under the delusion that your own principles for living can somehow be grafted onto those around you. My game is different from yours, and its rules are different. Life is short and fleeting—and in most cases very fragile. It isn't the life of a person that matters quite as much as what can be accomplished with that life."

"Then why avenge your son's death?" questioned Curt. "If life is of so little value, why spend your time and energy here?"

"Because several million dollars are at stake," Severon replied. "And because I am a businessman. When you take something of mine, you must pay for it. You took the life of my son, and I will take yours." He raised the gun. "Now, put the box down."

Cheryl wanted to scream. Curt came to stand beside her, yet his presence did nothing to comfort her. Even when he put his arm on her trembling shoulder, Cheryl found her body tensing even further.

Severon smiled at them with an evil leer that made Cheryl draw in a sharp breath. Would he kill them now?

"You may have already seen my friends overhead," Severon said as he put his own gun into his suit-coat pocket. "I wouldn't try anything foolish. They've been instructed to shoot you both if you so much as sneeze."

"Good thing I don't have a cold," Curt said snidely.

Severon stared hard at him for a moment, then turned to the box. He fumbled with it for several minutes before growling in anger and turning back to face Curt. "It's stuck."

"Yeah, it does that. I find that a ballpoint pen usually does the trick. I have one right here, if you need it. See, you just pry it between the lid and the box—"

"Then get over here and do it, and remember my men have you and your friend covered. One wrong move will see her dead."

"Relax, Severon. Your friends at the gate have already made certain I'm not carrying any weapons. They went over the car in detail, and they did everything but strip-search me. How could I possibly pose a threat?"

How indeed? Cheryl wondered, yet she prayed that Curt might be just such a threat. She wanted nothing more than for Curt to find a way to release them both from the clutches of Grant's father. Sitting there, helpless, she thought of every movie she'd ever seen, remembering the hapless victims and how they staged their own rescues. But this wasn't a movie. She had no carefully concealed knife in her shirtsleeves. She had no prearranged plan for an army of mercenaries to storm the premises and whisk her and Curt to safety by the sudden appearance of a blimp or fully armed jet. Her only hope was that God had listened to her prayers.

Curt walked to where Severon stood and reached slowly into his breast pocket. Cheryl tensed. She could tell by the look of concentration on Curt's face that he was about to make his move. She'd seen that look a hundred times before.

What can I do to help? What can I do?

Suddenly it seemed important to distract Severon's concentration. Cheryl began to strain at the ropes and rock the chair in place. She yelled from behind the gag, calling Severon every name she could think of—all of it coming out in garbled, incoherent groans.

It was enough, however, to make Severon turn. Just as he turned, Cheryl rocked the chair too hard, and it went smashing against the concrete floor. Lying perfectly still, Cheryl feared that the men overhead would riddle her with bullets. She could almost feel the impact of the bullets piercing her flesh. It was the nightmarish day of the DEA shoot-out all over again.

She heard the scuffle between Severon and Curt, but was unable to see the results. Overhead she could hear voices and shouted commands. There seemed to be a great deal of yelling and confusion. What in the world was happening?

Everything went silent. She tried to raise her head up enough to see, but it was impossible, so she waited silently for her fate.

"I've got your boss," Curt shouted to the rafters. "If any of you wants to play hero, now's the time."

"I think we've got them all, Curt," a man yelled down from overhead. "We picked up the ones at the gate and a man who claims to be piloting the plane outside. There doesn't appear to be anyone else around."

Cheryl saw several people move across the floor of the hangar toward where Curt and Severon had been standing before her fall. She longed to know for herself that all was well with Curt. She tried again to twist around. Just then a hand pressed against her shoulder.

"Relax, Cheryl; you're okay."

It was Curt, and his voice gave her instant assurance that everything would be all right.

He untied her gag and then cut the ropes away from the chair. Helping her to her feet, he assessed her from head to toe. "Are you hurt?"

"No," she managed to say, still tasting the oil on her tongue. "Are you?"

"Nah," he said with a grin, "I'm too tough."

She shook her head, and her legs went out from under her. Curt immediately grabbed her and put a supportive arm around her waist. "Come on. I'll put you in the car until this mess is taken care of."

"I thought he would kill you. He blamed you for Grant, and he said—"

"Don't think about it," Curt replied, hugging her close. "It isn't important now."

He opened his car door for her. "You stay here."

"Curt," she said, taking hold of his arm, "I have to say something."

He gave her such a look of understanding that Cheryl knew no words were necessary. "We can talk later," he said. "Erik and Christy are waiting for us at home, and the sooner I finish up inside, the sooner we can go to them."

"Erik's there?" she said with a voice that betrayed her interest.

"Yes, Erik is there," Curt replied with a grin. "He has something he wants to tell you. Seemed pretty important."

"What was it?" she asked, feeling a surge of anticipation.

"I think I'll leave that to him. You'll just have to be patient for once and do things my way."

Chapter 18

The last conscious thought Erik had was of the clock chiming three times. He fell asleep with his head on the kitchen table, only inches from where his sister dozed. His dreams were nightmares of confusion. He pictured Cheryl in a cage, dangling over a bottomless abyss. He couldn't reach her, and the hopelessness of the situation made him frantic.

At the sound of a car door slamming, he jumped. Unsure if he'd dreamed the noise, he glanced to where Christy had bolted upright. Apparently the sound had been real.

"What time is it?" Christy asked, getting to her feet.

Erik jumped up, his heart pounding fiercely against his chest. He glanced at his watch. "Five-thirty."

They hesitated at the table, their eyes asking the unspoken question of whether they dared look outside. The sound of another car door had them both running for the front door.

Christy beat him and threw the door open with such force that it banged against the wall, breaking the silence of the moment. They moved across the threshold and out on the porch to find Cheryl and Curt coming up the walkway.

Christy let out a shout and rushed down the porch stairs. Cheryl stepped aside as Christy threw herself into her husband's arms. "You're here! You're safe!" She was crying, sobbing, and kissing him all at once. Curt wrapped his arms around her and buried his face in her hair.

Erik held back. Shoving his hands in his jeans' pockets, he exchanged a look with Cheryl that spoke volumes. Curt and Christy moved up the stairs, and as they passed him, Curt leaned toward Erik.

"I told her you had something to say." He winked and went inside the house with his sobbing wife.

Cheryl came up the stairs rather hesitantly. She searched his face as

422

though looking for an answer to some unspoken question. Erik could no longer hold back. He crossed the short space and pulled her into a fierce embrace. For a fleeting moment, he thought she might fight him, but instead she only maneuvered her arms in order to wrap them around his neck.

"I thought I'd lost you," he whispered against her hair.

"I know," she answered softly. "I thought I'd never see you again."

For several minutes they did nothing but hold each other. *It's enough,* Erik thought. It was enough to know that she was safe and that God had answered all of his prayers.

He pulled away gently and looked down at her. The tightness of her worried expression softened, and she smiled. "Are you really okay?" he asked, fearful of the answer.

"I'm better than that. I. . .well. . ." She glanced away. "There are some things I want to tell you."

"Me, too," Erik said. "There's a porch swing on the east side. Why don't we go sit there and watch the sun come up?"

Cheryl nodded her approval and let Erik lead her past the front door and around the side of the stately Victorian home. Erik waited for her to take a seat before joining her. He didn't care what she thought as he put his arm around her shoulders and gave a little tug. Cheryl willingly snuggled down against his shoulder, tucking her head under his chin.

"I love you," he whispered, feeling his heart in his throat. He waited for her to tense, but she didn't. "I think I've loved you for a very long time now." He hoped she'd say something, but she didn't. *Maybe it's too soon,* he thought. *Maybe she will never allow herself to love again.*

"Look," he said softly. "I just wanted you to know how I felt. I know you've gone through a great deal. I guess I just want you to know that when you're ready to love again, I'm here waiting."

Cheryl moved away from him and eased back against the swing. She looked out across the yard before allowing her gaze to rest on his face. "I thought I was going to die," she said simply. "I found myself alone and terrified, and I kept thinking about what you and CJ had told me about God."

Erik grinned. "I wasn't sure you were listening."

Cheryl countered his smile. "I was listening." She grew sober. "I listened just enough to make myself think, and unfortunately at that time, thinking was the last thing I wanted to do. There were already too many things to think about. Grant. My father. The baby. Not to mention everything else related to the last year and a half of my life.

"I wanted to pretend that I could make it all go away. That nothing need ever hurt me again. I wanted to believe that I was alone, because that way I didn't need to worry about feeling anything for anyone."

"But you weren't alone," Erik said softly.

"No, I wasn't. I know that now. I found it out while I was waiting in the back of my kidnappers' van."

Erik shook his head. "What happened?"

"I realized that God really was Who you said He was. I wasn't sure how to go about getting Him on my side or putting myself on His side, but I prayed. I really, honestly prayed, and it gave me the courage to go on."

Erik reached out and squeezed her hand. "That's more than I'd ever hoped to hear."

She smiled and nodded her head. "It was more than I'd ever thought possible. I came to realize while I was there, stuck in the middle of nowhere with little hope of escaping, that God was truly there for me. Then I started thinking back to other times in my life when God must have stood by, watching me make my mistakes, knowing that I was too stubborn to be reached any other way. I knew then that He'd been there all along. Even when I was in the pits of despair. Even when I'd made the wrong choices with Grant. God was always there."

Erik quoted the verses from Psalm 139: " 'Where can I go from your Spirit? Where can I flee from your presence? If I go up to the heavens, you are there; if I make my bed in the depths, you are there. If I rise on the wings of the dawn, if I settle on the far side of the sea, even there your hand will guide me, your right hand will hold me fast.' "

"Yes," she whispered, and the look she gave him caused his heart to soar. "I tried to flee from God's presence, and believe me, I made my bed in the depths." She lowered her face. "I'm not proud of who I am, Erik."

"But you should be," he said softly. "You're a child of God. Forgiven and purified by the blood Jesus shed on the cross. He took your sins, yours and mine, and sacrificed His life to reconcile us with God. Give

Him the past and console yourself in the fact that He blots out your sins and remembers them no more."

"I like that idea," she said, twisting her hands in her lap. "But, Erik, the past is hard to forget. There are people who will no doubt help me to remember it on a daily basis."

"Probably. But there are those of us—me, for instance—who don't care about the past. We're far more interested in the future and what it might hold in store. The past only entangles us, and Satan uses that to steal away our victory in Christ. The future is our hope in God's ability to take us out of Satan's snares, and the present is where we must act in faith to believe He will do just that."

"And you can forget the past? Forget that I was adulterous with your sister's husband? Forget that I would have borne him an illegitimate child? Can you forget my part in this entire nightmare and still love me? That seems an awful lot to ask."

"But in Christ," he said softly, feeling the pain in her words, "all things are possible, and in Christ, all things are made new. You are a new creation, Cheryl. Why should I condemn you for that which you've thrown off?"

She moved back into his arms and laid her head back until they were cheek to cheek. Together they watched the sky lighten. The colorful fingers of dawn spread out in a blend of lavender, pink, and orange. It was a moment Erik always hoped to remember. A moment that bound them to one another. He would wait forever for her to love him.

Without warning, she got to her feet and looked back at him. "I'm ready," she said softly and extended her hand.

Erik's sense of hope fell hard. He got to his feet and reached into his jeans' pocket to retrieve his car keys. She, no doubt, wanted to go home. He pulled the keys out, but, to his surprise, Cheryl pushed them away and instead reached up to touch his cheek.

"No," she whispered. "I meant that I'm ready to fall in love with you."

Erik couldn't believe his ears. The keys dropped noisily to the porch floor. "You. . .mean it?"

Cheryl nodded, her eyes bright and clear. "I think I've been falling in love with you ever since you showed up at my door with your roguish grin and boyish charms. Facing death made me rethink a few things."

"Like what?" he questioned, gingerly touching her face. He was almost afraid it was an illusion. Her soft skin against his fingers convinced him that it wasn't.

"Things like. . .us. You made me feel whole. You helped me to see hope when I had none. You gave me love when no one else could reach me."

Erik pulled her against him, and with one arm around her waist, he lifted her face to meet his. "I can't believe this is happening."

"Me neither," she whispered.

He wanted to kiss her, to feel the soft sweetness of her lips against his. He lowered his head to meet her mouth, then hesitated, waiting a moment, as if for permission. Her eyes told him everything. He saw in their blue depths the desire and longing that seemed to mirror his own emotions. Pressing his mouth to hers, he felt her melt against him and sigh. She wrapped her arms around his neck and pressed him closer.

Erik wanted to yell out loud, and when he released her, he did just that.

"I love you, Cheryl Fairchild!" he exclaimed and lifted her into the air to circle round and round with her.

She giggled as he had never heard her do before. There was a definite joy returning to her life, and he thanked God that he could be part of it. He kissed her again.

This time the kiss lingered, and afterward, they simply held each other in the quiet of the morning. Erik felt as though nothing in life could be better. His emotions ran rampant, and his heart seemed to soar on the wings of the dawn. The chains of the past were broken, and now the future could begin.

A Gift of Wings

Chapter 1

Debbie Sanders reshuffled a stack of letters and finally opened the largest of the five envelopes. The card inside was another of her mother's attempts to keep Debbie's spirits up. Flowery in artistry as well as words, the card wished her a happy birthday, while her mother's handwritten note suggested Debbie not let the past ruin the day for her.

But while the day might not be completely ruined, it would forever be haunted by the events of the past. Nothing could change that.

Putting the card aside, Debbie turned to focus her attention on the computer screen. She took her position with Aldersson Enterprises very seriously. Brad and CJ Aldersson had opened yet another resort, this one specializing in romantic getaways and couple-oriented clientele. The Aldersson Inn was not intriguingly titled, but its reputation for elegance set amidst a Rocky Mountain backdrop would soon speak for itself.

Pulling up the registration files for January, Debbie could see that marketing and advertising had paid off. They were booked solid. The twenty-room lodge and five honeymoon cottages had been quickly snatched up. Granted, most of the early reservations were family or friends of the Alderssons', but nevertheless, the place was going to be filled to capacity.

Clicking on the information she needed, Debbie reconfirmed the guests who were scheduled to check in on opening day, January 5. Everyone's account seemed in order, and relaxing a bit, Debbie closed the file.

I just want to do a good job, she thought, realizing this was the fourth time she'd checked the file that day. Sitting alone in the resort office, Debbie wasn't prepared to hear voices outside in the lobby. She stiffened. Five years ago this very day, she had also heard voices coming from where there should have been no sound.

Her mouth went dry and her heart picked up its pace.

Five years, and all she had to show for it was a residual fear that seemed to nip at her heels at the most inconvenient times. Frank would have laughed at her silliness. She had once been among the best officers on the payroll of the Drug Enforcement Agency, and now she cowered in her office like a frightened child.

Determined not to disappoint Frank, Debbie pushed back from her desk and got to her feet. She looked heavenward, hoping somehow that her deceased husband could see her making a stand. But somehow, Debbie doubted it was all that important. Frank was dead—shot down during a raid on a crack house. Shot down the day before Christmas— her birthday—by a surprised drug dealer.

"Debbie, you in there?" a voice called out.

Debbie let out a heavy breath. Curt O'Sullivan had been her partner for several years while with the DEA. He was also Brad Aldersson's brother-in-law and the reason she had been given the job of managing the resort.

"I'm in here, Curt," she called and nervously wiped her damp hands on her jeans.

No doubt Curt remembered the day as well. He had probably come up early for the family's preopening celebration. Brad Aldersson had scheduled for his family to privately enjoy the lodge prior to giving it over to the public. A kind of run-through for Debbie and the rest of the staff.

"Ah, here you are," Curt said, beaming a smile toward her. "I've brought a friend. Hope you don't mind."

Debbie smiled. "I knew you were bringing Christy. This was supposed to be a place for husbands and wives, after all." She tried to sound jovial, remembering the holiday spirit.

Curt grinned. "Yeah, well, Christy is coming up with Brad and CJ. I've brought you someone else. He's going to stay here and celebrate the New Year with us."

Debbie frowned. "I thought this was going to be family only. Just the three couples—you and Christy, Brad and CJ, and Christy's brother. . .oh, what's his name?"

"Erik. Erik and Cheryl. Yup, they're coming, too," Curt said, leaning against the doorframe rather casually. "But this is someone else. An old friend. He popped in on me and I thought I'd bring him along. You know, just for the fun of it."

Debbie shook her head. "There's more to this, Curt O'Sullivan. I can tell by the way you're acting."

Curt pointed at his chest. "Who, me? I'm not acting."

"So bring in your surprise and let me gauge for myself what's going on."

He laughed and stepped back. "Okay, buddy. The coast is clear."

Debbie couldn't have been more surprised when Nathan McGuire stuck his head around the side of the door. "She's not going to throw anything at me, is she?"

Debbie felt her world begin to spin out of control. The past rose up like an apparition. Trembling, she crossed her arms and shook her head. "What are you doing here?"

"Merry Christmas and Happy New Year to you, too," Nathan said, coming into the room. "Is that any way to greet an old coworker?"

"Sorry, but we took down all the mistletoe," Debbie replied rather snidely. *Coworker, indeed. How dare he come here?*

"I can go find some," Nathan replied with a mischievous wink, "if that's all it takes."

Debbie took her seat at the desk, hoping to put some distance between herself and Nathan. "Forget it."

"So, anyway, Nathan didn't have any plans for the week and we thought—"

"Stop it!" Debbie said, looking up quite seriously. "I didn't work all those years in the agency for nothing. Why are you really here?"

"She's good," Nathan said, winking at Curt. "Definitely has a sixth sense for knowing when something's up."

"I know," Curt replied. "That's why she made a good partner."

Debbie slammed down a ledger. "Enough! My sixth sense didn't keep Frank from being killed, so take your flattery elsewhere. Just tell me why you've brought that…that…"

Nathan leaned down on the desk and grinned. "Great, all-around good guy? Wonderful friend? Trusted—"

"Oh, please, spare me!" Debbie narrowed her eyes. "I'm not in the mood for this, and you both know why. Don't try to cheer me up or play these games."

Curt came around and touched Debbie's shoulder. "Deb, we didn't mean to upset you. We know it's the anniversary of Frank's death."

Hearing the words didn't hurt as much as Debbie had thought they might. She missed Frank—missed their companionable relationship. They had understood each other so well, and because they both worked for the DEA, they knew the risks and job frustrations that each other faced.

But Debbie had accepted that Frank was gone. Missing him didn't mean that she hadn't learned to cope. Sometimes she even thought she was ready to date again—fall in love and marry. Sometimes. But not today.

"I'm really sorry," Curt said softly.

"I know you are," Debbie replied. "But, honestly, I'm all right." She looked up and caught something in Curt's expression as he exchanged a glance with Nathan. Her instincts were right. Something was going on. "Now, are you and the Quarterback Flash over there going to tell me what this is all about?"

Curt pulled away and took a seat. "There's a slight problem—nothing to get too worked up about."

"Right," Debbie said. "That's why you brought him."

"I didn't bring him—he brought me. I thought you might handle the news better if I were here to soften the blow."

Debbie felt her legs start to shake. "What news?"

"Simon Hill has escaped," Nathan replied quite seriously.

Debbie felt the world suddenly stop. Everything went silent. "When? How?" She looked to the two men for answers. "How in the world did the penitentiary let Frank's killer escape?"

"We don't have all the details," Curt began, "but apparently he clubbed a guard, dressed in his clothes, bribed another guard, and pretty much walked out."

"Just like that?" she questioned.

"Like I said, we don't have all the answers. It was thought best that we put some protection on you, since your testimony is the one that put him in there."

"But Hill doesn't know where I'm at. He probably thinks I'm still working in Denver."

Nathan spoke before Curt could get a word out. "They found this in Simon's cell." He pulled out a newspaper article for the Aldersson Inn and pointed to the photograph of Debbie with Brad. Debbie's face was circled in bull's-eye fashion.

Completely stunned, Debbie sat back and stared dumbly at the article. "He actually had this in his cell?"

"That's why we thought it best to have someone guarding you," Nathan replied.

"You?" she questioned, looking up. "Why you?"

"I'm so glad to see your enthusiasm," Nathan said, straightening up. His six-foot-three, 220-pound frame seemed to tower over Debbie. "They wanted the best man for the job. That's why I'm here."

"For how long?" Debbie questioned, looking to Curt for answers.

"For as long as it takes," he stated matter-of-factly. "Look, Nathan is the best, and you know that as well as anyone."

"I knew it five years ago. I know nothing about him now," she protested.

"Well, I still like my coffee black, and I love blackberry pie à la mode. I'm fond of skiing, snowboarding, and snowmobiling, but I also like swimming and scuba diving."

"I suppose this is your idea of comic relief," Debbie said, getting to her feet once again. She didn't know how to deal with the news she'd just been given. It was bad enough to have to face the possibility of danger, but to do it with Nathan McGuire at her side was almost unbearable. "I don't want a bodyguard," she finally said. "I can take care of myself."

"Nothing doing," Curt said, shaking his head. "You know better."

"I won't have this bozo following me around day in and day out. And I especially won't deal with his entourage."

"What's that supposed to mean?" Nathan asked, sounding almost hurt.

Debbie put her hands on her hips, hoping she could somehow appear intimidating, although at half his weight and a good seven inches shorter than his height, Debbie knew she probably didn't worry the man in the least.

"I've endured your womanizing before, as you both remember quite well. You might be a wonderful professional, but I don't trust anything else about you. I have a quiet life now, and I want it to stay that way."

"You're hurting my feelings," Nathan said, then offered her a quick grin. "Would it help to say I've changed?"

"No," Debbie answered flatly. "No one can change that much."

"Nathan became a Christian about four years ago, Deb," Curt threw in. "I've seen the change in his life, and I know it's genuine."

Debbie felt gut-punched. All the support for her argument seemed to fade. "I'm glad," she said, trying hard to acknowledge the news graciously. "I'm glad you've changed inwardly, but you've still got the same Hollywood good looks on the outside. Women are going to just naturally be attracted to where you are."

"You really think I'm good-looking?" Nathan questioned with raised brows. "Hmmm, maybe this assignment won't be so bad, after all."

Debbie rolled her gaze upward. "Take him away. I can't deal with him."

"I can't," Curt said apologetically. "You're just going to have to endure this."

A noise came from outside the front door of the lodge. With instincts honed from years of training, all three people sprang into action.

"You stay here," Curt said to Debbie as he pushed her behind the desk. "Get down."

Nathan pulled a gun from under his coat, while Curt reached down for the revolver he traditionally wore strapped to his ankle. Nodding, he cupped the weapon and moved to the side of the door.

The sound of the front door being opened caused the hairs on Debbie's neck to prickle. Her scalp felt electrified. She could hear footsteps on the hardwood floor. The door to the front desk area opened. That meant whoever it was now stood just outside her office.

With Curt on one side of the door and Nathan on the other, Debbie was inclined to crawl completely under the desk. If bullets started flying, she wanted at least the pretense of security. But instead of hiding, Debbie was frozen in place. Had Frank's killer really come back to see her dead, as well?

There was a dull thud-type sound as if someone had put something heavy on the counter. Then the footsteps sounded again, and glancing around her desk, she could see the highly polished shoes of her trespasser.

"Stop right there!" Curt called as he popped around the corner.

"Hands up!" Nathan declared.

Debbie would have laughed at the stunned expression on Brad Aldersson's face if the situation hadn't been so serious. Shaking, she got to her feet, as Curt and Nathan reholstered their weapons.

"I don't think this would be a very good way to greet the visitors," Brad said rather dryly. "Tends to put a damper on the romantic spirit of things, don't you think?"

"Sorry, Brad," Curt answered before anyone else could say a word. "But we've got some problems."

Brad nodded. "So I gathered from your telephone message. Guess you'd better fill me in."

Chapter 2

"And that's all we really know," Curt concluded, while Brad took in the information.

Debbie could no longer stand the confines of the crowded office and got up to leave. "I'm going to go make some lunch," she said and, without waiting for their comments, hurried from the room.

By the time she reached the kitchen, Debbie realized Nathan had dogged her steps. "I'm sure I don't need you to watch me make lunch."

"I'm here to guard you, and that's what I intend to do."

"Protect me from the pickles?" Debbie asked sarcastically.

"Look, you don't have to give me such a hard time. After all," he said, smiling, "we can be friends—we used to be friends—right?"

Debbie looked at him for a moment, catching the intensity of his brown eyes. He *was* Hollywood good-looking. His dark eyes and black hair betrayed the traits of a Navajo great-grandfather. His sharp, chiseled features were also reminders of an ancestry that once cultivated the Southwest with pride and great success. She remembered him talking about this once when they were working to break a code used by a drug ring. He had told her of Navajo code talkers during World War II and how he had relatives involved. But that wasn't all she remembered, and it was the other memories that troubled her.

Shaking the thoughts from her head, Debbie turned to one of three well-stocked refrigerators. "Do you like tuna salad?"

"It's all right," Nathan said.

"Is there something else you'd prefer?" she questioned, leaning back from the door.

"I'd prefer that we be friends," Nathan replied quite seriously. "I know this is a hard day for you, what with Frank and now this news, but you need me, and it would be easier if you'd put aside the hostilities and cooperate. I just want to keep you alive."

"I can keep myself alive," Debbie said, refusing to be swayed by his soft words. "I can take care of myself." She slammed the door, upsetting the punch bowl that had been placed rather precariously atop the refrigerator.

Nathan crossed the distance without warning and caught the bowl just before it crashed to the floor. "Yeah, you do a real good job of keeping yourself out of trouble." He handed her the punch bowl and grinned. "But with two of us on the job, you'll be just that much safer."

Debbie nearly growled as she yanked the glass bowl from his hands. "Just stay away from me."

"Not a chance, lady," Nathan replied. "Not a chance."

🙠

"I think we should move her to someplace less conspicuous and hard to control," Curt told Brad.

Nathan quickly agreed. "I think Curt's right. The resort is fairly isolated, but it is the one place where Hill realizes he can find her."

"I have a cabin a short ways from here," Brad offered. "You can only get there by hiking up or using a helicopter. And, I might add, the hike would require someone in excellent condition. You mentioned that Hill walks with a limp, so I doubt we'll be risking much there. Especially with it being winter."

"Sounds perfect. Can we borrow it?" Nathan asked.

"I wouldn't have mentioned it otherwise."

"Does anybody care what I have to say about this?" Debbie questioned.

Nathan looked at her sympathetically. He felt bad that she was having to endure all of this. He knew she'd rather have been left alone to mourn Frank on the anniversary of his death. "We care, but right now we don't have a lot of time. Simon has friends, and no doubt he left prison with a plan."

"Yeah, a plan to kill me," Debbie replied.

"Well, he's not going to be allowed to do that," Nathan said, reaching out to touch her hand. He wanted to offer her some reassurance that he would keep her alive. "But you're going to have to be cooperative."

"You know the routine, Deb," Curt said softly. "We have to move you out of here quickly and without anyone noticing that you've gone."

"We have some crates in the storage room," Brad said with sudden excitement. "We could hide her in there. Then I can have the delivery truck pull up and haul the crates out of here. We could have Nathan meet up with my helicopter, and I could fly the two of you to the cabin."

"Sounds like a plan," Curt said, nodding. "By leaving Debbie's car here and showing no signs of her leaving the premises, if anyone is watching the place, they'll think she's still inside."

Nathan looked at the woman he'd come to guard. A woman he'd long ago lost his heart to. Her beauty played out in an exotic, almost South Sea island way. She was all-American, but her dark eyes were alluring—almost bespeaking of a secret. Her long, black hair, now braided and casually pulled over one shoulder, glistened and begged his touch. She was every bit as beautiful as he'd remembered. The only difference was that he'd lost her years ago to Frank. Now he hoped she might come around to giving her heart to him—again.

That was the biggest reason he'd volunteered for this assignment. He'd held his distance, giving her time to grieve her husband's death. If the truth were told, he'd been grieving Frank's passing himself. Frank had been a dynamic man, a powerful leader, and a good friend. His loss had been felt by the entire team.

But more than this, Nathan had given them both time to get beyond their shared past. Beyond the hurt he'd imposed upon her—upon them both.

"I'll call the delivery service we used to haul this stuff in," Brad said, pulling out his cell phone. "Debbie, I don't want you to worry about a thing. We'll have you back here before opening day. You'll see."

"He's right," Curt said, giving her a smile. "I'm sure they'll have Simon apprehended in a matter of hours. This is all just a precaution."

"Sure," Debbie said, getting to her feet. She walked to the door and turned to look back at the trio. "I was taught the speech, too, you know."

"It's more than a speech," Nathan said, standing. "We have a vested interest in you."

"Oh?" she questioned.

Her dark brooding eyes wreaked havoc with Nathan's nerves. "Yeah," he finally replied, coming up behind her. "You're our friend, and we want to keep you alive." She said nothing, but the look on her face told Nathan he'd hit a nerve.

He followed her to a secured side door. This was the entrance to her own private lodge quarters. Sliding the key into the lock, she looked at Nathan as if he were standing on her coattail.

"You don't have to follow me everywhere."

"Well, just about everywhere. If the bathroom facilities are inaccessible to outside attack, then I won't have to follow you in there."

"Maybe I'll just take up residence in there," she said, turning the key.

"Nope, you're going to live in a box. At least for a few hours," Nathan replied with a grin. He reached out and touched her arm. He could feel her trembling beneath the soft warmth of her sweater. Her apparent fear sobered him. "I really meant what I said in there. I care about keeping you safe."

"I know that," she answered, almost sounding defensive. "I'm a job, and you don't want to ruin your good record."

"It's more than that."

She shook her head. "No, it's not." Then, as if reading his mind, she added, "It will never be more than that."

"You're bound and determined to keep me at arm's length, aren't you?"

"Absolutely," she replied. "It beats the alternative."

He tilted his head to one side, losing himself for a moment as he met her eyes. "Which is?"

"To be one of your many conquests," Debbie replied flatly, then added, "again."

"My what?" Nathan was genuinely puzzled. He knew his past had lent him a reputation of being a real ladies' man, but his inability to find what he was searching for was the reason for the long parade of lady loves. He had never been able to commit to any of them because they weren't what he was looking for. He might never have known that if Curt hadn't shared his own hope in Jesus.

Debbie turned and backed up against the door. "I'm sure you had little trouble walking away from our relationship, but it wasn't that way for me. If it hadn't been for Frank, I don't know what would have happened."

Nathan looked away in shame. "I was wrong to treat you that way."

"Yes, you were, but it's in the past."

"I'd like for it to stay in the past," Nathan replied. "I'd like a second chance."

Debbie looked at him for a moment as if trying to assign value to his statement. "So now you're back, and I'm just supposed to forget everything that happened?"

"Forget the bad; remember the good," Nathan replied. "We had something special once. I know we could have it again."

"What's the matter, Nathan? Have you run out of women in the Drug Enforcement Agency? Are you starting over again, and I just happen to be at the top of the list?"

"Aren't you being just a wee bit judgmental? Curt told you already I've changed. I'm not the same guy I was back then. Curt helped me to find out what was missing in my life. He helped me to see that the love I needed was from God, not from a woman or any other human being."

"Then you don't need any attention from me," Debbie replied rather sharply.

"Deb, please hear me out. When you left—when I sent you away— I knew I'd made a mistake. By the time I could see the truth for myself, you were engaged to Frank. I tried to comfort myself by believing it was only a rebound thing, that you were just doing it to hurt me—"

"Don't flatter yourself," Debbie said, her eyes narrowing angrily. "You and Frank were cut from two different cloths. Frank was sweet and honest—you couldn't come close to him on your best day."

Nathan couldn't deal with her anger. Maybe after she got used to the idea of him being around, she'd calm down and deal with him in a more civil manner. With his pride smarting, he looked at Debbie and held his hands up as if to ward her off—or surrender. "You go ahead and get your things. I'll wait here. I wouldn't want you to think I was crowding old Frank's memory too much." His tone grew increasingly snide as he stuffed his hands in his jacket pocket. "No, ma'am. Don't want anyone thinking I'm here to fill his shoes. I'm not sure I could even climb the heights of the pedestal you've elevated those golden slippers to anyway."

Smack!

Her hand slapped across his arm and chest almost before the words were out of his mouth, pushing him back. Glaring at him with tears in her eyes, Debbie turned away.

"How dare you," she whispered, barely able to speak.

Nathan instantly regretted his attitude. Here it was, the anniversary of Frank's death—the love of her life—and on top of that, Debbie was left to face a complete upheaval of her security. She had to leave her new home and be whisked away in a crate, all in order to keep her alive. And to top it off, Nathan had to make it just that much worse by losing his temper.

"I'm sorry. Please forgive me. That wasn't a very Christian way to talk," he finally said. She remained fixed with her back to him. "Debbie, I'm sorry. I really am. I miss him, too, and I honestly didn't mean to intrude. I thought maybe enough time had passed. I thought maybe I had a chance to make things right between us. I know now that I was wrong, but it doesn't change the fact that I have a job to do. Please just get your things. We don't have a lot of time."

He heard her sniff noisily and watched as she wiped her tears away with the back of her hand.

"I'm sorry I hit you." She turned, shaking her head. "This is just too much for me. I thought I could deal with it professionally, but I can't." She sobbed, and her expression turned from misery to one of deep-seated pain. "I'm sorry."

She quickly opened the door to her room and disappeared inside. She hadn't bothered to close the door behind her, but Nathan wouldn't have dreamed of intruding. He'd already done that and had made a big mess of everything.

Father, he prayed silently, *I could sure use some pointers in diplomacy. Maybe a few in the matters of the heart as well. I don't know how to help Debbie, but I sure seem to have a knack for hurting her. Please help me.*

Chapter 3

Brad's cabin didn't have a lot to recommend itself to either Nathan or Debbie. Solely dependent upon solar power and a gasoline-powered generator, the cabin was rustic at best.

"It's not much to look at," Brad said after depositing two bags of groceries on the counter. "It used to be an old hunting cabin. There was a narrow four-wheel-drive road up here, but a nasty rock slide eliminated that about a year ago. I bought it thinking CJ and I might one day build a cozy little hideaway." He shrugged apologetically. "At least it will afford you privacy."

"And security," Nathan offered.

Debbie nodded. "I suppose you're both right." She felt almost desperate in her situation but wouldn't have admitted it for the world. "How soon will you be back?"

Brad motioned at the bags. "We brought enough food for two weeks. I can't be making too many trips up here or it might look suspicious."

"But surely they'll have Simon Hill back in custody before two weeks are up," Debbie said. She gave Nathan what she knew was a pleading look for affirmation and added, "Right?"

"They're doing the best they can. It's a federal case, but I'm sure they've called in local and state help," Nathan replied. "You'll be back to work before you know it."

"That's right," Brad said with a smile. "Why not relax and enjoy the vacation? If the weather holds, you can have some incredible stargazing up here. Come on, let's finish bringing in the supplies and let me get out of here before somebody notices something."

Debbie followed the men outside, crunching through the ankle-high snow. The wind whipped at her coat, causing her to pull up her zipper. A low, moaning sound filtered through the trees as the breeze picked up. The sound struck a deep chord in her heart. She suddenly felt alone—alone like she had the day Frank had died.

Fighting her fears, Debbie turned to her companions. "What if the weather doesn't hold?"

Brad and Nathan were already unloading the helicopter, but Brad turned to reassure her. "Don't worry about it. The forecast is good. Even if a snow or two blows up, you have shovels and emergency supplies in the closet behind the door. Oh, and there are two pairs of snowshoes as well. Just make sure if it does snow that you come out and clear me a landing pad. We've had so little snow lately that I didn't figure I'd have any trouble setting down here today. See the markers around the landing pad? Those show me how deep the snow is. If the markers are covered, there's no way I can land. If they'd been covered today, I would have made you jump out." He grinned at her, as if the lighthearted comment could somehow make things better.

"We'll shovel out if it snows," Nathan said, stacking up two big boxes. Lifting them without any difficulty, he nodded toward the cabin. "Would you get the door?"

Still suffering a deep sense of shame and embarrassment from her nervous outburst hours earlier, Debbie decided to make the best of the situation. She nodded and went without a word to the cabin door.

Brad followed Nathan with the last of the supplies. Debbie felt an overwhelming sense of fear when he turned to go. Now she would be left alone with Nathan. The idea bothered her more than she wanted to admit. It wasn't a fear that he would do something inappropriate. It wasn't even a fear of Simon finding them. No, this was a fear of her own reaction to Nathan's touch—to his nearness. She was absolutely horrified to realize that with very little trouble at all, she could, again, come to care for Nathan McGuire.

"You'll have the cell phone if something comes up," Brad told Nathan. "Hopefully it will work, but there's no way to be sure. I tested it a few minutes ago, but that doesn't mean it will work a few minutes from now. It's the best we can do at the moment, however. I'll try to think up something else." He seemed to think on it for a moment, then shook his head. "I'll do what I can. I wouldn't use the phone unless you have to. No telling who else might pick up on it."

"We won't use it unless it's an emergency," Nathan agreed. "But call us when you know something."

"Curt plans to keep tabs on the situation and to let me know when the coast is clear and Hill is back behind bars. They're staking law enforcement teams at the inn. Hopefully, if Hill is planning something, he'll strike quickly. After he's captured, I'll come back up here and collect you two," Brad said, giving a little salute. "Debbie, don't you worry about a thing. You'll see. It's all going to work out. Now, let's get everything hooked up and the generator running, then I'd better get out of here."

All she could do was nod. She felt helpless to say or do anything else.

Moments later, Debbie stood alongside Nathan, watching the helicopter lift off and depart to the west. She looked at her watch and realized it would soon be dark. As if reading her mind, Nathan motioned toward the cabin.

"We'd better get inside and get things warmed up and figure out the arrangements."

She led the way, still saying nothing. Inside, Debbie glanced around the room. It wasn't much. A table and two chairs had been positioned against the south wall just inside the door. A small stove was wedged between two rather crude-looking counters. It looked serviceable and neat, but certainly nothing more. A sink and tiny refrigerator rounded out the kitchen portion of the room.

The living room offered little better. A couch and fireplace were the main attractions, while a wood box and long window seat bench were the only other furnishings.

"It's kind of like camping out with a roof, huh?" Nathan said, grinning.

"I'm not sure I've ever seen anything quite like it," Debbie admitted. "I haven't lived like this since I went on Girl Scout trips as a kid."

"You were a Scout? Small world. Me, too."

Debbie tried to relax and nodded. Nervous at the thought that they were completely isolated from the rest of the world, she rubbed her cold hands together. Her thin gloves did little to offer warmth, and suddenly the idea of a fire seemed the best motivation to move.

"I'll get a fire going," she suggested. "I'm pretty good at that."

"Don't you want to see the rest of the place?"

She swallowed hard. "I don't think there's much left. Just the bathroom and the bedroom."

"We might as well check it out for ourselves," Nathan replied. He went to the north side of the cabin. "You may choose what's behind door number one or door number two," he said, sweeping his arm across the space for dramatic effect.

Debbie smiled in spite of her tense nerves. "Door number two, please."

He grinned and opened the door with great exaggerated effort. "Ah, the bathroom, so to speak."

Debbie came to where he stood and peered inside. "I suppose it will do. At least we don't have to traipse outside in a snowstorm."

"That leaves door number one as the bedroom," Nathan said. He went quickly to open it and nodded. "This will do nicely. No windows—at least none that anyone could get through. We'll get the windows covered, and then no one can see in, either."

Debbie followed him into the tiny room. A double bed was the only furnishing, and it nearly filled the space. She saw for herself that the windows were barely more than narrow portals for letting in light. Nathan was right. It afforded plenty of security.

"This will be your room," he said, checking under the bed. "Nope, no hidden monsters or bogeymen."

"What about dust bunnies?" she asked.

He grimaced. "Plenty of those. I suppose the Aldersson maid isn't inclined to come all the way up here for cleaning."

"That's okay. I'll take care of it. I'll need something to do while I'm stuck here," Debbie said.

"Brad said there are some board games in the kitchen cupboard. We could always entertain ourselves with those."

"That's okay. I brought a book. But first, I think I'll give everything a good wipe down." She wanted to keep the conversation light and neutral. Cleaning seemed a good way to keep herself occupied. She shivered against the chill of the cabin. "I've changed my mind. First I'll build that fire."

"Why don't you let me worry about the fire?" Nathan said, following her into the living room. "In fact, why don't we unpack the groceries and find that take-out food Brad arranged for us. We can sit in front of the fire and have a nice supper. Then we can worry about spring cleaning or belated fall cleaning." Looking around the room, he chuckled in amusement and shook his head. "Well, it ain't much to look at, but it's home."

Debbie met his gaze. That was her first mistake. His warm brown eyes searched her face for some sign of agreement. She felt her breath catch in her throat. A memory of a day long past came to mind.

She and Nathan had gone along with Curt and another woman DEA agent named Cali Murdock to a public appearance to help raise money for a children's park. Children covered the carnival-like landscape while parents fought to keep up with their tykes. As community service, the agents had been placed in charge of regulating how many kids were allowed in and out of the station, called the moonwalk. As the children bounced up and down inside the completely enclosed area, squeals of delight filled the air along with the laughter of the agents. It had been a fun time, Debbie remembered. The kids had loved Nathan; she had loved him, too, or at least she thought she had. That was just before he'd ended their relationship in order to give more attention to some other woman. She'd mourned the loss, but then Frank had come into her life, and she'd found true love and contentment. Frank had helped her heal and forget Nathan's cavalier attitude, but Frank couldn't help her now.

"You look a million miles away."

Debbie shook her head. "Sorry, I guess I was just daydreaming."

"Bad memories?"

She grimaced. "Why do you ask?"

"Because your expression is the same one I used to see on my sister's face when my mother served liver for supper."

Debbie smiled and looked away. "Memories come in all shapes and sizes—bad and good." She went to the supply boxes and quickly changed the subject. "I guess your plan sounds as good as any. I'll get these unpacked, but if you don't get some heat going in this place, I'm going to be inclined to bury myself under a pile of covers instead of doing any work."

"We could snuggle together for warmth," Nathan teased.

Debbie dropped the box of cookies she'd picked up and turned rather abruptly. "Don't even joke like that, please. It's hard enough to be up here—isolated and without hope of escape—but if you go making me feel like I'm in as much danger from you as I am from Simon Hill, I'm not going to be able to function."

Nathan sighed. "Let's set some ground rules, okay? I'm not going to jump you, so put your mind at ease. You've made it abundantly clear that you want nothing to do with any romantic entanglements, and I've made it clear that I have a job to do. I'm not going to compromise you or force my attention on you. It wouldn't be professional, and it wouldn't be Christian. I have a new set of standards to govern my life, and I intend to live by them. I'm sorry that I joked about the snuggling. It won't happen again. In fact, you don't even have to talk to me, if you don't want to."

Debbie nodded. "Okay, just as long as you understand."

"I can't say understand is the word I'd give it, but I know my place, and I won't be the one to overstep the bounds."

He turned away from her and went to the wood box. Debbie watched him for a few moments, then went back to unloading the boxes of food. She felt better for having put her point across, but at the same time she felt as if she'd alienated the only friend she had at the moment. Could they live under the same roof for several days and not talk?

Then her mind went to his comment about actions that weren't Christian. Wasn't Debbie guilty of just such a thing? Nathan was only trying to keep her safe. He was an agent with a job to do, and she was fighting him every step of the way. Her attitude was unprofessional, and it definitely carried overtones of being proud and ungrateful. And why? Because he'd voiced an interest in romancing her? Because he suddenly realized what they'd had and lost?

With a sigh she began to silently pray. *I don't know what to do, God. I want to let go of the past and live my life in full. I want to put You in charge of my future, and yet I seem to keep grabbing it back from You. Nathan claims to have become a Christian, and I want to believe that he's changed, but he was so awful to deal with before. So full of himself and so bent on making everyone know how wonderful he was. And he hurt me.*

She cast a quick side-glance at Nathan as he blew on the kindling to encourage the fire. He was handsome; there was no way around that. And he'd already made it clear that he was interested in rekindling their old relationship. What was she supposed to do with that? Could she possibly reciprocate? Could she let go of the person Nathan used to be and accept that he had changed, that he was worthy of consideration? Of love?

Shaking her head, Debbie continued with the task at hand. Maybe when the matter of Simon Hill was dealt with, she could really start to analyze the situation and think about letting Nathan into her life. Maybe.

Chapter 4

Debbie retired early to the bedroom. Nathan figured she was exhausted from the ordeal of hiding out, but he also knew she was dealing with the tension of their isolation. He felt bad for having come on so strong, but in truth, his confidence in seeing a chance to get back into her life had made him overzealous. Now he realized that, like a frightened child, Debbie would have to be convinced of his trustworthiness.

Staring into the fire, Nathan thought of the past. His past. He had nothing back there to be proud of, unless it was his DEA work. Sometimes he felt that Satan tried to steal his future by reminding him of the things he'd done. The pastor had said that Satan had no power, except that which Nathan gave him—that God in Nathan was stronger and more powerful than anything the world could dish out. But memories had a way of sneaking in to undermine the foundation Nathan had built through his relationship with Christ. It was hard to let go of the past, especially when others were more than happy to remind him of what he'd been and done.

Debbie was that way. She'd only known Nathan prior to his change of heart. Frank's death had played a big part in Nathan's new life, although he wasn't sure Debbie would understand. Seeing Frank die, Nathan suddenly felt vulnerable, mortal. He and Curt had discussed the matter one night, and what Curt had said made sense. Aside from God, there was no peace, no hope, no life. Nathan began to see that for himself, and it wasn't long after that when he'd asked Curt to help him find his way to God.

But Debbie had no idea of how he'd dealt with his old self. She had no reason to believe that the arrogant ladies' man who had walked away from her desires for commitment was now the same man who shared a lonely cabin with her. Truth be told, as much as he'd hurt her, Nathan had no right to expect that she'd think anything but the worst of him. How could he ever explain that he'd done what he'd done out of fear? That he'd walked—no, he'd run away—from the intensity of their love because it threatened to swallow him whole?

In college, he'd quickly become a sought-after date, especially after becoming the university's star quarterback. Girls just naturally flocked to him, but they always wanted more than he could give. He'd date a girl three or four times, find the relationship growing intimate, and quickly move on before it got too serious. His friends called him "old love 'em and leave 'em Nate."

Commitment was just something that had never come easy to Nathan, and it wasn't something he intended to get caught up in. When he'd met Debbie, however, his attitude began to change. And that change terrified him.

He'd just transferred from Florida, where he'd known and worked with Curt O'Sullivan. There was a major drug-trafficking problem going on in the Denver area, and more agents were needed. Curt had suggested him for the position, and feeling ready for a change in his life, Nathan had left the balmy beaches of Florida for the dry mountain climate of Denver. His first day on the job, Debbie had walked in with Curt, and suddenly Nathan had known the truth. She was the one.

He'd never believed in love at first sight—probably still wouldn't believe in it had it not happened to him. She had been dressed rather casually in a DEA ball cap, sweatshirt, and jeans, but he'd thought her the most beautiful woman in the world. Her statuesque frame, model-like face, and dark eyes had captivated him immediately. But none of that held a candle to her laughter. When Curt had teased her about something, she had laughed, and her entire face lit up in genuine delight.

When their gazes met from across the room, she had flashed him a smile that melted his heart. They seemed destined for each other, but as the relationship grew closer, Nathan got cold feet. Feeling hemmed in and confused by the emotions she evoked in him, Nathan had put an end to their relationship and taken up rather quickly with one of the girls who worked in the office. His actions had devastated Debbie and for a time had alienated Curt.

The next thing Nathan knew, Debbie was spending her time with their supervisor. Frank was a good man, and he had apparently seen Debbie's need and pain and felt compelled to help ease her through the bad times. But within weeks they were engaged, and Nathan realized just how much he'd lost.

He never said anything to anyone. He was too embarrassed. He had somehow figured that by walking away from Debbie, he could dispel the feelings that so frightened him. But Nathan had been wrong. So very wrong.

The sound of the bedroom door opening pulled Nathan from his memories. He looked up to find Debbie standing there in jeans and a sweatshirt similar to what she'd worn the first day he'd met her.

"It's too cold in here with the door shut," she said softly.

"I didn't think about that, but I'm sure you're right. Why don't you warm up out here and leave the door open? Give it a few minutes and let the heat circulate," he suggested, "then go back."

She nodded and surprisingly didn't argue. Instead, she came out to the fireplace and sat down on the brick ledge that ran alongside the hearth.

For several minutes neither one spoke, then as if searching for answers, Debbie turned to him. "They will find him, won't they?"

"Hill? Sure," Nathan agreed. "It's impossible these days to get too lost. He'd have to leave the country to have much of a chance, and there's no way he'd be allowed to do that. They had notice of his disappearance within hours of his escape. I'm sure they'll have him back within forty-eight hours."

"I hope so."

"Don't worry. They want him back behind bars as much as you do."

"I suppose they'll stake out the inn. I feel so bad. Here it is Brad's big moment, and my past is ruining it."

"It's not your fault," Nathan reassured. "No one could have predicted this, and no one blames you. If Hill throws off the grand opening a day or two, Brad will understand."

"I just feel so bad, and for more than just the trouble with Hill." She looked back to the fire, seeming to struggle with something she wanted to say. "Nathan, I haven't been very nice to you. I'm sorry. I'm glad you've changed your life. I'm glad Curt was able to lead you to

450

Jesus. I haven't handled any of this very well, and I want to apologize."

"I don't blame you," Nathan replied. "I was just thinking about the way I used to act—the way I treated you. I'm ashamed to remember those times. I was out of control. There's no other word for it. Life in the fast lane seemed to be my only hope for forgetting how empty my life really was. I buried myself in my work and my social life, and still I went to bed every night feeling hopeless and in some ways useless."

Debbie nodded. "I know how that feels."

Nathan watched her for a moment. "I wish he were still here," he said, knowing that he really meant it. If he couldn't have Debbie for his own, he wished that Frank might still be alive to comfort her and give her hope.

"It doesn't hurt as much as it used to," Debbie admitted. "I miss Frank sometimes, but we really didn't have all that long together, and the memories are few." She looked up at Nathan. "It was a whirlwind romance, as you well know," she said, a slight smile forming on her lips. "I started the whole thing. Frank was too shy—just a friend. He always told me that he couldn't believe himself worthy of anyone who looked like me. He made me feel like the most beautiful woman in the world."

You are the most beautiful woman in the world, Nathan thought, but he remained silent.

"Frank had a great sense of humor, but it was his fierce loyalty that really drew me in. He would have walked through fire for his people. I had never seen that kind of devotion in another human being, unless it was my parents and their love for each other and for my sister and me."

"I didn't even know you had a sister," Nathan said, feeling safe to broach the subject.

Debbie smiled and nodded. "She lives in Maryland. She's a doctor. Has a husband and one little boy and practices medicine in Baltimore. She came out here last year and stayed at the hotel where I was working. Brad was training me to take over the resort, and Brenda—that's my sister—thought I was crazy. She tried to talk me into coming back east to live. My folks live in Philadelphia, so we would have had the entire family close together again if I would have moved back."

"So why didn't you?"

Debbie shrugged. "I don't know. I guess I really like it out here. I felt at home and at peace. I wasn't sure after Frank died that I could ever feel at peace again, but it's come with time."

"Sometimes time is the only thing that can heal our hurts," Nathan replied softly. He loved watching her as she reached her hands out to the flames. In those moments she seemed unguarded, thoughtful, yet content.

She surprised him then by looking up at him, almost as if she were studying him. "Frank's gone—I've learned to deal with that. He was a good man, and I loved him a great deal. Nothing will change that, but neither will anything bring him back."

Nathan wondered for a moment what she was trying to tell him. Why was she saying this unless she wanted him to know she was open to his interest in her? Feeling bold yet cautious, Nathan braved a question.

"The past is the past—for both of us. But what about the future?"

She bit her lower lip and looked to the ground. "I don't know. I guess once we get this ordeal behind us, we can talk about it some more. You really hurt me, though."

"I know." He felt as if she'd stuck a knife in his heart. "I never meant to. I was afraid."

She looked at him for a moment, then nodded. "I guess I know that. When you left me, Frank helped me to understand things. He told me men like you were running from themselves, not from anyone else."

"He was right. Frank was always good at figuring people out."

"He told me not to be too hard on you," Debbie said, looking back to the fire. "He said it wasn't personal."

"He was wrong on that count," Nathan said softly. "It was very personal. Too personal. That was the problem. I didn't know how to let it go on being that way. I didn't know how to deal with the intimacy of it all. I felt overwhelmed, terrified. If there's one thing I wish I could have you understand, it's that my love for you was, for the first time in my life, the real thing. I didn't know what to do with that fact. It demanded more of me than I knew how to give."

He heard her draw a deep breath and exhale. "Yes, well, as you said, the past is the past. I shouldn't have reacted so angrily to your reappearance in my life. I'm sorry."

"I understand. I just want you to know, beyond a shadow of a doubt, that I'm not the same man I used to be. I won't hurt you again—at least not intentionally, not like that."

"I want to believe that, but for now"—she looked back up—"for now, I just think it's better that we keep our distance. Your mind won't be on the job if it's on romancing me. And the same for me."

Nathan felt a surge of hope. "So you wouldn't be averse to my interest in you? You might consider letting something develop between us?"

Debbie got up, moved to the window, and, pushing back the heavy drape, glanced outside. For a moment Nathan thought he'd pushed too hard. Chiding himself for his eagerness, he almost didn't hear her reply.

"You were the last person in the world I expected to see today." She dropped the curtain and turned. Leaning back against the wall, she shook her head. "I didn't expect to feel this way. You've started something inside me. Something I didn't bargain for."

Nathan got up and moved to stand behind the couch. "You started something in me a long time ago. I know you thought it was only superficial, but I'm here to tell you it's much more than that."

Debbie looked at him for a moment, and Nathan fought against the urge to rush to her and embrace her. He longed for nothing more than to hold her in his arms and kiss her, but he knew he could never nurture their love by force.

"I don't know how to deal with this right now," she finally said. "I have to deal with one thing at a time, and right now, Simon Hill is the man I have to focus on."

"That's okay," Nathan said. "I'm a patient man. I waited through Frank; I can wait through Simon Hill. So long as I know I have something to wait for."

Drawing a deep breath, Debbie closed her eyes and nodded. She opened her eyes and Nathan saw the glistening of her tears. "Wait for me then," she whispered.

❦

The wind picked up sometime in the night and howled and moaned until Debbie thought she might go mad. Tossing to and fro in the hard bed, she thought of her openness with Nathan. Had she made the right choice? After all, she wasn't a child anymore. Surely those silly games of hiding feelings and keeping thoughts secret were more the kind of things college kids did. Dating and falling in love was different when you'd already lived through a world of hurts and emotions. When you were ready to settle down and build a future with someone, playing games held very little interest.

But was she ready to settle down? Could she give her heart to Nathan—trust that the changes in him were true? She'd felt a physical attraction to him since he'd first walked into her life so many years ago. His rugged, carefree appearance captivated most every woman she'd known. He had a way about him, and even the married women she'd worked with joked about how easy it would be to forget their husbands when Nathan McGuire was around.

On the other hand, Debbie had known that kind of attention for herself. She'd made money modeling in her early college days. It had paid the bills and helped offset her parents' obligations to finance her education. Plus, it had been fun. She'd talked to Curt's wife, Christy, on more than one occasion about that very thing. Christy had been an internationally acclaimed model prior to retiring to run a business designing custom wedding dresses. Christy understood the attraction and the pitfalls of leading the life of a model. Both women agreed that for a short time the fascinating lifestyle had held them captive, but only briefly.

Once Debbie had gotten interested in law and criminology, modeling soon took a backseat. She felt frustration and a sense of despair when the men around her took her less than serious in regard to her pursuits. All she wanted was to be treated as an equal, yet inevitably she was viewed as some sort of celebrity or plaything. Sometimes the men were less than respectful, and she'd endured her fair share of unwelcome advances. For some reason, many men seemed to think she'd naturally desire the attention. That's why it had been such a relief to be teamed with Curt O'Sullivan. Curt had been driven to learn more about the airplane crash that had killed his parents. The job at hand was more important to him than Debbie's looks or measurements. They'd developed a friendship and a bond of trust that Debbie took great comfort in. Curt respected her and treated her as a capable, competent partner. That had meant the world to her, and it was those thoughts that allowed her to finally drift off to sleep.

Sometime around dawn, Debbie woke up. The room was still dark, but a fuzzy light filtered in from the cloth-covered windows. Startled by her surroundings, she sat up and tried to get her bearings. The wind had died down, and the silence seemed almost eerie. Huddling there in the bed, she wondered if she should try to go back to sleep. She heard something in the living room and wondered if Nathan was also awake.

Grimacing against the cold, Debbie pushed back the covers and sat up. She'd gone to bed fully dressed, unable to bear the thought of sleeping without the warmth of her clothes—but also nervous about sleeping under the same roof with Nathan so close. She wasn't tempted to do anything wrong, but neither did she want to do anything to cause him any temptation. This setting was one born out of necessity and safety, not for rekindling old romances.

It was one of the reasons her confession to him had come with such great difficulty. Her attraction to him and desire to fight that attraction had fueled her anger at Simon Hill and her frustration at being displaced. But now, now that she'd admitted her interest, Debbie felt very vulnerable.

I can't lie to him, she reasoned as she slipped on her shoes. *But I also don't want to let things get out of hand. I don't want things to move too fast.* She glanced at the Bible she'd packed in with her things. She'd left it atop her suitcase the night before. Reaching for it, she opened to a verse in Isaiah.

" 'Those who hope in the Lord will renew their strength. They will soar on wings like eagles; they will run and not grow weary, they will walk and not be faint,' " she softly whispered the promise. Curt had shared this Scripture with her after Frank had died, and it had quickly become a favorite.

"I will hope in You, Lord," she murmured, closing the Bible. "I will hope in You and wait for my gift of wings."

"You're up kind of early," Nathan said from the doorway.

"I woke up and it was already light," she said, shrugging. She put the Bible on her pillow and got up. "What's your excuse?"

He grinned. "Oh, I have a whole list. A lumpy couch. A cold room. Hungry belly. Take your pick."

She smiled. "Well, I can't fix the couch, but I can stoke up the fire and make you breakfast." She wanted to be as amiable as possible—

show him that she could put aside the past and be pleasant. Pleasant, but not too pleasant. There was a fine balance to maintain.

He nodded. "Okay. Meanwhile, I'll go outside and check to see what's gone on in the night and whether or not we need to shovel any snow. I'll gas up the generator and get it running and bring in more wood. Deal?"

She nodded, suddenly feeling more at peace about their future. He was really trying hard to put her at ease. "Deal," she said softly.

Chapter 5

Day one passed without any mishaps or problems between them, but it was the strangest Christmas Day either Debbie or Nathan had spent. They read the Christmas story in honor of the day and what it meant to them, but they couldn't afford to ignore the situation that had brought them to the cabin. Debbie worked at cleaning the small rooms and felt less worried about Frank's killer as she observed Nathan's precautions. He seemed completely focused on his work, setting up ways to reinforce the cabin's safety—their safety.

By day two, boredom had set in, and by day three, Debbie knew they were going to have no other choice but to spend time in real conversation or she was going to go mad. She had avoided talking to Nathan for any long periods, figuring this would help to keep things professional. They chatted amicably over their meals and upon rising and going to bed. Otherwise, Nathan seemed to occupy himself in tending to the outside of the cabin, checking the perimeters, seeing that the landing pad was clear of snow, and, in general, avoiding her.

Debbie had thought this a very positive thing, but as the days wore on, her nerves began to fray. Why hadn't they caught Simon Hill? Where was he? The longer he spent outside of the prison, the less likely they were to find him. The thought was terrifying. Debbie longed to talk to Nathan about it, but it was almost as if they'd silently agreed to avoid the subject. That, and about a hundred other subjects that couldn't help but lead them back to issues of the heart.

On the fourth day, the skies opened up with a howling snowstorm, driving Nathan indoors. It was clear that they couldn't avoid each other. After all, the living room was the only warm place to be, and Debbie wasn't so proud that she'd trade off her own comfort for privacy.

"It looks pretty bad out there," Nathan said, after checking the window for what had to be the tenth time.

"Good," Debbie said, surprising them both.

Nathan turned and grinned. "Good? You're trapped high atop a mountain, with a raging snowstorm to keep you cabin-bound, a killer on the loose, and a less than desirable roommate, and you say good?"

"Well, the snow will keep Simon Hill from getting to us and. . ." She let her words trail off as she considered what she was about to say. Looking up at him, she added, "And you aren't a less than desirable roommate."

Nathan leaned back against the cabin wall. "Are you sure about that?"

Debbie nodded. "I wish you were less than desirable."

He grinned. "Well, I haven't had a bath in four days, and if you got closer to me you might very well change your opinion."

Grinning, Debbie shrugged. "I'm in the same fix, so I doubt it would matter that much."

"So, you wanna talk?" Nathan questioned casually. "I mean, unless you had someplace else to go."

Debbie thought of his words. They both knew fully well that they were avoiding anything personal, anything that even hinted that it might be a matter of the heart. Debbie caught his gaze and knew he was just as overwhelmed by his feelings as she was.

"I want to hear about how you came to the Lord," she said, feeling it was the only safe way to begin the conversation.

He looked surprised, but nodded very slowly. "I'd like to tell you about it." He motioned to the couch. "Why don't we sit close to the fire?"

Debbie crossed to the couch and took a seat with open eagerness. She felt only a slight hesitation when he sat down beside her. There was hardly more than two feet of space between them. Not much of a distance to cross. Not much at all.

"I hated what I'd become," Nathan began without warning. "I had no fear of life or death. I plunged into my work with a sense of 'live for today!' I went into my personal life the same way. Then I met you."

Debbie's heart began pounding so hard she was certain Nathan could hear it. "I asked about your acceptance of Christ."

"I know," he said, studying her with such intensity that she had to look away.

She cleared her throat nervously. "Go on, then."

458

"You made me realize that something was missing. It scared me. Scared me bad. I didn't want to need anyone or anything. I knew you were 'religious,' but I knew, too, that it wasn't for me. At least I didn't figure it was. The closer I got to you, the more evident my own emptiness became. You were content and happy. You knew what you wanted out of life, and I didn't know how to deal with that." He stopped for several seconds, shaking his head.

"I couldn't handle it, Deb," he admitted. "I felt myself getting more and more involved with you, caring more—loving more. I couldn't deal with the liability."

"Liability?"

"It was a risk to love you. I don't expect you to understand—"

"Oh, I think I understand very well," Debbie interrupted. "Why do you think I'm still alone, five years after Frank's death?"

Nathan grew even more serious. "I'd like to think it was preordained. That God was working to put us back together."

Debbie swallowed hard. Her breath came in short pants, and she knew Nathan would see his effect on her. She tried to clear her mind. "Let's get back to why you gave your heart to Jesus."

"I couldn't deal with losing you. Then Frank got killed, and I couldn't deal with that, either. Curt saw how far down I'd gotten. I started drinking pretty heavily, and I wasn't much good for work or anything else. Curt cared enough to get me sobered up and to lay down the law to me. He saw right through me and knew I was heartbroken over you. More than that, however, he knew I was missing something else.

"He talked to me about God and about his own past. He told me about seeking all kinds of solace after losing his folks in an airplane crash. Nothing worked. It actually took coming to Denver, meeting Christy, and getting back together with his sister to make him see that his comfort could have been had all along in the form of his relationship with God. His parents had taught him that, and he'd let it get away from him."

"I know," Debbie replied, "I went through part of that with him."

"I know you did. He told me that, as well." Nathan stretched and cast a sidelong glance at the window. "I think the wind is dying down."

Debbie sensed his uneasiness. The wind made it harder to hear if someone was trying to break in, but the storm would surely keep any intruder away. "So then what happened?" she asked, hoping to put his mind back on their conversation.

He looked at her and smiled. "I'd like to say that I understood everything and instantly accepted salvation. But that would be a lie, and I've promised myself not to do that anymore."

"Good. I'm going to count on that," Debbie said with a smile.

Nathan's voice lowered. "I promise not to lie to you again."

Trembling, Debbie folded her hands in her lap. She wasn't helping matters any by making comments. If anything, she was only steering them back into a dangerous area.

Nathan seemed to understand. He squared his shoulders and looked back to the fire. "Frank's death hit me hard. Harder than I'd like to admit. In some ways, I blamed myself for a long, long time."

"Blamed yourself? Why?"

"Because I envied Frank and wished on more than one occasion that he'd just go away. I kept thinking if he hadn't been there, I might have won you back."

Debbie didn't know what to say. She'd figured Nathan to have never given her a second thought. He was the one who had ended it, after all. He was the one who'd said he couldn't be a part of her life anymore.

"Frank called me the night of his death. He asked me to come in on the operation as a last-minute backup."

"I know. I remember. We were so shorthanded. Frank, himself, wasn't supposed to be there."

Nathan nodded. "I didn't want to come. I didn't want to have to work with him. But then he mentioned you were the one we were guarding, and I realized I wanted to be there. I needed to be there to offer you whatever protection I could. When things went bad, I nearly broke my neck getting to you. I had to know you were all right. But even in seeing you alive, I knew you weren't all right." He stopped and looked at her.

Debbie couldn't turn away from his gaze. He somehow had bonded her to him with nothing more than a glance. She wanted desperately to say something that might break the intensity of the moment, but her mouth went dry and words refused to come. Against her will, Debbie found herself transported back in time. She no longer saw Nathan. She was on the floor, holding Frank as he bled to death.

"I knew he was dying," she said, her voice sounding as far away as that day. "I'd had enough training to know they weren't going to save him from this." She fought the memory. "He wasn't even supposed to be there. He came in at the last minute because so many of the regular people were down with the flu." She shook her head slowly. "We went to the site—two houses, side by side. One held a drug lab; the other was supposedly nothing much more than where the dealer did business and lived. There wasn't supposed to be anyone in the second house. We'd already learned from surveillance that everyone was in the lab working."

"Only they didn't realize that the dealers had dug a tunnel between the two houses." Nathan's words sounded so far away to Debbie.

She nodded. "I was supposed to meet Simon Hill at the second house. We'd be all alone. I was going to buy the stuff, close the deal, and signal the rest of the team. Simon would have to cooperate. But it all went wrong." She felt tears come to her eyes. "There wasn't supposed to be anyone else in the house."

"I know," Nathan said, reaching out to touch her arm.

"Frank called him down. Told him the place was surrounded. Simon didn't seem overly concerned. He just sat there smiling. Smiling and nodding. Then we heard voices. Voices where there shouldn't have been voices." Debbie saw it all over again in her mind. She had reached into her bag for her gun, but it was too late. "Simon's people burst into the room and surprised us. Frank didn't even have a chance to fire his weapon. Simon emptied his gun into Frank at point-blank range."

Debbie shook her head back and forth. "I thought for a second that everything was okay. Frank had a vest on beneath his shirt, but two bullets had ripped into his neck and another made it through the top of his head." Tears streamed down her face. The horror of that moment cut her as surely as the bullets had cut through Frank.

Burying her face in her hands, Debbie sobbed. Nathan pulled her into his arms and held her. He said nothing. He didn't need to. He had been there. He had seen Frank die in her arms.

"I'm so. . .sor. . .sorry," she stammered between sobs.

"You don't need to be sorry for mourning the loss of the man you loved," Nathan replied.

"I wasn't the wife he needed," Debbie said, struggling to regain control. She pushed Nathan away. "Frank was old-fashioned. He wanted a wife at home and kids and a dog. He didn't want me on the force. If he hadn't been worried about me, he would have seen Simon had a gun. He would have killed him first. Instead he looked at me—it's my fault he's dead."

Nathan cupped her chin with his hand and forced her to look at him. "You don't know that. You can't spend the rest of your life second-guessing what might have been. What happened, happened. It's in the past, and no amount of blame will change it."

"I just feel so guilty."

He let go of her face and reached up to wipe her tears with his finger. "But you don't need to," Nathan replied. "It wasn't your fault."

Debbie looked away, embarrassed at having created such a scene. She reached into her jeans' pocket, pulled out a tissue, and wiped her face and blew her nose. She straightened her back and turned back to face Nathan. "He was a good man."

"The best," Nathan agreed.

"He deserved better."

"He got the best. He had you for a wife, a job he loved, and now he's in the best possible place."

Gratitude for his words and kindness rose up in her heart. "Thank you for helping me through this. I didn't plan to fall apart."

"Do we ever plan to fall apart?" he asked good-naturedly.

The minutes ticked by, Debbie began to grow aware of their silence.

"So you were telling me about your experience coming to God," she said, feeling so much better for having let out all of the stored-up pain.

Nathan shrugged. "Not that much left to tell. I realized I was lost, and Curt said there was someone Who was looking to find me. Someone who was willing to bring me back home—to show me the way."

Debbie smiled. "Sounds like Curt."

"He prayed with me, and I knew that I wanted the kind of relationship he had with God. I have that now—only it's my own personal relationship. I'm not riding on anyone's coattails or trying to be something I'm not." He looked at her, his expression relaxing a bit. "It's just me and Him. Do you know what I mean?"

Debbie nodded. She knew exactly what he meant.

"I thought you would," he said softly. Leaning closer, he reached up and drew her face to his. "I hope you will understand this as well." Kissing her slowly and tenderly, Nathan seemed to pledge his love for her in his kiss.

Debbie reached up and put her arms around his neck. It had been so long since anyone had held her, kissed her. She wanted to cry for the joy of it.

Without warning, a loud booming sound rose above the wind's relentless tirade. The lights went out, and only the flames in the fireplace lit the room. Debbie clung tightly to Nathan, uncertain if the storm was wreaking havoc on them or if Simon Hill had finally located them.

"You stay here," Nathan commanded, standing with Debbie at his side. "I mean it. Get in the bedroom and lock the door. Don't come out for anybody but me."

Nodding, Debbie watched him pull on his coat and pick up his gun. "Please be careful," she said, barely able to form the words.

"Hey, I'm the best, remember?" he teased. Then he sobered. "Now, go on. Lock the door behind you."

Debbie hurried to the bedroom and slammed the door behind. Sliding the lock into place, she leaned against the frame and prayed.

Chapter 6

D ebbie waited in silence as the wind continued to howl. From time to time she heard noises coming from outside, but fear kept her from even attempting to look out the windows. She glanced at her watch and realized that ten minutes had gone by. *It could take that long*, she reasoned, *to check the entire area—what with the storm.*

But after thirty minutes and still no sign of Nathan, Debbie's imagination began to play tricks on her. She even imagined once that she'd heard Nathan's voice calling her above the whine of the storm. Her imagination was running rampant as she thought of Simon Hill managing to locate them.

Rubbing her cold fingers together, Debbie wondered what she should do, how long she should wait. The room was terribly cold, and with the door closed, there wasn't even a hint of warmth to ward off the chill. She pulled on her coat and gloves and began to pace.

"He told me to stay here, and I know that's probably best," she argued to no one, "but he's been gone such a long time." She looked at her watch again. Forty-five minutes. Where was he? A nagging doubt played on her mind. Something was wrong. She just knew it. Had the killer found them? Had he hurt Nathan?

By the time a full hour had passed, Debbie realized she couldn't stand the wait any longer. Cautiously, she slid back the lock and opened the door a crack. Peering out into the living room, she saw the place was completely deserted. The fire was dying down from lack of attention, and there was no sign of Nathan.

She opened the door and stepped out. Listening, she tried to denote any sound that might not fit. The wind made it difficult at best to hear much of anything.

"Why couldn't we have hidden out in a beach house in Hawaii?" she muttered, checking the bathroom for any unwelcome visitors. She had no idea what she would have done if Simon Hill had jumped out at her, but she had to check nevertheless.

The house was clear, and Debbie's nerves settled a bit. She stoked up the fire and tried to reason that Nathan was fully capable of taking care of himself. But reason and emotion did battle for her will, and emotion won out.

"I have to find him. I have to know that he's all right." She pulled up the hood of her coat and tied it snug. Nathan would have a stroke if he found her out there unprotected, but he would just have to understand. *On the other hand,* she thought, *if he's hurt and needs help, I've already wasted an hour.*

She opened the door and felt the stinging ice and snow hit her face. The storm blinded her from seeing much farther than a foot or two in front of her.

"Nathan?" she called out and then repeated his name. No response.

Knowing he would have gone to the generator shed, Debbie crept her way along the side of the cabin to where she remembered the shed to be. The snow kept her from even being able to see it.

"Oh, God, help me," she prayed. She knew it would be pure folly to let go of the house and lose her bearings in the storm. Remembering a length of rope in the closet behind the front door, Debbie hurried back to the cabin. She could tie the rope to the cabin and use it as a guide to get her back to safety.

Finding the rope was easy. Figuring out where to secure it was not quite so simple. Finally, Debbie struck on the idea of tying it to the doorknob on the inside of the front door. She then wrapped it a couple of times around the knob on the front side for extra measure, then pulled the door shut as best she could. With the rope wedged in the door as well as tied, Debbie felt confident of getting back safely to the warmth of the cabin.

She hoisted the rope to her shoulder and let it out a bit at a time. When she retraced her steps in the direction of where she knew the generator shed should be, she gave the rope one last pull to ensure its security, then ventured away from the house.

Her bearings served her well. Inching through the storm, she made the edge of the shed without losing her footing even once. The thick snow swirled around her legs, chilling her to the bone, but Debbie pushed on. Her urgency grew with every step. She couldn't shake the feeling that she had waited too long.

Working her way along the shed, she came to the door. Pushing against it, Debbie felt relief when it gave way and opened into the dim confines of the shed. The room looked undisturbed. There wasn't any sign of melting snow, which would have been there had Nathan come to check the generator. The generator! It wasn't running.

Debbie felt panic begin to build. If Nathan had made it to the shed, where was he and why wasn't the generator running? She looked down at the rope, which was still gripped tightly between her gloved fingers.

"Oh, Nathan, please don't be lost in this storm. Please, God, don't let him be lost."

She looked back outside, the hopelessness of the moment overwhelming her. Snow swirled around her feet and blew in through the open door. The whiteout made it impossible to see. How could she possibly find him? If he'd gotten off base and wandered away from the cabin. . . She didn't even want to think of what might happen.

Debbie looked at the length of rope. There wasn't that much left. She could walk the distance of the rope, but nothing more. Determined not to give up, she remembered back to their first day. She reminded herself of the layout. The helipad was directly south. The shed was to the east of the house. Behind the house there was another small outbuilding. Nathan had teased that it was the bathroom, but Brad had assured them there was indoor plumbing.

Drawing on all her reserves of strength and hope, Debbie turned to leave the meager protection afforded her by the generator shed. As she turned, her eyes caught sight of a spool of wiring material. The roll looked new, practically unused. Debbie tied the rope to the leg of the generator and went to the spool of wire. She could use this instead of the rope. There was at least three times as much wiring as the length of rope. She could make it all the way around the house and out to the back. She was sure of it!

Unraveling a bit of the wire, Debbie secured it to the generator. She thought for a moment to tend to the job Nathan had originally come out to do, but the generator could wait. If Nathan was lost in the snow or hurt, he needed her attention more than the house needed power.

Feeling less confident of the wiring's hold than she had of the rope, Debbie tied the wiring off a second time by wrapping it several times around the shed's door handle. Then with a quick prayer for guidance, Debbie set off into the storm.

She kept her head down but followed the rope back to the house. She figured it better to keep her bearings and base herself off the house than to just wander aimlessly. She rounded the back of the house and looked up against the brilliant white of the blizzard. She couldn't see anything and for a moment worried that her search would be completely in vain. Maybe she should just wait out the storm and then go in search of Nathan. But her mind told her that later would be too late. Nathan needed her help and needed it now. She began to really fear for him, and that fear drove her into action.

As she moved away from the house, Debbie thought the wind lessened. For just a moment she thought she could see something; and then just as quickly, it was gone. Clinging to the wiring spool, she let out just enough wire to gingerly take a few steps. Step by step, she inched her way through the snow, painfully aware that she needed to be searching the depths of the snow for any sign of Nathan. *He could have fallen,* she reasoned. He could have lost his balance and hit his head. She tried not to think of the consequences. For a moment she saw Frank bleeding in her arms. She couldn't lose Nathan, not now, not when they'd just found each other again.

She swept at snow with her booted foot, praying she'd meet no obstacle in the form of Nathan's frozen body. She didn't. Finally, her perseverance was rewarded. She hadn't found the back shed, but she'd found a watering trough and that, she remembered, was only about six or seven feet away from the outbuilding.

Pressing forward, Debbie could have cried out in relief when she reached the solid wall. Patting her way along the side, she maneuvered to the door.

"Nathan!" she called out. "Nathan, are you here?" She tried to open the door, but it wouldn't budge. Pounding against it, she called out again. "Nathan!"

She was too stunned to be scared when the door finally gave way.

There, shivering and looking rather surprised, stood Nathan McGuire.

"So good of you to come," he said, his teeth chattering.

Debbie threw herself into his arms. "I thought you were dead. I thought Simon Hill had found you and killed you. I was so worried. You didn't come back." She chattered mindlessly in her relief.

He wrapped his arms around her. "I know. I know. I lost my way. I must have stumbled around out there for twenty or thirty minutes before finding this place. I figured I'd be better off with whatever shelter I could find. I tried to call to you. I thought you might have heard me."

"I did hear you," Debbie said, pulling back. "I thought it was my imagination. I heard voices and figured I was going crazy." She could feel how very cold he was and motioned behind her. "Come on. Let's get back inside the cabin. You need to warm up."

"We shouldn't risk getting lost again. You're lucky to have found me or this place."

Debbie held up the spool. "I tied off at the generator shed." She smiled. "I was a Girl Scout, remember?"

He laughed. "Good thing you were. I figured to keep you safe, rescue you from harm, but here you are rescuing me."

Debbie looked at him and realized the love that had rekindled in her heart. "I think we're rescuing each other," she said honestly.

He seemed to understand her meaning and nodded. "Well, we can discuss the matter more thoroughly in front of the fire."

"Right," she said, laughing. "Come on."

❧

Nathan watched Debbie as she hurried around the room, fussing over him. He liked the way she had lost her fear of whether or not Simon would crash in on their world. He liked the way she seemed completely devoted to caring for him. He could get used to such attention.

"I think the storm is over," Debbie said, pausing long enough to glance out the window. "Why, I actually see some blue sky out there."

"So when do you want to marry me?" he asked as she put a mug of hot chocolate in his hands.

Frozen in her steps, Debbie could only stare at him.

He grinned. He'd wondered how she might react if he voiced the question he'd been dying to ask for nearly five years.

"It isn't that hard a question," he teased.

She shook her head. "You're serious, aren't you?"

"I wouldn't have asked if I weren't."

"Marry you? Just like that?"

He shrugged and sipped from the mug. "I suppose you'll want a long engagement, huh? Time to prove to yourself that you're doing the right thing, time to get to know me better."

She sat down rather absentmindedly. "No, I wouldn't want a long engagement."

"So you *will* marry me?" he said, hoping he didn't sound as eager as he felt.

"Nathan, we've barely gotten to know each other again."

"We know each other, Debbie."

She shook her head. "It's been five years. I knew Nathan McGuire the selfish playboy, the headstrong, self-assured DEA agent, the man who couldn't commit. Five years ago, that's all we had."

"No, we had love, too. That was real. It was terrifying, but it was real," Nathan said, refusing to let her off the hook. "It's real now. I love you, Deborah. I've never stopped loving you."

Tears came to her eyes. "Frank said he could make me forget about you. That he could make me stop loving you, hurting over you. I wanted him to make me stop caring. I didn't want to think of you as anything more than a troubled bit of my past."

"I know your love for me didn't die. You might have buried it, but it's still there."

"But that would be wrong. I loved Frank."

"I know you did," Nathan said, nodding. "No doubt about it. You loved him and married him and for a very short time, you were happy. I can make you happy again. I know I can. If you just let yourself love me again. Just reach down deep into the recesses of your heart—surely you can find a bit of that old love. If not that, then I'll settle for new love. Fresh and untried. Please just say yes. I won't take no for an answer." He smiled to lessen the severity of his statement.

She stood so silent that Nathan worried she'd tell him no. Pushing back her long black hair and drying her eyes against the sleeve of her shirt, Debbie smiled. "You always were pushy."

He laughed out loud. "When I see something I want, I go after it." Getting to his feet, Nathan put his mug on the mantel and came to where Debbie stood. "And I want you, Debbie. I want to be the man you need—the man you love."

Debbie opened her mouth to speak, but instead, the cell phone began ringing.

"Ignore it," Nathan said. "I want to hear what you were going to say."

Debbie shook her head. "It'll keep. Answer the phone."

Completely frustrated, Nathan went to the kitchen table and picked up the phone. "Yeah?"

"Nathan, it's Curt. It's over."

"They caught Simon?" Nathan questioned. He could see the spark of hope in Debbie's eyes.

"Yes. He didn't go willingly. Cali Murdock had to shoot him. It's her first kill, and she's feeling pretty bad."

"I'm sure she is, but remind her that it was in the line of duty."

"I have," Curt answered, then added, "So how's Debbie doing? I'm kind of relieved to hear that she hasn't killed you yet."

Nathan smiled. "She's going to be considerably better after hearing this. She might even give me an answer to my proposal of marriage." Debbie began furiously shaking her head. She clearly didn't want Nathan discussing the matter with Curt.

"Oh, great! I knew we were leaving you two alone for too long," Curt said in mock disgust.

"Yeah, well, not long enough that she's given me a straight answer."

"Look, Brad said to tell you he'll be up to get you when the weather clears. Hopefully you'll be back here in time for tomorrow's New Year's Eve party. Why don't you at least give her that long to make a decision?"

"I'll think about it," Nathan replied. "I'll talk to you then."

He hung up the phone and looked at Debbie. The last thing he wanted to do was ruin the pleasant feelings between them. News of Hill's death could very well destroy the moment. Deciding to glaze over the details, details he really didn't have, he said, "It's over. Simon Hill is dead, Brad's hoping to come for us tomorrow, and Curt said you'd better say yes to my proposal."

He grinned broadly, then shook his head. "No, he didn't really. I promised I wouldn't lie to you, so I have to come clean. I think he would have said it had I given him a chance."

Debbie looked at Nathan for a moment and asked, "How did Hill die?"

"I don't have much information. Curt simply said he didn't come willingly. Cali Murdock had to shoot him."

"I see. Where did it happen?"

"I don't know. Curt didn't say."

Nathan crossed the short distance and reached out to take hold of her arm. "I've waited through Simon Hill. Now you can completely devote your mind and heart to me."

"Like you haven't held my complete attention for the last few hours." She tried to act casual about it, but Nathan could tell she was nervous. "I think you have a helipad to clean off. Brad can't land if you don't give him a clear space."

"If he can't land that just means I'll have you to myself that much longer."

"I'm not answering your proposal until I'm safely back at the inn," Debbie said, crossing her arms.

Nathan grinned and grabbed his coat. "One landing pad, coming up. Why don't you get on that cell phone and line up a preacher?"

Debbie gazed heavenward as if for strength. "Go!" she said, pointing at the door. "Go, and pray I don't lock you out of the house."

Chapter 7

Hill was first spotted near Debbie's old house in Thornton. They lost track of him after that, but someone called in from Longmont and thought they'd seen him with a couple of other men. All of them looked suspicious, so the citizen called in to the sheriff's office and they notified the federal authorities," Curt explained as Brad and CJ's New Year's Eve party swung into full force.

"But then he surprised everyone by turning up at the airport. If Cali Murdock and a couple of other agents hadn't been there on another case, we might have missed him altogether," Curt continued. "Cali recognized him, in spite of his attempts at a disguise. The agents called him down, and a chase ensued. The other men with him gave up, but not Hill. Cali ran him down, and when they reached the parking lot, Hill opened fire on her."

Debbie cringed at the thought and cast Cali a look of admiration and gratitude. "I'm glad you were on the job. I appreciate what you did."

Cali, who was still rather shaken over the events, nodded. "I couldn't let him go, but shooting him wasn't the end result I had planned for."

Nathan put his arm around her and gave her a hug. "Hill made his choices. He chose the end result—you didn't. You have to remember that."

"I know."

"Say, this is some party," Curt said, changing the subject. Glancing around the lodge's common room, he smiled. "I figured Brad and CJ would change their minds about it being couples only. I've hardly ever seen them leave their kids behind."

The idea for a close-knit couples celebration went out the door after Hill's capture and the end result was a crowd of family, friends, and even former and present coworkers on hand to ring in the new year.

Curt's wife, Christy, appeared with their fifteen-month-old son in

472

her arms. A rather petite five-year-old girl skipped along behind. "Jeremiah wants his father," Christy announced, so Curt held out his hands to take the baby.

"Why, Sarah, you've grown at least three inches since I saw you last," Debbie said to Curt and Christy's daughter.

"I'm going to school now," the child announced. "I can read."

"Good for you! You keep working hard," Debbie told the child. She smiled at Christy and added, "I'm sure sorry for ruining the holidays for you and your family."

"Nonsense," Christy replied. "They weren't ruined at all. We're just relieved to have you safe."

Nathan had moved away from Cali and had again taken his place at Debbie's side. Observing his casual embrace of Debbie, Christy raised a curious brow. "Curt mentioned you two were, well, getting closer."

"I think the entire Simon Hill matter was God's way of throwing us together again," Nathan announced. "I've long looked for a way to see Debbie and get her to put the past behind us, and thanks to Hill, I had the perfect excuse."

"You don't need an excuse to do the right thing," Curt replied. "Doing what's right is excuse enough."

"I know," Nathan answered. "I just wasn't sure Debbie would see it that way."

Just then, Curt spotted Christy's brother, Erik, and his wife. "I need to go talk to Erik before the evening gets too crazy." He shifted Jeremiah to his left arm, then winked at Debbie. "Don't get too carried away with the party spirit. If somebody asks you a tough question, be sure to think it through before giving him an answer."

Debbie laughed. "You know me well enough to know I weigh all decisions very carefully."

"Except for those taken out of your hands," Curt teased. "Like being imposed on by a former partner and whisked away to an isolated cabin."

"Well, I have to admit, if I hadn't seen the results on the news, I might have thought it was something you and Nathan planned out."

Curt looked rather smug and exchanged a look with Nathan that left the women all chuckling. "I think there may have been more to this than we know," Christy said, eyeing her husband. "Perhaps we'll never know."

"Oh, I think I already know," Debbie replied. "I had a very interesting talk with Cali. You know, the kind that has to do with who was assigned to do what and when. Funny thing about assignments and how sometimes people bribe people to change places and let them have certain jobs."

"Really?" Nathan said, stepping away rather casually. He looked up at the beamed ceiling. "Nice lighting up there."

Christy laughed all the harder. "Surely Curt wouldn't have had anything to do with it."

"I thought Cali looked tired," Curt said. "She needed a break. Nathan wasn't doing anything this week, and Cali had previously scheduled the week off for skiing."

"Like it did any good," Cali replied. "I got my exercise and then some."

"Well, I suppose my friends were only looking out for my best interests along with their own," Debbie said, smiling.

&

As midnight neared, Debbie found her spirits considerably lightened. The party and the atmosphere did much to heal her misery over Simon Hill and the terror he'd brought to her life. She'd given a great deal of thought to Nathan's proposal, and she knew in her heart that she very much wanted to say yes.

Watching Brad and CJ with their two boys and Curt and Christy with their children, Debbie knew that what she wanted more than anything was a husband and family. What worried her, however, was how she could ever handle being married to another DEA agent. The idea of sending Nathan out to do his job terrified Debbie. How could she kiss him good-bye, watch him leave for work, and not fear that he might never return? She remembered Frank dying in her arms and couldn't help superimposing Nathan's face over her now-dead husband's features.

On the other hand, Debbie wouldn't dream of asking Nathan to give up his job with the agency. He'd been involved for more than ten years. He had a good future with them, and to ask him to leave now would be wrong.

"You're looking awfully serious," Nathan said, slipping up behind her.

Debbie jumped. "You scared me."

"I didn't mean to," he said, pulling her back against him. "It's almost midnight," he whispered against her ear.

Debbie shivered, delighted by the way he could make her feel. She loved having his strong arms around her. He represented a pillar of strength in human form. God with skin on, she had jokingly admitted to Curt. Curt had admonished her not to put that kind of pressure on Nathan.

"We guys are only human," he had told her. "We try awfully hard to be all things to those we love, but if you go heaping unattainable attributes on us, we'll fail every time."

"So you're safe and sound," Nathan said, bringing Debbie's thoughts back into the present. "Do I get an answer to my proposal?"

Debbie pulled away and turned to face him. "I'm not sure I can give you an answer."

"Why?" he asked, seeming hurt.

"If I say yes, I'll betray myself. If I say no, I'll betray myself as well."

His expression was one of complete confusion. "I don't understand."

"Nathan, I can't marry another DEA agent. I can't go through that again. Losing Frank was just too hard. I can't watch you die as well. If I say yes, I'll never know another moment's peace."

"And if you say no?" he asked softly.

"No peace there, either," she admitted, pausing for a moment. "Because now I know that I still love you."

"Hey, you two, it's nearly midnight. We're going to start the count-down in about thirty seconds," Brad called from across the room where everyone else had gathered. "Don't forget, McGuire, she may have your heart after midnight, but the rest of you belongs to Aldersson Enterprises. I'm going to need you on the job bright and early tomorrow."

"What?" Debbie questioned. "What's he talking about?"

Nathan grinned. "I work for Brad now."

"Since when?"

"Since about eight hours ago."

Debbie felt overwhelming relief at this news. She wouldn't be the one to force him out of the DEA. He'd gone of his own accord. "And just when were you going to tell me about this?"

He shrugged. "It didn't seem important until now."

"Not important?"

"I quit the agency because I knew you could never deal with that side of life again," he said thoughtfully. "And I couldn't deal with the side of life that didn't have you in it."

"Ten. . .nine. . .eight. . . ," the others called from across the room.

"Marry me?" he asked.

"Five. . .four. . ."

Debbie nodded. "Yes. Oh, yes!" She wrapped her arms around Nathan's neck.

"Two. . .one. . .Happy New Year!"

Nathan's lips pressed firmly against Debbie's amidst the shouts and laughter. Melting against him, Debbie sighed at the wonder of God's timing.

"Hey, you two, the party is over here," Curt called.

The kiss ended, but Nathan refused to let Debbie pull away even a fraction of an inch. "We're having our own party," Nathan called back. "Debbie just accepted my proposal."

Cheers went up from the crowd. Even the kids, now sleepy-eyed and yawning, jumped up and down in youthful imitation of their parents' excitement.

"Well, I'd say we initiated this place in proper order," Brad announced. "A romantic engagement for a romantic resort. I don't see how we could possibly top the evening."

"Anybody know where there's an all-night chapel?" Nathan questioned playfully.

Debbie elbowed him and shook her head. "No way, buster. We're having a real wedding, with friends and family and a wonderful reception right here."

By this time everyone had come to gather around the newly engaged couple. Brad shook his head. "This place is booked pretty solid for the next few months. I think you'll just have to postpone your nuptials until the summer."

"Nope," Nathan said, holding tight to Debbie. "We're getting married within the week, or I'm taking her back up to that cabin until she changes her mind. She promised me it wouldn't be a long engagement."

Everyone laughed at this, and Debbie shrugged. "Guess I have to do what the man says," she said, sounding horribly oppressed. Smiling, she lay her head upon his shoulder. "He'll be dancing to my tune soon enough."

The laughter was interrupted by Jeremiah's howls of protest. "I'd say it's time to put the kids to bed," Curt said, trying to soothe his son.

"I think you're right," Brad replied, looking to CJ, who held their own sleepy two-year-old.

"I don't want to steal anyone's thunder," Erik said, looking rather sheepishly at the crowd, "but Cheryl and I have an announcement of our own." All eyes turned to the couple as Erik continued, "We're going to have a baby!"

"What a night!" CJ Aldersson declared. "Congratulations."

"Yes!" Debbie said enthusiastically. "How wonderful. I'll always remember this moment as one of the happiest in my life."

"I intend to give you many more happy moments," Nathan told her as the others gathered around to congratulate Cheryl and Erik.

Debbie reached up to touch Nathan's cheek. "And I intend to give you happy moments as well. So many, in fact, that one moment will blend into the next and you'll never know one from the other."

"Hmmm, I like that thought." He kissed her gently. "So where do you want to spend our honeymoon?"

Debbie pulled away and called out, "Hey, Brad, is that cabin available next week?"

"What cabin?" he asked in confusion.

"The one you flew us up to," Debbie replied. "I'm planning my honeymoon."

Brad laughed. "I can think of better places."

"Me, too," Nathan said, looking at Debbie with a rather surprised expression. "It was cold and dirty and—"

"And completely isolated and only accessible by helicopter," Debbie added, letting the full meaning of her words fall on them both.

Nathan instantly agreed. "Yeah, Brad. That place available?"

Brad nodded in full understanding. "I'll see what I can do."

"I like the way you think, Deborah soon-to-be McGuire," Nathan said.

He smiled at her in such a way that Debbie knew without a doubt she was making the right decision. Her heart soared with a lightness that she'd not known in years. A gift of wings had been given to her. A gift of hope that could only come from waiting for God to work out all the details of her life. The past could finally be laid to rest, and with it, Debbie knew that Frank would be pleased. She was at peace, happy and whole. That was all he would have ever wanted for her. It was all she had ever wanted for herself. God had given her a new start—a fresh new world to explore and a gift of wings on which to fly above the sorrows of the past. And He had given her Nathan McGuire—a soul mate with whom she could share the journey and the burdens of life. What more could she have asked for?

A Letter to Our Readers

Dear Readers:

In order that we might better contribute to your reading enjoyment, we would appreciate you taking a few minutes to respond to the following questions. When completed, please return to the following: Fiction Editor, Barbour Publishing, Inc., P.O. Box 719, Uhrichsville, OH 44683.

1. Did you enjoy reading *Colorado Wings?*
   - ❑ Very much. I would like to see more books like this.
   - ❑ Moderately—I would have enjoyed it more if _____
   _____
   _____

2. What influenced your decision to purchase this book?
   (Check those that apply.)
   - ❑ Cover   ❑ Back cover copy   ❑ Title   ❑ Price
   - ❑ Friends   ❑ Publicity   ❑ Other

3. Which story was your favorite?
   - ❑ *A Wing and a Prayer*   ❑ *Wings of the Dawn*
   - ❑ *Wings Like Eagles*   ❑ *A Gift of Wings*

4. Please check your age range:
   - ❑ Under 18   ❑ 18–24   ❑ 25–34
   - ❑ 35–45   ❑ 46–55   ❑ Over 55

5. How many hours per week do you read? _____

Name _____

Occupation _____

Address _____

City _____ State _____ Zip _____

HEARTSONG ❤ PRESENTS

Love Stories
Are Rated G!

That's for godly, gratifying, and of course, great! If you love a thrilling
love story, but don't appreciate the sordidness of some popular paperback
romances, **Heartsong Presents** is for you. In fact, **Heartsong Presents**
is the only inspirational romance book club, the only one featuring love
stories where Christian faith is the primary ingredient in a marriage
relationship.

Sign up today to receive your first set of four, never-before-published
Christian romances. Send no money now; you will receive a bill with the
first shipment. You may cancel at any time without obligation, and if you
aren't completely satisfied with any selection, you may return the books
for an immediate refund!

Imagine. . .four new romances every four weeks—two historical, two
contemporary—with men and women like you who long to meet the one
God has chosen as the love of their lives. . .all for the low price of $9.97
postpaid.

To join, simply complete the coupon below and mail to the address
provided. **Heartsong Presents** romances are rated G for another reason:
They'll arrive Godspeed!

YES! Sign me up for Hearts❤ng!

NEW MEMBERSHIPS WILL BE SHIPPED IMMEDIATELY!
Send no money now. We'll bill you only $9.97 postpaid with your
first shipment of four books. Or for faster action, call toll free 1-800-
847-8270.

NAME _____

ADDRESS _____

CITY _____ STATE _____ ZIP _____

MAIL TO: HEARTSONG PRESENTS, P.O. Box 719, Uhrichsville, Ohio 44683